THIRD WISH

A NOVEL IN FIVE PARTS

PARTS
1 & 2

by Robert Fulghum

Third Wish, Volume One
Part One: Witness
Part Two: Ariadne and the Jumwillies

Text © 2009 by Robert Fulghum

Ilustrations on pages 62–71, 87, 91–93, 97, 103–104, 137–138, 145, 148–150, 163, 166–168, 174, 204, 212, 219, 248, 254, 288, 295, 298, 303–305, 325, 331, 336, 339, 366, 369, 375, 379, 390, 394, 398–399, 404, 412–413, 423–424, 428, 437, 449–450, 460–461, 502 © 2009 by Karen Lewis
Music scores © 2009 by David Caldwell
Music companion CD, Tracks 1–5 © 2009 by David Caldwell

FIRST EDITION (English Language), 2009
Previously published in The Czech Republic by Argo Publishers, 2004

Library of Congress Control Number: 2008937176

ISBN-13 (2-vol. set): 978-1-60830-043-3

Manufactured in China

Slipcase and Book Jacket Illustration: Digital composite by Barbara Witt of work by Karen Lewis, Margaret Allen Dougherty, and Gretchen Batcheller
Book and Package Design: Barbara Witt
Copyediting: Kathy Bradley

10 9 8 7 6 5 4 3 2 1

becker&mayer! Books
11120 NE 33rd Place, Ste. 101
Bellevue, Washington 98004
www.beckermayer.com

ABOUT THE MUSIC

Music is an elemental dimension of being human. The music we carry in our minds reveals much about us. The music in the lives of the characters in this novel has been incorporated to provide a richer understanding of their humanity. The music would not be included if it were not essential. Please give the recorded music as much attention as the written word.

Parts One & Two - Tracks 1-5

Written and Performed by David Caldwell

1 - Cuckoo Not Song 3:07

2 - Alex's March 2:13

3 - The Jumwillies' Fight Song 1:07

4 - Alex and Alice 1:42

5 - Vasilev Ouranie 2:30

PART ONE

WITNESS

Including

The Cretan Chronicles of Max-Pol Millay

The Illustrations of Louka Mahdis

The Music of Soterios Tourlakis

To Begin With:

On the Greek island of Crete, there is a town called Hania.
By the harbor of that town is a cafe, named for a wind: *Meltemi*.
On the terrace of that cafe is a table - large enough to seat five.
That table is the center of gravity for the story I will tell you.

The table is there now, waiting. The chairs and tablecloth, the glasses and napkins, the plates and silverware are waiting. Inside the cafe, there is a barrel of wine. Outside, it is summer. A breeze from the sea breaks the heat.

All the major players of the theater of this book will sit at that table from time to time. In the end, they will sit at the table together. They will drink the wine from that barrel. They will honor the coincidences that have brought them together. Each has found a way through a maze to be there.

Being there is not a matter of fate, destiny, or the will of heaven.
They have been drawn out of longing for something and someone.
Each person is part of a love story - not the same love story - not even the love story they had once imagined. Nonetheless, bitter and sweet, old and new, for better or worse - love is their common ground. Far more than romantic love - the love of self and the love of life.

All of this is real. All of it.
Every person and place and thing in this book is real, existing on the bridges we use to cross over the border between fiction and not-fiction.
The table at the Meltemi is one such bridge.

It is at that table at the Meltemi that Alexandros Xenopouloudakis finally completed his one and only poem, written in Greek and English. Take note, read twice: It is the frame around the story I am going to tell you.

After the poem you will suddenly find yourself in Japan.
Surprise!

Οδηγίες Προς Οδοιπόρους

Θα σου δηλώσουν: Όλα τα ταξίδια έχουν γίνει.
Εσύ θα απαντήσεις: Εγώ δεν πήγα να δω ο ίδιος.

Θα επιμείνουν: Ο,τιδήποτε έπρεπε να πούμε, το είπαμε.
Εσύ θα απαντήσεις: Εγώ δεν μίλησα ακόμη.

Θα σου πουν: Ό,τι ήταν να γίνει, έγινε.
Εσύ θα απαντήσεις: Εγώ δεν τελείωσα ακόμη.

Σε προειδοποίησαν: Κάθε πορεία είναι μακριά,
κάθε πορεία είναι σκληρή.

Μη φοβηθείς. Εσύ είσαι η θύρα, εσύ κι ο θυρωρός.
Θα μπεις μέσα και θα προχωρήσεις. . . .

—*Αλέξανδρος Ευαγγέλου Ξενοπουλάκης*

Instructions for Wayfarers

They will declare: Every journey has been taken.
You shall respond: I have not been to see myself.

They will insist: Everything has been spoken.
You shall reply: I have not had my say.

They will tell you: Everything has been done.
You shall reply: My way is not complete.

You are warned: Any way is long, any way is hard.
Fear not. You are the gate - you, the gatekeeper.
And you shall go through and on . . .

—Alexandros Evangelou Xenopouloudakis

SANAA

Slowly.

Sanaa walked *slowly* down the stone steps into the steaming water of the outdoor hot spring pool. Shivering when the wind drove snow against her bare skin, she resisted the urge to hurry. Morioka had been emphatic: "Slowly, slowly - must go in slowly. Remember."

The particular minerals and high heat of this spring at Arima would serve to set the ink on her body. But until the ink reacted, quick motion in the water would blur the design. Morioka had told her to sit in the water up to her chin, stay as long as she could stand it, and then stay a little longer than that.

Slowly, Sanaa sat down in what looked and smelled like carrot soup. Hot! Hot enough to hurt. To take her mind away from the scalding water she concentrated on watching snowflakes drift into the steam and disappear. Snow becoming steam becoming water becoming steam becoming clouds becoming snow becoming steam. The seamless cycle.

Hot! Panic. Heart racing, gasping for breath, Sanaa scrambled out of the ferocious heat of the pool into the relief of the snowy cold. Calming down, she reached for her towel. And for the first time she noticed her arm.

The invisible tattoo was now visible.

Sanaa dried her face, put on her glasses, and looked again. Against the rosiness of her skin was the promised white filigree of Morioka's calligraphy.

She walked back into the dressing room and stood before the mirror.

Across her breasts and down her arms were poems in faint Japanese. Turning slowly she saw the image of Kannon, the goddess of mercy, laid as a lacy shawl across her shoulders and down her back. Like a formal *mi-e* of a Kabuki actor, she stood still, holding a pose that made the moment indelible in her memory. So. Just so.

But still not quite the real thing. Not a real tattoo done with steel needles. Morioka had refused her that. Sanaa thought he was testing her will. Using a staining ink mixed to match the color of her pale skin, he had decorated her body to let her see what it might be like to have the invisible tattoo. When he was finished she could not see the design. Only heat would declare the contrast between skin and ink.

And the hot water was only a substitute for the true catalyst: passion.

The invisible tattoo was meant to be seen in the heat of passion - the flush brought to the flesh by rapture - a gift made visible only by one's beloved. Moreover, he said this invisible tattoo would soon fade away. When Morioka explained this she had not replied. He wondered if she fully understood what he meant. She did.

Sanaa considered her decorated body in the mirror.

Who could she show this to? She had no audience for even this painted substitute for the real thing. There really was no one she cared that much about. At least not now. So why go on to have the invisible tattoo etched into her skin? All that pain and money and time invested in what? Amusement? Sex? Love? No. Would there come a time? Maybe.

Later, while sitting in a tea shop waiting for the bus to Kobe, Sanaa found herself thinking about what it might be like to have the invisible tattoo as a kind of trump card to play if she should ever find someone who so commanded her passion she would let the tattoo speak for itself.

Imagine that.

Sanaa looked down at her bare arm. Her skin had flushed slightly, and the delicate calligraphy of Morioka's poetry began to appear. Only a few inches of *kanji* showed before being covered by her sleeve. She couldn't read the old-style Japanese. She didn't know it was part of a famous court poem of the era of pillow-book writing, "Ecstasy come softly to me now . . ."

When Sanaa walked out of the tea shop into the blowing snow, she carried the heat of the hot spring with her. Pausing, she threw her overcoat around her shoulders like the cape of a confident, carefree traveler. She marched off toward her bus, laughing to herself.

It was the laugh that always came to her when absurd possibilities nevertheless appeared likely and welcome. Like fire-walking, having the tattoo was only a matter of will. And her will power had never deserted her.

At the bus station, she was the center of attention. People often stared at her, drawn by her vitality and intrigued by the contradiction between her young face and white hair. When she went up the bus steps ahead of her fellow passengers they were puzzled to notice that her expensive black leather boots did not match. One had buckles, the other had laces.

ALIAS SANAA

The next morning Sanaa was on a plane bound from Osaka for Paris.

The steward in the first-class cabin noted her name on his manifest: "Riley, A. O." It matched the name on her passport: Allyson Octavia Riley.

And in her purse, on a copy of her birth certificate, and on her driver's license, it was the same: Allyson Octavia Riley. By social custom and the law of the land, this, indeed, was her real name.

But it had never been real to her. From an early age she rejected it. And even though she still used it when necessary, it would always be a pseudonym to her.

She was the unexpected, late-coming last child, third daughter of John and Carolyn Riley. Her father had long wanted a son and an ally. Thus, "Allyson." He called her Al. She had never been his ally or his son. She was his baby daughter, but he denied her that role. When her father died, she decided never to use Allyson again, more in sorrow than in anger.

At various stages of her life she had been called Allie, Riley, O'Riley, Alice, Alley Oop, and Big Al, whatever suited sisters, friends, classmates, teachers, and family. None of these names were ever her own. But nobody ever asked her how she felt about it. "Without asking, you are born; without consultation, you are named; and without knowing when, you die," she said, quoting Fabuliste Curnonsky. While being born and dying were out of her hands, she was determined to name herself.

If it were left up to her, people would be free and even expected to re-name themselves when they became twenty-one. And again at fifty, perhaps. To forever be tagged by parental ego-need or family legacy seemed unfair to her. She was not a pet or a possession. Why not use a name for as long as it was useful - a day, a week, a decade - and get another when life called for it? Japanese artists did that, Hokusai for one.

As a child she imagined she had been adopted and someday she would discover her real name. As she grew older she adopted herself, and made a game of giving herself secret names as the situation suited her. As an adult, she often tried out new names when she was traveling.

Just now, in Japan, she was Sanaa.

A month before, she had allowed a man to think of her as a Roman Catholic nun named Alice O'Really. She had not introduced herself as such. The misperception was entirely his own doing. But she had allowed it. She had since felt some small remorse for the playful deception. She liked him. Still, if he was satisfied to see her as a nun, it was his problem. And she was amused at being Alice O'Really for a week. An Alice in a permanent Wonderland.

Her favorite social philosopher, Fabuliste Curnonsky, had said in his essay "On Being" that "Knowing a person's name doesn't tell you anything important about him. Knowing something important about him doesn't tell you his name."

(Actually, Fabuliste Curnonsky was the name she used when she wanted an authoritative source for an opinion that was, in fact, her own. She had enough sayings of Fabuliste Curnonsky to fill a small book.)

Her father had been an emergency room physician. One of the great ones, people said. Nobody was better in a crisis than he. His confidence under pressure was legendary. His medical students and attending nurses called him "Jack the Rock." In another life he might have been a great battlefield surgeon, a commando leader, or a spy. But his strengths did not apply to family life. At home, behind his back, his wife and daughters called him "the Lone Stranger."

His private enthusiasm was flying sailplanes. Another realm where he pushed his limits, alone. When his glider went down in the open sea off Santa Barbara, his body was never found. It seemed fitting to his youngest daughter - she never knew where he was when he was alive either.

She was far more like him than she knew or would admit. She had his brains, his confidence, and his steel. With what little time her father gave her, he taught her to play cutthroat poker, how to judge a fine wine, how to select a cigar, and how to sharpen a knife.

He insisted she take flying lessons. She soloed at eighteen.

Like him, she excelled at solitude. From childhood she had an amazing ability to be absolutely still - like one of those street mannequins who challenge you to make them react. She conveyed a promise of something interesting about to happen, while at the moment there was only coiled stillness.

She had two strengths her father lacked: a capacity for passion and an unwavering, open-eyed, creative imagination.

Her footwear was an example of her ability to consider the most ordinary things, pose questions, and act on her conclusions. More often than not, her shoes did not exactly match. She reasoned that since her feet, like most people's, were not identical but differed in size and shape, it did not make sense to buy matching shoes which usually were not comfortable for one foot or the other. Why compromise? Feet first.

Furthermore, since the two halves of human beings are not symmetrical, why should symmetry ever be the goal in clothing? She never wore matching earrings. The same for gloves and mittens and socks. Nor did she have any use for matching sets of dishes or glasses or napkins. Her table was set like a bouquet of mixed flowers, each place setting chosen to please the guest.

"Nothing in the world matches," said Fabuliste Curnonsky. "Don't fight it - cooperate with that."

Now, she is on the plane for Paris. Wearing two nearly identical red sandals, with unmatched socks. One with red and white stripes and one with red and white checks. When her seat companion strikes up conversation, she will introduce herself as Calliope - the name of the Greek Muse of epic poetry and eloquence. There is some truth in this. She has decided to accept her self-appointed role in the life of the man who still thinks she is a nun. *Amusing to be a muse*, she thinks. *Why not?* As Fabuliste Curnonsky said, "We are often just exactly who we pretend to be."

"Why can't you just be normal?" asked her exasperated mother.

She thought about the question and the next day left these words written with an indelible felt-tip pen on her mother's bathroom mirror:

*

There is a piece of music with a permanent place in Allyson's mind.

She composed it herself when she began cello lessons. When she learned to read the language of music, she realized she could write in that language as well. Her first attempt produced a simple, childlike piece to accompany a recurrent dream. The tune lodged in the jukebox of her mind and seemed to play itself at promising moments of transition. Whenever things were looking up, Allyson found herself humming what she called "The Cuckoo Not Song."

*

Meanwhile, the man who thinks of her as Alice, the nun, is in Greece, on the island of Crete.

CRETE

The largest Greek island. The last land in Europe before Africa.

It is November. Wednesday. Two o'clock. Steel shutters rattle down and slam shut. The shops of Hania are closing for the afternoon, as is the Cretan custom. Homebound traffic has snarled to a halt in front of the central market. Sounds of small-scale chaos: shouting, horns honking, the shrieking of a policeman's whistle.

Max-Pol Millay weaves his way through the car clutter toward the commotion in the middle of the street. A large man in a black leather coat is planted in front of an old gray Fiat sedan, beating on its hood with a walking stick in one hand and a furled umbrella in another. *Wham! Smash! Wham! Smash!* The man shouts, hits, shouts, hits. Crazed with fury. The fierceness of his rage intimidates even the policeman. The urgent screech of the policeman's whistle, the wailing hooting of an arriving ambulance, and the sirens of two police cars seem to fuel the man's assault on the hood of the Fiat. *Wham. Smash. Wham.* More police. More whistles. More shouting and horn honking. Pandemonium. *Wham! Smash! Wham! Smash!* The cane shatters. The battering stops. The assailant throws aside the remains of his broken cane and bent umbrella, staggers backward and collapses on the curb, gasping like a boxer decked by a low punch. Max-Pol can see his face for the first time.

"My God, it's Alex!"

Before Max-Pol can push through the crowd, the emergency team has lifted the limp gladiator off the curb, strapped him to a stretcher, and rolled him into the back of the ambulance. There's no blood or glass in the street. Only the hood of the Fiat is damaged, pleated from the blows rained upon it.

What's happened? Nobody knows. The car apparently did not hit anybody, but for some reason this old man stepped off the curb and attacked it with his cane and umbrella. Very strange. A vendetta, perhaps?

The driver, another old man, is helped from the car, apparently un-injured, but dazed and speechless. The police and bystanders are sorting things out in the usual Cretan way - pointing and arguing all at once. There's no fire, but a fire truck arrives just the same.

Max-Pol stares at the ambulance slowly howling away through the chaos. No doubt. It was Alex - Alexandros Evangelou Xenopouloudakis himself. None other. The last time Max-Pol had seen him - a month ago - had been in the Barcelona Zoo, calmly discussing the peculiar existence of the only albino gorilla in the world.

NIGHT TRAIN

The night train from Paris to Barcelona leaves the Gare d'Austerlitz at 9:15 to arrive in Spain the next morning at 8:00. Alongside the dark blue coaches on track 9 the platform master mechanically shouts at no one in particular, "Allez! Allez! Allez!"

A man in a brown jacket impedes the progress of hurrying passengers. He moves slowly along the platform walking backward pulling his loaded luggage cart. To the annoyance of those trying to pass, the cart swerves from one side of the platform to the other. Ignoring the muttered complaints of the inconvenienced, he muddles on.

His cart has a damaged front wheel. Pushed, it will only go in circles. Pulled, it lurches forward unpredictably. He is resigned to this cart. It fits the state of his life at the moment, which is also damaged goods. He drags cart and life on down the platform in a mood of amused belligerence.

His amusement is not shared by the officer in the blue uniform.

"*Bon soir, monsieur - vous allez ou vous venez*? (Good evening, sir, are you coming or going?)"

The platform master - ever alert for deviant behavior.

The cart puller replies with a gruff attempt at Gallic wit:

"*En retraite, j'avance.* In retreat, I advance - Napoleon said that."

"Ah, you are *English,* then?" (Alas, the eccentric English.)

"No, American."

"American - ah, well, then, but of course." (Naturally. Americans are not eccentric, just inane.)

"Your tickets, s'il vous plaît, and your passport."

The man in the brown jacket responds with a crisp salute:

"Certainement, capitaine - my papers."

The documents are superficially inspected.

"Bon, Monsieur Max-Pol Millay. I congratulate you. You have achieved your very car - enter, and left - cabine C. You will be at home on this train, monsieur, for it departs the station in the same way as you have arrived - by going contrary to the forward direction during several kilometers. It will back out of the station, you see. Au revoir - bonne chance."

*

In the passageway of the wagon-lit an attendant lounges against a window, smoking a cigarette. He has been watching Max-Pol's arrival and has overheard the encounter with the platform master. As Max-Pol struggles into the narrow corridor, the attendant comes to attention, makes a small bow, gestures toward the platform, and says, "Bravo, señor. Bravo! I, Josep Centenero, applaud your style. Never has anyone arrived at my car in such fashion. Backwards. Ha-ha! You will be at home in Barcelona, where we always do things our own way. Bravo! You have crossed the border into Cataluña already. Welcome!"

Holding out his tickets, passport, and a hundred-franc banknote, Max-Pol says, "Look, Señor Centenero, I've had a crappy day. I'm tired. I've never ridden a Spanish train - or even been to Spain. I don't have any pesos, and I don't speak much Spanish. Just take care of me. Understand?"

The attendant visibly brightens at the size of the banknote and this shrewd recognition of his authority and experience. The best kind of traveler, this one. Swiftly pocketing his advance tip, he takes charge of both luggage and passenger.

"Si. With pleasure, señor, I will put your bags away, and you will make your toilette as you please - washing the hands, the face, and combing the hair. I will assure you of placement in the lounging car, where you will have an aperitif and tapas. At ten o'clock you will have the dinner. I will make reserve for you the table."

"Ten?"

"Oh, si, señor, you are now in Spain. Ten is early, I admit, but it is still a dignified hour to eat. If I may suggest, you will eat the soup, the pilaf, the omelet, the salad, and the pears in wine sauce. These things are to-day fresh. The Spanish table wine is better than the wine of the French in the expensive bottles.

"Do not, I beg you, do not drink the coffee - it is instantly from the powder. As you are taking your dinner, I arrange the bed. Mañana, I wake you at an hour before arrival in Barcelona. You will not eat the breakfast on the train - it is in the little packages - for the tourists. You must take your coffee at your hotel when you arrive. That is all. Will you be satisfied?"

"Do it, Señor Centenero."

*

In due time Señor Centenero escorts Max-Pol to the dining car and on into the lounge section, where he indicates an armchair and table by the window. He turns and speaks softly to the bar attendant while gesturing with his head and hands. The skinny young man standing stonily behind the bar is immediately mobilized.

Señor Centenero explains, "Pepe will serve you at once."

Overseen by Señor Centenero, Pepe brings a tray of small white dishes: one filled with olives of several sizes and colors - blacks, greens, and browns; another of tiny dried-and-salted silvery fish; and a plate of pieces of octopus and squid in an oil-and-crushed-tomato sauce. A small bowl of hazelnuts completes this array of tapas.

On his next trip from the bar, Pepe brings a tray of miniature bottles of gin, vodka, whiskey, and sherry - and two small bottles of mineral water, one with fizz, one without. On his third trip, Pepe comes with two empty glasses, a bowl of ice, a saucer of sliced lemons, oranges, and limes, and a large linen napkin. He snaps the napkin in the air and drapes it across his customer's lap with extravagant flair. He smiles. "You have been served by Pepe." He bows. Señor Centenero bows. "Bienvenido a España."

*

As the train slowly backs its way out of the station through the railway marshaling yards, Max-Pol leans back in his chair and sighs. It is as he wished it might be. The night train from Paris to Barcelona. Food of another place. Service of another time. And no one he knows has any idea where he is or where he is going. It would take Interpol to find him.

Exile. Deliberate exile. Affirmative exile. To leave home, work, friends, and culture - to surface somewhere else. Exile, knowing that a new life will have to be constructed mostly out of the remnants of the old. Still,

12

for now, exile. Not as one banished, but as one going the long way around to be at home again in his own skin.

He is not going off to find himself. He knows where he is now. But for the first time in his life he hasn't planned exactly what comes next. And, for the time being, it doesn't matter.

He recalls three sentences from the notebooks of Albert Camus.

> *"I withdrew from the world not because I had enemies, but because I had friends. Not because they did me an ill turn . . . but because they thought me better than I am. That was a lie I could not endure."*

Max-Pol takes out a fountain pen and his journal, and writes:

> Letting go is not the same as giving up.
> Admitting you're beaten is not the same as defeat.
> Withdrawal with honor is not the same as running away.

*

Max-Pol has music in his mind, but it is music that cannot be written down easily, if at all. It is little, interconnected phrases of melody that come from his listening to recordings of Gypsy violin, flamenco guitar, Cretan lyra, and Indian sitar. A tune of his own is emerging from this mélange, but, for the time being, the music is as his life is - a work in process, but nothing for certain - only possibilities.

*

Max-Pol looks up at his image reflected in the window of the train.

Lifting his glass of sherry, he says, "Here's to you, Max-Pol - in retreat, you advance."

The train slows, stops, begins moving forward now, gains speed - southbound, through the night, to Spain.

THE DINING CAR

At ten, the woman in command of the dining car barged into the lounge and into Max-Pol's reverie. A short, stocky, duck-butted woman, with hennaed black hair caught up in a gold comb. Face painted in an elaborate mask of makeup - shades of pink, orange, and violet. Peacock blue uniform, high-heeled shoes of patent leather. A living advertisement for a small Spanish circus: Behold! The ringmistress.

She fired sudden bursts of condensed Spanish at Max-Pol. With a stubby finger, she jabbed at him and then jabbed at the single empty table, implying: *You. Come. You. Sit. There.*

Max-Pol obeyed her wordless summons and was marched to his seat. She jabbed again: *Sit.*

He sat. Warily. As a man might sit in temporary custody in a customs shed, confident he has nothing to declare, but fully understanding he is in the hands of petty authority, and it is less trouble to comply than to complain.

His captor snapped open the menu briefly in front of his face, as a prosecutor might hold up a piece of unconvincing evidence in court. Snapping the menu shut before Max-Pol could read a word, she jabbed in the direction of his sleeping car, firing another verbal burst in his direction. He recognized only "Centenero." Evidently the meal had not only been suggested, it had been ordered. The matter was closed.

She turned to stride away, only to find her passage blocked by the figure of an old man. Imposing enough to stop the forward motion of even the duenna of the dining car.

She let loose a verbal rockslide meant to sweep this elderly obstacle out of her way. To no avail. The old man was still there. He said nothing, nor had he moved. He looked at her in amused interest.

And winked.

The lady had made the age-mistake: the assumption that all old people have regressed to malleable children who can be pushed around. Sometimes one of these old children turns out to be a fully functioning adult, still capable of holding his own in the face of intimidation. The gentleman in the aisle was one of these. He eyed his opponent with all the composed confidence of an experienced champion of intimidation tournaments. She was about to be unhorsed.

(Pause.)

Consider this old man - make the calculated inventory of an experienced police detective - noting details at quick glance.

Size: substantial. About six feet tall, but not heavy. The man's size is not in his build but more in how he stands and carries himself: erect, self-confident. A briar-wood sturdiness.

Age: not really so old - younger - between seventy and eighty? Hard to say. Gray hair - freshly barbered. Tanned, weathered skin, smoothly wrinkled. A mild tremor in one hand. Carries a plain black cane, but doesn't lean dependently on it.

Face: patrician. The skin still stretched across high cheekbones without bagging into pouches. Full mustache hiding his mouth. Eyebrows not yet gray - black - thick and heavy in a single line crossing his forehead. Eyes deep set - green iris - the sclera clear white, not bloodshot. A long, noble beak of a nose and an equally long jaw and chin. What might first be taken as a small cleft in the chin is a scar that continues up into the lower lip.

Clothes: fashionable without flair. Not the style or condition of those of a man who has grown careless in his dress, living out his waning years waiting for death in clothes he bought years ago. Nor do they droop from his body like clothes on a hanger. They fit well, as if tailored.

A white, oxford-cloth cotton shirt. No tie, but around his neck a soft green silk scarf worn ascot style. Black wool V-necked sweater. A tweed jacket, with soft pigskin leather patches on the elbows and cuffs. Dark brown trousers in wide-wale corduroy.

Shoes: practical. Oil-tanned leather with rubber soles - meant for walking anywhere - with tops just covering the ankles. The right shoe has had an orthopedic reconstruction, with sole and heel twice the normal thickness, adapted for some malformation or injury.

Adornment: simple. Plain gold wedding band on the fourth finger of his right hand. No apparent watch. Gold and horn-rimmed glasses in his jacket pocket.

Smell: freshly scrubbed. Not the musty odor of the unbathed old.

In sum, comfortably and thoughtfully dressed. Neat, clean, well-groomed. Middle or upper class. The demeanor of an academic scholar, accustomed to well-deserved respect from the best of his students.

Conclusion: probably English - perhaps French. All appearances suggest a widowed, retired university professor in the Oxbridge-Sorbonne class - and financially solvent. A man of substance, security, and strength.

You would never expect that in his pocket was a red rubber nose.

*

Señora Perez, for that was her name, registered none of this.

The wink scrambled her thinking. Men did not wink at her. She raised her voice, upbraiding the old man for startling her, for blocking the aisle, and for not being able to see that the dining area was full. She pointed toward the seats in the lounge. He was unmoved.

He winked again. She took a deep breath. She looked him up and down. Now she saw him. She closed her mouth. She had at last noticed the full presence of her opponent.

He responded with the power of emotionless patience, speaking her language slowly, skillfully, as if using her rockslide to lay up a stone wall across the aisle. His voice was deep, throaty, thick. His Authority bigger than her Authority. She had fired a popgun, and now she was staring down the barrel of a very large cannon. A fully loaded cannon.

She might be in charge of the dining room, but he was emphatically in charge of himself and wasn't going anywhere she wanted him to go at the moment. For all she knew, he could be a *Very Important Person*. He rumbled on, slowly leaning in her direction as if he might topple on her at any moment.

Chastised, she bowed her head. Hearing laughter, she looked up to find the fearsome old man wearing a red rubber nose.

She backed away - giggling, bowing her head, making gestures of helplessness with open hands and shrugged shoulders.

She capitulated. Tears. Handkerchief. "Oh, señor, señor, por favor señor . . ." The dining-car audience laughed on. She laughed. The clown
standing before her laughed. The diners applauded. The unhorsing was
complete. The dining car was his.

*

"Pardon," said Max-Pol, gesturing to the empty chair at his table, "Si
quiere - s'il vous plaît - please join me." The champion of the joust
smiled with interest. The hostess sighed with relief. A welcome solution: "Muchas gracias, señor, muchas gracias."

Pocketing his red rubber nose, the old man limped to the table. His
former adversary hastened to pull back the chair for him. Hanging his
cane on the back of the chair, he sat amiably, as if the chair had been
reserved for him all along.

The courtly champion now showered his defeated adversary with
verbal roses in effusive Spanish. Disarmed by his flattery, she dissolved
into smiles and little bows and hand-wringing girlish gratitude.

Certainly. Certainly. There will be nothing but the best for the gentleman. She twittered off sideways toward the kitchen, shot sharp orders
to waiters and sharp stop-staring-and-eat-your-food looks at the rest
of the diners. Calm was restored to the dining car of the night train to
Barcelona.

"I like your red rubber nose," said Max-Pol.

"It is my secret weapon. Most disarming. It often gets me out of
trouble I don't want and into the kind of trouble I'm looking for."

The old man considered the younger man: Handsome, healthy, serious. He would guess forty, intelligent, open-minded. But not European.

"You are an American, I perceive."

"Is it so obvious?"

"Yes. The mix of language - accurate but not colloquial - spoken
slowly; your clothes and hair - trimly American in style and cut; and you
crossed your legs beneath you under your chair when you sat down.

"Furthermore, I must say that only an American would *back* down a
French train platform with such savoir-faire. Brilliant! A most notable
arrival.

"But forgive me. This is boorish. I am sounding like an immigration inspector. Since I am the recipient of your hospitality, let me thank you and introduce myself. I am Alex Evans."

"And I am Max-Pol Millay."

A firm handshake across the table.

"I must say your name doesn't sound very American."

"At birth I was named Maxwell Pollock Millay, but was called 'Maxie' by my mother, and it stuck all through high school. Like many young people I wanted something less childish and more sophisticated when I went to college, and I didn't want to be called 'Max' so I combined parts of my first two names into Max-Pol, that's all."

"I like it. It sets you apart. I have not known anyone named Max-Pol."

"And you are English?"

"You also observe as well – my accent, ascot, tweeds and so on – the little clues are always there, are they not?"

The men reconsidered one another. Substantial conclusions are reached in such moments. Like two male dogs of different ages, they had approached one another with stiff caution, making fundamental judgments.

Almost imperceptibly they each relaxed in their chairs. The verdicts were positive.

"Well, then," said Alex Evans, raising his magnificent eyebrows.

STRANGERS

Now began that conversation unique to strangers drawn close together by the coincidental circumstances of travel. A genuine intimacy is possible. It is not the confessional made to a priest, not the purgation directed by a psychiatrist, and not the confidences shared with a friend. This is the unique companionship reserved only for the fortuitous stranger, about whom one later says, "It seemed as if I had known him all my life."

Such a fellow traveler serves as an appellate court in the face of verdicts already reached by friends and family. The testimony given in this rehearing of a life is often edited - autobiographies are reconstructed out of facts, inventions, and yearnings. Just as often, the plainest truth is told.

*

"What takes you to Barcelona, Mr. Evans?"

"To visit friends - to enjoy the pleasures of Cataluña - and to sit in the sun, which does not shine in England at this time of year." Though his English was formal, clear, and concise, there was a trace of accent - tonal decorations suggesting birth outside England or long exposure to another language.

"You speak Spanish fluently."

"Well enough, I suppose. But I also enjoy speaking Catalan - that arrogantly peculiar language of the state of mind that is Barcelona."

"Did you grow up there?"

"Did I grow up there? - a very provocative question. I must answer both yes and no. Yes . . . and . . . no. I was not born there, you see, but it might be said that I did grow up there, in the sense that wherever events move one from adolescence to manhood, it is there you have grown up, however brief that time may be. Yes, it can be said that I grew up in Spain. But that is a long story for another time."

For the first time, of many times to come, Max-Pol got a reasonable and affable answer, but only to the question asked. Nothing more was volunteered, though much was implied.

"And you? What takes you to Barcelona?"

Alex's question came at the same time as Max-Pol's steaming soup, served not by a waiter but by Señora Perez herself. The saffron-yellow broth smelled of chicken and garlic. A lemon slice sprinkled with paprika floated on its surface. Appraising the soup gave Max-Pol time to consider how much he would say, since Alex had set the style of a cordial but circumspect exchange. What does take him to Barcelona? Wishes, sorrow, and affirmative exile - more. But that, for him too, is another story for later.

"I suppose I'm just another tourist, making my first journey to Spain."

Alex raised his eyebrows again, smiled indulgently, and changed course. "I am surprised to find an American traveling by train. Why not fly? You see nothing from the train by night, and the service is not so elegant these days."

"Yes, but I'm tired of airplanes and airports. I want to go slowly."

Congenial silence fell between them, filled by the rhythmic rackety-racketing of the wheels on the rails as the train settled into its mainline speed. After serving Max-Pol's soup, the duenna of the dining car approached Alex cautiously, delicately presenting the menu as if offering a large butterfly for his consideration. He ordered as if giving her seductive suggestions, not instructions. He winked again. She giggled as she hurried off to the kitchen, and quickly returned with another plate of saffron soup.

Max-Pol took the initiative, wading deeper into the waters of acquaintance. "How have you spent your life, Mr. Evans, if I may ask?"

"Of course. My field of interest is classics - Greece and Rome, mythology, history, philosophy, and drama - with a specific interest in archeology. And you?"

Far more quickly than Max-Pol expected, he was back in the witness box. He stirred his soup, buttered a slice of bread, and sipped his wine.

"Medicine has been my life. I'm a doctor - a physician in family practice in Seattle, Washington. I hesitate in telling you that because, as you might well understand, when you say you're a doctor, the conversation always turns entirely to medicine and illness. Suddenly, clinic is open. Right now, to be candid, I hate my work. And I hate having that feeling even more. So I'm taking an extended leave from it. I'll gladly talk about almost anything else except medicine."

Alex leaned back in his chair, reappraising his companion.

"Agreed. I completely understand and sympathize. I'm equally disinclined to invite an inquisition of my own field of interest. I'm satiated with the past. I welcome only the present. Will you spend much time in Spain?"

"No, I'm just passing through this time. I'm going on to Greece by ship - to Crete, actually. I was there for six months once before, doing a fellowship on the Cretan diet, and poking around in the roots of my family tree. I have a very small bit of Cretan blood in me."

"There's a vague story on my father's side about some great-great ancestor buying a Cretan woman out of slavery in Egypt, bringing her back to Crete to marry her in her village, and finally carrying her off to England, where they had nine children. It's probably genealogical hokum, but perhaps some part of my DNA resonates to Cretan soil. I know I'm drawn there. So, I'm going. Have you ever been to Crete?"

Alex was lifting a spoonful of soup to his lips. The question stopped him. He carefully replaced his spoon in his bowl, and looked up, his face flushed. In a voice now softened and slowed, he whispered, "Crete."

"Crete," he repeated, drawing out the word as if tasting its flavor.

He looked out the window for several minutes. When he turned back to Max-Pol his eyes were moist. "*Kriti,*" he said. "I must tell you the truth. *Eimai Kritikos* - I am Cretan. It is my native soil. *Gennithika stin Kriti* - I was born in Crete. Baptized and christened in the Greek Orthodox Church as Alexandros Evangelou Xenopouloudakis."

He turned away and looked out the window again, slowly stroking the side of his face with one hand.

(Silence.)

Pulling out a handkerchief, Alex dried his eyes and blew his nose without comment or apology, then returned his attention to his soup. When he had composed himself, he spoke again, his mood confidential.

"Zee-no-poo-loo-dah-kiss. With such a name - Alexandros Evangelou Xenopouloudakis - well, you can understand why it is easier in England to use Alex Evans. It is common with Greeks to make such changes because we have such vexing names. For example, the great soprano Maria Kalogeropoulou was better off as Maria Callas, do you not agree? And Domenikos Theotokopoulos, the painter, was probably glad to settle for being called El Greco. I forget about my christening name sometimes myself, but then, I have not been in Crete in more than fifty years."

(Silence.)

Interrupted by the arrival of Max-Pol's omelet, which was folded like a croissant and decorated like a salad, with little carved radish flowers and twists of onion and tomato. Max-Pol attended his omelet and waited for Alex to continue.

Alex changed the subject, gesturing at Max-Pol.

"You see, you give yourself away again. You cut your omelet with your fork in your left hand and your knife in your right. Then you put your knife down, transfer the fork to your right hand to eat. That is very American. Why? I do not know. It puzzles me. It is impractical, and Americans are nothing if not practical."

Max-Pol smiled, nodded, and continued eating while giving Alex an encouraging look. As a physician he had learned to delay his own questions, and to wait for what people were prepared to tell him.

Alex cleared his throat, rearranged his cutlery, poured some wine, sat back, and finally asked, "Do you know the history of the Spanish Civil War?"

"Yes, the general story."

"Well, I was a volunteer in one of the International Brigades. To fight is in the Cretan blood, we say, and since I was born too late to fight the Turks, the call to come and fight the Fascists was too strong to ignore. I wanted to be a man, and a man should act.

"A Cretan man should fight for something, somewhere, sometime. It is the *palikari* syndrome - the desire to be tough, bold, and engaged in what might politely be called affirmative brigandage. Ha. The Cretan version of Robin Hood.

"I came with the English Brigade, because I was studying in Cambridge at the time and was tired of books. We arrived in Madrid in the winter of 1936, and were disbanded in Barcelona in November 1938. I came to Spain as a naive, bloody-minded adolescent. I left as a bloodied and bitter man. That is what I meant when I said I grew up in Barcelona. Do you understand?"

"Yes, I understand."

"As with many men my age, those years have become the times of great memories - great purpose, war, danger, the mad rushing of the blood that comes from heroic fear, pain, and sorrow. All that. But for me it was also a time of monstrous, nihilistic stupidity on all sides. My stupidity as well. A cathartic catastrophe. I do not like to think about it, but . . ."

Alex paused, inviting a response with his lifted eyebrows.

Max-Pol considered Alex as closely as Alex had scrutinized him.

"I hardly know how to respond. But first, and please forgive my professional curiosity, may I ask why you wear an orthopedic shoe, limp, and use a cane? Were you wounded in the war?"

"Ah, that. How I would like to say yes. I used to lie and say I was wounded, just to add shine to my heroic image. But the truth is mundane - banal - absurd, actually. I fell down a flight of stairs. Running for shelter during an air raid in Barcelona, I broke my ankle.

"You know, those silly stairs are still there, and I have gone back to see them more than once. I shake my head in dismay. Ridiculous! Such a short set of stairs. I must have landed at some odd angle. The ankle was badly set by an English nurse. She did the best she could.

"But that is not the only reason for my limp. This old leg of mine has been my nemesis. Twice smashed up on other occasions. Repaired many ways, many times. It should be displayed in a museum of orthopedic surgery. Over the years the bones of the ankle have fused, the knee joint was replaced, and there are metal pins and plates in both upper and lower leg bones. If all this was not enough, the hip joint will have to be exchanged one of these days for a stainless steel version because of the accumulated wear from my awkward way of walking."

Alex eased the leg out into the aisle and contemplated it, patted it, and stroked it affectionately as he would an old and faithful dog. "But, thanks to the genius of the surgeons and the daily consumption of a few grains of aspirin, I can still walk a mile or two a day."

"You don't sound bitter about it."

"Bitter? No. Not at all. What good would bitterness do? I think I am very lucky, actually. I could have lost the leg entirely – there was a time when amputation was a real possibility. And I have pain only when I overuse it. Many people my age cannot get around as I can. No, I have been lucky." And he rapped his knuckles on the wood of the dining table.

"Believe me," he said, "I have had my share of times of feeling sorry for myself. More than once I have lain on a hospital bed in pain I thought I could not bear. I wished I were dead."

Alex looked out the train window for a while, stroking his face again.

"But in retrospect, I have at long, long last come to understand that this leg has made a better human being out of me. You see, as a young man I had size and strength and health and brains. With innate Cretan arrogance and a Cambridge education, I would have been unbearable. As it is, I know about suffering, bad luck, and despair. It has made a much more sensitive and sympathetic person of me. I am not rationalizing. I know it is the truth."

Alex smiled and continued. "I will give you a metaphor from the game of poker, a game I learned during the Second World War from some Americans in Egypt. I assume you know poker – you are an American man, after all. Well, then. Sometimes I have seen myself as one who has been dealt all the cards of a royal straight flush – in spades – *all* the cards except, unfortunately, the ten, which was returned to the deck in a misdeal. Do you know such a feeling? To come one card shy of an unbeatable hand – in a misdeal?"

"I can imagine."

"In such a situation, you still have choices. You can fold in defeat. You can stay in the game, but bet with caution. Or you can scare everybody else to death by bluffing and recklessly betting as if you were invincible - as if you still have the flush. Now you must rely on your guts, as Americans say. The Spanish say *los cojones sobre la mesa* - your testicles are on the table. Furthermore, you must consider why you are playing in the first place.

"Do you wish to win and end the game with all the money? Or do you wish to keep the game going because it is the playing that is the pleasure? What will you do? What will you risk? I am not sure how others would respond to my situation - either in cards or in life. But as for me, I have stayed in the game. And look - here I am!"

Alex threw up his hands and laughed heartily. He laughed on, softly repeating to himself, "Look! Here I am!"

He turned sober. "Forgive me for such a soliloquy, but tomorrow is my birthday and I am in a reflective mood."

"Really! To your birthday." Max-Pol raised his wine glass in salute.

"Salud! But it is nothing - a number only. No more questions or speeches. It is growing late. All the other diners have gone. Look - the attendants are waiting to close up. Perhaps we could continue our conversation another time - in Barcelona, perhaps for lunch? Will you allow me the pleasure of introducing you to a great cuisine?"

"I'd like that very much."

Finding that their compartments were in cars in opposite directions on the train, the two men made the parting pleasantries of thanks and goodnight. Max-Pol realized as he reached the door at the end of the dining car that somehow along the way, Alex had taken care of the bill.

He turned to say something and saw Alex in the kitchen, shaking hands with the chef. Alex was wearing his red rubber nose again, and his arm was laid lightly around the shoulders of the giddily grinning Señora Perez. Alex would no doubt get fresh coffee in the morning. The kind not made from the powder.

Alex caught Max-Pol's eye.
And winked.

*

During his childhood Alex often witnessed the parades of troops into
Heraklion from warships docked at the port: British, Italian, French,
and Russian. Grandly uniformed brass bands led the way, blaring forth
Ta-tah, Ta-tah. Whump, whump, whump! As soon as they passed through
the city wall, Alex would fall in alongside and march with them. The
music of those times spun around in his head and merged into a tune of
his own - a march. He could hear it now with full band at full blast. But
when he was in a get-up-and-get-on-with-it mood, he would whistle
the tune softly to himself. Not a trumpet call to battle, just a marching
song to accompany him when he mobilized himself from contempla-
tion to action. He was whistling his march when he went to bed on the
night train to Barcelona. He had a plan.

Alex's March

MISTER X

Name: Alexandros Evangelou Xenopouloudakis.

In Crete he was "Aleko" to family and friends - the common nickname for Alexandros. At Cambridge he introduced himself as "Alex Zenon," but when friends learned his real name they referred to him as "Al X" and called him "Al" to his face and sometimes "Al the Greek" or "Al the Cretan" behind his back.

He objected to none of these names. He believed that nobody is singular - all are many people, playing many roles in many theaters at once. It makes sense to have many names.

His private name for himself was Mister X. Other than the handful of members of his own family - all now dead - he was the only person he knew whose name began with X. It was an ancient and uniquely Greek letter. And the names of many ancient and unique Greeks started with it: Xenocrates and Xenophanes, the philosophers, and Xenophon, the historian, to name a few.

On the other hand, its form is ubiquitous and universal. X is used as a symbol as well as a letter, noun or verb, and abbreviation. X marks the spot. Boxes on forms are filled in with an X. In chemistry, Xe is the symbol for xenon, a rare gas often used in high-intensity arc lights.

In mathematics, X is a sign of both multiplication and an unknown. X means to cross out, delete, obliterate, or end. Almost everything unknown or unrevealed or mysterious is referred to as X. The X factor, Madame X, the X project.

Then there is the X-ray, a railroad Xing, and X used in games such as football and tic-tac-toe. X is found in the model names of cars - XL - and in the names of weapons projects - MX. Distilled liquor quality is indicated by the number of X's. XL and XXL are used to indicate larger sizes of men's shirts. X is used to indicate levels of sex and violence in films.

X stands for ten in Roman numerals. X is used to mean "you are here" on maps, and as an acknowledgment that "you are not here, but I seal this with a kiss for you" at the end of letters.

Alexandros Evangelou Xenopouloudakis liked X.

He heard his name called in the sound used at the beginning of so many words: experience, exciting, exam, exactly. X. It was old, mysterious, useful, and both simple and complicated at the same time. *Like me,* he said to himself sometimes. *I'm an X.*

He had one other name. A powerful name. But a name he would never know. His mother, Immanuela, called him "Darwin," but only in the hidden place in her heart where secrets are kept.

There was a sailor. Australian. Serving with the British navy during World War I. A large, quiet, gentle child of a man. On the way to the Far East through the Suez Canal, his ship put into the port of Iraklion for two days for repairs. Walking away from the port and into the neighborhoods, he asked a young woman for directions.

Immanuela.

She was lonely. The Cretan man to whom she was betrothed was himself a seaman, but she hated him. He beat her and used her badly. The Australian was the first man who treated her with respect and kindness. She was small, pretty, and vivacious. One thing led to another. It does not take much time for the fine thread of fate to bind two people together.

The only common language they had was beyond words.

He said he would come back for her, but she never saw him again.

She did not even know his name. She knew only that he came from Darwin, a town on the remote north coast of Australia. And she knew he was the father of her twin sons. One son died at birth. She never looked at the son who lived without thinking of Darwin, and so she called him Darwin in her heart as long as she lived. And she lived only three weeks, taking his secret name and his real father's identity to her grave with her.

Her sailor's name was Alec St. John. A bastard son of Viscount Bollingbroke, he shipped out to Australia as a teenager, where he volunteered for service with the Australian naval contingent sent to Gallipoli during World War I. At war's end he went back to Australia, where he took a job as a longshoreman, finally becoming captain of the port of Darwin. He never married.

Many times he thought of Iraklion and the Cretan woman who touched his heart. He thought of going back to find her, but assumed he would find only a woman who had loved many sailors. He did not know he was the only one. He never knew he had a son.

During World War II the port of Darwin was heavily bombed by the Japanese. The captain of the port, Alec St. John, was one of those killed.

The port captain's office was the center of the attack.

On the Japanese pilots' maps it was marked with an X.

MAX-POL AND ALICE

Max-Pol went off to bed, but not to sleep.

Sleep was impossible. The conversation with Alex Evans had stirred his mind, and the demon of the railbed stirred his body.

Overnight travel by train is romantic only from a distance, and is best experienced in a comfortable seat in a cinema. In films from a more idyllic era, a train is seen steaming across a river valley in the moonlit night, carrying well-dressed passengers in carefree comfort, smoothly rolling along toward adventure in some faraway destination. The reality inside the lurching wagon-lit would please only those who enjoy amusement park rides.

To Max-Pol it seemed his car must be tilting up off its wheels on one side and then the other as the train leaned and stumbled clumsily around curve after curve. Once, the movement reached such a crescendo of violence he feared that he would be rolled out of his bed onto the floor and trapped in his sheets like a mummy. Sudden stops flung him upright, looking wide-eyed out the window for signs of collisions or collapsed bridges.

He abandoned sleep. Three a.m. He got up. And over-optimistically tried taking a shower in the tiny combination bathing-stall-and-toilet. Only by bracing himself against one wall with one knee and against the opposite wall with one arm could he remain standing. With his free hand on the handle he tried to counteract the fluctuations of the water temperature from hot to cold, while weaving back and forth under the swinging spray of water, trying at least to get wet. His rhythmic movements rivaled the mating dance of some long-legged river bird. Cursing the train, he dried himself with a disposable towel the size of a dinner napkin and caromed his way back into bed.

The train moved onto a long stretch of smoother track, lulling Max-Pol into not-quite-sleep but another stage of consciousness. What came to him, once again, was August, and Alice O'Really - she of the third wish.

Alice.

He saw her again as he had first seen her, across the long wooden dining table at the summer symposium. Though the conversation around her is lively, she doesn't speak. She's not disengaged, but participates only by paying unwavering attention to whoever is speaking. At times she smiles, even laughs, but doesn't join the general banter of mealtime. Hearing disability? Speech impediment? Perhaps.

Maybe she has nothing to say? Silence can mean stupidity or wisdom.

There are other incongruities. Her long, thick, wavy hair is ivory white, but the skin of her face and hands is smooth, unblemished and unwrinkled. Is she prematurely gray or post-maturely young? She could be thirty-five or fifty-five.

There's a careful plainness about her.

A simplicity, elegant in its artlessness. No jewelry, no hair adornments, no makeup and no fingernail polish. No glasses, no watch, no ring. Her clothes reveal little. Good quality, but severely navy blue. Navy blue turtleneck and navy blue jacket and navy blue leather shoes.

Odd that her shoes don't match - one with laces and one without. Absentminded? Probably a navy blue mind and soul. Must be a member of some liberal order of Catholic nuns. A Poor Clare - something like that. Yes, a nun.

Max-Pol reads her nametag from across the table: Alice O'Really.

Odd spelling, but it fits. Irish Catholic. Max-Pol turns away. He's not Irish or Catholic, and not drawn to nuns, especially the aging, silent, contemplative, navy blue type.

The weekend passes. Here's the nun again. Navy blue, still. Sitting in the front row at a meeting, closely attending the speaker. Now sitting with another woman under a tree - writing notes back and forth on the same pad. Now making elaborate hand gestures in dealing with a member of the staff - signing, perhaps.

Max-Pol's mental medical chart description: *Middle-aged, hearing-impaired, self-denying, liberal Irish Catholic nun in no apparent distress.*

The first of many moments of surprise: After lunch she drives through the parking lot in a station wagon with a rowing shell mounted on top. Max-Pol walks down toward the boat dock. Watches her unload her shell, carry it down the dock, and slide it into the water. Easy. Like a craftsman with a familiar tool.

Max-Pol stops walking and watches as she peels off her navy blue sweatpants and top. Underneath she wears faded cornflower blue shorts and a yellow-and-white striped rowing singlet. Nice figure. Very nice. It's as if she changed bodies as well as clothes before going rowing. This rowing body is lithe, lean, and young.

She settles into her frail craft and sculls away from the dock with the comfortable authority of someone who knows exactly what she is doing. Stroking steadily, she moves off down the lake until she rounds a headland and is lost from sight.

Some nun. Max-Pol reran the memory again and again. Some nun.

What's she doing here?

For that matter, what's Max-Pol doing here?

*

The formal agenda of the weekend symposium on "Medicine and Microchips" had been enlivened by the keynote speaker on Friday afternoon - a famous neurobiologist. He asked the assembly of mostly medical professionals to engage their imaginations and consider what they would wish for if the world of microchip technology could grant their wishes. He reminded his listeners of the perils of ill-considered wishes as illustrated in children's fairy tales.

A father of four himself, he had found he had a flair for telling bedtime stories. As a hobby he had spent more time than he ever expected researching the history, structure, and relevance of fairy tales, knowing they give deep insights into the nature of humanity. Since so much of modern technology seems more akin to magic than Newtonian science, the speaker began with a reminder of the unforeseen consequences of treating magic casually.

Most commonly, he explained, wishes are granted because the receiver deserves the luck. Usually a basically good and thoughtful person, the wisher is liable to make unwise decisions under pressure. Wishes are rarely handled well. In fairy tales, the first wish is always extravagant and always made in the excitement of the moment. The second wish is usually made to repair the mistakes of the first wish. And the third and final wish is squandered in getting out of the mess created by the first two. In the end, the truth is discovered: The life the wish-maker had in the first place was just fine after all, and he lives, usually, happily ever after. That's the way it works in fairy tales.

The neurobiologist went on to find parallels in the wishes of modern medicine, but Max-Pol's mind had already left the meeting.

Fairy tales.
Three wishes.
Max-Pol had at least three himself, now that he thought about it.

The first had come true, but not the way he intended. He had paid dearly for that. Nevertheless, he was free to grant himself his second wish: exile - another life. Just get the hell out. And the third wish? That was more complicated.

After the coffee break, Max-Pol didn't go back to the meeting. Medicine was slipping away from him like a string of boxcars unhitched from the engine of his life. The latest developments in voice-activated diagnostic computers were of less interest than the actions provoked by the voices in his mind.

He looked across the table at the mystery lady in navy blue.
What kind of wishes would this rowing "nun" have?

*

As the night train to Barcelona eased into a lulling rhythm, Max-Pol drifted deeper into memory. Same weekend. Late afternoon. He sat daydreaming in a chair, alone at the far end of the long porch of the main meeting house.

He was vaguely aware that someone had moved down the porch and sat now in the chair next to his. A tap on his arm. The navy blue nun. She held out her notebook. Max-Pol read:

"Hello. It's me, Alice O'Really."

The message on the pad continued: "You've been watching me. I've been watching you. Weekend going quickly. Tell me about you. I have hearing and speaking problems. Read lips well. Talk to me."

Her expression was open, welcoming. She arched her eyebrows, inviting response. This time it was Max-Pol who was unable to speak. She had boldly eliminated all the hours of small talk it might take to get to such a familiar moment.

Max-Pol was certainly ready to talk - yearned for someone to talk to. But here? Now? With a nun?

In reply to his surprised silence, she retrieved her pad and wrote: "What would you do with three wishes?"

Max-Pol was disarmed by her ingenuous invasion of his reverie. Still, he was pleased she had come. Having considered her from a distance, it was enchanting to have her suddenly appear in his existential living room, as if she anticipated welcome. Up close she was far more attractive than at a distance. It was the absence of so much that drew his attention. He interpreted her simplicity as guilelessness.

He looked at her. No makeup. Healthy skin. Slightly flushed at the cheeks. Even features, long straight nose, freckles. Blue eyes under unplucked, still-black eyebrows. Nothing special, really, if you only examined the parts. But a face aristocratic in its unadorned austerity. A face Durer might have drawn.

As to her mouth: At rest, the slightest touch of natural grin in the upturned corners. Her smile was broad, and her laughter revealed slightly uneven white teeth, with a slight gap between the upper front two. A sensual, seductive mouth. If the rest of her face had been flawed, her mouth would more than compensate.

Hunch, intuition, or the what-the-hell spirit made Max-Pol respond as if he had been expecting her. It reminded him of a time when, walking down the street in a big city, he had seen someone coming toward him he thought he knew well but hadn't seen in a long time. When he got closer, he was wrong. But now, in this sudden appearance of Alice O'Really, the closer he got the more he felt a sense of recognition.

*

"Three wishes? Well, OK," he began.

"I hadn't thought about my circumstances in terms of wishes until this weekend, but I admit there's a familiar pattern in play. My first wish was to have something end. To be done with a very toxic situation. I don't want to unload the whole mess again now because I spent three years sorting it out, sifting it down, and shoveling the slag safely away. I may be kidding myself, but I think I'll never need to talk about it again. It's enough to say it's over, resolved, finished. I got my wish. Now I have to live with it.

"My second wish is about to come true: exile – another life. Leaving medicine and the medical model of my existence, which is built on illness and my obligation to heal. Can you imagine what it is like to spend every day of your life with sick, unhappy, needy people? People who will not take responsibility for their own health? People who mostly use you and lie to you and treat you like a garage mechanic? 'Fix me.' That's it.

"My second wish is to get free of this – to leave the life I have before I have no more life. Not to run away, but to just go on to the next phase of what I imagine my life to be. As a beginning, I'm going to go slowly by land and sea to Greece – to the island of Crete – to live outside my country and culture and personal history. After that, I don't know. I really don't know. And it's OK with me. All my life so far I've always known exactly where I wanted to go and exactly what I needed to do next to get there. And I've done it. For the first time, I don't really know. I'd like to reinvent myself. As what? I can't say. I want to be surprised."

Alice O'Really said nothing – but studied him so intently that Max-Pol looked away to escape what must surely come next. She started writing, but her ballpoint ran out of ink.

Boldly, she took his fountain pen out of his shirt pocket, uncapped it, and printed:

"Third wish?"

She turned her notebook around to show him. But he already knew what she would write. And he held his gaze on that place where her face would be when she looked up, because, first, he wanted to see the unwritten message expressed there.

She lifted her eyes to meet his. Her features were inviting – forehead wrinkling upward, eyebrows arching, eyes widening. Head tilting back slightly. Asking. Beckoning, as if she had opened a gate in her cloister and was encouraging him to cross the threshold between formality and intimacy. Her gaze held steady. The invitation remained on her face: "Yes?"

He hesitated. Looked away. Looked back. Looked away again.

Tearing the sheet out of her notebook, she held it up between them, her eyes just above the top edge of the page, her finger tapping the words:

"Third wish?"

So. He wished.

"I wish for a . . . Witness. It's hard to explain, but I'll try." As he heard himself assemble his wish aloud for the first time, he felt vulnerably foolish. Even a fairy godmother might find his desires cockeyed. He didn't tell her everything - the whole wish was too ill-formed and improbable - but what he did say risked enough. When he finished, he felt suspended in a rush of relieved joy - like a man who has just jumped from a plane and successfully deployed his parachute.

He was prepared for almost any response from her: antagonism, amusement, curiosity, confusion, even indifference. He was prepared for anything - except for what she actually did.

Tilting her head to one side, placing her chin in the palm of her hand, she studied him. Abruptly, she placed the piece of paper on the flat arm of her chair and wrote again.

Below "Third wish?" she printed, "Granted!"

She held the paper up for him to see, then she carefully folded it, took his hand in hers, placed the note in it, and closed his fingers over it. With her fist she lightly tapped his fingers, stamping an invisible seal on his wish. She made the sign of crossing her heart in promise, as if elevating his wish to a covenant between them.

Third wish. Granted.

Her eyes held him still in solemn silence, as she slowly graced her promise with a rising curve of her lips that might be a benevolent smile or a mischievous grin. Or both. She raised her eyebrows. Asking again: "Yes?"

His move. He could choose - to believe or not believe that she took him seriously. Maybe she understood, and maybe she was just as crazy as he was. But what's to lose? His desire for a new way of life included spontaneity.

So. He chose. A reckless choice, but why not?

Opening his fist, he held out the folded paper toward her, and firmly closed his fingers on it again.

"Done," he said.

Third wish. Granted. Accepted.

And now? Now what? His move again. To turn daydreaming into fact. To warrant her validation. What if he changed his mind later - and wanted to undo or at least revise his wish? No chance in a fairy story. In real life, maybe. If and when it came to that, he would ask her. Perhaps she would have some unused wishes of her own.

*

This memory of his encounter with Alice O'Really had become a short film played again and again and again in Max-Pol's theater of the brain. As he drifted deeper into sleep, he wondered where she was now.

*

She was in Japan. On a bus from Arima hot spring on the way to Kobe. Her mind was on the invisible tattoo Morioka had inked onto her skin. Today she was calling herself Sanaa. She liked the sound of it. Sa-naa. She had seen it in a travel article. It was the name of the capital city of Yemen, located in a small plain in the mountains in the far south of the Arabian Peninsula.

She was like that sometimes: remote, but unexpectedly open. So, she was Sanaa, for a day. But she was no more Sanaa than she was Allyson or Alice O'Really, or several other names she had used from time to time. She was still looking for a name of her own, one that made it clear she belonged only to herself.

As the bus coasted down the mountain road toward Kobe, she thought about Max-Pol Millay, he of the three wishes. She wondered what his real name might be and who he belonged to.

ALLYSON KNEW

She knew. Allyson Octavia Riley knew exactly what she had done that August. It was as if she had been wandering around in the alleyways of her mind, had opened an unremarkable door only to find that it led directly onto the stage of a theater where a play was in progress, in which there was a role for exactly the person she seemed to be at the moment. No need for "Excuse me, please, I'm not what I seem." She let it happen. Because if you are temporarily lost yourself, being found by almost anybody will do for the time being.

She might have explained. The truth was so awkwardly simple.

On Tuesday, the doctor had given her his verdict. Being a coxswain in competitive shell racing was over, or else her chronic laryngitis would become irreversible. Fifteen years of coaching and screaming and shouting at crews of women had done considerable damage. Polyps were forming on her vocal cords. The throat specialist who had treated her with tolerant good humor up until now was solemn. She must not use her voice for two weeks. Repeat. *Must not.* And she must - repeat - *must* give up being a coxswain.

The likelihood of surgery was real. The possibility of becoming permanently hoarse was genuine. Add that to the congenital lack of hearing in her left ear, and she would find herself permanently on the outskirts of normal communication. "Get a pad and write to people when you must communicate," the doctor had insisted.

She believed him. She would try. No, it was not good enough to try. She would do it. But she didn't want to talk about it to anybody.

While she was riding the ferry on the way to the conference, Allyson's suitcase had been stolen from her car. Leaving her with only the navy blue outfit she had on and her crew clothes.

Well, she thought, *for two days I can get by with what I have.* No matter how disoriented she felt with silence and the theft, she wanted to be away too badly to turn around and go home. Besides, this meeting was her last obligation to her job, and Allyson always met her obligations.

And that's how she came to be perceived that weekend as a hearing-and-speech-impaired nun. It was an obvious conclusion for people to make. But so what and why not? She was ready to be someone else. She could explain later to anyone who needed explanations. When someone called "Sister," she laughed. If they only knew.

What tipped the balance between fact and fiction was the almost prophetic screw-up on her nametag. Instead of "Allyson O. Riley" it read "Alice O'Really." She liked that. O'Really. It had an implied question mark after it - O'Really? And she liked "Alice." She had identified with Alice in *Alice in Wonderland* as a child.

It was the third wish business that got her in far deeper with Max-Pol than she intended. A mad, reckless throw of the dice, that. Who was she to grant the wishes of strangers? But so what and why not?

And though she found it hard to admit it to herself, he was the first man she had met in a long time she felt drawn to. And she wanted to know why. Though men had often pursued her, she had never pursued a man in her life.

And now? She would at least step through the looking glass he held up to her. From now on, for Dr. Max-Pol Millay, she would be Alice. He would be Wonderland.

WITNESS

"What do you want most now, Max-Pol?" The ultimate question.

Asked by the psychiatrist, Marcus Levine. The two men had been fellow students during medical school, and had become colleagues in medical practice. Max-Pol treated Marcus's children, and while Marcus was not Max-Pol's therapist, he had become a caring confidant during Max-Pol's personal crisis. The two men held one another in mutual esteem, professional respect and personal trust being only part of a relationship that also included playing poker and racing small sailboats together.

Now they were sitting by the fireplace in Marcus' home late on a rainy fall night, ceremonially drinking a vintage red wine. This was a farewell occasion. Tomorrow, Max-Pol would leave for Europe.

Marcus had first offered to be of help after the death of Max-Pol's wife and unborn child. The two men had met informally but regularly. Once the crisis had eased, the conversations continued as Max-Pol talked himself out of the practice of medicine and into indefinite, self-imposed exile in Crete.

Max-Pol rose and stood before the fire, warming his hands, composing his thoughts. Without turning around he spoke aloud, more to himself than to Marcus. "What does Max-Pol Millay really want now? What? I'm not sure I believe myself when I say I want to be alone and a stranger in a faraway place - to just get lost for a while.

"That's romantic in the most maudlin way, but I'm not sure that's me. It's not about grief. I can deal with that anywhere. Rationally, I know I wasn't to blame for what happened, but I still feel guilty. But, in time, that will ease. I know that. I don't see what I'm doing as running away or giving up, Marcus. I'm letting go and opening up."

Max-Pol walked over to the counter and refilled his wine glass. He sat down beside Marcus and stared into the fire.

"You know I'm not a loner - not good at solitude - but I'm 'peopled' out. Spending my days with patients whose problems are far worse than mine doesn't salve my own wounds. And well-meaning friends don't really fill the emptiness after a while.

"What do I want most now? I think I know, but I don't have a name for it. I want someone else in my life. But not a lover, not a companion, not a friend, not a wife, and not a muse. Not even a therapist - with all due respect and gratitude for the help you've been, Marcus. You got me across the coals. But there's something else in the way of a human relationship I really wish I had. Now."

"What would that person do for you?"

"Just *know*. Know what I was doing and thinking and feeling, without any responsibility to do anything in response - no advice or counsel or feedback. Just *know*."

"And if they knew, then you wouldn't feel alone?"

"Yes. I think so. It's selfish, isn't it? Is it too crazy to think there might be someone else who would be in the same state of mind? Someone who would want a reciprocal relationship? *I* know and *they* know. Period. No strings attached."

"You might be surprised. I've had several patients who expressed similar feelings. More common than you think - this contradictory need for accompanied solitude - being separated without being forsaken - wanting to be on a deserted island with someone on another deserted island within calling distance. Monastic, in a way - the quest for the cloister."

"How do you respond when patients want that?"

"I tell them I think it's a normal transitional need. If you are not ready for any of the more conventional relationships, but still don't want to cut yourself off from that sense of there being *another* - then someone who *knows* but doesn't require interaction can be essential to your well-being.

"Keep something in mind, Max-Pol - this is important: the number of workable models of human relationships is infinite. As long as two people openly agree on the nature of their contract with one another, anything is possible. As a psychiatrist I'm aware of some pretty unusual relationships that function quite well. Even so, people come to me because they're worried what other people might think or what society and culture approve of. They want the affirmation that society does not openly provide.

"You know examples of this yourself, Max-Pol. Gay couples, couples of non-traditional age differences, couples from widely divergent social and economic and ethnic backgrounds, and couples who are married but don't live together. Those are just the most common ones.

"I also am constrained to say that my experience confirms that almost any combination works for a while, and almost any combination inevitably changes."

Marcus wrinkled his forehead and looked away, lost in thought. After a long silence, he turned his attention back to Max-Pol.

"Witness. You want a *Witness*. Someone who *knows*. A keeper of the archives of your existence. And who requires nothing of you."

Max-Pol smiled in recognition. "Yes, I like that. *Witness*. It feels right when I say I want a Witness."

"Good," said Marcus. "And you may well find one. People tend to find what they look for, more often than not. But keep my admonition in mind: you are in a transitional state - in motion going *away* from one period in your life toward another. A Witness may be a temporary need. And a Witness may become something else. Take care - of yourself and of the Witness. You said 'No strings attached' - but strings always get attached. Don't forget that."

"You're a wise friend, Marcus."

"But not, I think, a candidate for your Witness. I hesitate to guess, but when you find your Witness I suspect it will be a woman. And, if so, I wonder about Laura's death. Would you tell your Witness?"

"I want to say *No*. But for all my confidence that I've settled the sorrow, I suppose it will rise up and catch me by surprise. Demons don't go away, they just lie low. Sooner or later I'll need to unload the whole story again. And I'd call you first. The Witness is for the rest of what goes on in my life from here on."

Marcus sat silently, wondering to himself who his own Witness was.

"So, Marcus, where and how does one find a Witness? Advertise?"

"Who knows? Keep your eyes open. One may appear where and when you least expect. Being lucky helps, but, as they say of teachers, they show up when the pupil is ready.

"However, you won't find your Witness just because you need one. You yourself recognize the essential reciprocity involved. You must be prepared to *be* a Witness yourself. That's important."

BARCELONA

CRASH! Max-Pol was jolted awake and *CRASH!* upright by explosions. Alarmed, he raised the curtain. The day had begun with a storm: black clouds, slashing lightning, bellowing thunder, and, lashing rain. Blasts of wind rocked the train. Not the affable Spanish autumn Max-Pol had expected. He muttered grumpily to himself, "Beautiful. Just what I need. Welcome to Spain."

*

The train eased into the Estacio Termeo de Franca, built for the Universal Exhibition of 1888 and refurbished for the 1992 Olympics. But the elegant station was deserted. The night express from Paris was the only train. Señor Centenero explained, "In España it is a holiday, señor. No porters. No taxis. But it is maybe Señor Millay's hotel has sent a car and driver for him."

And such was the case - a bellman walked along the platform with a sign: "Car for Señor Millay."

Alex Evans stepped down heavily from the train - looking as whipped and chastised by the journey as Max-Pol.

"Alex, my hotel has sent a car for me - come share it."

Alex nodded in weary acceptance.

They rode in grumpy silence, broken only by Alex directing the driver in Spanish, explaining that Señor Millay would be dropped off first and, if it was agreeable, the car would take Señor Evans on to his lodging in the foothills a little farther on. Agreed.

At his hotel Max-Pol was caught up in the busyness of unloading baggage. Only after the car drove away did he realize there had been no goodbyes and no arrangements to meet again. Max-Pol waved ruefully at the car moving off into traffic. Not a good morning. Still, Alex knew where he was if he wanted to get in touch.

Two days later, the hotel concierge handed Max-Pol a message as he passed by on the way to breakfast.

A Mr. Alex Evans wishes to return your kindness. If you have no other obligations, please join him for lunch at the Restaurant Quo Vadis, #13 Cr. Carmela, close by the Mercat Boqueria, just off the Rambla. Today at 2:00. Please leave word if you accept or decline.

"When he calls, please tell Mr. Alex Evans that I accept. Do you know anything about this restaurant?"

"Oh, si, señor. It is one of the oldest restaurants in Barcelona, in the hands of many generations of the same family. Since it is near the best market in the city, it always has the best of provisions. Professors from the university eat there for lunch. And it is a customary place for dining after the symphony or opera. A choice of excellence."

*

The Quo Vadis was as promised. It had an unpretentious entrance off a narrow side street, but when Max-Pol opened the door into a foyer, the first note of welcome was the thick, meaty aroma coming from the kitchen. Baskets of fresh mushrooms and fruits and vegetables were displayed at the kitchen entrance. Nothing flashy in the decor. Food was emphatically the specialty here, not fashion.

Beyond the kitchen, the dining areas were lit with warm yellow light from oil lamps. Dark wood fixtures and furnishings. Rust-red, terracotta tile floor. White linen. Fresh flowers - purple freesias. Middle-aged waiters in black jackets and white aprons. Soft strains of guitar music.

Max-Pol felt like going outside and coming in again, just to prolong this first impression - this warm, welcoming ambience that said, "Come, sit down, relax, eat, enjoy."

Alex was already seated at a table near the entrance to the main part of the kitchen, explaining later that since he could not possibly eat all the fine dishes prepared here, he liked to sit where he could feast on them with his eyes as they came from the kitchen.

Sleep and Barcelona had restored Alex's spirits. His mood was lively, his attire dapper - a touch of Spanish style in his dress. A sepia brown wool suit with wide lapels. A yellow- and white-striped broadcloth shirt, with a multicolored, floral-patterned tie and matching pocket handkerchief.

"Well, then," said Alex, lacing his fingers together and giving Max-Pol his most attentive look, "since this is your first visit to Barcelona and this restaurant, please allow me the pleasure of ordering for you. Is there anything you must not or will not eat? No? Then we shall begin with a small serving of a tangy chicken-liver pate and hot rolls, and an impertinent young wine of this region. Then, a soup - whatever they prepare for the day will be excellent. This is the season of mushrooms, and we shall have a sampling of five, each prepared in a different fashion. *Cabrito* - young goat - is a specialty of the house, and I will order it lightly grilled, with leeks.

"A muscular wine from the south should accompany this dish - a wine so dark it is called a *negro* - a black wine. Finally, I think a dessert of fresh green figs in cream - an espresso - and a small Cuban cigar. Will this be acceptable?"

Max-Pol nodded and smiled. "Si, Señor Evans. If I were a beautiful woman, I would feel overwhelmed by your courtliness."

Alex laughed. "No. No. If you were a beautiful woman, you would feel surrounded by danger - enjoyable danger."

"Let the danger begin," said Max-Pol.

Signaling the waiter, Alex carried on an animated conversation with him, placing an order that met the approval of the nodding waiter as well.

"Si, Señor Evans."

Alex turned back to Max-Pol. At ease in these surroundings, pleased at being a knowing host, without any prompting he began as if continuing a conversation with Max-Pol already begun in his mind.

"Well, then. War. You wish to know about the war in Spain. You, who have not been to war. You want to see wounds and medals. You want to know about Barcelona and Spain and me and the un-civil war. But you are avoiding asking me. And I am avoiding telling you. I am of two minds on this matter. I both *do* and *do not* want to speak of such things.

Do you understand?

"But let us not take the life out of this dinner by speaking of times of death and destruction. The events of the past will wait for us. But the food before us will not. Eat. Drink. Enjoy. We will walk and talk a little, after. Agreed?"

"Agreed."

The rest of the meal was given over to the pleasures of the feast, with short lectures on the merits of each course. As waiters came swinging through the kitchen door, they paused and showed Alex what they were serving to other guests. Dishes of tiny pink shrimp and black mussels, white oysters in beds of ice, fried purple squid and aubergines, and fierce spiny lobsters, still steaming from the pot. Alex made exaggerated episcopal blessings over each dish.

"And the wine," Alex said, "the wine! Taste it. The wine is the dangerous woman who courts *you*." He lifted his glass, drank, and continued. "The Spanish do not subscribe to the French foolishness wherein the so-called best wine is recognized only by experts and afforded only by the rich. Ridiculous! No wine can ever be the best, because we do not have the same tastes.

"Let the grapes be grown with care, let the weather be generous, let the winemaker know his trade - and you will have only *different* wines, not the *best*. Wine is good young and wine is good old. You simply must taste as much as you can in order to decide what you prefer. It is up to you."

Alex was equally eloquent on the subjects of table linen, cutlery, and china (plain, so as not to compete with the food), and coffee and cigars (dark, strong, fresh). It was almost five o'clock before they finished lunch.

Rising with a groan of pleasure, Alex said, "Come. We will walk, and I will tell you what you want to know. Or as much as I want to tell you."

Rambling

Alex steered Max-Pol out the door, across the street, and onto the Rambla. Now a tree-shaded pedestrian way, it was once the bed of a small river that became a moat following the line of the medieval defense walls of Barcelona. When the walls were demolished in 1776, the Rambla was remade into a great avenue running straight from sea to foothills. With its lofty plane trees and alfresco cafes, the promenade is lined with stalls selling flowers, birds, sweets and books. Alex and Max-Pol joined the ramblers, taking their time strolling, sitting, watching and being watched.

The Rambla begins to lose its charm as it opens into the Placa de Cataluña. Here, Alex suggested they walk a few blocks west to the university. From the outside, the university looked to Max-Pol like a great Midwestern American railroad terminal. Inside, however, the Moorish influence was obvious, with slender columns and interior courtyard gardens. It was to one of these inner sanctuaries that Alex walked with directed purpose.

The space was not large. Open to the sky but surrounded on all four sides by the four-story-high arcades of the building, the light of the courtyard was soft, the air damp and cool. Small trees flourished, along with flowers and moss. Water played from a single spout into a long, shallow pond. Water lilies. Goldfish. Peacefully quiet - not even the traffic noises from the main street just beyond the building could be heard. The timeless sense of sanctuary in a medieval cloister.

Alex settled himself on a stone bench.

He relit his cigar and puffed contentedly, slowly, blowing smoke rings. "Someday," he mused, "I shall get good at this and be able to blow three rings, one inside another. I have seen it done. I know I could do it."

Max-Pol nodded, waited.

"Well, then. This is the second time I have sat on this very bench in this very courtyard. The first time was on the twenty-eighth of October,

1938. It was the day of the final parade of the International Brigades that fought on the Republican side. They say 300,000 people lined the streets. But I had broken my ankle, as you know, and could not parade. And I did not want to parade. I had enough of the insanity of this un-civil war and was glad to have a reason to be out of sight. I came here alone to hide myself.

"I sat here. Exactly here. So very alone. For several hours. Every-body else went to the parade. The building was a filthy shambles then. Hundreds of refugees had been camping out in here. This pond was a cesspool.

"I was scared. In despair of my life. I wished I were dead. In coming to Spain I had thrown away every opportunity I had to get somewhere and be somebody. I would never be an English gentleman. I felt old and crippled and stupid. Nothing to look forward to. It was a bad day for Alexandros Xenopouloudakis. A very bad day."

Alex took a deep breath, remembered.

"And now? Here I am again. This time I feel young and healthy and much wiser than I did all those years ago - how many - can it really be fifty-seven years? Now, now I fear little, now I despair of nothing. The years have been good to me. Such a surprise. Such a life. Such a world."

Three saucy Spanish coeds laden with books walked briskly through the courtyard, chattering and laughing, smoking cigarettes. Clumpy black leather boots, mini-skirts, tight sweaters, long black hair, flashy makeup and flashy attitude.

Alex caught Max-Pol's roving eye, winked, and laughed.

"I also notice," he said, "but old age dampens the urges. For that I am grateful. I feel I have finally escaped from the grasp of a mad and furious master. It is enough to remember."

"You were going to tell me about you and the war."

"Yes. Well, then. In 1936 I was in England - at Cambridge University. Studying philosophy and classics and history. So young, so full of ideas and ideals.

"'Isms' were in the air – Marxism, communism, anarchism, and all those dreams of international brotherhood, the liberation of the workers in chains, overthrow of oppressors, and racial equality. You know the litany, I am sure.

"I was very much influenced by John Cornford, a research student in history at Trinity College, the great-grandson of Charles Darwin, and the son of a professor of ancient philosophy. Also a poet of great promise. He and Richard Bennett and Julian Bell were the center of an activist group who wanted to carry thought into action. They attached themselves to the view of Marx that the purpose of thinking was not just to interpret the world, but to alter it. 'Applied philosophy' was their battle cry.

"I sympathized. I was from a land oppressed for centuries by Arabs and Venetians and Turks. And I was restless myself. My life had become boring. You see, because of my size and strength I had been commandeered into rowing in a school eight. Yes, I, Alexandros Evangelou Xenopouloudakis, was once a Cambridge Blue.

"In truth it seemed the most useless thing in the world, to be rowing around backward in my underwear in the cold spring rain of England – going nowhere for nobody for nothing really important in the world. This was not applied philosophy. This was an escape from applying philosophy to anything but winning a silly boat race.

"When the word went out that Cornford and others were going off to join the Republican forces fighting in Spain, it seemed the most obvious thing in the world to do. We were intoxicated with idealism. With progress and freedom. A better world. Yes, of course, get up and go.

"Underlying all this was the example of Lord Byron, the great English poet, who was the epitome of the tragic hero. He had outfitted his own ship and sailed to Greece to fight in our war for independence, willing to sacrifice his fortune and his life for freedom. Though he died of fever at Missolonghi in April of 1824 without having actually gone into battle, he was given full military honors and a special place in the pantheon of the swashbuckling gods worshipped by the young and restless.

"Now, to be blunt, I think of Byron as a narcissistic ass, but that is another story. At the time, in 1936, Byron's life and writing inspired me greatly. And I literally thought of him every day because I was, by coincidence, living in the same room he occupied when he was at Cambridge in 1805. When the opportunity came to follow his example, I felt I had received marching orders from the spirit that shared my room.

"I quit the rowing crew, closed down my foppish life at Cambridge, and went off to the recruitment center of the British Brigade, which was in Paris at the time. I knew nothing of Spain, so I took with me a book of Spanish history and a Spanish language textbook. After some rudimentary indoctrination, we were slipped across the border into Spain and on to Albacete to be organized into fighting units.

"Fighting units. Ha. A joke. A dirty joke. We knew nothing about fighting. My one skill was pulling an oar in a boat - a lot of use that was. We drilled with shovels and broomsticks. Nevertheless, by fall we were in the trenches around Madrid. The closer the war came, the more I felt my Cretan blood rise - heroism and death were my heritage. Kill or be killed. I was a blind fool.

"But in time I learned how to kill with a knife, how to make petrol grenades, and how to maintain a rifle and pistol. Also, I became fluent in Spanish. More than once my ability with Spanish and English and French got me out of difficulty. I learned how to deceive and how to survive.

"I will not speak of the details of the next two years except to say they were insane. Much of what I remember of those times has been affected by what I have read since. But I can say that for all the glamour of the war written about by amateurs like Mr. Hemingway, the truth of the time was pathetic.

"Long days and weeks of boredom followed by a few days of berserk fighting and then long retreat marches. Days of digging useless trenches in the middle of nowhere for no purpose but to keep us busy until more useless trenches were dug. We were badly led, badly organized, and badly armed, and badly fed, and badly clothed. What a miserable time.

"The only use I made of philosophy was when we occupied the buildings of the Faculty of Philosophy and Letters at the University in Madrid. We stacked philosophy books in the windows to absorb flak and stray bullets. Ha. For once I was grateful for the verbiage of philosophers.

"As the war went on, our only reason to keep going was survival itself. All our idealism was trashed by the interests of the great powers and their ideologies: Russia and communism, Germany and Italy and fascism, England and capitalism. We were ground up in mills too large for us to see or understand or fight. And to make it worse, we fought among ourselves - communists, anarchists, and all the rest of the 'ists.' It became a struggle for control and power, not a struggle for ideals. What a bloody farce.

(Silence.)

"You know . . . the great mistake of Marx was thinking that the tie between members of the blue-collar working class was greater than the tie of language, race, religion, and cultural identity.
"Wrong. First you are a Greek, then you are a plumber. The everlasting mess in the Balkans or the everlasting mess in the former Soviet Union is the proof. Look at the Catalonians and the bloody Basques today. Still at virtual war with the rest of Spain, based on language and culture.
"Conflict always rides in on the horse of self-interest.
"But I digress.

"After taking brutal losses, the International Brigades were moved back again and again and again - until a commission from the League of Nations worked out a scheme to get us discharged and repatriated, and out of the way. We were an international inconvenience.

"Somehow, somehow, I survived without serious injury or illness. A miracle. Many of the men I knew well were maimed or killed. TB and dysentery and gangrene took more lives than bullets. I would have deserted except for personal loyalties and the fear of being killed or captured by fascist sympathizers behind our lines.

"But, as I say, we were withdrawn after the battle on the River Ebro in August. Thus I came to Barcelona. Most of us were in terrible condition.

I had some small wounds, had lost weight, was infested with lice, had raw sores all over my legs from some kind of infection, and was clothed in rags.

"But I had survived. My first real bath and first night in a real bed in two years I had here in Barcelona.

"I wandered around in relative freedom for three weeks. Would you believe I spent my time improving my Spanish, learning Catalan, and looking for loose women? Then I fell down the stairs and broke my ankle. It wasn't even a bombing run - the planes were dropping leaflets. How completely absurd!

"Everything around me and in me was chaos. Since all I had was a Greek passport, I could obtain passage only to Greece, not back to England. All my papers allowing me to be in England had been left in England. And the authorities were not persuaded by my story. Just go home - that's all they wanted us to do - go away - stop existing. How I hated going back to Crete.

"But, I admit, I was also homesick. So, another Greek found us passage on a Greek ship bound for Piraeus. And the next thing you know, I am hobbling ashore in Iraklion. Right back where I started. With nothing to show for it. *Tipota* - Nothing.

"And there, Mr. Millay, you have it. Thus ends the glorious saga of Alexandros Xenopouloudakis and the Spanish Civil War. And the rest of the nasty story here in Spain you know - Franco and all that. It is the business of history now. You can read it in books. It all seems a long, long time ago. I will not place on you the curse of old men's elaborate lies about the glories of war.

"Here is the truth: war is madness. Don't ever go to war."

Alex relit the stub of his cigar and smoked in silence.

"When the International Brigades held their fiftieth reunion in 1988 and dedicated a heroic statue of David and Goliath, Barcelona was not very interested. Actually, they were in denial - a conspiracy of silence about the Civil War.

"The Catalonians busied themselves celebrating the hundredth anniversary of the Great Exposition of 1888 - reviving dreams of success in commerce and industry, not 'isms.'

"The working masses now have jobs, health insurance, old-age pensions, cars, and television. Only teenagers dabble in anarchy. Dictatorship and fascism and capitalism won the war. And foreigners are welcome now only if they carry cash, not carbines.

"What a world."

Alex stood and stretched.

"Come," he said, and began walking out of the courtyard toward the street. "It has been an interesting day. I am tired and shall retire. If you would like, I will take you to visit the most exceptional sight in Barcelona.

"Yes? Tomorrow? Excellent. Meet me at the main entrance of the Mercat Boqueria and I will introduce you to a little breakfast specialty of this city. Say - at ten o'clock?"

They shook hands and Alex hailed a taxi.

Max-Pol's hotel was only three blocks away, but the shops had reopened for their evening hours, and Max-Pol went in search of a store that carried English-language books. Something big and thick on the Spanish Civil War. Alex may have been done with the history of that time, but Max-Pol was not.

PARTING

Alex was as sunny as the morning when Max-Pol met him at the market entrance. Max-Pol was not. He had spent the night fighting the Spanish Civil War - first in his reading and then in his nightmares.

"You look haggard," Alex observed. "First, an espresso - a double. Some fresh orange juice. And then, a *xuxo* - choo-cho - sweet bread dough, deep fried in boiling coconut oil, filled with flan pudding, dipped in the hot oil quickly one last time, and rolled in granulated sugar. Delicious. I shall have at least two. Not a healthy diet, I admit, but I do not worry about such things anymore."

From the breakfast counter Max-Pol surveyed the great market hall hung with the raw corpses of sheep and goats and chickens and rabbits. He decided to add a spine-stiffening, mind-loosening shot of cognac to his wake-up meal.

"Well, then," said Alex, patting his stomach and Max-Pol's, "we are prepared for the day. Let us go to see the most unique sight in all of Barcelona. Absolutely nothing like it in the whole world, I promise."

Out on the street, Alex waited until a taxi of the right color came along. Any bright color would do, but not black - black was for funerals and the pompous. Red was his choice today. As they settled into the back seat, he directed the driver, "Vamos a ver al Floc de Neu, me explico?" The driver laughed and replied, "Si, señor, to the zoo."

At the zoo, Alex bought the entrance tickets and hustled Max-Pol along in the direction of the great apes until they came to a large, glass-walled enclosure. Sitting in striped sunlight, eating a head of lettuce one leaf at a time, was Floc de Neu - "Snowflake" - the world's only albino gorilla.

An enormous, pink-skinned anthropoid with sagging breasts, seemingly outfitted in a white fur jacket, pants, and hat. He sat in regal silence. Occasionally he turned his famous face in the direction of his audience. Overhanging brow, flat nose, squinty eyes, and cockeyed smirk. Unmoved by the antics of the anthropoids outside his cage, he turned back to his lettuce. Snowflake had been here more than thirty years. Though his offspring had been many, none were albino. He was still the one and only.

"Hundreds of thousands of people have come to see him," Alex explained. "He is a cult idol. Every child in Barcelona knows Snowflake. He is better known than Franco or the king or the prime minister. There are Snowflake dolls and Snowflake storybooks and souvenir Snowflake photographs. I wouldn't be surprised if they sold his feces. When he dies, they will stuff him and put him in a museum. He is the totem of Barcelona - this five-hundred-pound freak of nature.

"If you wish to see the rest of the zoo, please feel free. There is an entertaining dolphin show in the aquarium, and I recommend a look at the hippos and rhinos. As for me, I have been invited by friends to join an excursion to see the saffron harvest near Tarascon. I will return on Friday. Perhaps we can meet again later in the week. We might see some of the Gaudi buildings together. I would especially like to see what they've done to the Sagrada Familia."

"I'd like that," said Max-Pol, "but I'm leaving Friday morning - going by boat to Greece - to Athens and then Crete."
At the word "Crete," Alex stopped and turned to face Max-Pol.

Silent for a moment, as if searching for something more important to say, he sighed, "Well, then." He cleared his throat. "You have my card. If you are in England on your way home, please come visit me in Oxford. I would like to hear about your sojourn in Crete. This is not a polite offer. I do not make polite invitations. You are invited. Write, if you wish, but do not expect a quick reply. I am notoriously terrible at correspondence."

"I promise. Let me walk you to a taxi." Max-Pol began making all the remarks of reluctant goodbyes: with thanks, polite amenities, and hints of unfinished conversations.

Alex held up his hand, interrupting Max-Pol's chattering. He took Max-Pol's hand in both of his. Gazing steadily into Max-Pol's eyes, he said, "I will not tell you goodbye. I have a phobia about goodbyes, especially prolonged ones. But I will say I have thoroughly enjoyed your company. You have the rare gift of listening well. Let it be enough for us to expect the good fortune of meeting again sometime soon - soon. Fare you well."

Before Max-Pol could reply, Alex smiled, turned away, and stumped off toward the zoo exit without looking back. Despite his solemn words, there was something casual and light about Alex's farewell. As if he was a lot more certain than Max-Pol that they would meet again. As if he intended that to come about.

Max-Pol watched Alex hailing a taxi outside the zoo.

"I have been your Witness," he said quietly to the distant figure. "Did you know? Would you understand? But somehow I don't think you will be mine."

Satisfied with his capacity, and comfortable with not yet having a Witness of his own, Max-Pol turned back to take one more look at Snowflake. There was a lull in the crowd of visitors, and the gorilla had moved to the front of his cage with his nose against the glass, giving Max-Pol a chance to stand face-to-face only a few feet away. They stared at one another.

Max spoke with respect, "We only come to see you, but we cannot ever know you. Are people really any different?"

Snowflake turned away, and walked slowly across his cage and through the door to the solitude of his inner world. Max-Pol did the same, thinking as he walked, *My cage is just much larger than his.*

*

An early-arriving storm front moved into Spain overnight, forewarning one of the harshest falls and winters in the Mediterranean in living memory. Poseidon roiled the seas early and long. With winds on the Beaufort scale at 9, Max-Pol's ship would be delayed for some days.

Crete was where he wanted to be - not in Barcelona or sick for days at sea. By plane, he could be in Crete in hours. To the airport, then.

By nightfall of the next day, Max-Pol was in Hania, on the north coast of western Crete, sitting by an olive wood fire in lodgings overlooking the old Venetian harbor. All that was missing was a companion.

Alex Evans, for example.

Or even a silent nun.

ALICE AND THE DEVIL

The woman Max-Pol knew as Alice O'Really, and who called herself Sanaa while she was in Japan, was by now in Paris, at a dinner party with French and American friends.

"How do you make a pact with the devil?" she asked in a husky voice. "I mean, if I lived in medieval times and wanted to cut a deal with Satan, how would I have actually gone about it?"

Professor Michaux peered at her through the top half of his thick bifocals. He was intrigued by the contrast between her young face and ivory hair. He paused to gauge her intentions. Throughout the dinner she had sat across the table from him without speaking. She had paid close attention to his declamations about his field of study: the influence of the occult on medieval thought. But she had not engaged in conversation. She was poised, admirably dressed in a pale blue silk dress, and, though silent, appeared intelligent and sane enough.

(It was just as well he had not noticed that her shoes did not match. Intelligent people usually made complex calculations about the reasons, but rarely ever did the obvious thing and asked. Had she been on the other side of the equation, Alice would have asked. Asking was one of her rules of thumb for living a wide life.)

"Mademoiselle, in all the years I have taught the history of the occult, never has anyone asked such a question of me. Why, if I may inquire, do you wish to know?"

"I may have made a pact with the devil. I'm not sure. Or I might want to do it someday. It might be useful to know exactly how."

"Are you serious?"

She laughed. "Oh, not in a literal way, Professor. I understand that making a pact with the devil is a well-worn metaphor for thinking about doing something wicked for the sake of personal gain. But I wonder if it's always been a metaphor. Is this merely a turn of phrase, or was there a time when people really thought they made actual pacts with the actual devil? And if so, is it still being done? And how? And is it always done for an evil reason?"

Her questions drew silent attention from the other guests.

"Mademoiselle, I am a historian - not a practitioner of black or white magic. I am a student of rites of the past, not a believing participant in such rituals in the present. However, I'm told witchcraft is very much alive. I can only tell you that in medieval times the literature was full of references to pacts with the devil. The church certainly believed it could be done.

"I will give you a copy of the English translation of my book, in which you will find one form reportedly used in making demonic contracts. I shall mark the pages for you. It was not always carried out in the service of evil, but sometimes solely in the service of self-interest, though it is not a whimsical enterprise in any case. As to what you do with this information, that is in your hands. You will be careful, I hope. One never knows, does one?"

*

Page 33, *The Influence of Occult Magic on Medieval Thought,* by Henri Michaux:

> *"In order to obtain wealth, fame, or power, or to possess a certain man or woman, contracts were to be written in one's own blood on unblemished parchment, stating what was desired, in exchange for all or part of one's soul. Rolled and tied with strands of one's own hair, the pact was to be hidden behind the high altar in a cathedral at midnight. The devil was expected to do the rest. It was believed that the maker of such a pact could be relieved of his obligations by the intervention of a saint who had successfully confronted Satan."*

*

On Tuesday morning, at the close of the early mass, Father Jean-Pierre was not aware that he had stepped on a very small roll of paper tied with white thread, and left lying on the floor behind the main altar of the Cathedral of Notre Dame.

Shortly after, a sacristan, tidying up the altar area, picked up the flattened packet and dropped it into the wastebasket in the vestibule as he went in to change out of his vestments.

LOUKA MAHDIS

In Crete, Max-Pol had an unexpected visitor - a most welcome one: Louka Mahdis (Loo-ka Mah-dis).

A tall, handsome young woman. An accomplished scholar/athlete - she rowed crew at Harvard - and on the international level. Restlessly nomadic - extended stays in Russia, Mongolia, France, and now Greece.

First and foremost a talented artist - drawing, painting, and mosaics.

Her mother was a third generation Greek-American and a medical colleague of Max-Pol Millay. When she set out to travel in Greece, her mother suggested she contact Max-Pol in Crete. Not only was he a social friend of the family, Max-Pol had been the family doctor since Louka was a teenager. She felt an unpaid debt to him for helping her through a difficult medical and personal crisis during her college years.

Max-Pol welcomed her visit and gave her travel suggestions. He also shared his written accounts of his experiences in Crete. He called them his "Cretan Chronicles." Since he was deliberately not writing a journal of his inner life, but more an objective observation of life on the island, he thought Louka might find them useful in her rambles around Crete.

Intuiting that the Chronicles were of more than casual importance to Max-Pol, she decided to illustrate them. A month later - the day she left the island - she made Max-Pol a present of her sketchbook - giving him a graphic view of Crete through her eyes and talent. Those drawings and paintings and notes became a permanent part of Max-Pol's Chronicles.

Later, he went to the places where Louka had sat to draw and paint - places he had often been before - and realized he had missed exquisite details of the landscape and life of Crete. Her annotated sketchbook enhanced his feeling for Crete with skills Max-Pol did not have. And her work made him open his eyes to what he had seen but not noticed.

She was not his Witness. But, unknowingly, she made him a more perceptive Witness of his own life. She did not give him drawing lessons. Louka Mahdis gave him memorable lessons in looking.

Debt paid.

And paid with amusement. Louka Mahdis is the name she chose to use for her Cretan sketches. Somehow Jaxom Lewis was just not Greek enough. *Loukoumades* is the name of her favorite Cretan dessert, made for her by Max-Pol.

A Sketchbook of Crete

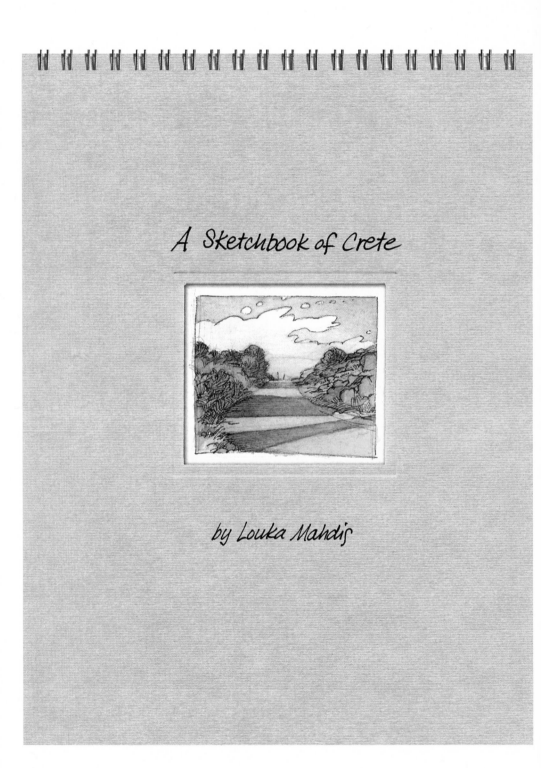

by Louka Mahdis

A walk through Rodopos

CRETE – A BRIEF GUIDE

↑ (pronounced 'Kreet' in English, 'kreety' in Greek)

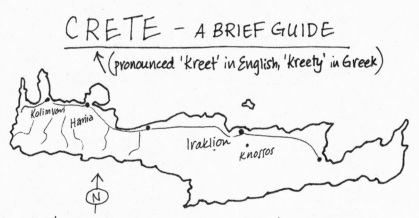

The largest Greek island. In the southeastern Mediterranean, almost equidistant from Africa, Asia, and Europe. Agean Sea on north, Libyan sea on south. Europe ends here. Africa is the next landfall.

About 160 miles long (250 km), it varies in width from about 56 miles (34 km) in the middle to about 7 miles (12 km) at its narrowest isthmus, between the gulf of Mirabello & the coast of Ievapetra. About 3,235 sq. miles in all (8,380 sq. km) — comparable in size to the island of Jamaica. Cold and wet and windy in winter, hot and humid and windy in summer.

Just over a half million people. Language- Greek (!) with Cretan dialect. English & German common as a second language. Crete has a cultural relation with the rest of Greece similar in many ways to Corsica's with France or →

64

Long walk along one road...

Tree by the road - soft shadows
jumbled rocks, crumpled red earth,
blooming sage

<u>AHA!</u> Thistle caught in the act
of blooming-lush, impossible purple
in a dry, spiky wrapper. Almost up
to my knees. A luminous landing-
pad for visiting bumblebees.

Hillside in full afternoon sun-
Strong silhouette against the sky
Bushes have their own little shadows
lime, red, orange, and may migrate
away any moment-hedgehog fashion

65

→ Sardinia's with Italy or Hawaii's with the United States. Alike and included, yet unique and separate. Became political part of mainland Greece in 1913 after 15 years of autonomy and almost 350 years of Turkish rule and 430 years of Venetian occupation before that.

Legendary birthplace of Zeus and home of Minos, the Labyrinth and the Minotaur, Theseus and Ariadne. Setting for endless escapades of the ancient Greek gods.

Unique history. Beginning in about the sixth century B.C.E., Crete was ruled by Minoans, then by Mycenaeans, Dorian Greeks, Spartans, Egyptian Ptolemys, Romans, Arabs, Byzantines, Genoese, Venetians, Ottoman Turks, and Germans in turn. Final liberation from Nazi occupation in 1945.

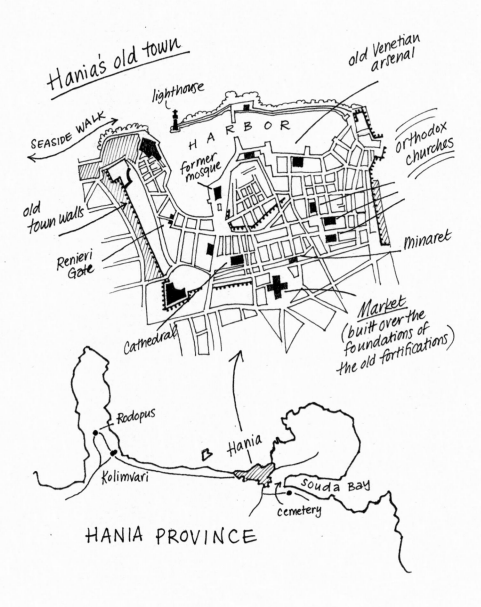

Hania's old town

old Venetian
arsenal

lighthouse

SEASIDE WALK

HARBOR

orthodox
churches

former
mosque

old
town walls

Renieri
Gate

Minaret

Market
(built over the
foundations of
the old fortifications)

Cathedral

Rodopus

Hania

Kolimvari

Souda Bay

cemetery

HANIA PROVINCE

Inner harbor of the old town   Morning

HANIA = (pronounced 'han-YA' in English <u>and</u> in Greek... also spelled 'Chania' and 'Canea'.)

Capital city of western most prefecture of Crete, with a population of 35,000 plus another 15,000 in nearby villages. Known in Minoan times as the orchard city of <u>Kydonia</u> - the Minoan word for quince.

Quince - <u>Cydonia oblonga</u> - is the common English name of a tree whose flowers have five petals and whose fruit has five lobes. This fruit doesn't have much flavor until it is overripe and falls off the tree. That moment is clear because the smell is unique - a lush, sweet aroma detectable at some distance. It is the smell of decadence.

The ruins of the Minoan town remain largely unexcavated beneath the inner city. Hania, then, is one of the longest continually inhabited town sites in the world - perhaps 5,000 years. Mentioned in Homer's Odyssey.

Like its namesake, the town has the feel and smell of decadence about it.

solid blue

pale grey-dun

grey dun

· running water · toaster sounds ·
· slap slap of hands passing
dough ·
· coffee grinding
· birdsong · cats

glowing peach

warm wood frame

Sound of pigeons:
buttery cooing

shadow

panes grey

a little darker, but not much

brown brown

white-washed steps

Violently blue sky - all else in shadow ~ light

warm dun-peach

olive-forest door

blue street with whitewashed step

ochre door
warm dun stone
blue slate street
w/ dun grout

Green & wht checkered cloth under white cover

shaded yellow butter wall

another good door

pepto-bismol wall with gold stone edges

straight green

bouganvilla in sun/shadow dapple
as sun moves in, table becomes luminous
conversation just around the corner...

dk red plastic
(darker pink)

chocolate
(semi-sweet) door

Late Morning walk in Hania - crooked streets and unexpected doorways.

69

One favorite corner on Angelou street

...just before coffee   Angelou Street

MAX-POL TO ALICE

The first time Max-Pol checked his e-mail in Crete, he found this brief message: "Third wish? Mail to Alice O'Really in care of A. O. Riley, Hotel De Lutece, 65 rue Saint-Louis-en-l'Ile, 75004 Paris."

Max wondered how she got his e-mail address. What was she doing in Paris? What's the connection between A. O. Riley and Alice O'Really?

Never mind.

Answer.

*

Kalimera, Kiria Alice:

I give you the respectful form of a Cretan morning greeting. Though, in truth, for myself I should say "kalinichta" which means good night, even though the sun is coming up, because I'm going to bed after I print this letter. I've been up all night. In university days I often did this. I stayed up nonstop to finish something because the juice was there, the thoughts I had been waiting for suddenly came all at once.

So is it for me now. I've been wrestling with your granting of my third wish. As you recall, I said I wanted a Witness for my life. I still need a Witness.

When I told you this in August, I didn't expect you to understand or take me seriously. But you did. When you made the gesture of granting the wish and accepting the role, I was surprised. And though I'm still flying blind with regard to you, some kind of uncommon trust was generated in our conversation. Enough trust for me to address you at least once in the role of Witness.

To clarify: I don't want a correspondent. Letters to friends are easy enough, but they have constraints. Your friends already know you or think they do. And you write in light of that knowledge, fulfilling the scripted expectations.

I used to wish I had a twin sister. That would be a perfect solution. I don't want a muse. Not in the traditional literary sense. Someone else said that a muse is a woman cooked up in writers' heads, propped up like a voodoo doll on a pedestal and then persecuted with illusions, obsessions, and fantasies. A piece of narcissistic nonsense. You may have thought that's what I wanted. No.

I don't want a literal witness to my life. Not a companion or lover or wife or fellow traveler. They lead to the boredom of predictable domesticity. Too many compromises.

I need, I <u>wish</u> for someone to witness the evidence of my solitude. Being there. And knowing. It would be enough.

You in your silence, and your granting of a wish, qualify you for the place of Witness in my life. The job is yours if you still want it. You may have changed your mind by now. I know we're both dancing around this, but my caution is a reflection of how important the idea of a Witness has become to me. I have experimented with being one to others, and I realize the possibilities.

I'm writing what I think of as my Cretan Chronicles, which are a fairly straightforward account of my experiences here. The first job of a Witness is simply to read my Chronicles. Read and know. That's all I ask.

There's more to say, perhaps later, but this is enough for now. You either get it or you don't. If you don't, you can write me off as a strange person. If you understand, you will know how to respond.

Some thoughts on the Chronicles I'm enclosing along with this letter: This writing is not intended for publication but for pleasure. For the past three years I've been through an internal wringer, squeezing out the poisons of the past. What I'm writing now is a way of getting outside and beyond and over all that. It's not confessional, either. You'll not find my old dark and dirty secrets here. Just the newer, brighter, and cleaner experiences. Above all, not analytical. It is not the whole me, but it is all I'm prepared to reveal now.

Sincerely,
Max-Pol

DREAMS AND MEMORIES

Max-Pol put his letter on top of his Chronicles, slid the stack of paper into a manila mailing envelope, sealed and addressed it, and tapped it with his fist, giving it the same invisible stamp of approval Alice O'Really had given his third wish after folding it into his hand in August. Done.

Exhausted, he walked through the apartment, alternately closing window shutters and removing his clothes, dropping the latter on the floor along his route toward bed. In this artificial morning darkness, Max-Pol groped his way between the sheets, rolled over on his stomach, and floated into an oblivion made sweet by the lack of schedule or obligations.

Max-Pol slept his way into another part of his mental movie made at the conference in August.

*

Just as he accepts the granting of his third wish, the final dinner bell rings. He and Alice rise and walk quickly toward the hall, arriving too late to sit together. During the meal, Max-Pol realizes he has done all the talking and none of the asking or listening. It's her turn. He will insist. He also wants to get his favorite fountain pen back. She kept it. On purpose or absent-mindedly?

But he doesn't see her after dinner. And hasn't seen her since.

The next morning, Friday, as he goes out for breakfast, Max-Pol finds a note from her in a plastic bag hung on the door handle of his room, explaining that she regrets having to leave early, but she has obligations to attend a rowing regatta.

"The granting of the third wish was a serious move on my part," the note says. "Believe me."

Max-Pol goes out on the porch to check. Her car and rowing shell are gone. He wonders how someone who is speech and hearing impaired can be involved in a rowing regatta. He asks around, but turns up little more than he already knows: She roomed alone. She was a good listener and a nice person. Several people think she might be a nun - from a Catholic hospital or a girls' convent school. Why does he want to know?

WAITING

A week passed.

Max-Pol settled into life in Crete. He had exactly what he wanted in the way of a place to live. A medical school colleague was one of five Cretan cousins who had inherited their grandfather's property in the old Jewish quarter of Hania. He urged Max-Pol to use the family's apartment until the following summer.

Jammed against the Venetian defense walls of the inner city, the houses of the district had grown upward in a series of small living quarters added like unskilled bees might build a higgledy-piggledy hive. At street level, the old buildings faced onto dark, narrow lanes; the cousins had remodeled a top floor into one large apartment with a terrace overlooking the inner harbor and the sea beyond. Natural pine wood and white walls and wide windows gave the rooms an airy feeling, in contrast with the gloomy spaces below.

The cousins used the apartment only in summer and were glad to have it lived in. It had an uncluttered, impersonal quality about it, making it easy for Max-Pol to make himself at home. Moreover, a somewhat elderly Mercedes sedan was included. All in all, a splendid arrangement.

Another week passed.

He should have been happy.

But after two weeks, the edge was off the pleasure.

No response from Alice. He became anxious.

And annoyed because he didn't really want to feel anything. His feelings spiraled down into a familiar, muddy funk.

All he asked was a simple acknowledgment that she had received and read what he had sent. What was taking so long? Had he done something stupid? Wrong address, no postage? More than once he checked his briefcase and the car - maybe he hadn't even mailed the envelope.

Was she traveling? Of course, then, her mailing address would be checked only occasionally - perhaps by someone else. Could they have made a mistake in forwarding the mail to her? Maybe they hadn't put on the postage stamps. Had someone else intercepted her mail? Was she ill, injured, dead, kidnapped? Had she entered a cloister? His capacity for theorizing became almost, but-not-quite, amusing.

Worst thought: what he wrote had put her off.

She wasn't really interested.

That's it. She changed her mind about being involved at all.

Three weeks.

Most of all, the anxiety itself bothered him. Why should he care?

He had simply been wrong about her, that's all. His usually reliable intuition had failed him. It was a mistake to unload so much on a stranger. He had read too much into his impression of her and had projected his need onto someone who could not fulfill it. He took a chance - it didn't work out.

Rethink. Try again.

*

At the height of his frustration, the reply from Alice came.

On the last day of the third week, a call came from Manolis, the manager of the private postal service in Hania where Max-Pol had arranged to receive his mail. Manolis had once worked for UPS in Chicago, spoke jivey English, and hung on to a hip Chicago style. He still faithfully followed the Chicago Bulls basketball team.

"Yo - it's Manolis - hey - you got an express box here."

"Where from?"

"Spain. Barcelona, Spain."

"Who from?"

"Lemme see - it's a Pilar Azul Pujol - some Spanish dude."

"Pilar is a woman's name, Manolis, but I never heard of her."

"Well, she's heard of you - definitely got your name on it."

"I'll be right over."

Pilar Azul Pujol?

The package was indeed from Spain. With a return address of the Hotel Jardi, Sant Josep Oriol 1, Barcelona. Removing the ripcord to open the box and pulling out some packing tissue, Max-Pol saw several envelopes and packets.

"Who's the Spanish babe?"

"I'm telling you, nobody I ever heard of."

"Sure, sure. Must be your secret lover."

Young Greek men have a one-track mind when it comes to foreign women. "What's in the box? Something sexy, I bet."

"Thanks, Manolis. I'll let you know. If she's young and single and beautiful and looking for trouble, I'll put you in touch right away."

"Forget beautiful, Max-Pol. Young and single and looking for trouble is enough for me. Wine and music and romance will make her beautiful."

"Manolis, you're obsessed."

"Hey, I'm young and handsome and Cretan. A living Greek god – that's me. I'm only doing my job. Love – it is my destiny." With this, he raised his hands over his head and did a couple of dancing, wheeling turns behind the counter while snapping his fingers and shouting, "Opa! Opa!"

"I'll take my box home."

"Lemme know if she sent her picture."

Max-Pol hurried back to his apartment.

FIRST WITNESS

Max-Pol emptied out the box on the table in his kitchen.

Three large, pale blue envelopes - sealed and numbered: #1, #2, #3.

Three small packets wrapped in a darker blue paper and black twine. Also numbered: #4, #5, #6. And three small boxes likewise wrapped and numbered: #7, #8, #9.

One of Max-Pol's habits - a habit his friends find intellectually less than admirable - is to read the last pages of books, especially novels, before he buys them. He wants to know where the author will leave him. If there is a miserable ending - a catastrophe - or a cliché-ridden resolution to the story or a slam-bang, stonewall, dead-end finish, then he doesn't want to read the rest of the book. Not his style.

A book doesn't have to have a happy ending - just an ending that contains possibilities for what might happen next. Max-Pol thinks a good novel should finish with implications for a sequel. A continuation. And the imagining of that sequel is the pleasure given to the reader. A reader should be led to do some work during and afterward.

In this spirit, Max-Pol opened the little box marked "#9" first.

Carefully wrapped in a clear plastic bag were three small cigars about the size of his middle finger. The elaborately filigreed red-and-gold ring said "*Romeo y Julieta - Habana*." Sincere cigars with specific purpose - made for those who appreciate a fine cigar but who don't want to spend the couple of hours required to smoke a much heftier size. These cigars were fresh too. Still moist and springy - not long from a humidor. A box of long wooden matches was enclosed, along with a folded note. Opening the note, Max-Pol found words written on stenographic notebook paper in handwriting he had seen before - part print and part cursive letters, in a familiar shorthand style:

Saw you smoking cigar walking on beach last summer. Enjoy.

The note was signed in ink with a calligraphic fountain pen nib. Max-Pol's pen? Most likely. As for the matter of the name, Pilar Azul

Pujol, there would probably be an explanation somewhere else in the mystery packages, but all uncertainty was past.

"Hello, Alice O'Really," said Max-Pol.

*

He sat down in a chair in the same way he might ease down into a warm bath. Slowly, with pleasure and relief. Taking out one of the cigars, he nipped its end with his teeth and lit up, using one of the slender, cedar-wood matches from Spain.

From the beginning, then.
An envelope. The big one marked "#1."
Inside, a single sheet torn from Alice's notebook:

"Received your Chronicle about the trip to Spain - read it - several times. If that's all you want to know, stop here - throw away the rest I've sent." The note was signed in a cursive flourish: "Pilar Azul Pujol, Witness."

Underneath the signature was a postscript - "If you wish to send more, the address is the same: Hotel de Lutece, 65 rue Saint-Louis-en-l'Ile, 75004 Paris. Mark 'Please Hold'- not to arrive before Nov. 15."

The second big envelope.
Several sheets of blue paper stapled together.
First page - one word in big block letters:
"!COINCIDENCE!"
Second page - in cursive handwriting:

"In and out of Spain this fall - including first week October - sentimental journey - spent junior year college doing Spanish at Univ. of Barcelona - Catalonian blood runs in family from way back - through New Spain, New Mexico, Santa Fe, Santa Barbara - great great great great grand somebody - conquistador mythology.

"Made up secret name for myself that year - Pilar Azul Pujol - college-kid silliness then - nostalgia now - Señorita Pilar Azul Pujol - Spanish Gypsy Flamenco Queen - dancing wildly by firelight with clacking castanets, and rose in teeth - !Ole! - still like the idea - smells of "la vida nomada" - the nomadic life.

"Living a taste of "la vida nomada" now - traveling - seeing art."

More pages - different kinds of paper, but all some shade of blue.

"Art lecture: Picasso was influenced by Velasquez was influenced by El Greco was influenced by Titian was influenced by Bellini - specific paintings - to see you must go to Venice, Paris, Madrid, Toledo, Barcelona. Final stop is Picasso Museum in Barcelona - has 50 paintings P. did from Velasquez's painting "Las Meninas." Next stage - Pilar Azul Pujol influenced by Picasso - Ha."

And underneath, a quick rendering in watercolor pencil and wash of the little princess who is the central figure in *Las Meninas* - in one of the many styles of Picasso.

Next page not strictly a page - a pale blue paper napkin - with just a series of words, written in pencil:
    figs, saffron, pomegranates
    quince, garlic, tangerines
    beets, cinnamon, aubergines

The napkin was printed with the name of a restaurant:
"Cafe Bolivia - Barcelona"
Other than a slight smudge of bright red lipstick on one corner of the back of the napkin, there was no explanation.

The fourth page had a rough map drawn on it. Gaudi's Sagrada Familia cathedral was marked in the middle, with several of the main streets leading away from it. Three blocks over and five blocks up was an X and the comment: "Pilar Azul Pujol, Gypsy Flamenco Queen, lived here."

The last page had several ticket stubs stapled to it: one from the Barcelona Zoo, another from the Mount Juic funicular, another from the Picasso Museum, and the last, a used subway ticket. The first three were dated in the first two weeks of October - this October just past. The subway ticket was dated in November. Two separate visits?

Max-Pol thought, *So Alice O'Really et cetera, wandering blue nun, was in Barcelona in October. Oh really? We must have been there during some of the same time.*

*

And they had been.

They went to the same museum – the one Alex Evans called "The grim prison of Picasso's painting."

Max-Pol had been just as intrigued as Alice by the rooms hung with Picasso's childlike reactions in oil on canvas to what is considered Velasquez's finest painting. This display is one more sign of Picasso's genius and artistic courage. Anybody else might be content just to look with admiration at a great painting like *Las Meninas*. But not Picasso – he responded with hundreds of sketches and drawings, and with fifty or more paintings of all or parts of *Las Meninas*. As if he had decided, as successful and famous as he already was at the time, to take a spiritual lesson acknowledging the mastery of Velasquez.

And Velasquez must have done something similar in his own way in reaction to El Greco. And El Greco, in turn, must have looked at Titian's work with the same kind of appraisal. This chain of creativity emphasizes that art is often a form of innovative plagiarism. Picasso would probably have said, "Of course – what took you so long to notice?"

Max-Pol opened the third big envelope. Three sheets of computer printout stapled together with a smaller cover note in handwriting. His fountain pen again.

Threes – trinities – fascinate me – nine pieces from my collection:

Yesterday, today, tomorrow
Nothing, something, everything
Infinity, eternity, immunity

Yes, no, maybe
Discern, perceive, behold
Body, soul, spirit

Id, ego, libido
Liberty, equality, fraternity
3 bears, 3 blind mice, and 3 little pigs

Wabi-sabi (Japanese)
the beauty of things imperfect, impermanent, incomplete
the beauty of things modest and humble and common
the beauty of things unconventional, asymmetrical, and unique

82

Albert Einstein's three rules of work:
1. Out of clutter, find simplicity.
2. From discord, make harmony.
3. In the middle of difficulty lies opportunity.

Three observations of Fabuliste Curnonsky:
1. The more things change, the more they are the same.
2. Everything looks better at a distance.
3. Things are never quite what they seem.

Three important women:
Louise Colet
Camille Claudel
Blanche Monet

Three musical forms:
waltz
sonata
scherzo

Three spirits:
zeitgeist
haeligeist
poltergeist

As Max-Pol opened and read the contents of the first three envelopes, he placed them in order on the kitchen counter and considered them. Too cabalistic to completely comprehend. A collection of little mysteries to solve. Sort it out later.

He turned to the three small envelopes.

In the first were three postcards of works of Picasso. A goat theme: his ludicrous bronze nanny-goat. A charcoal and blue-wash rendering of a recumbent goat. And a three-panel drawing of the goatish god Pan, playing pipes while gamboling about with full-breasted women. The mischievous side of genius.

In the second envelope, three postcards of the facades of Gaudi's buildings - Sagrada Familia, La Pedrera, and Casa Batllo. The solemn and soulful side of genius, turning stone and steel into sensual forms.

And in the third small envelope, a small, thin notebook - on its cover a note saying, "From the arboretum gardens of the Univ. of Barcelona. Inside are pressed flowers, all shades of blue and purple - crocus, foxglove, lupine, and several whose names I couldn't remember. So I named them myself: blue query, purple bruise, and fairy of the night."

Two small boxes remained.

In one, a plastic holder containing a worn silver coin with uneven edges. The accompanying note said: "Greek - from way back - the time of Alexander the Great - bought at coin market in Placa Real."

And in the little box marked #8, a small clear-glass bottle with a folded note visible inside. The corked top of the bottle had been sealed with melted wax. A small card suggested: "Throw this in the sea - perhaps it will find me - or someone like me."

The contents of the envelopes and boxes were now spread out all over the kitchen counters, tables, and chairs. Relighting the stub of his cigar, Max-Pol walked around looking at this exhibit of the mind of Alice O'Really at work. What to make of all this?

"Think. Don't jump to conclusions, Max-Pol," he said aloud.

Max-Pol's life experience had consistently proved that nothing would cause more trouble in any relationship than mind reading. That was near the top of the list of things he had learned the hard way. It would be a big mistake to try to figure out exactly what Alice was telling him.

She had done what he asked - she had read what he sent her - she had been his Witness. She had given him a choice about the rest - open or not. And she had not asked him for any response. She had only spent something of herself on him, and sent gifts. Unique gifts. Max-Pol was free to make of them what he might. If he wished to reply, he had an address.

And what could he really conclude about her now? He got up and walked slowly around the exhibit again, flexing the rational muscles of his mind. What did all this tell him about Alice O'Really Pilar Azul Pujol whoever?

Creative and imaginative.

Doesn't waste words.

Interested in art - knows a lot - and is somewhat artistic.
Attends details - much careful thought invested in this box of stuff.
Observant, thoughtful, reflective.
Uses a computer - but prefers handwriting.
Has her own idea of punctuation - influenced by Spanish?
Year in Spain - some Catalonian blood - must speak Spanish.
And. She has taken much closer notice of me than I realized.
What is not here is also interesting.
Nothing about being a nun. Nothing. A non-nun presentation.
And nothing much personal about the present - precisely where she is or what she does for a living or why she went so far beyond what I asked her to do.

Well . . . wonderful! he thought.

Max-Pol poured himself a glass of wine, walked out onto the balcony overlooking the sea. Warm sunshine, cloudless sky, fresh breeze from the northwest - the direction of Spain. Lifting his glass, he addressed his invisible companion:

"Here's to you, Alice O'Really Pilar Azul Pujol! Whoever you are, let us continue."

CRETE IN NOVEMBER

Rain. Rain. And rain again. And then more rain.

A week of this. As if rain were a new product on the market and the weather gods were holding an international exposition in Crete, demonstrating every possible variation of rain available.

Rain came in twenty sizes of drops, ranging from globs to minuscule mist. Falling straight, and then wind-driven, slashing sideways, whirling in spirals and loops, rising up instead of falling down. A convention of meteorologists would have been dancing in the streets. Almost everything they had ever read about rain was on exhibit. The basic textbook on available degrees of wetness would barely cover the range of this delugeous week.

Now it is morning. The rain show is being followed by an air and sea show. Beaufort scale 10. The north wind rolls the Aegean over the breakwater and into the old Venetian harbor of Hania. Waves of salty sea water scour the deserted stone quay. Though packed with restaurant tables and umbrellas and tourists in the dead calm heat of August and September, the waterfront is abandoned to the sea now on this November morning.

This first big storm after a dry summer and fall is a welcome housekeeper, sweeping and washing and cleansing. The air is sweet to breathe again. When the skies clear, the highest peaks of the mountains will be tipped with snow.

November is an in-between time in Crete. The time of the tourists has passed. The time of the olive and orange harvest is coming. Construction work is halted by weather. The pace of commerce slows. And the coffee- houses fill with men of all ages and occupations, as if some vast conspiracy were under way - one more Cretan uprising being planned.

The oldest coffeehouse on the waterfront is called the Parliament. If the affairs of state were left to the men who regularly gather here, every problem would be settled in a week. So the customers think. Only the taxi drivers know more. So say the taxi drivers.

On such a day, in such a time, Max-Pol is getting coffee lessons.

(FROM THE CRETAN CHRONICLES OF MAX-POL MILLAY)

This is my neighbor speaking. He really talks this way.

"You will not know Crete if you not spend the time in the kafenion (traditional coffeehouse). And you must not attend the kafenion if you not know the Greek coffee. And you must learn coffee Cretan style, not like Athens, you know. I teach you. We have coffee school in my shop just for you, ola kallah? OK?"

This is Kostas Liapakis. He's the caretaker of the flat in which I live. He has appointed himself my caretaker as well. His shop occupies the ground floor below my apartment. Basically, Kostas is a rug merchant, or so you might assume with only a glance at his merchandise.

He does have many rugs, but the cave-like depths of his store are piled high with other textiles of many sizes, weights, and colors. Bedspreads, couch covers, wall hangings, and blankets. All are old. They are the many parts of the dowries of many women, made in preparation for marriage. Everything has been woven by hand in the villages from handspun wool and cotton and linen yarns, and colored with natural dyes from plants.

Kostas Liapakis has collected these over years of traveling among the mountain villages. He parts with his treasures out of economic necessity, but with reluctance. For when these lovely old things are gone, there will be no more, because those days and ways are gone. When he can no longer obtain these things, Kostas will find something else to do.

Call him a caretaker of the past, a dealer in sentimental history. This is surprising, because he is only forty years old. He's wiry, manic, strong, clever, and comic. He could be a success at almost anything entrepreneurial.

Kostas Liapakis declares, sweeping his arms around the treasures of his shop, "Me, I not like the future. Me, I not like the present too much either. Me, I love the past. I love the yesterday. It is my style, you know." And the pleasure of the past includes the Greek way of coffee, Cretan style.

88

As you see, Kostas speaks English with a twist. It's not his accent; the actual words are correctly pronounced, but the order and tense are his own construction. He simply has his own way with English. It charms his English-speaking customers. I don't mean to make fun of him. I like his verbal gymnastics; they work in his favor.

"Must have fire. Must have water. Must have coffee. Must have sugar. Is be all you need. From these you make any kind of coffee you need, and you cannot know what kind of coffee you need unless you try many ways."

Professor Liapakis lectures as he sorts out his equipment on a long wooden table: a single-burner gas stove, a brass coffee grinder, two small brass pots with long handles, a short round stick of wood, a pitcher of water, a jar of oily black coffee beans, a jar of sugar, assorted spoons, glasses and tiny cups with saucers.

The brass coffee grinder resembles the casing of an artillery shell, which has been stamped and carved with intricate designs. "Turkish," he says, "from the old days, but we not speak of Turks." He makes a spitting gesture toward the floor. And smiles. "Turks, is not all be bad. Me, I had a Turkish girlfriend once in Marseilles." He holds his fingers together and kisses the tips. "La, la, la. A dancer. You know. With the belly, so." Pulling a dishtowel around his gyrating hips and torso in demonstration. He laughs. "You understand?"

Rolling up his shirtsleeves and removing the top of the grinder, Kostas pours in coffee beans from the jar. Replacing the top, he attaches a crank handle to the protruding axle and hands the grinder to me. "Hold with one hand. Also knees. And grind, grind, grind."

As I muscle the crank a few turns, the smell of coffee fills the room.

"Stop, stop," shouts Kostas. "Smell this coffee. Smell this coffee. This moment is be good. This moment I like. Is be first taste of the coffee. Not in the mouth, in the nose. Smell."

Yes.

When I finish grinding, Kostas removes the bottom of the grinder and shows me the fine dark powder I've produced. With a finger he touches the coffee and then his tongue. "Try, try it. Is be second taste of the coffee. Beans taste fresh, no?"

Yes.

"First we make sketo. Plain. Simple. One spoon of coffee, water, no sugar. Stir with wooden stick - only wood. Boil. Pour. Drink." With the hot flame the small pot boils quickly. Kostas pours the roiling froth into a tiny cup and sets it before me. "Wait, wait a little. Is be third taste of coffee - thinking how it will be, wanting to drink."

I wait. Yes. I want coffee.

"Now, taste. A little taste only."

Hot. Bitter.

"Now drink a little. Always only top, never bottom."

I drink.

Hello! That's coffee.

"This is, as I say, sketo. Plain. Only for the strong or stupid. But some like it so. Me, I do not. I think is not be right for you also."

Agreed.

"Take a little water. Take a little cookie. Now is make metrio. Medium. One measure water. One spoon coffee. One spoon sugar. Boil."

He makes. He pours. I taste. Better.

And on through gliki and gliki vrasto and names I cannot pronounce or remember. No matter, because they all have to do with just a touch more sugar and a touch more boiling, and pouring next to the cup or pouring from higher to get more foam; very delicate details, to be sure.

But here is the truth; there really are only two kinds of Greek coffee: without sugar and with as much sugar as you can possibly stand. In an hour I've had ten tiny cups of liquid coffee candy and ten tiny almond cookies. My body vibrates with a caffeine and sugar high. Coffee school has a ferocious effect on my nerves. I need air, movement.

Enough, enough. I must go to the market before closing.

North entrance of the city
market in Chania - always a
bunch of motorcycles and scooters
parked out front. Busy Busy!

Darkest - rectangles and arches
stand out against dun/cream stone
bleeding to city grime black at edges.
Grey steps w/dirty edges, light tops
sky is lightest and clock face
clear, cool cloudy light.

inside: soaring spaces, cream walls
hanging lights

91

Market bustles from early in the morning till about
2 in the afternoon when folks begin to close up shop
for the day. Sketched 'till I got hungry, then found a
seat in an impossibly tiny closet of a cafe and lunched
on tomatoey, fresh fish stew. Over coffee - sketched this
fish merchant across the aisle as he packed his wares
away into boxes of ice.

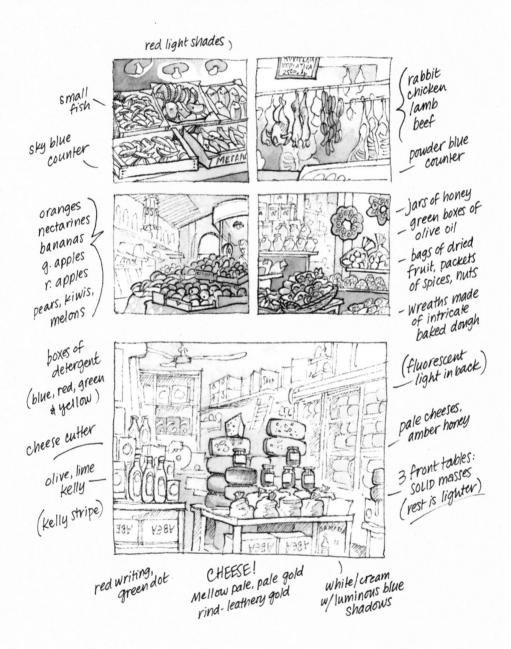

red light shades

small fish

sky blue counter

rabbit
chicken
lamb
beef

powder blue counter

oranges
nectarines
bananas
g. apples
r. apples
pears, kiwis,
melons

Jars of honey
green boxes of olive oil

bags of dried fruit, packets of spices, nuts

Wreaths made of intricate baked dough

boxes of detergent
(blue, red, green & yellow)

cheese cutter

olive, lime kelly

(kelly stripe)

(fluorescent light in back)

pale cheeses, amber honey

3 front tables: SOLID masses
(rest is lighter)

red writing, green dot

CHEESE!
Mellow pale, pale gold
rind- leathery gold

white/cream
w/luminous blue shadows

(CHRONICLES CONTINUED - 2)

The market closes at two o'clock on Wednesdays. It's the same on Mondays and Saturdays. Only on Tuesdays and Thursdays and Fridays do shopkeepers reopen their doors, somewhat reluctantly, from five to eight in the early evening.

On Sundays, of course, nothing is open at all. This once was the year-round rhythm of commercial Crete, which is appropriate to an island in the Mediterranean Sea where life is, even yet, primarily rural and agricultural. This is still the pattern for the six months of the year from October until April.

Between Easter and the end of September there's a different pattern of life. The change began only twenty years ago. Its cause is mass tourism. The Cretans look upon this annual invasion of tourists much as the Eskimos look upon the annual migration of caribou. They must be taken advantage of while they are around - the consumption of the consumer. In the tourist areas, stores and restaurants and tavernas are often open twenty-four hours a day in high season, and the streets are crowded at all hours of the day and night.

On this November Wednesday, commercial activity in Hania shuts down at two o'clock sharp. Homebound traffic is stalled on the main street as I weave my way through the car clutter with my plastic bags of groceries.

A half block ahead of me there's a commotion. I hear shouting, banging, horns honking, and a policeman's whistle. As I get closer I see a man in a black leather coat beating on a car's hood with a walking stick in one hand and a furled umbrella in another. His walking stick breaks, and he loses his balance and falls down. When he sits up and turns his face toward me, I recognize him. It's Alex Evans. What's he doing here? I thought he was in Spain.

Before I can make my way through the crowd, the ambulance crew has carried him away on a stretcher.

I took a taxi to the hospital, arriving as Alex was being carried into the emergency room. Finding a nurse who spoke English, I explained that I was a friend of the patient and also a doctor and would like to be useful if I could. She asked me to wait. So I paced up and down and worried.

I was a little surprised to find that I cared so much about the well-being of a man I didn't really know all that well. After a long hour, Alex was brought out of the emergency room in a wheelchair. He seemed as surprised to find me in the hospital as I had been to see him collapsed on the curb in town. I held out my hand and he clasped it firmly.

"Are you all right? Can I be of any help in any way?"

"Ah, Max-Pol. How very sorry I am that we meet again under such circumstances. Yes, yes, I am all right. At least my body is all right. I have not been injured or had a heart attack. Not even a stroke. I have momentarily lost my mind and made a complete fool of myself in public. My pride has wounds, but the rest of me is quite fit."

"I don't understand. You weren't hit by the car?"

"No, it is the car that was hit by me. It is a long story and now is not the time to tell it. I may be in a little trouble with the police for having damaged the old man's car. I assure you that I need nothing, except perhaps some clever excuse for what I have done. Please tell me where you are lodging and I shall be in touch with you when all this passes over."

Two policemen stood by, waiting. I gave Alex my address and telephone number. He shook my hand with confident firmness, smiled, winked, turned to the two policemen, and laughed the foolish laugh of the repentant, holding up both arms in surrender. Slowly he stood up. His size and his age and his voice regaining authority now. "Take me away."

Disarmed, the police walked down the hospital hallway with Alex lurching between them. Their treatment of him was deferential and solicitous. They had come to take charge of him, but now it was Alex who was in command. Señora Perez, the duenna of the dining car, would not have been surprised.

(THIS, TOO, SHALL PASS - CHRONICLES - 3)

Two days later, Kostas Liapakis came to my door with an envelope and a package. "A man has come to my shop. Kirios Alexandros. A large old man with much life in him. Is be looking for you. You know him? He says me give you these things."

The note said, "Alex Evans thanks you for your kindness and asks that you meet him tomorrow morning at ten at Cafe Kronos, at the bottom of the stairs on the west side of the main market."

Unwrapping the package, I was surprised to find a framed piece of stitchery I'd seen hanging on the wall of Kostas's shop. I'd admired it but not asked to buy it, sensing its personal value to Kostas. Kostas read the embroidered words aloud:

"Ki auto tha perasei"

He smiled. "This, too, shall pass. Is be very old. From village of Sfakia. I know you like, but you not ask to buy. Kirios Alexandros he ask me of you and I tell him we be friends and how you like my things. He says me, I want to give him something, and he says me why, and I say I want to give you something also, and when I show him what, he says it is be right. So, we both give you. He knows I not sell such things. But he is be Cretan, you know, and he has the honor, you know, and he will do me something someday. You understand?"

"Yes. And now I owe both of you."

Kostas smiled. I was getting the picture.

Debt and the honoring of debt is a Cretan specialty.

Like the coffee, it is best taken with sugar.

fresh
orange juice

foreground brightest
background lightest
mid ground- MED.
silhouettes, No true black

manilla canvas

plants- backlit,
soft greens
palms= silhouette

ΔΙΑΦΟΡΑ
ΜΠΑΚΛΑΒΑΔΑΚΙΑ
ΕΡΓΟΛΑΒΟΙ

coffee-
second cup
already !?!

Cafe Kronos - just down the stairs
from the west entrance of the market.
Alas! No loukoumades at this time of
year. On the baker's advice, I console
myself with 2 kinds of baklava instead,
and a mysterious almond cookie.

(CHRONICLES CONTINUED - 4)

Friday morning at ten at the Cafe Kronos. It is best place in
Hania to get "loukoumades" (loo-koo-mah-dez, meaning "little-
round-balls-of-doughnut-dough-deep-fried-in-boiling-olive-oil-
and-covered-with-honey-and-sesame-seeds-and-served-fresh-and-
hot"). The Cretan version of the xuxos of Barcelona. I am becoming
a dough ball gourmet. They are not good for my health, but, taking
my lead from Alex, I don't really care. Soon I may know as much
about doughnut holes as Kostas Liapakis knows about coffee.

Now I've come to hear the story of Alex Evans and the Fiat
fracas.

Alex is to people as fine sailboats are to rowboats. A kind of
foaming bow-wave goes before him; an invisible energy that
makes you aware of his oncoming presence. When he tacks into
the Cafe Kronos, the customers and staff pay attention.

Today he is wearing Greekness. He's adopted the costume worn
by older, middle-class Cretan men in winter: stout black shoes,
dark blue wool pants, and burgundy-red V-necked sweater-vest
over a white shirt. Black leather jacket, and black wool cap in
a semi-beret style. In one hand, a new cane - this one a sinewy
shepherd-style crook.

In the other hand, a string of amber komboloi (kom-bo-loy)
beads that Greek men flip rhythmically back and forth when idle.
This outfit wouldn't do at the Quo Vadis in Barcelona, but here, it's
exactly right. It's another example of his use of protective color-
ation. He has a Holmesian fondness for disguise.

The usual large greetings from Alex and so on. The waiter
stands by.

Portocalatha (fresh-squeezed Cretan orange juice) is what I
need. Coffee is out of the question. After the morning at Professor
Liapakis's coffee school, it may be days before I want coffee again.

"Orange juice? You order orange juice?"

I explain about coffee school.

Alex laughs and orders cappuccino.

"Cappuccino? You order cappuccino?" I mimic his tone of incredulity.

"Of course. Don't you know? Greek coffee is for old men and tourists. Nobody drinks Greek coffee unless they have no choice. And besides, it is not Greek. It is Turkish. We did not have such coffee until the Turks brought it. It is the coffee of the time when we were poor and oppressed, when we cooked with charcoal in the fireplace. It is boiled. Boiled! Boiled coffee is terrible. It is the sign of the false gourmet of our time who wants to make a fetish out of the necessity of old ways.

"I make an exception, of course, for our friend Liapakis, who is a sentimentalist to the core of his soul. But, really, this Greek coffee affectation is like the obsession with chili in your country. In that case, the original purpose of the hot peppers was to kill the taste of leftover mashed beans mixed with rotting meat. It is the way of the poor. Now, middle-class Americans have contests to see if their taste buds can be permanently damaged by chili peppers. This is macho madness, not fine eating.

"As to coffee, do not mistake me. If you want nostalgia, go with Kostas to a mountain village kafenion full of old men, and have Greek coffee. You should do so, mind you. Nostalgia has its uses and charms. But if you want good coffee, and you want your stomach happy, take steamed espresso with hot milk. I understand why Kostas likes Greek coffee. He likes living in the past. Me, I like living in the present."

As if on cue, the waiter appeared with cappuccino.

And I waited for Alex to tell me what he wanted me to know about yesterday's uproar in the street.

"Well, then. As you see, I am in good health and spirits. I have had to pay out some drachmas for damages to the old man's car and dignity, and a fine for 'public disorder.' I paid for the ambulance and the hospital as well. And, of course, I made a contribution to the, shall I say, 'benefit fund' of the police. An expensive business, my little street theater.

"Fortunately, it turns out that the police magistrate is my distant second cousin. We have not seen each other since childhood. He was easy on me. He might have put me in jail for a night."

Alex turned and stared out the window into the rain the way I had seen him do on that first night - stroking his face, looking at something far off in the distance - something only he could see. I waited. Maybe the time had finally come for him to tell me a long story.

"Really, I must apologize," he said. "I admit I am not being completely honest with you. I suppose there is some comedy in what I have done. Someday I shall truly laugh about my misbehavior. No doubt you will recount the incident to your friends as a classic example of Cretan craziness. But you do not know everything. And I feel I owe you the whole story. You, in a way you do not know, are involved."

Another pause - another distant look - another sip of coffee.

"Well, then. As I told you on the train, I am Cretan. Born here. Christened here. Much that was good came to me here as a young man. And also much evil. I left Crete in 1941 after the German invasion, and have not returned in all these last fifty-four years. Nor did I ever intend to return. But our conversations in Spain turned my mind toward Crete.

"As you may recall, the night we met on the train was my birthday eve. I was in that reflective mood forced on one by anniversary occasions. When you said you wanted to spend time here because you wanted to be in the presence of deep history, I realized I had a longing to return. To be in the presence of my own deep history. Some failure of nerve has kept me away. That says it: A failure of nerve.

"Enough time has passed, however. Even I will not be alive and healthy many more years. So. I came. First to Hania, to see how it would feel to be again in Crete. And you know, it has been both as wonderful as I hoped and as awful as I feared. Still, I am grateful to you for both the provocation in Spain and your concern expressed yesterday. Furthermore, I am really glad to see you. Somehow, I expected a reunion sooner or later. I trust you have received my gift from Mr. Liapakis."

"Thanks for such a fine present. And, if you don't mind my asking . . ."

"About the car attack? You have a right to know. And I feel the need to tell someone."

Alex paused and sipped his cappuccino, looking directly at me this time. When he finally spoke again, his voice was lowered in confidentiality.

"There is a rage in me about Crete. A rage. My rational side has kept this rage bricked up in some vault in my soul all these years. But it is a fire, this rage, which has never gone out. The rage is fueled by childhood memories, by experiences in the war, and by everything Cretan I have despised and from which I wish to escape.

"Much that is charming in Crete to the visitor is maddening to anyone who was born here but who wants to be a civilized member of the Western world."

Another pause, longer this time. A slight glazing over of his eyes. A look out the window again. A sip of coffee. A throat-clearing cough.

"All right, then, I will tell you. This old man was driving his car in the middle of traffic in such a single-minded, self-interested way, honking his horn at anyone and any vehicle in front of him. Pushing, pushing, pushing. Nagging the world at large. So self-important in his old car, as if he owned the street, as if he is the center of the universe.

"This is very Greek. Even more Cretan. 'The rules do not apply to me,' we think. Everyone for himself first, and then family, and to hell with anybody else. It is why Greeks do not stand in line or pay attention to lanes on the road or traffic signs. It is the same in international relations. What appears to others as cheating or breaking the law or lying or stealing, we see as cleverness. 'Above all, be clever.' That is our motto. Cretans think they have a license that says each may do whatever he wants, whenever he wants, anywhere he wants. Whatever he can get away with. That is clever.

"I have fought this in myself all my life. I hate it. I hate it. I hate it." Wham! Alex slammed his fist onto the table hard enough to rattle spoons, coffee cups, and the other customers, who had been listening.

"Forgive me. As I say, I was crossing the street, irritated by this old man, and I am crossing the street with the green light in my favor, though it was about to change, and this old man honked at me and that little honk was just enough to undo all the powers of my restraint.

"The wild beast of my rage smashed through the walls of its prison - this rage against selfishness and Greekness and age and death and loneliness and failure and being crippled and God-only-knows-what-all.

"And I took it out on the old man. Or at least, thanks be to God, on his miserable old Italian car. If he had stepped out to accost me I would have killed him. I would have beaten him to death."

The whole coffee shop was silent. Nobody spoke or moved. Though they probably did not understand his English, they felt his rage.

And I, too, was startled and speechless. Here was a side of Alex I did not know. The dark side, as extreme in its intensity as his heartiness.

Alex called the waiter, gruffly ordered a brandy.

"Make it two."

Alex lowered his voice again. "Max-Pol, my friend, it is not with any pleasure that I tell you this truth about myself. But you have been included in my life by coincidence or luck or fate or whatever. I do not really believe in such things. Yet here you are and here am I. Unknowingly you helped bring me to Crete and unknowingly you have witnessed this crisis. What can I say? You are entitled to know."

"Is there more?"

The brandy came. Seven Star Metaxa. The waiter had intuited Alex's taste. The best. We drank in silence, until Alex asked, "Do you ask as a physician or as a man?"

"A man."

"Well, then. Do you have a car?"

"Yes."

"I would like you to drive me to Souda Bay. I want to see a grave there. Some part of my life is buried in it."

Souda Bay Cemetery

Graves seem numberless- shining in the sun like slabs of salt. All alike until you step close enough to see that each name, inscription, story is unique...

Looking across Souda Bay - Four flags flying color against dark blue. Exact, proud shadows snapping in the breeze.

Registry- cool, silent marble building. Refuge from sun and sound. Name after name in the green-covered binders

Found Pendlebury's headstone strewn with fresh flowers. Evidently am not the only one seeking him out... look up and down the rows of white marble markers. One white-bearded gentleman watches me from a bench in the shade, calmly, hands folded over his cane. The breast of his dark jacket is strewn with medals. When I look up again - he is gone.

Souda Bay, just east of Hania, is one of the finest natural harbors in the Mediterranean Sea. Eight kilometers long, it is protected on the north by the rocky hulk of the Akrotiri peninsula, and on the south by the massive Malaxa escarpment, which rises steeply to the final heights of the Lefka Ori, the White Mountains, at eight thousand feet.

If its east entrance could be blocked and Souda Bay drained, more than five thousand years of maritime and naval history would be found: Minoan grain vessels, Roman wine boats, Turkish galleys, Venetian men-of-war, British cargo ships, Italian torpedo boats, and a German submarine, just to mention a few. Paradoxically, at the south end of the bay is one of the two most beautiful and carefully kept parks in Crete.

Well off a main road, surrounded by a substantial olive grove, is an arboretum of exotic trees, flowering shrubs, and cultivated roses. These encircle an open field of well-mowed grass. And there, in orderly rows, 1,564 nearly identical tombstones stand between the park entrance and the edge of the bay. This is the Commonwealth Cemetery, containing all the bodies of non-Greek soldiers and sailors and airmen and civilians buried in Crete since the first incursion of the British in the late nineteenth century.

Most are from World War II. Most were young. Most were from New Zealand and Australia. Many of the New Zealanders were native Maori. Also here are sons of Italy, France, Poland, Yugoslavia, Wales, England, Scotland, Canada, South Africa, and even India. All buried a long, long way from home.

The tombstones bear names for 772 of those buried here. The rest, 792, are marked with the phrase "Known only to God." The cemetery is also a memorial to those missing in action, fallen into the sea from ships and planes, lost in some remote mountain crevice dead of wounds, or blown to oblivion by bombs and shells.

Fifty years after the war the cemetery is still meticulously tended. The Commonwealth War Graves Commission is responsible. The trees are trimmed, flowerbeds spaded, grass fertilized and watered into an even greenness. The walks are regularly raked, the marble entranceways swept, and the decorative ironwork railings freshly painted. No trash, wires, or power poles mar the environment. Birds sing. A cool breeze wanders up the bay from the open sea.

So lovely. So awful. So sad.

The only other place like it in Crete lies west of Hania, on a hill above the beach at Maleme (Mal-eh-may) - an equally beautiful site, and equally well cared for. It is the cemetery of the German soldiers of the same war. All the dates on the stones there are between May 20, 1941, and May 13, 1945. Orderly rows of black stones marking the graves of 4,412 paratroops and mountain division troops. Most of them young, dying in the first three days of the third week of May in 1941. The view from the cemetery is over the green fields and sandy beaches where they landed - and beyond into the wine-dark Aegean Sea.

So lovely. So awful. So sad.

Alex got out of the car with less than his usual energy. He led the way through the gate of the Commonwealth Cemetery, saying, "I've never been here. I want to find the registry."

In the marble pavilion, just above a hanging desk, was a small bronze door, behind which Alex found the grave-registry volume. Placing it on the desk, thumbing through, he located what he wanted. He read aloud:

"Pendlebury, John Devitt Stringfellow, Captain, 115317, 10-E-13."

As we walked across the stone platform, down the steps, and onto the grass, Alex slowed his pace. A sobering environment, this. His personal energy seemed siphoned away by the emotional magnetism of the cemetery. I followed, stopping when he stopped, moving on when he moved. The long row of ivory marble stones in aisle ten was marked again and again with the phrase:

Soldier of the Great War - Known Only To God.

Except one. Number 13. The engraved words were succinct:

Captain J. D. S. Pendlebury.
General List. 22 May 1941. Age 36.
He has outsoared the shadow of our night.

Alex took off his hat and dropped it on the grass. He leaned on his cane. For the first time since I've known him he looked old, even frail. He wept without wiping away his tears. Sinking to his knees, he buried his face in his hands.

Feeling uneasy about trying to comfort him, I walked away. I was as unprepared for the depth of his grief here as I was for the size of his earlier rage in the Cafe Kronos. From a distance I kept an eye on him. In time he recovered, regained his feet and composure. After wiping his eyes with his handkerchief and blowing his nose, he looked up and motioned for me to rejoin him.

Putting his arm on my shoulder, he gestured at the headstone before him. "This . . . this . . . is the . . . grave . . . of the father . . . of all the life I have had . . . since I was thirteen years old. I know I have the habit of avoiding revealing myself by saying it is a long story for another time. Here . . . here
. . . is another long story. But not for another time. For now, if you don't mind."

We walked over and sat on a bench in the late afternoon sun of November, looking out across the grass and stones and bay and sea. I listened while Alex Evans brought John Pendlebury back to life.

(CHRONICLES CONTINUED - 6)

Alex began, "Before I can tell you about John Pendlebury, I must tell you a little more about Alexandros Evangelou Xenopouloudakis. Bear with me.

"I was born in 1915 in Iraklion, in the old city inside the Venetian fortress walls. I was born a twin, but my brother was born dead. And my mother died three weeks later.

"Like many Greeks, my father was an ordinary seaman in the British merchant marines. He was at sea when I was born. I remember him as a man who came with laughter and presents, which soon changed to anger and abuse before he went back to sea again. Somehow, I became convinced he blamed me for the death of my mother. Who knows the truth of the matter?

"Relatives raised me - aunts, cousins, grandmothers. And with much care, really, but I was never attached to any one member of the family for very long, nor did I live in one house for long. Even as a child I was physically large, intelligent, and independent.

"I was often out and about on my own, everyone in the family thinking I was being looked after by some other member of the family. They were kind enough, and generous as well. Greeks are good with children. But I was, in reality, orphaned and alone.

"To be sure, it was an exciting time to be alive. Crete had been freed from centuries of Turkish oppression in 1898, and had been an autonomous state until enosis - unification - with the rest of Greece in 1913. We could stand up and breathe as free people again. Great optimism was in the air. Education and culture flourished.

"Our schools were new, our teachers enthusiastic, and our sense of the future was hopeful. Such things had been extinct in Crete for 400 years. How our culture survived the domination of the Venetians and the Turks is a wonder. And now, now, all Greece was being led by a Cretan! Eleftherios Venizelos, the most important political figure of our modern history. Finally, our day had come.

"If that wasn't enough, our history was being dug up at Knossos, stunning the world with the glories of our past. My cousins were working in the excavations at Knossos, and when I was twelve I begged them to get me work there. They came home with such amazing tales of kings and queens and palaces.

"I wanted to see for myself what was happening, and so they got me a stupid job doing no more than chasing goats and sheep off the property and bringing water to the workmen. A disappointment. Still, I was working at Knossos."

It was getting cold and windy. Alex stood up, stretching his bad leg. He pulled his black cap out of a pocket and settled it on his head. I thought we might leave. But Alex sat down again. As he said, there was still the "long story" to tell.

"There was one very special reason for my wanting to be at Knossos. My maternal grandmother told me that her grandmother had been married to an English archeologist. That was all she knew. Family mythology, perhaps. Like your family story about the Cretan woman who was bought out of slavery and married to your distant English ancestor. Who knows what truth is in these tales? No family likes to be ordinary.

"Nevertheless, my grandmother's yarn was enough to fire my interest in the English archeologists working at Knossos. I hung around them, studied them, imitated them, and quickly picked up the English language. At thirteen, I believed English was a voice buried in me from my ancestor, which may not be far from wrong in that I do have a facility with language. I take no credit for it. It just is. Like my size, it was a gift of birth.

"Seeing that the English archeologists were interested in potsherds, I combed the landscape for broken pottery while only halfheartedly chasing goats. When I found something, I carefully marked the spot as I had seen the real archeologists do, and then washed and cleaned my gleanings, wrapped them in paper, and gave them a number. I hid them in a clay water jar. They weren't much, really - little bits and pieces of painted clay. But I felt I was being an archeologist.

"That very first summer, in 1928, I found an elaborately decorated and almost undamaged pot, complete with lid. Well, actually,

I did not just find it. You see, I was doing a little excavating of my own. And inside the jar were quite a few little clay seals. I thought I had struck gold. This was a find! I was overjoyed.

"But I was also afraid. Terrified, actually. What I was doing was strictly forbidden. I could be punished and fired. I told only my cousin. But he told one of the English archeologists, and the next thing I knew I was in trouble. Or thought I was.

"My cousin came, bringing this tall Englishman with him.

"His name was John Pendlebury.

"The same man who is buried there."

Alex pointed toward the grave in plot 10 E 13.

Gusts of wind whipped off the water and into the trees around us. Alex shivered, and sighed. "Now I will tell you about John Pendlebury. He was only twenty-four years old that summer, but he had been singled out by the great Arthur Evans to succeed him as curator of Knossos. The personalities and characters of the two men were much the same.

"Moreover, Pendlebury had been both a star scholar and a star athlete at university. He took a First in classics at Cambridge, with a distinction in archeology. He was awarded the Cambridge University place in the British School of Archeology in Athens, and from there he had come to work at Knossos."

From his wallet, Alex produced a faded black-and-white photograph laminated in plastic. A tall, well-proportioned young man dressed in full native Cretan costume. A particularly appealing face - his intelligence and energy and vitality were apparent. "Pendlebury," said Alex.

"He was not only fluent in Greek, but he used the Cretan dialect and was as interested in all the ordinary aspects of the Cretan life of the present as he was in the Minoans. He would eat and drink with the workers, and accompany them to their homes and kafenions. He became adept at the acrobatic style of Cretan dancing. Having been a champion in the high jump at Cambridge, he could fling himself far higher in the air while dancing than any Cretan. They loved to see him dance. They invited him to every feast and wedding and christening. He could make speeches and sing and recite lines from Homer. Oh, he was much loved by the Cretans. They always addressed him with respect, but, since they could not easily pronounce his name, they called him 'O Kirios Blebberry' - the dear honorable Mr. Blebberry."

Alex's voice trailed off. He stood up. Laughed. "Grace was in every bone and fiber of that man," he said, pointing at Pendlebury's grave.

He sat again, deep inside his memories, and murmured, "My God, those were great times. Great times . . ."

Several minutes passed before he remembered my presence and continued. "You see, Pendlebury had one of those personalities founded on curiosity - about anything and everything, anytime, anywhere - old or new. In all my years, I've never run across such an intellect. Not only did he serve as curator of Knossos in the spring and summer, but in fall and winter he was the director of excavations in Egypt at Tell El-Amarna. I know he learned Arabic and was probably as much of a local legend among the Egyptians there as among the Greeks here.

"I tell you, Max-Pol, despite what must seem as my exaggeration, this truly was a singularly remarkable man. Such men really do come along from time to time.

"Digging at Knossos was not enough to occupy him. Oh, no, not him. He wanted to know every other possible ancient site on Crete, and see it firsthand. He wanted to check all the ancient references to distance for accuracy, and he wanted to walk the routes taken by the Minoans between their centers of activity. In less than ten years he walked all over this island. I am quite serious when I say no man before or since has seen as much of Crete on foot.

"And he was a prodigious hiker, legendary even among the Cretans, and that's saying something. My God, could he walk! Few could keep his pace. Many times I went with him the year I was eighteen, and even I, who was younger and stronger than he, was often pressed to keep up with him.

"Fifteen miles in three hours over rough territory before resting was nothing to him - a common walk. It takes a strong man to move in such fashion. And he could do it day after day. Nobody ever knew or loved Crete like John Pendlebury. Nobody."

"When the war broke out, he went home to England to join a cavalry regiment. Then he was attached to a special operations group to be trained in resistance and intelligence, and sent back to organize partisan forces in Crete. When the Nazis invaded mainland Greece, he was all over Crete setting his organization in motion.

"When the Germans invaded Crete by parachute on May 20, 1941, Pendlebury was in Iraklion. After taking part in early fighting in the city, he was on his way by car to his headquarters at Knossos. Just beyond the Canea gate, his car ran into parachute troops who had fallen well beyond their landing target, in a place neither they nor Pendlebury expected. There was a firefight, and Pendlebury was gravely wounded. A German doctor of the paratroops examined him, bandaged him, and moved him to a nearby house.

"The next day, the Germans came again, grilled him for information. And when he refused to talk, they took him outside and shot him to death in cold blood. In cold blood. Once in the head - twice in the heart. I was not there, of course. All of this I learned later. There were witnesses.

"Two Cretan women - wives of workmen from Knossos - buried him in a nearby ditch. But the Germans came back next day to locate his body and get his identification. They had learned about Pendlebury, and wanted to make sure he was dead. To be certain, they also took his glass eye."

"Glass eye?"

"Yes, a glass eye. I forgot to mention that Pendlebury had lost an eye in childhood and had a glass eye. One more improbable fact of the man. It never seemed to bother him. He would take it out when he was drinking and put it on the table in front of him. It scared Cretans half to death. When he was off in the mountains he would leave it behind on his bedside table. His housekeeper would not even enter the room. Often I have wondered what happened to that eye. It must be somewhere. I hope you do not think it strange of me to say that I wish I had it."

"In that grave over there lie the remains of the most remarkable man I ever met. And believe me, I have met many. All I've told you is true. The stories that were made up about him afterward make him seem mythological in stature. I assure you the facts make him exceptional enough. If he had lived, if he had only lived, he would have been even more of a legendary figure in Crete. His feats during the resistance would have made him a hero. As it is . . . as it is . . . as it is."

Alex dried his eyes with his handkerchief.

He rose and walked toward the field of gravestones. He turned back to me. "The sun is going, and I am getting cold. Let us walk and I will tell you the part John Pendlebury played in my life."

I followed him across the cemetery grass all the way down to the edge of the bay, to the first row of headstones, and then, as if he were reviewing the slain troops while reviewing his past, Alex began a start-and-stop walk that would take us back and forth in front of every grave.

"As I say, Pendlebury took an interest in me, especially when he found how readily I had learned English. One of the tasks Evans had put off for years was the washing and sorting and assembling of potsherds that had been boxed and set aside while the more exciting discoveries were being made. The job needed doing.

"Pendlebury was of a more modern school of archeology than Evans - one that stressed that a great deal was to be learned from the smallest pieces of an archeological puzzle. He moved me to this work. And I must say I was quite good at it, succeeding at putting some pots together where even he had failed. We often worked side by side for days. Over the next five seasons I became not only his assistant but an honorary member of his family as well. I went almost everywhere he went."

Alex interrupted his story at times to stand in front of a grave as if he recognized the name on the stone. I realized that he must have been involved in the Battle of Crete and might have known many of these men.

The headstone of a New Zealand private - age nineteen.

"As I say, I worked alongside Pendlebury every day and went

with him everywhere. On his marathon hikes - to his dinner table - and I stood in the background while he had conferences with Arthur Evans at the Villa Ariadne. I knew his wife, Hilda White, and I held his son, David, in my arms when he was a baby. Hilda was thirteen years older than Pendlebury, which made her old enough to be my mother, which in some ways she became.

"The young archeologists would hold lively conversations in the late evenings on Pendlebury's verandah, talking about everything imaginable: poetry, electricity, food and wine, dogs, history, insects, and languages. My understanding of the mind and interests of a well-educated man was formed by listening to them."

A sergeant of the Black Watch battalion - age thirty-four.

"Pendlebury encouraged and directed my education. He gave me books - a world atlas, for example, and an encyclopedia. He grilled me on what I was learning in school, and corrected my English. He began speaking French to me, and when I proved an able student, he taught me French while we sorted potsherds.

"He told me of his life. We had much in common. He was an only child, the son of a consulting surgeon to St. George's Hospital in London. His mother died, his father remarried, and Pendlebury was sent off to boarding school at an early age. Though he continued to write to his father the rest of his life, he never lived with him again after boarding school. You might say he had been orphaned, like me."

A New Zealand corporal - a Maori name - age twenty-three.

"When I finished gymnasium second in my class, I was eighteen, fluent in English and French, and much affected by my association with the cultured British. I dressed in their style and adopted their mannerisms. But in doing so, I crossed over a forbidden line with my family. Both they and I contributed to the alienation, I suppose, but at the time I simply thought they resented my advantages. My father certainly did.

"He had come to hate the British because on their ships all foreigners were treated as woggish servants of Empire. We had terrible rows when he was at home. If I had not been so much bigger and stronger than he, he would have beaten me. But he was afraid of me. I could feel his fear. The last time I saw him, he spat on me and disowned me. I was more relieved than hurt. It gave me reason to acknowledge the truth: John Pendlebury had become my father. Now more than ever I was determined to be an Englishman."

An English airman. "Known only to God."

"Pendlebury arranged for me to continue my education in England, first at a preparatory school, and then at Cambridge. At the end of the summer's work at Knossos in 1934, he bought me passage to England, where I was taken in by his father, who was glad to give me what he had not given his own son.

"You might think I wanted to become an archeologist. Not in the least. Matching potsherds for five seasons had cured me. Archeology was becoming tedious, boring, dirty work. My hunger was for cleaner occupations. I wanted to think for a living. I went up to Cambridge to do classics, with a special interest in philosophy. And, well, you know the next chapter. Idealism and Spain and back to Crete in 1938."

Another soldier of the Black Watch - age twenty.

Alex remained silent as he walked and stopped and walked and stopped. He seemed reluctant to open the pages of the missing chapter - his part in the war years in Crete. As we came to the grave marked 10 E 13, I prompted him: "And then?"

Alex was standing in front of Pendlebury's headstone.

"I had a miserable time of it when I got back to Crete from Spain. Lost years. Mostly back at Knossos in season and sitting around kafenions in the winter. War was in the air. An anxious time. When I heard Pendlebury had returned to Crete, I went to find him. He was living in a small roadside building on the grounds of the Villa Ariadne. We had a marvelous reunion.

"I wanted something useful to do. I was a veteran of war now, not a schoolboy. He recruited me to work for him in the resistance, though I was hardly fitted for life in the Cretan underground. My limp, my size, and my Englishness, you know. So I helped with logistical plans, drew maps, and learned to use a radio. I was Pendlebury's aide-de-camp. Though I'm sure he didn't and couldn't tell me everything, I could guess most of it. I knew the war was coming. Here. To Crete.

"I should explain that my father was in Crete when I returned from Spain. He had deserted from the British merchant marine because he didn't want to get conscripted into armed service. He was not willing to fight or die for the British. He disdained my experiences in Spain. How could I be so stupid? In his eyes I was a fool. He said I had ruined my life. We had a terrible fight - a real fight - with fists. He literally broke a chair on my back, and I broke his nose. Blood everywhere. The kitchen of my grandmother's house was a shambles.

"Neighbors forced us apart. As I was going out the door I glared at him, and he spat on the floor again. I spat back. This is serious, this spitting. Cretans do this whenever they mention the hated Turks, for example. It is a supreme gesture of loathing and contempt. At that moment, if I could have gotten my hands on him I would have killed him."

The hard look on Alex's face slowly softened.

"And in a way, in a way . . . I suppose I did kill him." Alex turned and looked out over Souda Bay to the open sea.

"How?"

"Those of us working for Pendlebury compiled lists of people we could not trust. Suspected communists, Nazi sympathizers, and those who were known to be anti-British. I put my father's name on that list. For fair reasons, mind you. He was as anti-British as they come. But still, he was my father. In my panic, I left that list behind with many other papers when I fled the Villa Ariadne the day the Germans came.

"Later, while I was in Cairo working in British intelligence, I saw the names collected of those Cretans who were collaborating with the Germans. My father's name was there. The Germans must have found the list I left behind and co-opted or compromised the men. Mind you, not a few had collaborated willingly. Perhaps he was one of them. Who can say now?

"When I saw my father's name on the list, I said and did nothing. When the civil war broke out in Crete at war's end, those in the resistance who had fought with the British had one agenda: to capture and eliminate former collaborators.

"I know that my father was killed just after the war, but I don't know by whom or for what. I don't even know where he is buried. Reason says it is impossible to know at this distance in time what the circumstances were and what part I actually played in his death. Much is conjecture. Still, my feelings are a confused stew of guilt, triumph, relief, and sorrow. More times than I care to remember I have managed to bury these feelings, deny them, only to exhume them once again.

"This is why I have stayed away from Crete all these years. I could bear not knowing. What I feared was knowing, afraid of finding out a truth I could not live with. And this is why, when I returned to Crete this time I have stayed in Hania. To go to Iraklion is to walk around in an emotional minefield. I may go. I may have to go. But not yet."

Alex turned away, his gaze fixed on Pendlebury's grave.

"As I said, the day the Germans dropped on Crete I was at the Villa Ariadne. We had no warning. I know now that Freyberg, the New Zealand general in charge of the Commonwealth troops, was well informed about the details of the invasion, because the English had broken the German codes. The Enigma business, you know.

"London did not want the Germans to suspect. Freyberg was given decoded signals from the famous Enigma interceptions by the one officer cleared to receive them, and after reading them he was required to burn them. Which he did immediately.

"None of his staff was allowed to read and consider the information. Freyberg was overly cautious in moving troops into precise positions because the Germans might begin to suspect the

Enigma code had been broken.

"This was tragically stupid, because there were only a few obvious places to protect, and the Germans had no forces for a sea invasion from mainland Greece. Only by air could they come. It is said that Freyberg was on his balcony having lunch when the first paratroops came out of the sky. He said, 'Right on time.'

"This wasted intelligence and misplacement of troops cost many good men and women their lives, and cost Crete its freedom. At the end of the first day, two platoons with machine guns could have denied the Germans use of the airfield at Maleme, and the invasion would have failed. Two bloody platoons! What a shame. What a goddamned shame."

Alex's eyes remained fixed on Pendlebury's headstone.

"The last I saw of Pendlebury he was rushing off down the driveway of the Villa Ariadne to Iraklion to see for himself what was happening. He was in his captain's uniform, and fearlessly enthusiastic for what then seemed the beginning of some grand adventure he had prepared for all his life. He shouted, 'Wait here for me. I'll be back.' I waited as long as I could. He never came back. And I never saw him again."

Alex stepped closer to the headstone, touching it and stroking it.

"How strange it is now. How utterly strange. When last I saw him, I was twenty-five and he was thirty-six. He was still a father figure to me. And now . . . here I am . . . eighty . . . and he will be thirty-six forever. Now it is I who feel like a father visiting my son's grave. Damn it all . . . God damn it all."

Tears again.

"Peace to him. Joy to the worms," said Alex.

It seemed right to leave Alex to his thoughts and walk back to the car. I pulled a blood-red rose from a bush growing between the headstones of row 10 E. At a better time I would give it to Alex. As I passed through the cemetery gate, I looked back. Alex was talking again - this time only to John Pendlebury.

We drove back to Hania.
Slowly and in silence.

THE FLOURISHING LIFE

Max-Pol finished writing his account of the afternoon at Souda Bay with Alex. Instead of satisfaction, he felt exposed and oddly self-conscious. He went into the kitchen. The Alice artifacts were spread out on the kitchen table. Witness. What will she think of his Chronicles?

He went back to his desk. Calling on his physician's capacity to look objectively at whatever facts lay before him, he read through his Chronicles. He could not avoid what he recognized. When he finished, he wrote his reaction in the form of a commentary to be inserted into the Chronicles before he sent this installment to his Witness.

*

Why have I written at such length about Alex?

On re-reading these Chronicles, I realize that I have not done what I said I would do: Write an objective description of experiences in Crete, while avoiding talking about myself.

How can I deny the obvious?

In these long accounts of life with Alex I reveal myself.

I write about him to write about me.

Since I don't take notes or carry a recording device while we are together, everything about Alex passes through me, and is shaped and embellished by who I am and what I value.

I confess that at times I feel as if I am becoming Alex.

Make no mistake, I'm not writing fiction. The facts are real and accurate. But, like the work of a portrait painter, the final picture is also a self-image. I am the artist who chooses the brushes and the colors and point of view. I choose the pose.

It's clear, isn't it? I want to have as rich and adventuresome life as he has had. I want to be as strong and as self-aware as he is. I want to allow the same range of emotions he allows: joy, rage, passion, and sorrow. Living as long a life as he has is not as important as living as wide a life.

I envy him his size.

Not his physical dimensions, but the size of his very being. Walt Whitman's line comes to mind: "I am large. I contain multitudes."

It's not that I'm inhibited or shy or afraid. And I don't despair.

I may yet fill out the frame of my life. I am also large, and I also contain multitudes. And I may yet get up, throw open the doors and windows of my life, and go outside.

I think Alex has experienced these same feelings. His account of Pendlebury's life reflects this same spirit of profound regard. Not envy, but respect for the exemplar.

Pendlebury's life was a paradigm for Alex.

And his life, in turn, is a paradigm for mine.

I would not want to really be Alex or live his life. Of course not.

I would not want to be Pendlebury either.

But I do know what I want:

To be around such men because they have led a flourishing life.

And have it said of me: Max-Pol Millay led a flourishing life.

Dear Witness, self-deception is such a fog sometimes.

I suppose you have been aware of what I'm doing all along.

Does that change anything?

Shall we continue?

*

Hania, evening.

Kalispera, Kiria Alice:

You acknowledge my Chronicles with inspiring provocations. Such gifts! If you were nearby, I would ask you to elaborate on the artifacts of your existence you chose to send me. And that would be a mistake, would it not? Like asking a poet to explain a poem line by line. The pleasure of the elaboration is mine.

But one train of thought I don't want to dismiss. In your sets of threes there are names I recognize:

Louise Colet. I know her. She was Flaubert's muse when he wrote "Madame Bovary," or so say the literary historians. But she was both the living model of the main character and Flaubert's mistress for several years. Furthermore, she may have been an active co-author of the novel. Flaubert burned all the letters she wrote to him while he was working on the novel. Suspicious, isn't it?

Camille Claudel was accepted by Rodin as a pupil when she was nineteen and he forty. Talented in her own right, too. I've seen her sculpture in the Musée Rodin in Paris. She became his model and lover. Another candidate for muse for those who think that way. The strain of the relationship curtailed her creativity and contributed to her having to be placed in an asylum for the last thirty years of her life. Rodin drove her crazy.

Blanche Monet. I'm not sure. Was she the stepdaughter who became his daughter-in-law and then his companion for the last decade of his life after his wife (her mother) died? She was a painter too, I think. But her work was totally submerged in the ocean of his talent.

It's no idle accident that you list these three women. All three were drowned by the male chauvinism of their times and the success of the major male figures in their lives. Are you one of these women? Is this a cryptic code about your experience with men?

Just for the record, I am not one of these men.

What I know about you is enigmatic. Nevertheless, I begin to feel some certainty about your own unstated wishes. Is it that you want a Witness of your own for whatever is going on in your life? Or more? If so, then I offer reciprocation - a gift in return.

Here's a set of threes of my own. The rules of the game:

An open mind.

A level playing field.

Equal rules for an even match.

In the meantime, I send you another installment of my Chronicles.

Max-Pol

ALICE IN PARIS

Midnight in Paris. In her bed, Alice drifts down into sleep.

As has happened off and on since childhood, she hears a story being told or else tells herself a story - she's never been sure which. But she is certain that the story has not changed over the years. She knows it by heart:

"Once upon a time, far away and long ago, there was a bird. A very unhappy, young, little, girl bird. She had older sisters who were bigger and stronger and prettier.

And they were mean to the little bird. When their parents came to feed them, the little bird got very little food because her sisters stepped all over her and pushed her out of the way. And they said she was ugly and not like them at all.

One day the little bird's sisters flapped their wings and flew away and never came back, and the parents never came back either. The little bird was afraid. But she tried flapping her wings and to her surprise, she could fly! And so she flew away all by herself. She landed on a tree. She met an owl. A lady owl. And she was nice to the little bird. The lady owl asked the little bird why she was so unhappy, and the little bird told her story.

And then the owl explained: "It is very clear: You were born in a strange nest. Cuckoos lay their eggs in nests built by other birds, you know, but I can tell you, I know cuckoos, and you are not one."

"What am I?" asked the little bird. "I do not know," said the owl, "you will have to find out for yourself. You are just what you are and not something else. But remember: you *are definitely not a cuckoo.*"

As always, by this point in the story, Alice was fast asleep.

She was afraid to try to make up the rest of the story. It was her own childhood version of *Cinderella* mixed up with *The Ugly Duckling,* but she never knew how it ended. Did the ugly duckling become a swan or some other bird? Alice had once written in chalk on the headboard of her bed:

BUT NOT A CUCKOO !

122

Fabuliste Curnonsky

On the wall over the headboard of her bed in Paris, Alice taped some of the sayings of Fabuliste Curnonsky, written on napkins, notebook paper, blank pages torn from the ends of books, hotel scratch pads, and an airline boarding pass. Alice likes the informal atmosphere of reflective sagacity they create.

Alice was inspired to create alternate personalities by Fernando Pessoa, the most creative Portuguese writer of the twentieth century. He wrote most of his work in the guise of several dissimilar personalities whose biographies he created as an act of metafiction. He called these "heteronyms."

The writings of these separate figures were distinct, even contradictory. In going this route, Pessoa acknowledged human capacity for multiple states of being, and extended that as far as possible into giving life and work to his own inner community.

Another inspiration came from a line she saw chalked on a wall: "Don't believe everything you think."

And she didn't. But that didn't stifle her mind. Go ahead and think it, consider it, let it go when it doesn't make sense, and keep it when it does.

Someday she will collect all the wall scraps into a book of the thoughts of Fabuliste Curnonsky. She has a box full of them now. Over her bed in Paris at the moment are these, the important ones at the moment:

Everything looks better at a distance.
Anticipation and memory are more agreeable than experience.
Nothing is often exactly what it seems to be.

Romance is easy. Love is hard.
Sex can be safe. Love is always dangerous.
You need not fear men or women, only the ones you know well.

There are promises that must never be kept.
There are questions that must never be asked.
There are truths that must never be told.

SECOND WITNESS

Only a week went by before Manolis called Max-Pol.

"Hey, hey, Mr. Max-Pol, you got a package. And it's from some Greek chick in Paris - oooo-la-la. And she lives at the same address where you sent the package to the Spanish babe last week. How many women you got stashed in Paris?"

"Manolis, you're not going to believe this, but I don't know any Greek women in Paris. And besides, you're not supposed to be looking so closely at my mail."

"Yo, chill, Mr. Max-Pol, at least I didn't open it and read it."

"OK, Manolis, what's her name?"

"Hypatia Loulaki Xetrypis."

"What?"

"Hypatia Loulaki Xetrypis. Listen. I'll sound it out for you in Greek: He-pa-TEE-ah Lou-LAH-ki Ksee-TREEP-is. Could be Cretan. I know a guy named Xetrypis from Sfakia. And *loulaki* is a Greek word for blue. Hypatia, I don't know. But it's a babe's name for sure."

"Never heard of her, Manolis."

"Yeah, right. Listen, my cousin is coming over your way on my motorcycle. You want I should send your package? Special service."

"Sure. Thanks."

"Lemme know if this Greek babe sent her picture or is coming this way."

Manolis is always open for business.

*

Fifteen minutes later there was a sharp, hard clicking of heels on the stairs followed by a sharp, hard rap on Max-Pol's door. When he opened it, a package was thrust at him from the hands of an extremely sharp-looking young woman. Long black hair, assertive makeup, black leather jacket, skin-tight jeans, and knee-high black leather boots with high heels. Everything about her had an erotic edge.

"You Max-Pol Millay?"

"Yes. You must be Manolis's cousin."

"He tell you that?"

"Yes."

She laughed. And went off down the stairs, still laughing.

Hearing a motorcycle crank and roar, Max-Pol stepped out onto his balcony just in time to look down on the street and watch the flashy young woman clear the pedestrians ahead of her with a riding style as assertive as her makeup.

"Opa, Manolis, Oh-pa!"

*

As Manolis had said, the address on the box was the same as that of Pilar Azul Pujol. But the sender was indeed Hypatia Loulaki Xetrypis. So far there was Alice O'Really, who received some of her mail in care of A. O. Riley, but who sent some of her mail under the name of Pilar Azul Pujol, and now, Hypatia Loulaki Xetrypis.

As before, Max-Pol opened the package, pulled out the newspaper stuffing in the end, and slid out the contents. Blue envelopes and blue gift-wrapped boxes, again numbered 1 through 9.

Alice.

He unfolded the newspaper stuffing. The *Paris Soir* of three days ago. From ingrained habit, he picked up the small package marked #9 first. He sniffed it carefully. Cigars again. Cutting the twine and ripping off the paper, he opened the little box. Yes. The same as before.

Alice has good taste in cigars. Or knows somebody who does.

Lighting up, Max-Pol reached for the big envelope marked #1. He guessed it would be the Witness report. And guessed right.

*

"Received your Chronicles. Read it carefully several times. If that's all you want to know, stop here. Throw away the rest I send."

Signed, "Hypatia Loulaki Xetrypis, Witness."

At the bottom was a P.S. "If you want to send more Chronicles, send to me in care of A. O. Riley - same address. Will be away during the holidays, but back mid-Jan."

Max-Pol compared this note with the first response from Alice. The handwriting was different and yet alike, as if the writer was experimenting with graphic style. But it was the same blue ink and the same pen. His, he was certain.

The second big envelope. Pages stapled together.
A steno notebook page, with big block letters:
"!COINCIDENCE AGAIN!" and in smaller letters, "or maybe."
Stapled to it was a long letter on pale blue stationery.
"Pay close attention, because what I want to tell you gets complicated.

In an artist friend's studio I found a copy of "The Cretan Journals" of Edward Lear - you know, "The Nonsense of Edward Lear" - he of the Jumblies and Pobbles and the Owl and the Pussycat and limericks - more sense than non-sense. Seems he was on a drawing and painting trip to Crete in 1864. In village of Apodhoulou he was at a house built by Robert Hay in 1828. Footnotes say he was an English archaeologist who built the house for wife, Kalitza.

GET THIS: she was a Cretan woman carried off to slavery in 1821 to Egypt. He saw her there, bought her, married her, and brought her back to Crete. Then he took her to England to live in Amisfield, in East Lothian.

SEE? Get the connection? English archaeologist - Cretan slave? You said Alex told you about his family mythology - the Cretan woman who married the English archaeologist - and you told him about the Cretan slave woman bought and married by your ancestor. Put it together. Possible - POSSIBLE - you and Alex Evans are somehow blood kin from way, way back. Thin blood by now, but consider it. Get the book. Must be available there. Harvey & Co. publisher, Athens, 1984. See pp. 88 and 113.

"Well I'll be damned!" said Max-Pol.

He stood up, grabbed his wallet off the counter, rushed out, down the stairs, and up the street to the English-language bookstore at the end of the harbor quay. Yes! Lear's *Cretan Journals* was in stock. He flipped through the book. Found page 88 and then page 113. The facts were just as Alice had said. While they did not in any way prove he and Alex were necessarily kin, the coincidental possibility was stunning.

Max-Pol bought two copies of the book, and walked back to his apartment in a mild daze, saying, "Cousin Alex, Cousin Alex" over and over to himself. As he neared home, he picked up speed. What more surprises would Alice or Pilar or Hypatia or whoever she was have in store for him?

*

He ripped open the big blue envelope marked #3.

Several pages clipped together. A handwritten note:

> If I were Greek, my name would be Hypatia Loulaki Xetrypis - always wanted last name to begin with X - the mysterious Madame X - always be last on lists - X for experimental - X for blue movies - X for Xmas - X for unknown - Xe for chemical xenon - everything gets marked with an X - and X marks the spot - you are here - and seals with a kiss.
>
> X is my favorite letter.

Another coincidence. Something else to share with Alex Evans - Mr. Xenopouloudakis. Kirios X. Too much.

"And Hypatia is my archaic role model.

"Born in 380 A.D. in Alexandria. Became a teacher, astronomer, mathematician, inventor, physical scientist, and philosopher. Way ahead of her time. Studied in Athens. Never married because she said she was wedded to truth. Murdered by Christians for being a pagan philosopher.

"She married the wrong truth."

Another page - threes again.

> Tricycle, bicycle, unicycle
> A squared plus B squared equals C squared
> Bell, book, and candle
>
> Morning, noon, and night
> Tournay, yestoslay, Temorah (James Joyce)
> Good morning, good night, goodbye

Brahma, Vishnu, Shiva
(creator, preserver, destroyer)
Father, Son, and Holy Ghost

Three rituals of Samsara Sailon
1. rituals of remembering
2. rituals of reforming
3. rituals of revival

Three elements of Buddha-hood
1. emptiness - the Dharmakaya
2. oneness - the Sambhogakaya
3. uniqueness - the Nirmanakaya

Three great rules of altruism
1. No act of kindness is ever wasted.
2. No act of mercy is ever wrong.
3. No act of generosity is ever empty.

*

Max-Pol stretched, stood up, walked to the cupboard to pour a glass of wine. And changed his mind. Something celebrational was required. Something Greek. He found a gift-boxed bottle of Seven Star Metaxa, the best brandy in all of Greece - a gift from Alex. He had been saving it for a special occasion. If this wasn't a special occasion, what was?

Two fingers of Metaxa. A fresh cigar - one Alice had marked "for emergencies." This was an affirmative emergency. He wanted to tell someone - to share his - share his what? - joy, pleasure, excitement, confused delight? All of that.

Max-Pol's actual expression was simpler. With glass in one hand and cigar in the other, he pushed open the doors of his balcony with his knee, walked to the railing, and shouted at the traffic below:

"I'M VERY HAPPY!"

Puzzled pedestrians looked up at him. He waved. Several waved back at him. He laughed and shouted again, "I'M VERY HAPPY!"

This time there were tears in his eyes.

*

There was still more on the kitchen table.

Three small envelopes.

In the first, a piece of wide blue grosgrain ribbon - the emphatic bright blue in the Greek flag, a white stripe running down the middle. And with it, an explanatory note:

"Famous contemporary French performance artist, Sophie Calle, follows interesting people around for days, like a spy. Takes their pictures and then writes their biography. Decided to try it. But not so extreme - just follow for a few blocks or minutes. Followed older woman all in black into arcade of Palais Royale and into ribbon shop specializing in military decorations. Whole wall full of rolls of ribbon. The piece included is for some great Greek honor, worn in sash across chest with whoopee medal. When you win a medal, use it."

Second small envelope.

A ticket to Cezanne exhibition at the Grand Palais in Paris, with his *Une Moderne Olympia* painting on it. And a scribbled note written on a small blue Post-it: "Cezanne's response to Manet's scandalous 'Olympia.'"

Third small envelope.

Three postcards of three different versions of Cezanne's paintings of Mont Sainte Victoire near Aix-en-Provence. All three had a small X marked at the bottom of the mountain. The accompanying note said: "Picasso lived and is buried in his chateau at the village of Vauvenargues - here - at the foot of Cezanne's personal mountain. I wonder how often Picasso thought about that?"

Two small boxes left. One square, one long and thin.

The latter contained a calligraphy pen made from bamboo, with a narrow nib at one end and a wide nib at the other. Max-Pol recognized a fine writing tool when he saw it. The strip of emery paper wrapped around the pen and held with a rubber band testified to its professional quality. Such a pen always came with sandpaper suited to the grain of the pen, to keep its working edge free of fuzz.

Max-Pol also noticed that the nib was sliced at the correct oblique angle for use by someone left-handed. Someone like Max-Pol. Alice would know if she looked carefully at the nib of the fountain pen she took from him. Did this mean that she, too, was left-handed? Must be. Or else she had just picked a fine pen without knowing about the nib.

Maybe that's why her handwriting was inconsistent when she wrote him - she was trying to get used to his pen?

He could not say. There was no accompanying note. All he had beyond the pen was the pleasure of using it.

Finally, the little square box marked #8. A cube, actually - one that might contain something the size and shape of a golf ball. Max-Pol unwrapped it slowly, not wanting to bring the present experience to an end. He untied the twine instead of cutting it, and peeled the tape off the paper carefully, unfolding the paper and setting it aside. A small blue box with lid.

Lifting the lid, he found shiny, multicolored, star-shaped confetti, which was the packing material for something round and red. Max-Pol fished it out, scattering confetti on the kitchen table. The object was a red rubber clown nose, split in the middle so that when he squeezed it open, he could put it on the end of his nose, and when he let go, it would stay. A nose like the one Alex had on the train.

Max-Pol stuck the red rubber ball on his nose. Then he dumped the rest of the shiny-star confetti on his head, picked up his cigar and Metaxa, and went into the bathroom to look at himself in the mirror. He grinned. And said to his slightly inebriated companion in the mirror, "I really am very happy." He lifted his glass and clinked it against the glass of the clown in the mirror, who seemed altogether as happy as he.

Opa!

GIFTS TO THE WITNESS

When Max-Pol was ready to send another set of his Chronicles to Alice, he felt unwilling to simply ship them off as-is. What extra gesture was required? Gifts?

For two days Max-Pol turned over the rough possibilities in his head like stones in a polishing tumbler. And then it became clear: Why complicate the uncomplicated?

Accept what she sent on face value. Alice was sharing some aspects of her own life in her own way. Why should she not? She asked no response. She began no conversations. She asked no favors. There were no hooks in her gifts that might catch him. She had witnessed his writing. And he had witnessed her way of expression. Leave it there.

Witness for Witness.

Hard. A physician was trained to extend questions, and to consider all available data. In short, to leave no stones unturned when working a problem. But now? All his intuitive wisdom told him to leave the stones alone. For one thing, he wasn't working a problem. But he might create one if he started playing detective again. Do no harm.

Alice likes things that come in threes.

He could add to her collection from Greek sources.

She likes blue.

Max-Pol would find some blue wrapping paper for the Chronicles.

As he put the parcel together, Max-Pol caught himself speculating about where Alice really was and what she was doing and why she had invested herself in being his Witness. He stopped himself, and said aloud,

"Just send the package, Max-Pol."

MAX-POL'S THREES

From Greek mythology and history:

    First, the gods
        Zeus - heaven
        Poseidon - the sea
        Hades - the underworld

    Three Fates, the makers of Life - the daughters of Night
        Clotho carries the spindle, spins the thread of life.
        Lachesis determines the length of the thread.
        Atropos carries the shears, cuts the thread of life.

    Three Furies - the avenging spirits
        Alecto - unresting
        Megaera - jealous
        Tisiphone - avenger

    Three Graces
        Aglaia, Euphrosyne, and Thalia
        Attendants of Aphrodite

    Three Sirens
        Leucosia, Ligeia, and Parthenope
        Sea nymphs, part bird, part woman, who by their seductive
        singing lured sailors to their death on rocky coasts.

    The three elements of Greek tragedy
        Olbos - happiness and prosperity
        Hubris - insolence and pride
        Ate - infatuation, loss of judgment, disaster

    Themes: the Muse, the Mask, the Maze

Three is a perfect number, according to Pythagoras, the great Greek mathematician - it has a beginning, middle, and end, and cannot be divided in half.

The next day I stopped in to see Kostas at his shop. It was feeding time for his "employees" - a dozen or so cats. He fed them fish heads every morning, and they kept the mice out of his carpets. Nothing personal. He didn't treat them as pets with names. They simply worked for him, and he paid off. "Is be business only, you know?"

The oriental-patterned wrapping paper Kostas used for his shop was exactly what I needed to wrap Lear's Cretan Journals as a present for Alex. But Kostas wanted to look at the book first, since it was about the past.

The plates of postcard-size illustrations, with soft watercolors and loosely handled details in pencil, pulled Kostas into the Crete of the last century. I went with him, as he lovingly turned the pages.

Alex appeared at the shop door, whacking his cane on the doorframe to get our attention. He lumbered into the shop, good-humoredly grumbling, "Just what do you think this is? A library? A rag shop? It is a kafenion, the service is lousy, and the waitress is lazy and ugly!"

Kostas reluctantly put down the book and went to get coffee from the real kafenion at the end of the alley.

Alex sat in Kostas's chair, picked up Lear's Cretan Journals, and began looking through it. I said nothing. I watched this uncanny man with deep pleasure. We might be blood kin ever so remotely. An unexpected legacy.

"Lear!" he exclaimed. "A wonderfully preposterous, wonky man. How many hours I have spent reading his collected nonsense to my children. The Jumblies, the toeless Pobble, the Owl and the Pussycat. And his nonsense cookery! That inspired many a fine uneaten dish in our house. I remember his recipe for making an Amblongus Pie.

"It begins, 'Take 4 pounds (say 4 ½ pounds) of fresh Amblongusses, and put them in a small pipkin.' Then he goes on and on with boiling and seasoning and the late addition of a pigeon, cauliflowers, and any number of oysters. And the grand ending says, 'Serve up in a clean dish and throw the whole out of the window as fast as possible.' Ha.

"Oh, and there is the Bountiful Beetle, who always carried a Green Umbrella when it didn't rain, and left it at home when it did. And, (Alex stood to declaim):

> There was an old man of West Dumpet
> Who possessed a large nose like a trumpet;
> When he blew it aloud, it astonished the crowd
> And was heard through the whole of West Dumpet.

"I don't know whether Lear was limited in his rhyming skills or nonsensically clever, but he always ended his limericks with the same word as at the end of the first line. The children found it wonderfully predictable and would always shout out the expected word or phrase. Anticipation of their part kept them alert all through the recitation. West Dumpet, indeed.

"But I must say I didn't know Lear was ever in Crete."

He sat down and turned to the front of the book to find the publisher's name, and found there on the first blank page what I had written, "For my possible cousin Alex, from his possible cousin, Max-Pol" and, underneath, a note, "see pp. 88 and 113."

Intrigued, Alex read the text, smiling broadly as he realized the implications. "Wonderful!" he shouted. "Yes! Cousins!" he roared as he launched himself up out of the chair in my direction, and tripped over the edge of the rug just as Kostas came through the door with the tray of coffees.

Opa! Kostas never saw Alex coming. Only a slapstick comedian could have timed the wreck better. Kostas stumbled backward out the door with Alex falling toward him. The coffee tray was flung into the alley, in among the fish-head-eating pussycats. Crash! Cats yowled off in all directions. Shutters banged open up and down the alleyway. People came running out of the shop next door. Only to find Alex and Kostas lying there, laughing too hard to get up.

After the victims were untangled and the mess cleaned up, Alex was left to explain things to Kostas while I went for another round of coffee. When I returned, they both sat beaming, like two crows that had just shared a fresh mouse between them. A little metal tray was on the table - three small glasses and a bottle of tsikoudia (see-koo-dee-ah) - the Cretan multipurpose white lightning celebratory drink with a proof so high you can use it to disinfect wounds, remove grease spots, or start diesel engines.

"Well, then. My dear Max-Pol, I shall not assault you again, but you have experienced my joy at the prospect of kinship between us. Alas, we shall never have actual proof, of course. There were many women taken in slavery in those old days. Many. And there were many English archeologists wandering about Egypt as well. Too many.

"That your great-grand-something-or-other could have been kin to my great-grand-something's wife, well, it is a working hypothesis. If we ever have our DNA examined, we might have certainty. But, as Cretans say, blood is blood." Kostas solemnly echoed him, "Blood is blood," and busied himself pouring glasses of tsikoudia.

"Consider, however." Alex paused, then continued reflectively, "This is the positive side of an agnostic position: We cannot prove it is not true, can we? It is, as I say, a working hypothesis. And also a working conclusion. There is a Cretan concept - in Greek it is ex-adelphia - which covers all relatives in the area of second cousins, in-laws, and the rest. We are at the very least ex-adelphia to one another, and therefore . . ."

Alex rose to address me with solemn formality. "I, Alexandros Evangelou Xenopouloudakis, shall from this moment ever after, consider you, Max-Pol Millay, my cousin. It is our decision. What can we lose?"

In the same spirit, I rose and replied, "And I, on my part, agree, cousin Alex, so shall it be, from this day forth!"

Kostas gave the two of us a standing ovation, passed out the tsikoudia, and Alex and I drank with our arms linked between us, bringing our faces almost nose to nose. It is the Cretan custom between men who wish to confirm a close bond. You cannot avoid looking in one another's eyes.

Alex said, "I further propose we adopt Kostas Liapakis into

our family. He is as likely to be blood kin to us as we are to each other."

"Absolutely," I replied.

Alex explained in Greek, raising his eyebrows in question.

Kostas seemed frozen still for a moment. And then a slow warmth seemed to enter him, working upward from his toes and ending in a stupendous grin. "Malista. Ola Kallah. Ex-adelphia. (Understood. OK. Cousins.)"

Alex declared to Kostas, "We, who are no better or worse than you, accept you, who are no better or worse than we, as our cousin."

We repeated the tsikoudia-and-linked-arms ritual with Kostas. It was a bit complicated for three, but we managed it.

Alex then suggested we consider an ancient Cretan custom for establishing blood brotherhood. "Each man bares his arm in turn, while another man takes his knife and makes a slight cut at the wrist. Then they clasp each other's forearms so that the blood from the cut at their wrists mingles."

Alex translated this in graphic detail to Kostas.

"Nai, nai (yes, yes)," he exclaimed, "is be the old way. I know this."

The medical side of my mind urged against it. I declined the honor. "Being cousins is a matter of the soul," I said, "not the body. Exchanging human blood is dangerous."

"But of course," said Alex. "It is the Cretan way to do dangerous things."

I could see they both thought I was just too chicken to go for the knife-and-blood ritual. They smiled knowingly at each other. I might be part Cretan now, but never ever as Cretan as they. They would not push the blood ritual. Not now.

We cousins sat back in our chairs, basking in the goofy pleasure of our relationship. Alex fished around in his jacket pocket and brought out his komboloi beads. Sometimes called "worry beads" or "patience beads," their use is ubiquitous among Greek men, especially Cretan men.

Rodopus peninsula - from a drive along Crete's western coast

rocky blue bay

Minoan ruin? perhaps!

Cliffs and olive grove

road w/olive trees

great telephone poles

village

big cactus

road w/geraniums

Late Afternoon Snapshops - Notes from a walk through the countryside...

cats asleep

chapel steeple

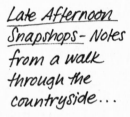
moss hugs the road and rocks stick up

little elderly ladies (and one gentleman)

view

Olive tree

Usually twenty-five matching beads, more or less, loosely strung on a cord. One extra bead at the end, along with a tassel. A komboloi resembles a rosary, but its purpose is secular, not religious. The Cretans say they play with their beads while the Roman Catholics have to pray with theirs.

Most often made of silver, amber, or plastic, the beads come in a wide variety. Men twirl them, work little hand tricks with them, or finger them repetitively. And nobody has a definitive explanation for their existence or continued use, despite the many stories told as truth.

Truth has a short life in Crete. Myths are preferred.

I have seen Alex use his komboloi often. Though men usually have several sets, Alex always had this one. Black Sea amber, perhaps from the days of the Viking traders. Irregular in shape, buttery orange in color. Smooth to touch, attesting to their great age and long use. The tasseled end included a thin silver disc, with remnants of both Arabic and Greek writing on it, worn now beyond decipherment.

"Hold out your hand," said Alex.

I complied.

He looped his komboloi over my wrist with all the dignity of a king hanging a decoration around the neck of an honored peer of the realm.

I felt knighted.

"I give you my komboloi. These beads are quite old, very valuable, and I have had them for a long time. They have been a trusted companion. How I got them is a long story for another time, of course. But it is enough to say that I am much attached to them. It is for this very reason that I want you to have them - not new ones, but these that are precious to me.

"You will keep them. From time to time, out of habit, I will reach into my pocket for them. And it will please me to know where they are. It will give me reason to think of my cousin, Max-Pol. From time to time you will run the beads through your fingers and think of me. Thus we will always be in touch."

Speechless, I took the komboloi in my hands, fingered the beads, and smiled, shaking my head. It was the best I could do - this wordless expression of great pleasure.

Alex and Kostas began their customary woofing and barking in rapid-fire Greek. Alex explained. "Kostas is a little embarrassed to have you know his thoughts, but he says you do not look very Greek, and your name is not at all Greek, and that we must give you a Greek name. I agree. But we do not agree on a name. Kostas takes this very seriously. If we three do agree on a name, you understand, you must be properly christened by a priest. It is required. I am not sure how you would feel about that."

This was not a time for argument. "I'm open to the possibility. It is, as you might say, another working hypothesis."

"And speaking of names," said Alex, "Since you are now family, it is my wish and command that from this day forth you call me by the name used by my closest friends and family - 'Aleko.' Agreed?"

"Yes. Aleko. From now on. But never call me Max.

"Agreed."

Kostas and Aleko conferred in turbocharged Greek again, too fast for my comprehension. When they want to include me, they speak slowly, simply, deliberately. When not, they simply raise the RPMs.

"We have achieved consensus," said Aleko. "We shall put this matter of a Cretan name for you in the pot to simmer on the back of the stove. Meanwhile, Kostas would like to give us both a gift - to show us something on this occasion. It is still early in the day, the site is not too far, and if you don't mind?"

As usual, the services of his chauffeur were required. And a cousin must not let a cousin down. Seeing my willingness, Aleko rose, clapped his arm around Kostas, jabbed toward the doorway with his cane, and shouted, "Onward! Onward!"

To elaborate:

Aleko and I have an unspoken agreement. I am his personal driver, available to chauffeur him almost anywhere he wants to go. I have the use of my friend's elderly blue Mercedes sedan, rumored to have once belonged to a bishop. The dignified style and questionable provenance of my chariot appeal to Aleko. I provide the car. He provides the adventure. With him in command even the most ordinary errand may become a memorable excursion.

Aleko and Kostas have formed a close friendship. A Cretan version of Don Quixote and Sancho Panza, with the two of them sometimes reversing roles. Aleko admires Kostas's love of the past. Kostas admires Aleko's knowledge. Since it is winter and business is slow, Kostas gladly closes his shop at any opportunity to join us. The old Mercedes sedan suits his style as well.

Whenever there is a break in the weather, we spend our time bumbling along the lanes and back roads of the region west of Hania. I drive and listen to Cretan music on the radio, while Aleko and Kostas hold good-humored shouting matches with one another over some fine point of Cretan tradition.

The two of them conspire to improve my language skills along the way. My clumsy Greek is too formal and too much like the mongrel version spoken in Athens. I am required to attend their private academy. I must speak as a Cretan. Be that as it may, Aleko and Kostas do not agree on just how a Cretan should express any given idea. Which means that our excursions are seldom tranquil.

More than once they rode together in the back seat barking and woofing and braying at one another - drawing pictures and writing words on scraps of paper, while I pushed on as best I could. And more than once I got us lost because they were too absorbed in debate to direct me.

On such occasions, the special virtues of both these men would shine. Never did either ask, "Where are we?" in a way suggesting disappointment or concern. My getting lost was simply not a problem for them. They are never lost. Oh, they might never have been to the exact spot before. But lost? Never! And it was against their principles to resort to a map. For them maps are for the faint-hearted. Maps are for sissies and tourists. Maps are just lines and words on paper. Above all, maps mean no surprises.

This isn't just the usual arrogant male thing. It is the way the two of them look at the world. They see any lack of knowledge as an opportunity.

On our trips the Fates and Graces become our tour guides. The response is never "Where are we?" It's always, "Look, look, where we are now! Thavma! Katapliktiko!"

Getting lost is a superb circumstance for them, much to be appreciated.

Some results of getting not-lost: A tour of an olive oil mill and the gift of a fresh bottle of olive oil from its owner; a walk in a citrus grove and the gift of a bag of lemons; an inspection of a wood-fired bakery and the gift of a loaf of fresh bread the size of a spare tire.

We've come back with honey, almonds, cheese, walnuts, spring water, roses, vegetables, wine, and wild greens for salad. All from the innate generosity of Cretans who willingly share their life stories, their occupations, and the fruits of their labors with strangers who are interested in them. And Aleko and Kostas are interested in everybody and everything. Strangers? Never!

Moreover, we've been lectured on local ways of raising donkeys, sheep, goats, pigs, and chickens. We've been assured of the best sources of Cretan boots and shepherd's crooks. And history. History is alive everywhere in Crete.

More than once I thought we would not get home before morning because several old men unraveled the tales of all the resistance activity in their area - beginning with the Germans and going back through the Turks, Egyptians, Venetians, and Romans. Getting acquainted with a local priest who wanted us to see all the fragments of Byzantine frescoes on his church walls took just as long.

None of these experiences are on maps or in guidebooks.

Kostas explained, "Is be Crete. Is be Island. Not be lost. If you go in mountains, in villages - in Crete is always be fine time. Anywhere. Is be fine. No worry, you know. Is be Crete. Ola kala. (It's all good.)

And now we are off again. Only Kostas knows where.

(THE OLIVE TREE - CHRONICLES - 8)

I was instructed to drive out of Hania on the coast road westward. As we passed through Maleme, Aleko pointed toward a hill above the town, saying the German military cemetery was there. A trip for another day.

At Drapanias, we turned south on a secondary road, driving through endless groves of olive trees. With Kostas pointing the way at intersections, we reached the tumbledown old village of Vouves (Voo-vays). Its location high on a ridge well away from the coast was evidence that it had been built centuries before, when the raids of slave-taking pirates drove the native Cretans to inland sanctuaries. From up here, you could see trouble coming a long way off.

Kostas called for a halt. "Is be here - here." We parked, and walked uphill. Kostas pointed a little way ahead and said, "Is be oldest olive tree in the world. Is be two, three thousand years old."

No signs. No fences. No railings. Just a shaggy old tree in the middle of an old village. But what a tree. We later calculated it would take ten or twelve people holding hands to encircle it. It isn't exceptionally tall, because it has been trimmed and tended. It was hanging full of olives - still a working tree.

Aleko knew all about it. He had read its story in a science magazine, and he was excited to see it firsthand. He walked around the tree, touching it, admiring it. "Katapliktico," he murmured, "just marvelous."

Kostas struck up a conversation with a Greek woman sitting on a nearby doorstep, peeling potatoes. Yes, indeed, it was The Tree. From way, way before the time of Christ. The village knew it was very old, but scientists had come from the Technical University at Hania and confirmed its antiquity. At least two thousand years old. A great tree. And twenty-two kilos of oil last year - maybe more this year.

Aleko explained that the difficulty in determining its age lay in the impossibility of using a coring method, as is commonly used for sequoias or the bristlecone pines. Olive trees usually die out from the center, while continuing to grow outward.

The center of this old tree is an empty room - a space large enough for both Kostas and me to climb inside it. The outer trunk is a gnarled complex of growth, carefully tended and nurtured by its caretakers. Splits and scars have been painted with a protective coating to deter insects, and the upper branches have been thinned and trimmed to prevent the tree from being damaged by high winds.

We stepped back and admired this living monument to perseverance. Despite everything destructive thrown at it by nature for centuries - disease, wind, fire, drought, and flood - it had survived. And continued bearing olives each year. I felt like getting down on my knees in homage.

I admired the villagers for their respect for the tree, in not turning it into a living souvenir stand. It was as if the tree was an ancestor. A respected and revered great-great-great-great-grandfather tree. The oldest living member of the family.

I picked up the black shriveled olives from the ground beneath the great tree. I could clean them of the meaty flesh, dry the kernels, and get a silversmith to drill them out and string them together on a chain. I gathered enough to make a new komboloi for Aleko.

He will be the only one to have patience beads made from the fruits of the oldest living olive tree. I will give it to him as a gift at New Year's, when Greeks exchange small personal presents, shouting "Chronya Pollah!" - literally, "Many Years!" - wishing that you may have them. The wish I have for Aleko, my cousin, Alexandros Evangelou Xenopouloudakis.

World's oldest olive tree

MONA LISA MOVES

In her apartment in Paris, She-of-Many-Names sat in a windowed alcove in a distracted state of mind, undisturbed by the thunderstorm over the city. The thrice-read Cretan Chronicles of Max-Pol Millay lay in her lap. In her left hand she held the page he had included acknowledging that he was writing autobiography, addressing his inner landscape and life as much as the landscape and life of Crete. Alex and Pendlebury and even Kostas were characters who existed in both realms. She had intuited as much. She read it again. She wanted to hear these stories from him in person.

She sat very still, staring out at the falling rain. Crossing her hands over the manuscript in her lap, she smiled ever so slightly. As a teenager she had visited Paris with her family, and had been taken to the Louvre to see the *Mona Lisa*, which she never actually saw because the room was so crowded and the famous painting was behind security glass and so far away.

In the museum's shop she had bought a postcard of the painting, and spent idle time with a small mirror learning to imitate the pose and the smile. Even now, whenever she was feeling seriously conflicted, she assumed the mask and pose of the *Mona Lisa*.

She wondered what Max-Pol would think if he could see her now. Would he recognize the pose? Most people didn't. But would he? Moreover, would he see beyond her imitation of Lisa Gherardini into the confusion behind the smile? Should she tell him what she was thinking?

No, not yet. But she wanted to. And therein lay the conflict.

She knew her response to his Chronicles had already revealed much about her, if he would notice. It seemed that he had. And that thought brought her both pleasure and distress. There was no way around it – she was drawn to this man across the demarcation line of Witness into a relationship she could not or was unwilling to name. But the possible consequences of responding to the attraction cautioned her.

She paced her apartment, allowing a fantasy to unfold. What if she made a surprise trip to Crete? Just cut through all this Witness business and showed up? Take a chance. Witness the reality firsthand, not the interpretation of it.

No. But suppose she just observed at a distance? Not declare her presence. She could disguise herself without much effort, especially if Max-Pol was not expecting her. People don't see what they are not looking for.

She laughed.

She had done crazier things in her life.

Village of Kolimvari - view from above the monastery

med.
blue sky

feathery
green tree

tree trunk
painted
white

light catches
edge of table

Cafe where the communists gather
ALSO - a barbershop inside next door

tile

weathered
peach

upstairs light
is warmest

greydoor

faded red can
blue bucket,
pink flowers

The Argentina at 10:00 am: Manoulis spies me sketching and appears at my elbow with a cup of piping, dark coffee and a glass of fresh juice. Holds his mustache with one hand and clucks approvingly at the drawing...

overlooking the sea above Kolimvari

On Second Thought

Before sending his next Chronicle to Alice, Max-Pol reconsidered what he had written. He thought he should write something like a preface – part explanation and part confession.

*

Dear Witness:

In the spirit of my reflection on my last set of Chronicles, I forewarn you that while I have kept the façade of reporter, what you are about to read is more autobiographical than ever.

The events described are accurate, the adventures true, and the essential character of the conversations faithfully related. But this Christmas cake of experiences I have baked for your acknowledgment comes in several layers. Some of the layers reflect my own wrestling with matters of religion and philosophy.

I surprise myself. Freed from the demands of medical practice, my mind seems unwilling to take a vacation and determined to get down in the basement where the elemental machinery is and make it work.

I first wrote at unreadable length. I have reread and rewritten and cut this text to make it as succinct as possible. Still, it is long. You may not be interested in religion or philosophy, but since the ideas are profoundly important to me, I ask your indulgence.

Witness my struggle to have a firm existential base on which to stand.

Christmas.

Aleko and Kostas announced they were taking me to church on Christmas Eve. Church? This was unexpected. Neither had ever spoken to me about religion. Neither seemed to have any particular affection for the Greek Orthodox Church. No antagonisms, either. The subject simply had never come up.

And I am not drawn to cathedrals or churches - Greek Orthodox or any other kind. For me, they are monuments to how badly human beings can deceive themselves. When it comes to religious matters, I am agnostic, skeptic, and an unwavering cynic.

To an outsider like me, the Greek Orthodox Church seems to be mostly about death. I see the priests and monks and bishops as self-important in their Byzantine finery. Their long hair and beards seem vain, their daily black dress seems life-denying. The cookpots they wear for headgear make it hard for me to take them seriously. Their obsession with black mourns a Jesus who suffered and died and went away, not a man who triumphed over his own death and might live in the hearts of people still.

If I had my way, servants of the church would wear workman's overalls and flowered shirts, and carry tools.

And there would be dancing and laughing in the church in memory of a man who brought Good News about life. As it is, every service in the Greek Orthodox Church seems like a funeral to me.

So why do I care? Am I more religious than I want to think? I won't go on. Nobody wants to hear what I think of religion.

Ninety percent of the people of the world believe in God, so the pollsters say. So be it. Besides, it's Christmas. Sour sentiment is unwelcome.

Aleko and Kostas laid their plans - a conspiracy between them. Kostas was in command this time. "Is be surprise. Big surprise." First we would go to church, then we would have dinner. The service was in a special place to the south of the village of Kolymbari.

Which meant leaving in the evening around ten o'clock and having dinner at "another special place" around two o'clock in the morning, back in Hania. I was to dress warmly and bring a flashlight. "It will be memorable" was all Aleko would tell me.

Christmas Eve.

A clear, cold, still night. New moon. Just the smallest movement of air from the south, out of the Libyan Sea and Africa, filled with sweet fragrance. The smell of Christmas in Crete is orange blossoms instead of fir trees.

We drove along the coast for half an hour, turning south at Kolymbari into the foothills toward Spilia, and then turning off on a narrow road leading west up a steep ridge. All along the road people were trudging uphill in the same direction. We parked at the end of the road and followed a lighted pathway toward a grove of trees at the face of a cliff. Ahead of us, I could hear liturgical chanting.

Rounding a corner of rock, the volume of the chanting increased. I was surprised to see a huge crowd of people, standing in a great cave, lit by candles and torches. Kostas explained that this cave was the site of the hermitage of a very holy monk - maybe sixth century or earlier - whose bones could be seen in a glass box in a chapel off to one side of the cave entrance.

Special Christmas Eve services have been observed in the cave for over a thousand years. The liturgy is four hours long, but the cave is usually full by 9 o'clock - everyone standing. On a stone platform built against the back wall of the cave stood a massed assemblage of priests from the surrounding villages. Perhaps twenty-five of them, in elaborate vestments of gold and crimson and green and purple. In their midst stood the legendary Irineos - Bishop of Kissamos and Selinon, who always dresses in plain black. He's said to be one of the great Cretan social reformers of all time, and at eighty-four can still deliver an exhortation of inspiration on any occasion.

Off to one side were ten liturgical chanters, all men - flanked by flags of church and state, massed candles, and incense burners.

Adding a touch of realism to this mystic setting were animals in a crèche, unwittingly adding amusement to this formal occasion, keeping the crowd smiling. Several very nervous sheep, a lively black-and-white bull calf, two skittish black goats, and a solemn donkey - all brushed and beribboned, wearing unusually large brass bells, and making antiphonal responses to the liturgy - braying, baa-ing and bonging. There had been a pig as well, but he escaped and was being pursued downhill by several young men.

The mood was unlike anything I've ever experienced in a religious setting. Hardly the Byzantine funeral I expected. More than anything else it felt like a social event. The community was simply present while the liturgy was performed - even if the community was also talking, laughing, and coming and going. Kostas said you were just supposed to come to show your respect. Light a candle, kiss the icons, and share the sweet bread while walking back to the village with your family and friends in the light of a new moon on the eve of Christmas.

Aleko said, "It is simply that community itself is sanctified."

I imagine that people came to that cave long before the Christian era - in Paleolithic times and Minoan times - as long as there have been humans here - and they will continue to come as long as humanity lasts. Come to stand in awe in a mysterious place in the mysterious earth in the mysterious winter darkness and acknowledge everlasting amazement, whatever names it is called, whatever songs are sung, whatever sounds are chanted.

A powerful experience. I admit I was deeply moved.

We drove all the way back to Hania without speaking - each deep in his own thoughts. Three sometimes-wise men sharing the blessed bread between us, as we continued the celebration, riding along in the quiet cave of the car, still in the company of the wonder of it all.

In Hania, the restaurants and tavernas were emblazoned like small cruise ships docked in the harbor of the darkened city. Lights. Music. Laughter. The feast was on. Greeks fast before Christmas Eve services and break the fast as soon after church as possible. Unlike that of most Western countries, the Greek holiday season doesn't begin until December 24 and it continues through January 6, Epiphany.

Though some Western-style commercialism is creeping in, along with Santa Claus, presents are exchanged at New Year's, and they are small and personal in nature. The Cretans do not focus everything on the single meal on Christmas Day. They eat for two weeks. Beginning, as I have said, at two in the morning on December 25.

Kostas Liapakis's cousin owns the restaurant we patronize, the Amnesia. The name seems appropriate because the meal, featuring boiled sheep's head, a Christmas delicacy, is one I would just as soon forget. The conversation, on the other hand, affected the way I have looked at everything ever since.

The comfortable piety expressed by Aleko and Kostas at the cave at Spilia surprised me. They kissed the icons, lit petitionary candles, followed the liturgy, and crossed themselves often, as is the Orthodox custom. Exposing my ignorance, I asked: "Are you both practicing members of the Greek Orthodox Church? Believers, in other words?"

They looked stunned. And then gave each other a raised-eyebrow look I interpreted to mean, "How can this intelligent man ask such a stupid question?"

Aleko said, "If you are Greek, then you are Greek Orthodox. If you are Cretan, you are the most Orthodox of all. Period. It is part of your character, your cultural tradition and your soul. It is in the soil you stand on."

Kostas chimed in, "Like the taxes and the death. A Greek not give his taxes, depending on how is feeling about the government, but a Greek for his country will give his life. Maybe we not be always inside the church, but the church is be always inside us."

Aleko gave Kostas an exuberant slap on the back. "Yes! Exactly, Kostas. Let us drink a little kokinoh krasi (red wine) to that."

And he poured a measure of wine into our glasses. We toasted the Greek Orthodox Church and Kostas and my supposed enlightenment, but not death or taxes. We spat on death and taxes.

"Your question knocks at the great door of Truth. Allow me to respond," said Aleko. "Fear not, I shall be succinct." Pouring wine again for us, he sat silently for a moment, characteristically touching the fingers of one hand to his forehead, gently tapping, calling to attention the employees in the workshop of his mind.

Kostas and I sat back in our chairs.
Looking away, closing his eyes, Aleko turned to us.

"Well then, class, I give you three phrases to consider.
        One: Multiple working hypotheses.
        Two: Multiple working conclusions.
        And three: Parallel praxis.

"Please repeat the phrases after me, so as to impress them on your minds." We repeated. Multiple working hypotheses, multiple working conclusions, and parallel praxis. Kostas looked puzzled, and Aleko marched him through the notions in Greek. Satisfied, Aleko continued.

"The first is a seminal concept in science. I am told that this idea was first expressed at the end of the last century by an American geologist. Chamberlin, I believe.

"Multiple working hypotheses."

Aleko let the phrase sink in as he drank his wine and scrutinized his students for signs of early confusion. Satisfied with our attention, he continued.

"Onward, then. Our Greek forefathers, that famous old Gang of Three - Socrates, Plato, and Aristotle - believed that ideal truth could be known but that it was hidden like a needle in a haystack. Philosophy was a great game of hide-and-seek.

"They began with a single hypothesis: truth exists and is knowable, and if knowable, then it is employable - it can be used. That's like saying God exists and can be found, and, if found, then engaged.

"You are certain of these things from the beginning - it's just arriving at these conclusions that is difficult, like seeing the top of a mountain above a fog. You know it must be standing on something, but you have to go and find out what. And when you discover its base, then you figure out how to climb it."

Aleko translated all this into Greek for Kostas, and Kostas nodded his understanding. Kostas enjoys playing the fool at times, but he's play-acting. Even with ideas, he follows the horse-trader's primary rule: Never appear to know too much.

"I continue. By now in science we have learned that far better answers to basic questions can be attained if we open-mindedly pursue several different hypotheses at once. The mountaintops above the fog may indicate the presence of real mountains - but they may also be optical illusions, dreams, hallucinations, or fantasies. We must pursue these possibilities.

"Currently, for example, there are those who are examining all available data on the theory that the universe may be expanding.

Others take the point of view that the universe is either pulsing or in a steady state. All must conjecture just how much matter there is in the universe in the first place. I briefly mention only a few of the many lines of investigation.

"All begin with a 'Suppose that . . .'

"All those investigators are aware of, and have or should have, respect for the work of the others. This is the nature of the idea of having multiple working hypotheses. One does not start with a conclusion and work backwards to find evidence to support that conclusion. One starts with respect for many possibilities, and tests those many possibilities, irrespective of the conclusion.

"If you always start with a conclusion, you will find no surprises - only the evidence you need to support that conclusion. If you start with as much evidence as you can, you will almost always be surprised at what you find. The idea of multiple working hypotheses is on the side of surprise, not certainty.

"Katalaves? (Understand?) Are you still with me?"

We nod. So far, so good.

"Now, I happen to know some of these thinkers personally - astronomers and astrophysicists and chemists. One of the most famous is a devout Roman Catholic - a Jesuit. Several others are practicing Orthodox Jews. They are neither fanatics nor liars. One might reasonably ask how they can profess a certain religious faith based on a belief in a personal God and, at the same time, be successful working scientists. Simple. They have reached a place in their lives where they have multiple working conclusions. Please note we have come to my second concept:

"Multiple working conclusions."

Aleko paused to translate for Kostas, who had a now-let-me-get-this-straight expression on his face. Aleko took out his pen and wrote several words on a napkin. The two of them got into their barking and woofing and braying routine, pointing in the direction of the local church and the heavens and the wine. Kostas finally shrugged his shoulders, raised his eyebrows, and held out both hands open. This is the Cretan way of saying, "Maybe, maybe not."

Aleko returned the gesture. They laughed.

"Well, then. When you have reached multiple working conclusions, it means that you can run your life in the face of truths that may be irreconcilable but not necessarily incompatible. For example, I can fully participate in the liturgical celebration of the Greek Orthodox Church of the birth of the Son of God. There is deeply satisfying emotional truth there.

"And . . . And . . . I can walk outside, look up at the stars, and acknowledge the fact that the pictures from the Hubble telescope published last week reveal that there are at least fifty billion more galaxies like ours than we thought. All with multiple solar systems, planets, perhaps life, even creatures like us, with gods and multiple working hypotheses like ours. Another kind of truth.

"Both are satisfying in a different way. It is the same to say that I live on the basis of both Newtonian physics and quantum physics. It is why I have a photograph of the Andromeda nebula on the wall of my study alongside a photograph of me and my friends at the greatest lunch we ever prepared. It is why those people can stand there in the cave at Spilia awed by great mystery, and reply to it with great community. That's there. We are here. These truths do not interfere with one another. Do you see?"

Kostas had a puzzled look on his face.

Aleko translated. Kostas still had a puzzled look on his face. Kostas made his "maybe, maybe not" gesture again, but this time picked up his wine and said, "Stini-ya-sas (To your health)." Meaning he was not sure he agreed with all that was being said, but he was having a good time.

Aleko paused, reflected, and resumed. "Very well, put it another way then. Place one hundred thoughtful men and women on a hill at sunset in a rural landscape. People from many walks of life, from many lands and cultures. Ask them to prepare a written response to share with the rest of the group.

"Some will write poems. Some will write facts. One might write music. When the experience is finished and the results produced, there will immediately be problems. They will not have used the same letters, or words of the same language. Even so, they will have talked of many things - sky, clouds, and trees. Yet they will have seen a different tree, a different cloud, and the same sky in a different light.

"Shall we come to blows over this? Divide into hostile camps? Who shall say that what this man says is true and what this woman says is not? And what shall we do with those who do not wish to speak but who can respond only by dancing or singing? Each can respect the truth of the other. We have here another example of multiple working conclusions."

Kostas understood this without translation. "Malista, malista."

"Bear with me. I am almost done. We come to my final notion: "Parallel praxis."

"Parallel is a word you know - and praxis is that old Greek word that is more than the English word 'practice' suggests. Praxis, for me, means the whole working out of one's truth from its beginning to its end - including motivation and thought as well as action.

"Praxis is always in motion, never at rest. Always in process, never settled. But one may operate on more than one line of truth resolution at once, especially when there is a great difference in scale. As an educated man, I can follow the exploration of the mysteries of the universe with enthusiasm. As a Cretan, I can attend the service as we did tonight with a full heart. As a citizen, I can work for the continuation of democracy with all my being. And as a despotic and tyrannical host, I can insist we drink more wine.

"All of these are true statements. I believe all of these. This is who I am. There you have my metaphysics. I am finished."

I nodded. I understood. I agreed.

Aleko turned to Kostas. More barking and woofing and gesticulating with hands and shoulders, punctuated with shouts of Nai, nai! and Ohi, ohi! ("Yes, yes!" and "No, no!"). Finally, Aleko took out his pen again, and on a napkin he drew the sign for infinity. On top of that and slightly crossways to it, he drew still another infinity sign. Finally, he drew a third infinity sign across the other two. It looked like a multi-bladed propeller.

Kostas stared at it. Looked up with his best foolish face and said, "Flower? All means this? Truth - flowers?"

Aleko is stunned. Pleased. Delighted. And amused, in that order. "Katapliktico! Kostas," he shouted. "Marvelous! Yes! Truth flowers." And he roared with laughter. "You can say that, Kostas. Truth flowers." Kostas was not quite sure that what he said was what Aleko understood, but he was pleased that Aleko was pleased.

And I was pleased to find that philosophy is still alive among the Greeks. This was the first but not the last example of this ongoing habit I was to witness, especially among Cretans.

Once again the wine was poured, the glasses clinked together. We were in the presence of yet another truth - the truth of great companionship. We would no doubt hear more about multiple working hypotheses and multiple working conclusions and parallel praxis in times to come. But not tonight.

The night was almost over. It was five o'clock in the morning. Time for me to go home to bed, though many Greeks were still at tables in the Amnesia, eating, drinking, laughing and singing, and would still be there at sunrise.

Such a night!

Merry Christmas, indeed.

THE LIGHTHOUSE

Wide-awake, in the mellow mood that is the gift of wine and profound conversation, Max-Pol ambled along the harbor front in welcome solitude. He was satiated by the experiences of the last twelve hours: the service in the cave, the food at the Amnesia, Alex's philosophical dissertation, and the intense pleasure of the company of his two "cousins." The most memorable Christmas Eve feast of his life.

He walked away from the sounds and lights of the town toward the empty darkness of the open sea at the harbor entrance. Sitting down on a bench at the water's edge, he consulted his watch.

5:30 a.m., December 25.

"Christmas Day," he said aloud.

"I have no plans. And no obligations. No family to see, no presents to give, no turkey, no tree, no carols. Nothing. And that's just fine."

Thinking he heard footsteps on the quay behind him, and thinking his friends might have followed along behind him, Max-Pol turned around and called into the darkness, "Aleko? Kostas?" No reply.

And then another name came, as from his unconscious, and he called out, "Alice?"

(Silence.)

"Why did I say that?" Max-Pol asked aloud.

"She's not here. Wishful thinking? She might be here. She could be. Alice would do something like that. It's not that far to come - Paris to Athens to Crete, or even a direct holiday charter - here in half a day. She might even come, watch me from a distance, and leave without saying anything. Just being a Witness. An invisible Christmas gift, Alice-style."

He looked at the lighthouse.

How many hundreds of years had it been there?

A beacon that both eased the anxiety of those searching for the way into safe harbor and warned of the rocky shoals on either side of the passage.

162

He stood and slowly turned to face the silence behind him, and called again, softly this time,

"Alice . . . are you there?"

(Silence.)

Confused about which he wanted most - Alice or not Alice - but convinced he was alone, Max-Pol stood, stretched, and walked back to his apartment.

PERSPECTIVE

Not long after New Year's, Cretans begin asking each other:
"Where are we? In what season?"
They answer, "*Oute afto, oute ekino.*" - neither this nor that.
People say, "I can't believe it's still January."
Or "How can it already be February?"
And some protest, "Only yesterday, *yesterday*, it was last year."

There's an ancient explanation. Chronus, the Titan of Time, being idle after serving as midwife to the child of the New Year, wishes to regain center stage in the lives of men. He knows that so soon after the holidays they cannot yet recall just what month and day and year it is. He summons them: "Come - come back to the timetable and the almanac." In his self-interest he befuddles minds, forcing frequent checking of watches and repetitive inspection of calendars.

As if meant to intensify this confusion, the halcyon days arrive in Crete now. Halcyon is the Greek name for the kingfisher bird that is said to lay its eggs on the surface of the sea. For the fourteen days of incubation, the nursemaid sea remains agreeably tranquil. For human beings, these are simply days of peaceful weather - a period of false spring - with lucid skies, temperate winds out of Africa, the prophetic greening of the countryside, and the adamant early flowers.

Taking advantage of these conditions, Pandora, the caretaker of hope, seduces minds toward inclinations of optimism and confidence. One may momentarily feel that good must ultimately prevail over evil in the universe, and one's own troubles will be resolved. This, too, has its Greek roots, for Aristotle's doctrine held that the universe and everything in it is developing toward something continually better than what came before.

But, of course, experience says these restless, roseate, and timeless conditions will likely prove as false as the appearance of spring in February. It is too good to last. A modern realist acknowledges only a pessimistic optimism.

Still, be that as it may, sitting mindlessly for an hour drinking coffee in the first sun of such a day in such a season is in itself a true thing - a worthy occupation. If friends are present, so much the better. Profound and open-eyed folly is best enjoyed in good company.

terracotta roofs, dk green shutters

darkening brick against light sky

minaret from the time of the turks

strong shadows on pink wall

faucet shrine

blue grey
red!

pink

gold

gold/dun stone

maroon

patchy

peach/ faded cream

darkens toward edges

Shrine of the red shirt

caramel wood door

'Τοπ Χαναϲ'- (Tope Hanass) comes from the Turkish name for the gunpowder magazine, which was located just a little ways around the corner. The building still stands

Typical Hania dog

A low, practical, mutt of a model with a long body and short, stumpy legs - spends better part of the day asleep...

THE MELTEMI

In just such sunny circumstances, at eight on a Monday morning, Max-Pol and Alex and Kostas are on the west side of the stone quay of the venerable Venetian harbor of Hania, having breakfast together at their favorite kafenion. It is named the Meltemi - for a very specific wind that blows from the northwest in the Mediterranean during August, bringing welcome cool weather to Crete.

(A term of endearment comes from this wind - meltemaki mu - meaning "my little breath of fresh air." And those who habituate the Meltemi kafenion refer to themselves as the Meltemi-maki-manians *- meaning "the crazy Meltemi crowd.")*

Max-Pol and Alex and Kostas, members in good standing of the Meltemi-maki-manians to be sure, have moved their table out into the sunshine, close to the water's edge.

On the table before them: tall glasses of fresh orange juice, small cups of steaming chocolate-frothed coffee, and plates piled with fire-gridded toast. On a tray: jars of thyme honey, lemon marmalade, and black fig jam.

Kostas has provided an antique ivory linen tablecloth from his nearby shop. Alex has brought flowers from an early trip to the market - bright red anemones picked wild in the mountains and care-freely arranged in a burnished copper vase. Max-Pol puts three Cuban cigars on the table.

This is a small-scale farewell breakfast. Alex is going to Iraklion. Max-Pol is leaving for Athens and Delphi. And Kostas is going nowhere. He must stay by the bedside of his mother while she suffers along toward death.

Despite this cornucopia of comestibles and the celebrational occasion, the three men sit in fraternal silence, leaning back in their chairs, eyes closed, taking the morning sun like turtles on a rock. From time to time one or another stirs - stretches arms and legs, and makes yawning noises before lapsing back into sedentary somnolence. Apollo's arriving chariot has mesmerized and sedated this triune brotherhood into bliss.

Kostas is not accustomed to being awake and abroad at such an early hour. He's considering not opening his eyes. His body accepts his consideration. Slowly his breathing lapses into regularity. He snores softly.

Alex whispers, "Now there is a contented man, Max-Pol."

"No, just an exhausted one, Aleko. He was up most of the night with his mother again. Even as tough as she is, I don't think she'll live long. Kostas asked my advice as a doctor, and I looked in on her last night. From what he told me it seems she has congestive heart failure, arthritis, lungs badly affected by TB when she was younger, and now, of course, she hardly eats. I wouldn't be surprised if she has other problems - cancer, for example. I told Kostas it's likely she will get pneumonia, and that will be the end. A welcome, blessed end. All I could do was to reassure him there's nothing more he can or should do.

"At first I wondered why she wasn't in a hospital or a nursing home, but now I understand. You would understand as well. She *is* in a nursing home - Cretan style. Kostas is taking care of her at home, as he both wants to do and is expected to do. As you know, people here, especially the old, go to a hospital if there is a chance they may get well - but they stay at home to die.

"His sister and a cousin help out. His mother has never been in a hospital and is not about to go now. It's just as well. She sleeps most of the time. She's getting loving care. One day soon she will just not wake up.

"Kostas is as tough as she is. He will do whatever he needs to do as long as he needs to do it to make her end comfortable and peaceful. Staying up all night with his mother isn't onerous. He says she stayed up all night with him many times. Now it's his turn. His clarity on this is admirable. I don't know anything about her life or how his father fits into the picture, but from what I saw last night, Kostas' deep affection for the past includes her."

The bells of the cathedral peal, marking the end of the morning service and stirring Kostas. His face has the soft, slightly puffy quality of a small child not yet fully awake. He sits up, rubs his eyes, unselfconsciously crosses himself, and just as automatically, reaches for his coffee with one hand and his cigarettes with another.

"*Ahman, ahman.* Is be early - too early."

Despite the sorrow of his late-night vigil, Kostas has rallied to say goodbye to Max-Pol and Alex. The thought of losing his mother doesn't make losing the company of his friends any easier, even if he knows they will be gone only for a week or two. Like Alex, Kostas does not like goodbyes, even temporary ones. Goodbyes dip water from his well of grief, which is deep. Kostas has an inborn talent for melancholy, a personal attachment to nostalgia, and a Cretan capacity for emotional excess. Added together, the sum is a tearful state.

"Me, is be sad, you know. A fine day for sad."
Alex and Max-Pol cannot help laughing. Such a Cretan thing to say.
"A fine day for sad."
Their laughter masks their own anxieties.

Alex has decided he will, after all, go home - to where he was born - to where he began growing up - to Iraklion and Knossos, toward the central part of Crete. Rationally, he knows that all of the figures of that part of his past are dead. Mother, father, grandparents, uncles, aunts. Only cousins may be there - and even many of those members of his generation are likely gone by now. Dead or migrated. There is nothing to be afraid of. He will find what he looks for. Nevertheless, he is fearful of what he may find.

Far more than Max-Pol realizes, it is he who has enabled Alex to spill out the past and sort through the pieces. For a time Alex thought to invite - even press - Max-Pol to go with him. But. No. Not now. Later. Providentially, Max-Pol must make a trip to Athens to tie up loose ends to do with visa, passport and banking, and to buy books.

Alex will go home. Alone.

"Well, then. When you return from Athens, it would be my pleasure to have you join me in Iraklion. I will enjoy showing you the Minoan world from the point of view of one who helped dig it up. I know where some of the bodies of the past were buried and where some may be buried, yet."

Max-Pol has been hoping for this invitation from Alex.

"Aleko, I'll come. I should be back in a week. I have to put some things in motion in Athens and then come back in a couple of days to get the results. In the meantime, I thought I'd take your suggestion to see Delphi - it's a good time of year to go, what with this nice weather and it not being tourist season."

"Delphi! Delphi! Yes! Excellent time to go! The ancients always went early in the year, you know. You will enjoy the scenery - there will be snow on the mountains. But it is also a dangerous place to go - always has been."

"How do you mean?"

"Delphi is the prime representation of a grievous flaw in human nature - the insistent desire to know the future. This vexatious yearning kept the oracle of Delphi in business for centuries. It keeps astrologers in business today. It is why people still throw the I-Ching coins and use tarot cards. Do you not hear people speak of consulting Lady Luck, who is either with you or against you? The oracle was no more and no less than Lady Luck.

"And our pride or arrogance - our weakness or our strength - is that we think if we know the future we may take advantage of it - or else, if it is against us, we can change it to favor us. History is littered with the wreckage of the lives of men who tried."

This is exactly why Max-Pol is somewhat anxious about his trip.
He, too, wants to know the future.
He, too, knows better.

ALEX GOES HOME

A taxi has been waiting for Alex farther down the quay, the driver lounging on his part of the rock with his own turtlish friends. Alex has shifted from relaxation to restlessness.

He is ready to go.

"I have an appointment at Knossos tomorrow at noon. With the current curator of the site - the same job Pendlebury once held. With luck I may be invited to stay in the Villa Ariadne."

As Alex rises to leave, he says to his cousins, "Come with me to my taxi, I want to show you something."

He calls to the driver, who opens the trunk of the car.

"Look!"

In the trunk is a matching set of luggage - three old-fashioned suitcases: large, medium, and small. Cinnamon brown, oil-tanned, hand-stitched harness leather, with brass hardware, outside straps, and thick leather handles. The bags, despite the appearance of antiquity, are unblemished and unscarred. They are, in fact, brand new.

The last time Max-Pol had seen Alex's traveling equipment, Alex had the latest bulletproof nylon-and-steel, airline-style, roll-aboard luggage.

Alex lifts out the smallest of the bags and hands it to Max-Pol.

"Look at this - look at the craftsmanship, smell this leather, feel it. These are the last of their kind. When I was a young man, I wanted bags like these. The luggage of a gentleman, a world traveler, a bon vivant. All I could afford was a canvas sack.

"Now nobody wants these - they are out of style. The shop that makes them here is going out of business, and these bags were on sale for a fraction of their cost. At last I can afford to travel in the style I wanted when I was young. Now I *am* a gentleman, a world traveler, and bon vivant.

"My time has finally come. From a practical point of view, I do not need these. For my soul, for going home, they are required."

Kostas, the lover of the past, is so impressed that he unloads the other two bags, lines all three in a row, and stands back to admire both the luggage and the man who owns them. In effusive Greek he praises the bags and Alex. With care, he replaces the luggage and inspects Alex. Laughing, he whisks a few pieces of lint off Alex's coat, and flicks dust off Alex's shoes with his handkerchief.

"Moment, moment," he says.

And runs back to the breakfast table to get a bright red anemone, which he places carefully in Alex's buttonhole. Alex unwraps the cigar Max-Pol gave him. Kostas offers him a light.

And with the feigned dignity of a royal ambassador entering his chariot, Alex folds himself into the taxi, waving his hand in benevolent blessing out the window as the taxi takes him away.

On the road back toward home.

ALEX ON THE ROAD

"Take the new road all the way" was the longest sentence Alex spoke aloud for the next two hours. For all the pleasantries of his leave-taking, he was in a dark and pensive mood fraught with both yearning and foreboding.

The return to Iraklion was intimidating, and Alex was not easily intimidated. What troubled him was the ease with which someone his age could wander off into the no-man's-land of nostalgia. Age can make one passive, which leads to ennui - deep boredom - and out of some need to structure one's time it is easy to become absorbed in the past.

Alex was aware of his dilemma. He had spent his life studying the past - history and philosophy and language and culture. But he had avoided his own past. He would not have come to Crete but for having had his memories awakened by Max-Pol. And he would not have come to Iraklion if being in Hania had not been so splendid. These coincidences mattered.

He wondered: Why was he so determined to go back to Iraklion?
Perhaps he should have gone with Max-Pol to Delphi.
Alex had a question for the oracle, but not about the future.
Alex wanted to know how to change the past.

Hearing about Kostas's mother opened a long-closed room in Alex's mind. An empty room. Nothing was in that room. And never would be. It was the room of memory reserved for his mother. What kind of person was she? He could not say. What did she look like? He would never know. She died three weeks after he was born. His life for hers.

Unlike some who lose a mother early in life and fill their emptiness with imagination or stories told by others or even an album of pictures, Alex had deliberately closed the door on that emptiness, and left it as it was. He could live with nothing. He knew too many men whose maternal shrines were filled with angst-laden details left behind by mothers who were destructive. Better no memory than bitter memories.

So what was he going to Iraklion to find? What purpose would it serve to find her grave and the grave of his father? At the very best, he would find only names and dates on marble, hardly enough to furnish that room in his memory.

For that matter, every name he could remember from his childhood would probably exist only on a stone now. There would be no reunions, no excited calling out, no greetings, no arms around, no celebration.

On the other hand, there would be no recriminations, disapprovals, or remonstrations. The dead have nothing to say. The courtroom of the past would not be in session, unless he managed to keep it open in his heart.

Why could he not stamp "case closed" on the evidence and leave it be? Strange. One of those everlasting conundrums one must live with - a collection of yes-no items one could acknowledge and accept but never fully resolve.

Alex reflected on the truism that men tend to marry their mothers. But if you had no experience of a mother, how could you seek some-one like her? His own marriage had been wide, but not deep. He and Gwyneth had an adult peer relationship. She was as strong in her own way as he.

Never had she taken him in her arms as a mother might comfort or pamper a child, nor had he asked for that. To be sure, there had been affection between them - desire and passion early on - and kindness, even exceptional generosity in later years. But Gwyneth was not his mother, nor had she ever tried to be. And her closeness with her own mother and father meant he had never had to be a parent surrogate for her.

His daughters had never tried to mother him, either. Though if he ever accepted their invitation to come out to Australia they would no doubt smother him with insistent care, treating him as an old child. Even affectionate condescension is still condescension - it is not truly maternal. He might meet them in a bar somewhere, but go out to Australia? Never.

In some respects, the girls were strangers to him - always had been. Interesting strangers - strangers he admired and respected, but people not of his world. They had grown up in a very different milieu in a very different time, and were bound to be very different from him.

Sports consumed their lives. Games when children, field hockey and rowing when adolescent, and now tennis and golf and sailing. They and their children and husbands lived and ate and breathed athletics. They owned a chain of sporting equipment stores, taught sports, played in leagues, and had a house full of trophies and sporty knickknacks. They spent the evenings watching sports on television. Australia was perfect for them. It was a sports-mad world.

Not for him. Australia was a country with no long history or deep culture - no mind, only body. When he found out one of his sons-in-law had written a best-selling book on the philosophy of Australian football, Alex knew he would never find a home among his relatives in Australia.

How surprised he would be to know his father was Australian, buried in Darwin. He might appreciate the unrelenting irony of it all.

Well, then. There was to be no mothering in his life.
Like his leg, he had lived with it - compensated for it.
Nobody was ever dealt the whole deck of cards.
Some hands had a queen - some did not.
But. Still. Be that as it may. He missed something dreadfully.
Something to do with tenderness. An unrestrained intimacy.
In an odd way, he knew he had looked for it.

There was an ongoing fantasy with which he sometimes indulged himself when walking alone in a city. It may have started out as a dream, but now he recalled it with such vivid clarity that it only just barely lay over the line in the world of events that never really happened but seem as real as if they had.

Alex recounted the story softly to himself, as if he had an invisible companion in the car riding with him to Iraklion.

"As I walk I see coming toward me some distance away, the familiar figure of a woman - someone out of the past, someone I am longing to see but never expect to meet again. She looks up. She recognizes me. We stop in stunned disbelief. Can it be true that we have found one another at last? We run to meet each other, and throw our arms around one another. The climactic moment comes when she takes my face in her hands with the greatest tenderness and says something to me that makes me cry. I cannot hear what she says – the sound fades out. Even so, it is the most joyful moment of my life. But it has never happened. I only imagine that it has. It haunts me. I don't know if I have found the one true love of my life . . . or . . . my mother."

Alex had imagined it so many times that he could easily direct the scene down to the last detail. There was something strangely satisfying in knowing he had translated his need into a piece of visual poetry that he could recite to himself at will. It might be the only taste of that longed-for reunion he would ever have.

Alex had come to the conclusion that imagination was more satisfying in many ways than reality. He had had an imaginary companion all his life: the twin brother who died at birth, a brother nobody had told him about until he returned to Crete after the Spanish Civil War. His father had thrown it up to Alex: the dead brother would have been different.

Alex didn't think so.

Why did the brother die? Alex didn't know. Was he an identical twin or fraternal? Again, Alex didn't know. Nonetheless, what he learned resolved his vague sense of incompleteness. For a long time, when alone, Alex entertained himself with imaginary experiences with his twin – his double. When he looked at himself in a mirror, he always saw his twin – even held conversations with him. His name for his brother was Achilles, he of the fatal flaws.

When his own identical twin daughters were born, Alex was elated. He lived out his twin fantasy through them in a most satisfying way. Through them he learned what it might have been like if his brother had lived. The girls were true soul-mates. Inseparable – sometimes inhabiting a private world and speaking a private language. To this day they lived close by each other, were in business together, often dressed alike, and were as difficult to tell apart as when they were children. He envied their doubled life with its mirror quality.

The envy wasn't sorrowful. Alex never felt sorry for himself, or at least not for long. It was not his way to dwell on what might have been. And it was the infusion of that spirit that guided him as he arrived in Iraklion.

He remembered reading that Nikos Kazantzakis had written his own epitaph for his tombstone. *"I hope for nothing. I fear nothing. I am free."*

Such a sentiment could be expressed only by a dead man, Alex thought. Anyone alive and sane was not free of fear. The Furies and the Nemesis would always be there to snatch you up and carry you off. But to recognize them was not to submit to them. Anyone alive was free to have hope for what yet might be. Alex believed that as long as one lived, freedom was a direction of intention, not a fixed condition.

Alex reached a decision. He would not go looking for the troubling part of his past in Iraklion at all. Whoever was buried there - wherever they were buried - let them stay buried. The houses and streets he had known as a child - leave them as they were in the memory of childhood.

He would go back to Knossos, where so much that was good had happened to him. He wanted to know what a new generation of archeologists and potsherd-washers were making of history. He wanted to see the site with fresh eyes.

With his mind settled, Alex relaxed and leaned back in his seat. Looking out the window, he saw that they had arrived in Iraklion. It was not the city he had left. It was the Iraklion that had risen from the destruction of German bombing during the war. How utterly amazing it was that people had forever found the courage to get up off their knees, to fight back, to rebuild, to push on. This was never to be underestimated.

Of *this* Iraklion, he was not afraid.

As the taxi wound its way through the streets of the inner city, Alex began composing a nonsense rhyme to amuse himself.

The dipthong is wild and quite hairy
Not really the sort you would marry
Of dugongs and biltdongs I'm wary
Their songs are too long and will vary.

Alex laughed. Dactylic trimeter. He should recite it to Max-Pol.

Through his rearview mirror, the taxi driver watched the old man cackling to himself. He wondered what had changed him from a grumpy silent man to this jovial passenger entertaining himself in the backseat? Alex caught the driver's look, waved, and considered translating his Lear-ical poetry into Greek. Now that would be fun!

When the taxi pulled up at his hotel, a reinvigorated Alex emerged.
Home again.
But on his terms.
Taking the new road all the way.

IRAKLION, PRAGUE, AND HANIA

February. Morning. Early.

In Iraklion the day is cold, the sky cloudless, and the north breeze sharp off the sea. Undaunted by the weather, Alex is back in a taxi again by eight o'clock. Layered up in his warmest clothes, he is bound for the Palace of King Minos, the Villa Ariadne, and the Stratigraphic Research Museum.

Alex's spirits rise as reliably as the sun.

At this hour, in this season in Iraklion, the tourists have not yet stirred from the sanctuary of their hotel coffee shops. Alex will have his own sanctuary in Knossos, and its museum of memories to himself for a while. When the crowds arrive, he will visit the non-public precincts to see what the pick-and-shovel brigades have discovered in the last fifty years.

Unannounced, a one-man meeting of the Spherical Learical League has been called in his mind. The beginnings of nonsensical Learisms form:

The aubergines spam on the bushes of myrtle . . .
turtle . . . fertile . . . wirtle . . . girdle . . . hurdle . . .

In Prague, Alice sleeps the sleep-that-knows-no-reason-for-waking, cozily buried under a white feather comforter on her bed in room 9 of the Inn of the Ostrich. She has come to Prague for the music. Last night she attended a performance of Mozart's *Don Giovanni* in the same opera house where he once conducted. In her dreams, she is onstage in the music. Outside, it is snowing.

In Hania, Kostas Liapakis is sitting by a woodstove in the front room of the Meltemi kafenion. He is shouting encouragements to the goddess of fortune, Tyhi, while rising slightly out of his chair. "*Nai, Nai, Nai!* (Yes, Yes, Yes!)" The game is backgammon and the dice are going his way. When business is nonexistent, as it will be on this cold and windy morning, he comes to his "office" to do "business" with other "businessmen" of the neighborhood. Playing backgammon is the only way to keep money in circulation in the winter. At the moment, for Kostas, "Business is be good – very good."

POLLY

In Athens, Max-Pol sits at a table in his hotel room filling out a label for a package he will leave at the front desk to be sent off by air express.

To: Hypatia Loulaki Xetrypis
In care of: A. O. Riley
18 Quai de Bourbon
75004 Paris, France

The plastic mailing pack contains an envelope wrapped as a gift. Bright blue-and-white-checked paper, broad red ribbon. Inside, the most recent installment of the Cretan Chronicles of Max-Pol Millay.

His Witness has been much on his mind. He hasn't heard from her since he sent his last Chronicles, but then she travels often. Surely something will be waiting for him when he returns to Hania.

But the cloud of doubt dims his sunny optimism: What if his declarations shifted the relationship too far into the personal? What if she . . . what?

"Just send the package, Max-Pol," he said aloud.

*

When Alex suggested to Max-Pol that he might enjoy visiting Delphi, he was enthusiastic. He needed to go to Athens, anyhow. And Delphi was on his list of places to visit during his time in Greece. In his reading he noted that the ancient Greeks felt the best time to consult the famous oracle there was early in a new year. Alex had confirmed it. "It is the time to go, so go," he said. "Maybe the oracle still inspires those who respect prophecy."

While Max-Pol is too literal-minded to take such thoughts seriously, he wouldn't mind knowing a little more about the future.

The front desk calls. His taxi is waiting.

*

Greek taxis are driver-owned small businesses on four wheels. Their drivers are not desperate, low-paid nomads at the bottom of the economic heap. Most are middle-class entrepreneurs who use their vehicles as cars-for-hire to go anywhere, anytime, for many purposes. In a city, these ubiquitous cabs often serve as a small-package delivery service and a non-emergency ambulance. In the villages, the conservative, gray-painted version of the taxi is usually the only means of public transportation. More often than not, the automobile chosen for this all-purpose work is a standard, sturdy Mercedes built for long service and reliability - a rolling statement of confident competence.

The drivers are likewise a confident and competent lot. The epitome of affirmative attitude. A Greek taxi driver would probably not turn down a passenger's request to be taken to South Africa or across Iraq. It is only a matter of price, with cash in advance, of course.

When Max-Pol asked about going to Delphi, the concierge of his hotel explained that unless he wanted to endure the scheduled formality of a tour bus experience with strangers, the most comfortable, enjoyable way to go was to hire a taxi specializing in taking foreigners to historic sites. It would cost less than renting his own car for the day, and would eliminate the stress of driving himself. He, the concierge, just happened to have connections with a driver with an excellent reputation. One day at Delphi would be enough. Mr. Millay should go early to avoid the horrors of Athens traffic, and come back late for the same reason.

Agreed - and so arranged.

At seven o'clock the next morning, Max-Pol came down to the lobby, package and guidebook in hand. He waited while a woman completed her business with the concierge. A small, well-groomed young woman - short black hair, fine features, and modest makeup - dressed in a black leather coat cut like a suit jacket, black turtleneck sweater, black leather trousers, and black leather boots - the fashionable look in Greece among the younger generation. Everything black.

Kostas looked on this style with distaste - "Is be *putana*-look, you know. Prostitute. All these days girls want to wear black and this and this and look like hoor." Max-Pol rather liked the look himself. He didn't know any woman who dressed like this, prostitute or not. His curiosity was aroused.

"Parakalo, Mister Millay," said the concierge. "This is your driver."

The woman turned and gave Max-Pol a soft, sensuous lopsided smile - raising her upper lip higher on one side than the other. A stop-you-dead-in-your-tracks kind of smile. Max-Pol was captivated. She offered her hand, saying, "Calimera, Mr. Millay. My name is Polydora Vlachou. Please call me Polly."

Max-Pol stared. Driver? Polly? Oh, really?

Lamely, he shook her hand and, heeling like a trained pooch, followed her out to the older-model Mercedes sedan waiting at the curb. The standard orangy-yellow shade, washed and polished - in exemplary condition.

Polly held the rear door open for him. Current editions of newspapers were laid out on the seat - *USA Today*, *Herald-Tribune*, and the Sunday edition of *The Times* from London. On top of these were a folded map of Greece and a guide to Delphi.

In a basket on the floor was a thermos of what later proved to be hot coffee, along with a bottle of spring water, and an assortment of fruit: tangerines, apples, pears. And a napkin. Cotton, not paper.

Max-Pol's expectations about a long taxi ride were being revised by the minute. And would be completely revised by day's end.

*

As the taxi pulled into traffic, Polly anticipated Max-Pol's question. "I expect you are surprised to have a woman driver. There are not many of us in Athens."

"I'm also surprised by the quality of your English."

"Thank you. I was for a number of years a stewardess with Olympic Airlines on their international routes between Athens and the United States - most often to New York and Boston. As with many Greeks, I have relatives in the States and I've spent holidays traveling around your country.

"Excuse me - I'll join you in conversation as soon as we're out of the Athens traffic. In the meantime, please feel free to have a coffee from the thermos and look at the newspapers." In the rearview mirror she flashed him her wry, lopsided smile and turned her full attention to the business of driving.

Max-Pol relaxed. He was in good hands. He fished the book review section out of *The Sunday Times,* poured himself half a cup of coffee, and leaned back in settled comfort. But he only pretended to read book reviews. What he was trying to read was the mind of the self-assured woman who had taken charge of his life.

Other than her appearance and the thoughtful gestures made for his comfort, neither she nor the interior of the car displayed anything revealing personal interests or style. There were none of the usual saint's medals, plastic flowers, political stickers, or smoking accessories he had come to expect in Greek taxis. He had not seen a purse in the front seat as he entered the car. And the radio was not turned on, so there was no way of knowing her taste in music. Again she anticipated his thinking.

"Would you like to hear some music? I have several tapes - classical, American jazz, and a few Greek things."

"Play something you like. I'm interested in other people's taste."

"Malista. Recently I went to the Megaron to hear Maria Farandouri in a Lorca -Theodorakis concert. I have the tape. Would you like to hear it?"

"Sure. I know a little of Lorca's poetry and Theodorakis's music."

Polly pushed the cassette into the tape deck, and the rich, throaty alto voice of Maria Farandouri, accompanied by solo Spanish guitar, filled the car as Polly smoothly negotiated the still-quiet back streets of Athens on the way to the National Road north.

In half an hour the city was left behind. The highway traffic thinned out. The dreary jumbled clutter of the suburbs of modern Athens gave way to the open countryside. And the dingy smog gave way to clear skies, open all the way to the mountains of Attica.

As the taxi reached cruising speed and the voice of Farandouri faded, Max-Pol opened the map of Greece. Polly, unfailingly attentive, noticed.

"We'll stay on this highway until just before Thiva - old Thebes - and then turn off and go through Aliartos, Levadeia, and Arachova. Delphi is just beyond. Do you follow on the map? It's about two hours' drive, but I usually stop along the way.

"The countryside is beautiful at this time of year. Even though it's still cold, the signs of spring are already there. I like to smell the air and hear the quiet. It's a relief to shift the mind away from Athens as soon as possible. I find that I drive more slowly and sanely after stopping."

"You certainly know how to make this trip enjoyable."

"We've worked very hard to gain a reputation for service."

"We?"

"Yes, I have a partner, my sister, and we have two cars – and because we don't want to risk our lives picking up fares on the street, we've specialized in taking foreigners where they wish to go. We have connections with the major hotels, several embassies, and some international corporations. We speak seven languages between us. But our main asset is our reputation for service."

Before Max-Pol could ask one of the dozen questions forming in his mind, Polly shifted conversational gears as smoothly as she shifted the gears of the car in traffic.

"The concierge told me only that you were an American man who wanted to visit Delphi for a day. There are several ways to visit Delphi. I don't have a canned trip. I've read many books about the site and made many trips there. If you'll tell me more about your interests, I'll be able to plan the day in a way that satisfies you."

Max-Pol somewhat surprised himself with the ease and the comfort he felt in telling this very professional taxi driver a good deal more about himself than about his interest in Delphi. He described his occupation and his sabbatical in Crete in much the same way he had talked with Alex Evans the first time they had met on the night train to Barcelona. Polly was even easier to talk to. She listened with unfeigned interest. From time to time she gave him her great smile, which only encouraged further revelations from Max-Pol.

He was also somewhat surprised that he was speaking person-to-person and not man-to-woman. For all her attractive qualities, Max-Pol sensed the fading of the gender factor between them. Perhaps it was just that he had noticed the plain gold wedding band on the appropriate finger of her hand at the top of the steering wheel. Perhaps it was that she wasn't wearing perfume. Perhaps it was a lack of any innuendo in her responses to him – no male-female overtones at all.

Puzzling.

Polly brought the conversation back to Delphi.

"If the oracle were still in business, what would you ask?"

Once again Max-Pol surprised himself. For a moment some smog in his mind cleared. The face of Alice O'Really appeared in that clearing. What would you ask the oracle? An Alice kind of gambit.

"I would like to know what to do about a relationship."
"Coming or going?" asked Polly.
"That is the question," replied Max-Pol. "Exactly the question."
"I'm glad I don't need to ask that for myself."
"You're happily married?"

Her eyes met his in the mirror. She smiled, but the smile was not for him - it was for what she was about to tell him.

"You might put it that way. I've had the same companion for fifteen years, and our lives have merged in such a satisfying way that I rarely question the longtime stability of the relationship.

"Since you are young, a doctor, and an American, you will probably not be shocked if I tell you my companion is a woman. I call her my partner or my sister for reasons of social convenience, but we're not relatives in that way - we are much more than sisters.

"It's accurate to say that for all intents and purposes, we're married. An unimaginable notion in Greece, but it is the case. Katalaves? You understand?"

"Katalaves. And I'm neither shocked, nor surprised. As one who spends a lot of time hearing about people's difficulties, I'm glad to hear about a relationship that works. I'm aware that studies have shown the most satisfying and long-lasting companionships are between two women. It's the quality of the relationship that counts, not the box it fits in or the label on the box."

"Maria and I don't fit into boxes, and we don't spend our time with other people who do. In a male-dominated culture like Greece, it's not always easy for a woman to go her own way, but Athens is not so Greek - it's really a big international city, and we find we can live a very satisfying if somewhat unconventional life.

"The name of our relationship is just what it is - the companion-ship of Polydora and Maria. We believe it's for life. We've sworn to one another to make it so. We had hard times in the beginning. Bad times. Her family is very large and very small-town, and they tried everything to separate us. They've even threatened violence. Much bitterness there. But trouble only brought us closer together. Fifteen years this June."

"Congratulations. Mind if I ask how it came about?"

"Maria and I were both flight attendants. We became friends. We shared rooms together when we had layovers in the States. We traveled together on vacations. We had much in common - coming from small Greek towns, wanting to get away, wanting to deal with our lack of interest in men.

"We became very close. We were a welcome solution for one another to a common problem. We both wanted and needed someone else in our lives. Affection led to the desire that becomes passion. We two became one.

"The Olympic Airlines scheduler didn't approve of our relationship and started making it impossible for us to be together. Since being together had become the most important thing in life for us, we quit our jobs. My uncle was retiring from the taxi business. He offered us a good deal, so we bought his car and license.

"Using connections from our airline days, we developed our clientele with care, and now we have two cars and a successful business. We've been lucky, but we've worked for our luck. Being open-minded and discreet, we've developed some very interesting trade. If we ever wanted to write a book, we could tell some pretty amazing stories about the lives of some very important people. But Maria and I say, 'Live and let live,' you know?"

Polly eased the car off the freeway and down a gravel road between fields newly greening toward springtime. She stopped the car on a slight rise in the middle of a vast agricultural plain that had once been the bed of a lake, drained long ago.

"Come, stretch your legs."

They walked a ways in silence, immersed in the almost palpable fecund freshness of their surroundings. When they returned to the car, Max-Pol didn't ask if he might ride in the front seat; he simply opened the front door and got in. It seemed like the natural thing to do.

DELPHI

The myth says it was here on the craggy slopes of Mount Parnassus that Zeus's son, Apollo, met the muses and became their leader. Ever after, the site of Delphi was associated with inspiration - with the infusion of new vision, whether in the arts or in the affairs of state. From about the eighth century B.C., Delphi was known for prophecy.

The need for Delphi arose out of the human conviction that the world is ruled by invisible supernatural forces. Since the Greeks had no sacred book, they relied for guidance on those persons who possessed the ability to commune directly with the gods. The devices of oracular divination were many. The will of the gods was read from the entrails of sacrificed animals, from the patterns made by flights of birds, and above all from the utterances by certain individuals who communicated with the gods from within a trance.

The oracle of Delphi was always a young woman - the Pythia. She purified herself in the waters of the sacred spring, chewed the sacred laurel leaves, sat on a tripod in the sacred inner sanctuary of Apollo, and gave largely unintelligible messages to priests who interpreted her responses to those who questioned her.

It is said that the questions were always clear, but the replies were not. The ambiguity meant the odds of reliable prophecy were in favor of the oracle.

The Delphic oracle was successful often enough to give Delphi a primary place in divination. Temples and treasuries, statues and tributes, and great riches were heaped up there in time. The Pythian Games were held there; the stadium and theater give only a glimpse of the creative and physical energy expended over centuries in tribute to Apollo and his spokeswoman.

As much as divination, the grounds of the Temple of Apollo offered a place to display evidence of power and property. Victorious city-states and rulers commemorated their battle successes with monuments to themselves at Delphi. Kings displayed evidence of their greatness there. Delphi became like great cathedrals or modern museums, whose splendors are associated with the names of the rich and powerful. Power - proof of the affirmation of the gods – must be seen.

And from time to time, some megalomaniac such as the Roman emperor Nero would trump everybody's card. To demonstrate his meta-power over both men and gods, he had the shrine ransacked and its treasures carried off to Rome.

Closed by the Christian emperor Theodosius the Great in 394, the buildings of the sanctuary crumbled into decay and were abandoned in the seventh century. Further destroyed by fire and earthquake, the site was buried by landslides.

Shepherds built a village where Apollo once ruled, and for the next eighteen centuries, generations of very ordinary people lived out their lives on what had once been considered the center of the earth and the home of the oracle of the gods. The ordinary village of Kastri lived and lasted longer than the great Sanctuary of Apollo.

In 1891 the French Archeological School and the Greek government appropriated the site, moved the village, and excavated Delphi. What remains today are the heaps of broken marble bones of the sanctuary, and the memories of the people of the village of Kastri.

*

This is a succinct summary of Delphi's history that Polly gave to Max-Pol as they wandered up the Sacred Way. Max-Pol told Polly about Alice in between stops at the various stoas and stumps of statues, the restored Treasury of the Athenians, and finally at the forecourt of the maze of stones marking the small temple building that was the heart of the Sanctuary of Apollo.

"Look." Polly opened a pocket guide that contained photographs of each major structure on the sanctuary grounds. Each photograph came with a plastic overlay on which was drawn a conception of the original building, so that you could see the ruins and then see a reconstruction when the plastic page was placed over them. "You can see what *is* and what *was* at the same time. Clever."

"Now I can grasp the impression it must have made," said Max-Pol.

"It's my opinion," said Polly, "that an intelligent person would have gotten as far as the porch of the oracle's temple, read the inscriptions, and gone home."

"How so?"

"Across the *pronaos* – the facing – just over the doorway – were three expressions. *'Gnothi Safton'* – Know yourself – was one. *'Pan Metron Ariston'* – Moderation in all things – was the second. And the third was the Greek letter epsilon – which, as you know, is the same as the letter E in English. Nobody then or now knows what the letter meant, but I think its ambiguity must have been deliberate. Two parts of wisdom are known and the other remains always to be discovered."

"So," said Max-Pol, "if you really worked at self-knowledge and you were mindful of the difficulties arising from excess, and you were aware of the place of mystery, you would have enough knowledge of the nature of the future to not need to ask the oracle anything further."

"Exactly. Take this relationship you would ask the oracle about. I would guess that it may be that you do not know yourself as well as you should in considering this matter. You need another person in your life more than you want to admit, but you're not content with a conventional relationship."

"True."

"And you want to give yourself over to your creative side, but again the conventional view is that an artist of any kind leads a socially irresponsible existence – mostly for himself. Yet you have a powerful need to be useful to others. But are the arts not useful, only in a different way? The ancient Greeks thought medicine was an art, by the way. And is that not true still?"

"Yes."

"And you have come to that middle time when age and experience should naturally reorder the life of any man. Or woman."

"True."

"Perhaps she is in the same place. And you, without knowing it, are doing for her what she is doing for you. You may be her Witness – you know – that other person?"

"Yes, Witness for Witness. That occurred to me, but I hadn't really given it much thought recently."

"Think about it, Mr. Millay."

Polydora gave Max-Pol her lopsided power smile.

"Think about it."

*

Over lunch, at a restaurant with a view all the way down the valley to the Gulf of Corinth, Polly told Max-Pol a story he would recall several times in the next weeks.

"One winter when I was still working with Olympic Airlines and not yet fully involved with Maria, I was in New York on a layover, and I was going to be alone on New Year's Eve. That afternoon I went to Brooklyn to a Greek bakery and bought a *vasilopeta*.

"It's a plain round cake, dusted with powdered sugar. We always have this cake at midnight on New Year's Eve. A coin is baked inside the cake, and when the slices are shared out, whoever finds the coin in the cake has good luck for the year to come. Do you know about this?"

"Yes. I shared a vasilopeta with friends in Hania this New Year's, but I didn't get the coin."

"Well, this time I had a sure thing, you see. I was going to have the whole cake to myself and was sure to get the coin. I thought it was funny when I bought the cake. But it made me sad when I cut the cake and, of course, found the coin."

"Why sad?"

"I was stupid. I had cheated myself in a way. Luck in this is never a sure thing. It is the risk taken when you have at least one other person involved. There must be someone else. And you must take the chance and cut the cake. Luck may be shared, but never controlled."

*

Max-Pol and Polly returned from Delphi earlier than expected. For one thing, the wind was blowing hard and cold - not a good day for lingering outside amid the great jumble of marble. And the maze of the marble ruins numbed Max-Pol's mind after a while.

He was not disappointed, however.

He had spent a day with a shrewdly candid woman who had a wise view of human relationships, especially unconventional ones. She didn't profess to any prophetic ability, but she had some fine common-sense advice. His memory of the day had little to do with the dead past and its stones and statues. When everything else he saw that day faded, what he would remember was the knowing smile of Polydora Vlachou.

Now, on the desk of his hotel room was a heap of laurel leaves from a tree whose trunk and roots reached way back underneath the ancient Temple of Apollo into the primeval earth beneath it. Polly had picked them and given them to him.

Alongside the leaves was a bottle of water he had drawn from the sacred spring of Castalia at Delphi - water drunk for centuries by those who wished to be inspired by the muses - water he would share with Alex and Kostas.

And there was a 100-drachma coin from the change he had gotten when he paid the bill for lunch. He would save it for a vasilopeta cake. A cake baked for two.

He looked forward to Alex's first question. "How was Delphi?"

Max-Pol would tell him that it is not true that Pythia, the oracle, no longer exists. These days she drives a taxi. Her name is Polydora. And when Alex asks what he means, Max-Pol would smile, as lopsidedly as possible, and take great pleasure in giving Alex his own excuse back to him:

"That, dear cousin Aleko - that - is a long story for another time."

(CHRONICLES CONTINUED - 11)

When I returned from Athens and Delphi, Kostas had a message for me from Aleko. "Any problem?" I asked Kostas.

"Ohi problema - is be laughing - ola kalah - say this and this and this, you know, and give this number for you."

When I called, Aleko was his usual effervescent self.

"Max-Pol! The anemones cover the hills here - come on!"

He went on to say that going home had not been as difficult as he had imagined. All was well and I must come and bring Kostas if at all possible, and also bring a rug to sit on and picnic equipment and cigars.

I had expected something more sober and thoughtful. This let's-have-a-picnic spirit surprised me. But, yes, I would come tomorrow. By ten o'clock.

Kostas couldn't leave - he was in mourning for his mother - but he could provide the required rug and a picnic basket, as well as all the necessary equipment and ingredients for making Greek coffee al fresco. It was his way of coming along in spirit.

Setting off early, I arrived in Iraklion to find Aleko impatiently encamped on the steps of the Hotel Atlantis.

"Look," he exclaimed, "I have supplies!"

And he opened bags filled with tangerines and oranges, bread, wine, cheese, and even onions and eggplants.

"Why onions and eggplants, Aleko?"

"Because they are beautiful. Look! Just look." And he arranged the crimson red onions and the deep purple eggplants carefully on the white marble steps, like objects in an art gallery. He stepped back to admire his exhibition. "Orea? Yes?" He always has time and an eye for Beautiful.

The doorman was not impressed, but Aleko was a paying guest, and probably generous with tips. With the indulgent patience of a mother picking up a child's playthings, he helped Aleko re-bag his treasures and load them into my car. One long, fat package intrigued me, but no doubt Aleko would reveal its contents in his own good time.

"Take Knossos road," he said, "and tell me about Delphi."

As Aleko had promised, the fields and roadsides beyond Iraklion were carpeted with bright red anemones, and also white daisies, pale lilac anemones, and several varieties of small yellow flowers. The orange trees were in blossom as well. Aleko waved his hands toward the landscape in approval.

"Good work," he shouted to the flowers, "Orea, poli orea."

As we approached Knossos, he began his guided tour.

"We shall begin with the grand view. Pass on by the site of the palace and up toward the head of the valley. Take a left across the river bridge, and then come back inhis direction by taking that road you can see winding up the mountainside opposite where we are now."

I parked the car. We walked to a low stone wall to sit.

"Well, then," began Aleko. "Of the great Greek ruins, all but Knossos have commanding and dramatic locations. The Acropolis stands above Athens. Mycenae overlooks the Plain of Argos. Delphi hangs high on the slopes of Mount Parnassus. Olympia spreads out handsomely across its broad river valley.

"But look here: Knossos. Unique in its unpretentious environment. A small hill, called Kephala, in a small valley, at the confluence of a small river, Kairatos, and an even smaller stream, Vlychia. The sea is not far, but you can neither see it nor hear it from here. There are mountains to the south, but the great snow-covered range of Mount Ida is not visible from Knossos. The site is so ordinary. So homely, in its lack of distinction.

"It may be concluded that the glory of Knossos lay in the minds of those who built it and kept its creative energy flowing for centuries. And its glory lived on in the minds of those who revived its stones and in the imaginations of those who come now to view its remains. Its glory was and remains internal."

And so it seemed to me. There was nothing that took my breath away, especially when I followed Aleko's instruction to hold my hand over the view of the Palace ruins so as to block it out and see everything else.

A modern road runs through a green valley given over to typical Cretan agriculture. Groves of olive trees, vineyards, cultivated fields of vegetables, clusters of village houses, small herds of goats and sheep, and the standard stony hillside.

Only in the center of the view is something different.

When I took my hand away, the site dominated my eye and my imagination. The ruins of the temple/palace of Knossos.

What strikes most visitors are the reconstructions made by Sir Arthur Evans. Disapproved of, even reviled by the professional archeologists, but much appreciated by the general public. To the best of his ability and the knowledge available to him at the time, Evans rebuilt small sections of Knossos to both protect and define his excavations. From these rooms and columns and frescoes you can see what Evans surmised - what Aleko would call the evidence of a working hypothesis.

From our hillside vantage point the rusty-orange pillars of intact porches and stairwells gave me the feeling that only yesterday an earthquake had brought down the rest of the buildings. The tourists clambering antlike around the ruins seemed like survivors of the catastrophe.

Below us, and between us and the ruins, a farmer was working in the deep soil of the well-watered valley. His intensively cultivated market garden was showing early growth - probably onions, squashes, asparagus, cucumbers, and carrots - the crops of this season. A flock of small birds followed his hoeing, pecking at worms and bugs. On the edge of the field, a woman picked wild greens and anemones. She called to the farmer occasionally, holding up bunches of the blood-red flowers. He stopped his work, leaned on his hoe, and smiled and nodded at the woman waving flowers at him.

Aleko pointed in their direction. "Look at them - husband and wife probably. People hardly any different from them have been living in this valley for six-thousand years - doing exactly what they are doing. Planting and harvesting. Raising goats and chickens. Picking olives - pressing grapes. Eating and sleeping. Giving birth and dying. As I come to the end of my own life, what

197

continues to astonish me is this simple on-going-ness of the human enterprise in spite of everything that would interfere."

He rummaged around in one of his canvas bags and produced an unlabeled bottle of wine and two glasses. "This wine is from this valley, I got it yesterday from the taverna where I ate dinner. You cannot buy it. It is available only as a gift from the tavern owner to those who praise his food. He owns the vineyard on the far slope, and he is certain that the vines have their roots in the ruins of Minoan houses lying just under the surface. This is deep wine - profound wine - wine with history in it."

"Aleko, I have a little something to add to this wine," I said. Reaching into my satchel, I brought out the bottle I had filled at Delphi. "Here's sacred water from the Castalian spring - something to mix into the historical wine of Knossos."

"Katapliktiko!" said Aleko. "Marvelous. You astonish me."

We mixed the wine and water in our glasses. And poured a small libation on the earth - for the gods. Touching our glasses in celebration, we drank in eloquent silence.

"Well, then. Here before you is the root source of one of the great myths. King Minos, the Labyrinth, Theseus, Ariadne - the lot. I could give you the classicist's versions, citing sources in Greek, Latin, German, and English. I could give you the interpretations of Freud and Jung. I could go on for days, if not weeks. 'Poli-blah-blah-blah,' as the Cretans say - a whole lot of words. If you are interested in these scholarly analytical views, I can provide you with a shelf full of books.

"However, I shall only give you a shorter and more human view. Let us say there was a king, whose wife gave birth to a retarded and deformed child. 'Not my child,' said the king. 'She must have been sleeping with wild animals. Lock the kid up, out of sight.' In time, word got out that the child had grown up so crazed he would kill anyone who came near him. Meanwhile, the king had conquered around and about and demanded tribute from his vassal cities in the form of some teenagers, one of whom was our hero, Theseus.

"Imagine him as a studly young contemporary Athenian in jeans, leather boots and jacket, sunglasses - swinging his komboloi as he gets off his motorcycle. The king's daughter, Ariadne, immediately falls in love with him, tells him how to kill her mad brother, and how to escape from the Labyrinth using a ball of string. Done. Minotaur slain. Theseus escapes with Ariadne. They live happily ever after for about a week. He dumps her on the beach at Naxos. She may have been pretty, but she was, after all, from a highly dysfunctional family, and probably a little weird herself.

"There. I have, I admit, been a little free in my interpretation. Yet something like that is at the bottom of the longer tale, don't you think? These ancient stories get reshaped into myths over thousands of years. A myth is a kind of public ferryboat. It carries us across a sea of experience to another shore. But the other shore is an illusion. The ride is always a round trip, back to where we started. And our ticket never expires. We may ride as many times as we wish.

"The basic story does contain the foundation stones of truth. Power, greed, desire, evil, misfortune, danger, love, rejection. The lot. Myth is the wrapping paper of truth, because it is more safely given and received that way. You are free to unwrap it or not."

He paused to see if I was overwhelmed with information.

I was.

"Enough of that. Look out here - in the valley," said Aleko, standing and pointing out over the scene below us. "Much has come and gone here. A fast-forward film of the last six thousand years would show huts and hovels, palaces and temples - rising and falling and rising again. Endless pillage. Invading armies marching in one end of this valley and out the other.

"Archeologists have dug it up and carried it off, and tourists have come to take a look and carry home photographs. Plague has come and gone. Fire, earthquake, volcanic ash, great storms, floods, and drought. All this has passed over and through this place. Imagine!

"And, yet, after every wave, calm returns. It is as you see it now. And a man and a woman tend vegetables and call out to each other in the spring sun. For all I know about this place - for all I have seen and done here - it is this fundamental sacred simplicity that speaks to me. It defies all Fates and Furies. The meek inherit the earth. Blessed are the people of peace.

"When I came here at age thirteen to work, the valley was going through a bare and stony stage. Its activity revolved around the excavations, which looked much as they do today. Now, as you see, that era is also over. The pine trees and cypress have come back. The valley is full of villages and farms once more. And Knossos itself has become a Cretan theme park, featuring the traveling human zoo.

"Yesterday I walked all the way around the outside of the fence, looking in. People from every corner of the world were on display. Caucasians, Asians, Africans, Indians. This processional visitation is as amazing to me as the immobility of the stones of the past. Schoolchildren should be brought here to see the people as well as the ruins. Can you imagine a teacher saying, after a unit on Asia, 'Let's go out to Knossos to see some Japanese and Chinese and Koreans - it is their migration season? It is a lost opportunity.'"

He shook his head in mild disgust.

"Now, look across there just above the main road - just north of the edge of the site of the palace. That large, plain building is the Stratigraphic Laboratory and Museum - not open to the public. Inside, students are still sorting potsherds as I did almost seventy years ago. And just to the right of it, you can see the Villa Ariadne in its gardens. And a little further on is the Taverna, the place where Pendlebury once lived.

"And almost anywhere you look, in any direction, just under the surface are the still-unexcavated ruins of Minoan civilization. At its zenith there were probably a hundred thousand people in this area. What remains are the bones of a culture preserved in these ruins below. See all those deep green patches? Wild fennel. Wherever you see it growing, the soil has been disturbed at a deep level, which means something very old is there, waiting.

"Consider. There were no defensive walls built around this area. Little that has been uncovered speaks of militarism or the glorification of conquest. The frescoes show plants and animals and fish and people - all in a comely style. There is evidence of a lightness of the spirit that has reigned here for a long, long time. Though, in seeming contradiction, along with that calm loveliness, the Minoans evidently had a special reverence for wild bulls and deadly snakes.

"Of course, the myth of the Minotaur cannot be ignored either - the half-man/half-bull beast of the Labyrinth, who annually devoured virgin adolescents. That story is based on some kind of bizarre reality.

"Some say Knossos was the palace of kings. Some insist it was a great temple complex. Others say both. We will never know. All we have are multiple working hypotheses, as well as multiple working conclusions. Whatever the truth may be, it fascinates us still, and draws us to it.

"In Egypt there are a thousand sites larger and richer, but the focus is on men who thought themselves divine, who were obsessed with death and the afterlife, not this one. Here at Knossos, something more emphatically human happened."

Aleko was deep in thought. He turned to me.

"Why and how it ended, well, we do not know that either. But all the considerable evidence points to a windy spring day in 1380 B.C. when the last great palace burned and fell into ruin, keeping its secrets for the next three thousand years. It was a day not unlike this one, perhaps. Pendlebury's summary is best. I can quote by heart the lines from his Guide to Knossos:

> 'And with that wild spring day, something went out of the world which the world will never see again; something grotesque, perhaps something fantastic and cruel, but also something very lovely.'

"And for all we know about this palace, we still know so little of the ordinary human events that took place within its walls. Let me give you a different example of the line of my thinking. Consider the Villa Ariadne over there - named by Evans for the maiden of the myth."

We shifted our gaze to the flat-roofed stone complex standing so stolidly on the green hill west of us - partially hidden by pines and palms and arbors of vines. Aleko pointed and continued:

"In 1905 that was a sloping, stubbled field. A year later an Englishman had planted a house there - a house not of this place - one designed with Victorian sensibilities and Evans's notions of how to beat the Cretan heat in summer. The sleeping rooms were built below ground level behind thick, shuttered walls.

"In that house Evans sorted out Minoan history, planned excavations, and wrote volumes about his discoveries. Half of the most important Mediterranean field archeologists of the nineteenth and twentieth centuries passed through the villa's doors, along with many rich and famous people who were curious about Evans's work.

"Elaborate banquets were held in that villa, and fancy balls. The workmen from the dig gathered there on its front steps to be hired and instructed and paid and fired by Evans. And I've no doubt that not a few babies were conceived in the villa's basement as young couples occupied its sleeping rooms over the decades."

He laughed.

"When mainland Greece fell to the Germans, King George and Prime Minister Tsouderos stayed in the Villa Ariadne. It was the seat of government for a few days before the King left for Hania. Pendlebury used the villa as a planning center for resistance. The British had a field hospital there during the first days of the German invasion. Surgeons tended the wounded in its main rooms - blood, pain, and death were in that house then.

"After the Allied surrender, the German general staff met there, and its commanding officer lived in the villa in grand style during the occupation. At the end of the war, the Resistance leadership returned to the villa, and the Germans came one last time - to sign the surrender documents.

"After the war, the Villa Ariadne was used by the combined British and Cretan leadership as a headquarters for the efforts to defuse the civil war. And today - it is used by the Greek

Archeological Service for meetings and summer quarters.

"All these things - and more - in only ninety years.

"But, consider: If a great earthquake and fire should destroy it today, and the ruins remain buried for three thousand years, not one bit of what I have told you would be found by any future archeologist excavating the mound. Hopes, fears, pain, sorrow, joy, excitement, conception, death, delight, companionship - nothing of this richness of the human spirit would be found. Yet, these are the important things - the human things."

Aleko wrinkled his nose in disdain as he concluded, "Those experts who dig up the Villa Ariadne someday will probably label it 'Late Proto-Palatial XV' and call it an extension of the priest/king/ cult, lustral basins and sacrifical sites, included. Ha. Poppycock!"

He stood and stretched his arms, embracing the view.

"Well, then. Enough. You have my view and opinion. What I want to know about ancient Knossos cannot ever be found - only surmised. It lies not in ruins, but in our imaginations."

sun, but
dark edge...
glow within

cloud
pine

red columns
black tops
gold stripe to front
fragments of mural-
blue sky, red bull.

HOT Bleaching light
Bare blue sky
Babble of a dozen
diff. languages as
tour groups pass by.

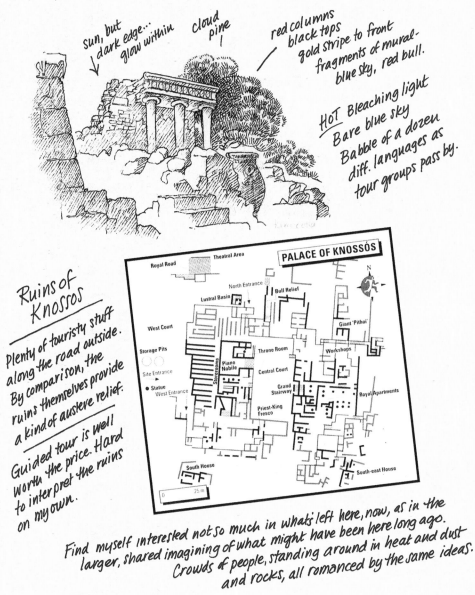

PALACE OF KNOSSOS

Royal Road

Theatral Area

North Entrance

Bull Relief

Lustral Basin

West Court

Giant 'Pithoi'

Storage Pits

Throne Room

Workshops

Site Entrance

Piano
Nobile

Statue
West Entrance

Storerooms

Central Court

Grand
Stairway

Royal Apartments

Priest-King
Fresco

South House

South-east House

0   25 m

Ruins of Knossos

Plenty of touristy stuff
along the road outside.
By comparison, the
ruins themselves provide
a kind of austere relief.

Guided tour is well
worth the price. Hard
to interpret the ruins
on my own.

Find myself interested not so much in what's left here, now, as in the
larger, shared imagining of what might have been here long ago.
Crowds of people, standing around in heat and dust
and rocks, all romanced by the same ideas.

"Enough of this. How about some of this great bread and cheese and fruit?" And Aleko began setting out the picnic.

As we ate, he stared off into space, eating with one hand, stroking the side of his face with the other. I sensed that he had wandered out of the labyrinth of Knossos into the labyrinth of his mind.

Giving me his most mischievous smile, he asked, "Shall we have a meeting of the Spherical Learical League?"

When we discovered we were 'cousins' by way of Edward Lear, we also found we had in common a fondness for limericks and word play. As any child knows, there's much sense in nonsense, and while Aleko and I enjoyed the light-hearted exercise of the mind in composing ridiculous rhymes, we both understood the serious aspects of the exercise. It bound us together in cleverness, just as those who work cross-word puzzles are united by an affinity for words. But there was more. Nonsense, while sometimes pure fun, is often a code for what may be too difficult to address more openly.

Being very pleased in finding someone who appreciated nonsense, Aleko had proposed we form the Spherical Learical League in honor of the rotund Mr. Lear, and challenge each other in rhyming games. "To keep our wits sharp," he said.

I suspect that Aleko never offered to play unless he had a few lines at the ready. It wasn't exactly cheating, but let's say, to be charitable, there was a certain advance preparation for the spontaneity involved. As usual, and as evidence of my suspicions, he led off:

"The jumwillies spume on the bushes of myrtle."

I added: "Advancing the key in the voice of the turtle."

"Good. His father was rippled, her mother was fertile."

How about: "The flaming ducks refused the first hurdle."

"Bravo! And we didn't use wirtle or pirtle or squirtle."

My turn next:

"Ragabag cooking is quite complicated."
Aleko: "Cleaning each one is a job that I've hated."
"This would not have happened if they'd never mated."
"But with the right sauce I'm quite satiated."

Unstoppable, we continued:

"Hoist it up high and set it on fire."
"Put out the ketchup, we're eating a tire."
"Break out the lute and break out the lyre."
"When we're all finished we'll roll in the mire."

And the worst was:

"Hell's bells, I missed her - painting on my sister."
"Luscious lips and pointed tips and plastered little blister."
"We go down to threeway town, a gypsy queen and mister."
"When we find the other kind, she'll shout and say we blissed her."

"Such minds," declares Aleko, "should be exhibited in museums."
"Or locked up, say I, where they don't harm other people."

The shift to nonsensical Learical poetry put Aleko in a high good humor. He handed me the long, fat package. "Open it, open it - there are presents, from me to both of us."

I snapped the string and tore off the brown paper.

Kites! Five octagonal wood-stick-and-oiled-paper kites of an antique design - three broad stripes of pale yellow, pink, and green, with a deep red flower pasted to the center. Not for a long time had I seen such kites - and not for an even longer time had I flown one.

Aleko explained as he assembled the kites. "These are not toys for children only. This coming Monday, the twenty-sixth day of February, is a national religious holiday called Kathari Deftera - Clean Monday. This day marks the end of Carnival and the beginning of Lent - forty days until Pascha - Easter. But we are going to fly them today - the day calls for it - Monday it may rain."

"Why Clean Monday?"

"Traditionally, homes, especially kitchens, are scoured in a symbolic cleansing of the spirit. Housewives scrub the kitchen pots and pans to get rid of the fat and grease of the feasting of the carnival times. During Lent we are not supposed to eat meat or dairy - only vegetables and fruits, bread, and a little oil. On Clean Monday, after the housekeeping is done and a special lunch is eaten, everyone goes outside to fly kites. We used to make our own, but now the stores are full of commercially made models. Still, we fly them."

"Why?" I asked. "What do they have to do with Lent and Easter? I don't remember anything in the Bible about flying kites."

"Tradition. It's tradition. The edge of myth. Which means nobody can say for sure. There are many stories about this - something to do with sending one's spirit up toward God, becoming as a child, letting go of some things and holding on to others at the same time. Lent is a time of freedom from bad habits and of holding one's appetites in check - creative tension - and tension is required for kites to fly. I do not know for certain. It is all reasonable, is it not? Make of the symbol what you like. Me, I like any excuse to fly kites."

"Why five kites?"

Aleko paused - thinking.

"Well, tradition again. Three are for the Holy Family. One for the little boy, Jesus; one for Mary, his mother; and one for Joseph, the husband of Mary. And one for you and one for me. We'll put them together, carry them up to that fence line above us, and see if we can get them all up flying at once."

Throwing off his outer coat, rolling up his sleeves, and tossing aside his cane, Alex busied himself. Tails must be made from newspaper, yokes adjusted, and balls of twine tied to each kite. When all was ready, my job was to run up the hill toward the fence with the string, while Alex launched the kite into the air.

"Wait, wait! Steady. Now! Pull! Pull!" One by one he tossed each kite, and I got it flying well enough for him to tie its string to a fence post and move on to the next launch. Aleko gauged tail weight and yoke placement perfectly for the light breeze blowing over the hill from the northeast. With our enthusiasm and technique, we could have launched a hundred kites.

When all were flying, Alex moved up the hillside with astonishing agility for his age and handicap. He lost his cap but let it go, hair tousling in the wind, shouting, "Malista! Malista!" We flew each kite out to the end of its string and moored them to the fence posts.

"Wine!" demanded Aleko. "We need wine."

I went down and fetched back the glasses and the wine and the bottle of water from Delphi. Alex poured and mixed our drinks. And from my pocket I produced two small cigars. We leaned back against the flowered grassy bank below the fence line, drinking our wine, smoking our cigars, and watching our five kites gently nodding about over the ruins of the Palace of Minos - over the flowering fields, over time and space and history beyond expression.

We watched utterly content, until we both fell asleep in the seductive sunshine of early spring.

The smell of coffee woke me up. Aleko had set up Kostas's stove and was preparing the Cretan brew, using the water from Delphi. "This is sacred coffee," he announced, as he poured up the little cups of black death. Perhaps it was after drinking such coffee that the oracle spoke in tongues.

As soon as the coffee ritual was complete, Aleko, with his accustomed energy, packed up and was ready to go. At his insistence, we left the kites flying - in the capricious care of the gods of the sky.

Aleko's itinerary for the day took us next to the Stratigraphic Museum on the hillside across the road from the ruins. This unadorned building proved to be a high-ceilinged warehouse whose four sides enclosed a substantial courtyard. In every room and all across the courtyard there were tall shelves of labeled boxes, and tables spread with broken pottery. Pieces flat and curved, pieces with handles and lips, pieces plain, and pieces painted with elaborate designs in white and black. The tables were attended by several young men and women focused intently on the task of restoring this ceramic jigsaw puzzle into meaningful forms.

Having been here the day before, Aleko was welcomed with enthusiasm. And teased about it being about time he came back and finished his work. Many of these same boxes of shards had been left behind as unfinished business when the war came to Crete. Alex swore he recognized some material, claiming that if he couldn't figure out how to put it together it would never be done.

We didn't stay long. "I have lost my interest in puzzles," Alex explained after we made our goodbyes and started down the path toward the Villa Ariadne. The gray stone mansion was still in its winter state - flaking green shutters closed, outdoor tables and chairs stacked against walls, dry leaves accumulated on stairs and walks.

Aleko stopped in front of the villa. "The Germans came up both sides of this gravel driveway," he said, "and I - come, I will show you what I did." We walked around the side of the house on a path underneath a grape arbor, to stand behind the house. Alex pointed at the back door and then toward the far end of the backyard.

"I went down those steps - across this yard - and over that high stone wall into the fields in seconds. I would bet money that you could not easily get over that wall now. Only if you are scared to death can you do it."

We walked to the wall, smoothly faced with squared stone, standing higher than Aleko's head. "Ha. You see. I set a record for getting over this wall that will never be broken. Pendlebury, who was a champion high jumper in school, would have been impressed."

I was struck by Aleko's continued high spirits and good humor. I expected nostalgia and sentimentality. Instead, there was this lively bantering - this jovial vitality. It baffled me.

"Well, then, come on - we have other sites to see," Aleko announced, more like a driver of a tour bus than the leader of a walk through his personal past. He led me back down the driveway to the group of buildings by the entrance gate - a collection of white stuccoed offices and living spaces. Laundry hung in the side yard, and children's toys and bicycles lay about the porch.

"Behold the Taverna - called that because it was an abandoned tavern that Evans bought and turned into quarters for his staff. Pendlebury and his family lived here. And the library that once was in the villa is kept there now. I took a look at it yesterday. Many memories there, many. But we should not again disturb the family living there now. Come on."

We walked a little farther on and stood at the gate to the world of the Villa Ariadne. Traffic whizzed by on the highway a few feet in front of us.

Alex turned to look back up the driveway toward the Villa Ariadne. His mood became somber, his voice low, his eyes moist.

"The last time I saw John Pendlebury - the last time - he was going through this gate. And the last time I saw Manolaki Akoumianakis, he was going through this same gate. Manolaki had been Evans's chief assistant through all the years of the excavations. A great man in his own right - as intelligent as Evans, though without formal education.

"Manolaki had heard that his son had been killed fighting with the Cretan division against the Italians in the north, and he vowed to fight in his place, even though he was now an old man. Pendlebury told him the hill over there where we spent the morning was a crucial defense position, and Manolaki and some other Cretans went up there to hold it.

"He was killed. A needless sacrifice. His son was in fact alive. He came back to find his father's body and buried it up there somewhere."

Tears welled up in Aleko's eyes as he turned to me.

"Max-Pol, forgive me, but I did not tell you the whole truth this morning. I did not want to invade your memories with mine. The extra kites we flew up there were not really for the Holy Family. Two were for us, yes. But one kite was for Manolaki. One was for John Pendlebury. And the other was in memory of all those in my life who have come and gone from this place." I looked across the valley and up. The kites were still flying.

We walked in silence back to the car parked in the lot outside the ruins of Knossos. I asked Aleko what he wanted to do and where he wanted to go.

"Max-Pol, this has been a hard day, but a good day. I have been determined to keep two working conclusions functioning today - to allow and respect the memories of the past, and at the same time to leave them be, without further excavations. To treat them lightly, gently, but to leave them where and as they are.

"Nostalgia is a worm that eats the soft tissue of the soul. The idea comes from nostos - return - and algos - suffering. You suffer because the yearning for the home you remember is always spoiled by what is there when you go back. You can go home. But you will be sorry you did.

"Odysseus invented nostalgia. 'Return home' was the driving force of his adventure. And he learned the hard way. As the poet, Cavafy, wisely observed, Ithaca had nothing to give him except the journey itself.

"I could spend a month here and in Iraklion - walking over every inch of ground of my history. I could go and look for the graves of my family. But to what purpose? It would add nothing to the rest of my life. I am glad I came this far. I am glad to leave. My mind is settled. I have better things to do than dig around in graveyards. Let us go. Back to Hania."

I could almost hear a large key turn in a large lock on this labyrinth of his life, as Alex turned to me with eyes clear and features firmly set in a broad smile of graceful benediction on this extraordinary day.

As we drove away, he looked back once more.

"The kites . . . they are still flying," he said.

(CHRONICLES CONTINUED - 13)

The day began to fade away into early twilight.

We collected Aleko's anachronistic leather luggage from the porter at the hotel, and left Iraklion through the Canea Gate in the massive Venetian walls. I remembered Aleko saying Pendlebury was killed here, but he said nothing as I turned the car onto the broad national highway and headed west toward Hania.

Sunset.

The road climbed up and out on the cape that is the sea end of the Kouloukonas mountains. A most uncommon sight lay in the cloudless western sky: the thin crescent rind of a three-day-old moon rising just below the planet Venus, the brightest light in the evening sky. The sky was so clear that the rest of the moon could be faintly seen, palely lit by earthshine. This conjunction of planet and moon and shining earth would have been enough to provoke the prophetic urge in astrologers of old.

Aleko was silent.

THIRD WITNESS

Despite the long day and late hour, Max-Pol climbed the stairs to his apartment two steps at a time. Unlocking and shoving open the door without closing it behind him, he went straight to the kitchen and flipped the light switch.

Yes! It was there - an express box on the kitchen table.

He had left his apartment key with Kostas, in case something came from Alice while he was away in Iraklion. And there it sat. The perfect ending to a perfect day.

He checked the shipping label.

From "Marie-Pascal Ramboulet" this time.

She, of course, just happened to have the same address as Alice and Pilar and Hypatia, with their mutual benefactor, A. O. Riley. Max-Pol smiled. She had become a quintet. The apartment must be getting crowded.

Without bothering to go back and close the door or take off his coat and cap, Max-Pol sat down at the table and tore open the box. Surprise! Instead of envelopes and small packages, there was a collection of draw-string bags of several sizes, made of cloth - silk, velvet, cotton - in shades of blues and whites - flowered, striped, paisley, and plain. None of the bags was numbered. He was on his own as to the order of opening.

He lifted the bags to his nose, searching for the anticipated cigars, and wasn't disappointed. Three big ones this time - the cigar shape called *triangulares* - seven inches long, tapering from the size of a nickel at one end to the size of a dime at the other. Hand-rolled. Fresh. Davidoff brand. Hefty, enduring smokes. About as fine a cigar as could be obtained anywhere. Aleko would be very impressed. And sooner or later will ask where Max-Pol obtains his cigars. The answer is a long story that's getting longer and longer.

Max-Pol examined the rest of the bags. He was aware of a subtle but unmistakable difference in the character of this latest response. What?

214

A prettiness? Yes. Softer, more feminine. Lacking a structured, formal, rational feel. And the bags seemed to be one-of-a-kind and made to order. Bags to keep, not throw away. Time and thought were in the making of these soft, sensual pieces of art, whatever else they might contain.

He touched them carefully, ran his fingers over the textures and patterns of the cloth. These lovely wrappings were in themselves more than a report from his Witness. And the quality of her gesture matched his desire for something more from her.

Having no instructions to follow, Max-Pol opened bags at random, starting with the smallest. Inside, wrapped in pale blue tissue paper, he found a faceless and grotesquely fat female figure about four inches high, made of pitted gray stone. Her breasts and belly and behind had a swollen heaviness about them. Familiar. Where had he seen this? The first words of the accompanying note reminded him: Venus of Willendorf - museum reproduction from Natural History Museum in Vienna - always thought she was a lot bigger.

Max-Pol had seen this figure in a slide presentation in an art history course in college. It had been found in a cave near Willendorf, Germany. Maybe twenty-five thousand years old. A primary reference in Western art. He, too, had thought it would be larger. A surprise in size and a surprise to get a fertility symbol from Alice. What to make of that?

Other bags had more to say about Alice being in Vienna during the holiday season. Postcard reproductions of the paintings of Breughel - *Hunters in the Snow*, *The Peasant Wedding*, and *The Wedding Dance*. Paintings Max-Pol had admired when they were discussed in art history class. Paintings full of life and energy - indoors and out. People alive - coming home from hunting, people about to dance, people about to feast. Surely Breughel could not have posed such scenes - everything in them was in motion. A photographer might catch such images, but a painter? That was his genius.

More postcard reproductions: sections of Gustav Klimt's immense Beethoven mural in the Secession Exhibition hall: great blanks of space edged with extraordinarily complex arrangements of angels and demons - dominated by the swollen-bellied Eve and the muscular figure of Adam - all lit with backgrounds of gold leaf, like modern icons.

One flat, flowered silk bag held a napkin, with the notation that it was from the coffeehouse in Vienna frequented by Freud. Written on the napkin in pencil were nine words - as on the napkin from Barcelona:

sepia	tangerine	celadon
pentimento	tambourine	indigo
oxymoron	tarantism	lapis lazuli

Max-Pol was tempted to see these words as a crossword puzzle of sorts - to be solved. On the other hand, she might simply like the look and sound of certain words.

Don't puzzle, he thought, *move on to the next surprise.*

Another small, flat bag had two black-and-white photographs in it: a cello alone, leaning against a plain white wall, and then a close-up view of the cello with one hand on the strings and one hand holding the bow. Both hands were female, but they did not belong to the same woman. The left hand on the strings was young - with slender, sinewy fingers, and short nails neatly shaped for playing a cello. The hand holding the bow was aged, twisted like a tree root grown to fit the shape needed for holding a bow. The nails were unpolished, and the diamond ring on the fourth finger was impressive. The note explained:

"My cello - my hand, and the hand of Mme Lumière, my teacher."

This was news. Alice played the cello or was learning to play? Where? Vienna? Paris? She didn't say. But here was one more piece of information that did not square with his impression that she was hearing-impaired.

Another bag contained only a small, irregular, nondescript stone about the size of a peanut. The stone had a hole through it, as if it was to be strung on a necklace. "From a path Monet walked between his house and the Seine - in winter."

One final bag, long and thin, blue-and-white striped cotton.

Rolled up inside it, tied with a strip of the same blue-and-white cloth of the bag, a page of threes:

Hermes, messenger of the Gods - three signs:
1. Talaria - winged sandals
2. Petasus - winged cap
3. Caduceus - gold staff with wings and two serpents

Theban Trilogy by Sophocles:
1. Oedipus, the King
2. Antigone
3. Oedipus at Colonus

Prayers for three kinds of people - Nikos Kazantzakis:
1. I am a bow in thy hands, God, please bend me or I shall rot
2. I am a bow in thy hands, God, bend me but do not break me
3. I am a bow in thy hands, God, bend me - who cares if I break

Lemma trilogy:
1. If there is a dilemma, is there a lemma or trilemma?
2. Or an omnilemma, maxilemma or minilemma?
3. How about a nonlemma, exlemma or lemmanalysis?

*

With all the bags opened and the contents laid out before him, Max-Pol sat motionless. His mind worked in several directions at once.

Stop it, he thought.
Speculation would only drive him into a maze.
Not now, but someday, he would ask her to explain.
Face to face.

He rose, took off his coat and cap, and went out to the front hall to close the door he had thrown open when he came in. He went to the kitchen for wine, a glass, and an ashtray. He sat down again to contemplate the array on the kitchen table. If he were in court, how would he approach a jury with this? What did the evidence suggest?

Something was missing. The puzzle lacked a border - an enclosing, defining edge - as if he was to provide that this time. There was no perfunctory note from the Witness saying she had read his Chronicles. She had not explained "Marie-Pascal Ramboulet," as if she took it for granted that by now he would know she had created a French name for herself in the spirit of the other self-christenings. As if she presumed he would have some understanding of her personal style by now.

He sensed . . . what? Melancholy? Solemnity? The gifts had a quality of loneliness about them. He could not say exactly why. Perhaps he was projecting his own needs on hers. Or maybe he wished she had these feelings. Multiple working hypotheses.

She must know that he would puzzle over every item for meaning. Was she teasing him? What was she trying to tell him? Or was she simply trusting Witness for Witness.

He knew what he was doing. He was projecting his needs - imagining her, creating her, fashioning her into an "other" who fit the irregular, empty space in his own puzzle.

Max-Pol shook his head. Yes. No. Maybe.

He went to bed exhausted, but deeply satisfied. Such a day. With Alex in Iraklion and Knossos - the kites - the sunset - the starry-night ride home - the box from Alice/Pilar/Hypatia/Marie-Pascal. As sleep came for him, the last thing that went through his mind was Learical:

> *There once was a girl with five names.*
> *She was good at incredible games.*
> *She met a young man, holding fire in a pan*
> *And . . . she remained the girl with five names.*

THE EYE OF ALICE

Five days passed. As Max-Pol passed Kostas's shop, Kostas shouted at him from somewhere in the back room and rushed out to meet him.

"Is be package for you. Please. Come inside. I have customers, but not long - buy nothing. Come. Sit. Wait. Have a little tsikoudia. I make coffee. Sit. Sit." When Kostas is in a mood for hospitality, there are no options. Max-Pol sat and watched the way of Kostas with customers.

Kostas divides clientele into several categories.

First, there are those who only want to look around. If he feels their interest is genuine, he will unfold and show his wares with as much enthusiasm as if they had come to buy a specific item. Sometimes show-and-tell leads to liking-and-buying.

Then there are those who want to buy a cheap rug to take home. He will tell them politely where find souvenir rugs - he has none to sell.

Lastly, there are those who ooze, "I have money, much money," but who don't appreciate the real value of his antique weavings. They want to play bargaining games with him because they think they are clever enough to take advantage of him.

Kostas holds such people in contempt. He does not want his things in their houses. "Is be like give my children to devils." To such people he declares his shop is an art gallery, but is not open for business today. "I sell nothing, nothing," he declares, ushers them out, locks his door, and walks away.

But for those who sense the historical value and irreplaceable beauty of what Kostas has - who appreciate such things as much as he - Kostas will unfold everything he has for them, give them a long discourse on how such things were made, and insist they sit for coffee. To them he offers his passion and knowledge - and he will always find something for them at a price he and they can afford. More than once Max-Pol saw him with such customers early in the morning and found him still with them hours later, saying over and over, as he unfolded a weaving or a rug:

"Look! Look at this. Is be beautiful! Feel it. Is be beautiful."

All the lifting down and unfolding and displaying and refolding and putting away has kept him lean and strong. "Is be my exercise, you know - lifting up and down - up and down. When the shop is finish, me, I go to America - be wrestler like on the television, you know - Kostas the Carpet Man is be killer - Ha."

His customers of the moment are lookers in more than one sense of the word. Two young, pretty, blond German girls. A special category for Kostas. "No be business, this. Is be entertainment."

The entertainment didn't last long, and Kostas rustled around making coffee. Max-Pol asked for his package. "Oh, in back - Manolis's cousin carry it - you know this cousin? Is also be entertainment - Ha."

*

Kostas brought the coffee and the package, which was from Paris - from the familiar address of Alice/Pilar/Hypatia/Marie-Pascal. Another one? So soon?

Inside, nested in shredded blue paper, was a small gift-wrapped box. Shiny, slick yellow paper, bright blue-and-white satin ribbon. Inside the box, a dark blue velvet bag. Inside the bag was what Max-Pol first thought was an antique silver pocket watch - the kind with the snap-open cover over the face of the watch.

Max-Pol pressed the knob at the top of the silver casing.

Instead of the face of time, or even the face of Alice, there was only the image of the blue-green iris of a human eye. The photograph of the eye had been developed in such a way that all but the iris had been eliminated, leaving only a jade mandala on a black velvet background. Stunning.

He handed the open silver case to Kostas.

"Is be eye, you know. Beautiful, this eye. Katapliktiko! Beautiful." He closed the case and opened it again. "Never have I seen such a thing. Woman? You know this woman?"

Max-Pol was silent. What is the answer to the question? Does he know this woman? Yes? No? Maybe? Someone who knows him a lot better than he knows her? He didn't have the answer to those questions, and he wasn't ready to invite Kostas into his workshop of speculation.

"It's my sister, Kostas. It's her way of saying she is keeping an eye on me. We haven't seen each other for a long time."

Max-Pol smiles feebly.

Kostas grins. He doesn't believe him.

"Nice. Me, I like to see the rest of your sister sometime. Opa."

*

Max-Pol did not share with Kostas the note accompanying the gift. Later, in his apartment, he read:

"Eye portraits popular in the late 18th century in England and France among the aristocracy and royalty. Often painted in watercolor on ivory and set in little jeweled frames or lockets. The first is thought to have been commissioned in 1785 by Mrs. Fitzherbert, secret wife of the Prince of Wales. The prince regent responded with a tiny painting of his own eye.

These keepsakes were popular – they were unidentifiable except by the recipient. There are collections of these portraits in several museums. Eyes not the only part of the face depicted – sometimes the mouth – or an ear.

A photographer who has a shop nearby specializes in these portraits of just the iris of the eye – remarkable what's there in the details. Each iris in the world is unique. No two alike – not even in the same person. I know a lot about this. Helped develop security systems based on eye identification. More about that some other time. Thought you might like to have a reminder of the Witness who reads your writing – an image of the eye through which your words pass."

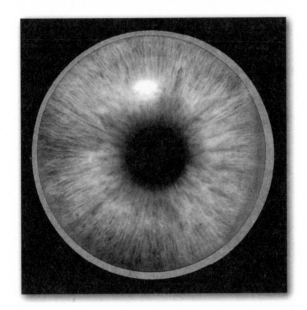

THE GYPSY RUG

Max-Pol meandered around Hania in a blissful daze.

The combination of the gift of the eye from Alice, the experience with Alex in Iraklion, and balmy weather made him euphoric. He ambled along the harbor and crossed the main street, singing to himself.

BLAT! BLAT! BLAT!

An air horn broke his mood, warning him out of the middle of the street. A burly six-wheel cargo truck muscled its way slowly through the morning busyness of Hania, calling attention to itself with its horn and a squawking loudspeaker system. High, red cab, matte aluminum truck body, no commercial markings. The irritating, rasping voice from the loudspeaker repeated a phrase in a dialect of guttural Greek.

BLAT! BLAT! BLAT!

As the truck moved nearer, Max-Pol looked through the dusty windshield into the face of a young woman holding two small children in her lap. They stared at him as frankly as he stared at them. A man was driving with one hand and holding a microphone up to his mouth with the other. Swarthy, black-haired, brown-eyed people - the man with a grandiose mustache - the woman and children with colorful kerchiefs tied over their hair.

As the truck jostled by, Max-Pol saw that its cargo area was filled with rolled-up rugs. Riding on top of the rugs was an adolescent girl, barefooted and wearing clothes that could compete with a peacock's display: loose-fitting trousers of emerald green, white apron, yellow-and-red-striped shirt, a patterned shawl of myriad shades of blue and pink. A scarlet-and-black headscarf crowned curly black hair. An exotic, olive-skinned face, with delicate features, almond-shaped eyes, wide smile, white teeth, crimson lips. A living odalisque. An apparition out of the *Arabian Nights* - not what commonly adorns the tailgate of a cargo truck.

Gypsies, real Gypsies, thought Max-Pol.

Whatever may be said about the disappearance of Gypsies, these no-madic rug sellers still invade Crete from time to time in truck caravans. Nobody knows where they come from or where they get their rugs. The Gypsies live behind a partition in their trucks when the weather is bad, and camp outside in river bottoms when the weather is good.

They sleep on the carpets, and when the carpets get worn and dirty, the Gypsies claim the carpets are antiques, though even an unskilled eye can see that the backs of the rugs have the uniformity declaring them machine-made. The Gypsies swear the rugs are made by hand in Iran, Iraq, Turkey, Afghanistan, or anywhere else you would like them to have been made.

Max-Pol quickly walked to Kostas's shop.

"Kostas, there are Gypsies in town," said Max-Pol. "I want to buy a Gypsy rug. What do you think? Come with me and help me bargain with them."

"Why you want this?"

Max-Pol wanted to send something unique to Alice in response to her gift of her eye - a real Gypsy rug - but he was not about to try to explain that whole story for Kostas.

"It's for my sister, Kostas - she has the Gypsy spirit."

"Is no buy from these people in truck. Rugs be from machines, you know. Gypsies sleep on rugs. Is be dirty. Is be nothing to have - nothing. Me, I have for you something real Gypsy - very special, you know - for your sister. Not in my shop. Not for sale. In my house I have. Come."

It was the first time Kostas had invited Max-Pol to his home. Lock-ing the doors of the shop, they set off - out of the narrow crooked streets of the old city, through a gap cut into the Venetian fortress walls, and down the wide promenade fronting the open sea.

Kostas's apartment was on the second floor of an aging neoclassical mansion built in the cultural revival at the beginning of the nineteenth century. The foyer was unadorned, as was the hallway: plain walls paint-ed white, flaking here and there to expose the color choices of previous inhabitants. An atmosphere of decadent sadness prevailed.

They climbed a sagging spiral staircase to a tall mahogany door.

Kostas unlocked and pushed open the door to reveal what Max-Pol imagined a sultan's harem bedroom might look like. Unabashed opulence.

High-ceilinged rooms with floors and walls covered with wool tapestries and silk curtains and linen weavings in ivory and red and black and gold and orange and pink. The furniture was likewise covered with multi-colored pillows, shawls, and blankets. The dowry treasures of who knows how many Cretan brides.

"It's a museum, Kostas."

"Yes. Is be my museum - what I love - all."

"You live here?"

"No, not now. Is be living in apartment of mother now. Sometime we will come here with Kirios Aleko and I tell you this and this and this, you know, about these things. Now I show you for sister."

Kostas opened an iron-strapped wooden chest. The smell of camphor and sandalwood seeped into the room as he lifted out lace tablecloths and folded lengths of finely woven curtains.

"This."

He unrolled a small, lightweight rug - about two by three feet. Soft, fine-textured. Intricate, many-colored Oriental pattern of pale blues and greens on three sides, with a plain dome-shaped space of crimson red in the middle.

"This I have a long time. Is be Muslim - rug for making pray only. I tell you. Once I am in prison in France - only for few days - a problem with papers for working, you know. And in this prison with me is be this Gypsy man. Young man. Why in prison? Because be Gypsy. Only that. He say me - help me - help me - have wife, children - waiting. So. I like him. I help him - only needs money, you know - little money. I have. We go out of this prison together. He say me - not all people help Gypsy people. I say you thanks and this and this and this, you know. Me, he give this rug. He say his rug is go everywhere with Gypsy - everywhere. Is be real Gypsy rug.

"Me, I cannot sell. Me, I cannot use. No pray this way in Greek church, you know - Greeks stand up at God, not be on floor waving up and down, up and down. But I like this rug. Orea, poli orea. Very beautiful. Your sister like this rug. Take it. Take it."

When Kostas gives, you must accept. An adamant, compulsive generosity is part of the Cretan character.

"*Sas ep-haristo poli, Kostas, para poli!* You have a great talent for giving," said Max-Pol.

And thought to himself, *AlicePilarHypatiaMariePascal, the Gypsy queen, will love it. She has a talent for receiving.*

EASTER

In Crete, Easter is not a holiday weekend.

Pascha is a holy season, defining the quality of daily life long before the formal religious celebration. Cretan Easter is a communal state of mind - even more pervasive in spirit than Christmas. December 25 is only a birthday, after all. So say the Cretans. Everybody has a birthday. But the rebirth-day at the heart of Easter is another matter. Resurrection from the dead is the ultimate miracle.

Christos ahnesti! - Christ is risen! - is the greeting.
And the reply is *Alithos ahnesti!* He is risen indeed.

Great Lent begins forty days before Easter, with the celebration of Clean Monday - the day of the scouring of kitchens and the flying of kites. The spirit of the fast is still observed in the villages by most people, and observed in the cities by the older generation. While no meat is eaten, the rest of the fasting diet is a matter of personal conviction rather than rigid rules. Fruit, vegetables, bread, and some fish are common fare, and on some special days people eat even less. Such restraint is meant to focus the mind on the larger sacrifice of Jesus.

At the same time there is in the air an anticipatory joy.

The glory of spring in Crete is coming on with a green rush - the earth is reviving, launching flowers from its soil. Along with the return of abundant life, the Easter season is a time of return for those Greeks of the Hellenic Diaspora. Daily conversation is filled with talk of reunions - who is going home elsewhere in Greece and who is coming home to Crete - especially from America, Australia, and Canada. Easter always means an in-gathering of family in a back-to-the-village migration.

Houses and churches are being cleaned and repaired. Gardens are being groomed. Lambs are being fattened for the slaughter. Orders are being placed for cakes and pastries. Wine barrels are being tapped and the wine tested. Kitchen supplies are checked and replenished. The self-control of the forty days of fasting will be compensated by the three-day indulgence of appetite beginning at two o'clock on Easter morning. It is the sweetest time of the year if you are Cretan. There is a word for this season of about-to-be: *ahnoixi* - spring - which comes from the verb "to open."

Whatever one's religious convictions or lack thereof, it is a moving experience to be caught up in this soulful celebrational season. One might easily begin to believe that Jesus lived out his life nearby, that it was the Turks who crucified Him, and that when He comes again, He will first appear in Crete and host a great feast. At Easter. One could believe that. It is, as Alex reminds Max-Pol, another working hypothesis.

*

A large contingent of Kostas's extended family is coming from Chicago. And Kostas's fifteen-year-old son will arrive from Germany, where he lives with his mother and stepfather.

(Alex and Max-Pol do not know about this son. Kostas has not told them. In case the son does not come - or in case the son has become a skinhead - one's friends do not need to know everything.)

In a burst of seasonal fervor, Alex Evans has invited his daughters and their families to come all the way from Australia to join him in Crete. They have not yet replied, and they will not come, but he has convinced himself they might. They have never experienced Easter in Crete. This is the year they must. There may never be another chance to be with their grandfather for Pascha.

Alex is acting as if they are already on their way. He is shopping for clothes for himself, and making preliminary arrangements for lodging for his family. He has a grand feast in mind as well.

(Kostas and Max-Pol do not know about all this. Not yet. In case the family does not come. One's friends do not need to know everything.)

This morning Alex is meeting Max-Pol at the Meltemi for coffee before going on a joint expedition to the market to research cheese. Alex has announced he is in a mood for cheese, never mind why.

"Calimera, Kosta! Ooo eeneh o Kyrios Max-Pol?"
Alex has found Kostas in his "office" - at the Meltemi, playing backgammon on an outdoor table in the sunshine of this fine March day.

Kostas replies in bursts of jackhammer Greek, saying and pointing: Look - Max-Pol is over there - across the harbor at the end of the jetty.

Alex can see Max-Pol sitting on the high stone wall, talking with another man. Kostas goes on, explaining that Max-Pol is with Kostas's cousin, Michael, who has come early from Chicago because he wants to get away from much sorrow. He was married only six months when his wife was hit by a car. She died a month ago. And, and, and so on.

Kostas says he and Michael and Max-Pol were having coffee, talking, when for no apparent reason, Michael started crying. And when Max-Pol found out why, he asked Michael to go for a walk. Kostas had the feeling he should not go along. So - there is the story. Kostas gestures again across the harbor. "Is be there. Is be coming soon back."

Alex looks again at the two figures out on the jetty. Max-Pol's hand is on Michael's shoulder. They sit gazing out at the rolling sea without speaking.

"Malista," says Alex - and, saying he will go to the market and come back, he leaves Kostas to his backgammon.

*

An hour later, Alex returned from the market heavily burdened with an armload of flowers - red anemones and white narcissus and purple iris - a long, crusty two-kilo loaf of fresh bread, and a whole cheese about the size and weight of a bowling ball. He had worked up a sweat, worked up an appetite, and, as he walked, he had been working up the details of a lovely story. Absentmindedly talking to himself, Alex pushed his way through the pedestrian traffic with his baggage, and people gave way to him like small cars confronted with a loaded cement truck on a narrow bridge.

Alex had surveyed the market in his single-minded quest for good cheeses. At the chosen shop he had asked for samples of French Brie, Danish blue, Dutch Gouda, and English Cheddar, all of which he could see in one corner of the display case.

The man behind the counter, almost as large and imposing as Alex, considered him in amused contempt. The man announced that although Alex was speaking Greek, he must certainly not be Cretan. Alex replied

230

that, on the contrary, he was indeed Cretan, but he had not been home in fifty years - he was now living in England.

"Well, well," the man bellowed, "I will speak in plain English, then. You should be ashamed of yourself! Ashamed! These," pointing with disdain at the small imported products wrapped in fancy foils and cellophane, "these things are not cheese! They are not fit to eat! They are foreign excuses for cheese!"

Alex backpedaled cautiously. "Well, I just thought . . ."

The man gestured expansively at the great whole wheels and smaller rounds of cheese piled like stone battlements on top of the counter and on the shelves behind, most the size of small tires or concrete building blocks. Pale blue and gray, and tinged with oozy green and hairy black molds.

Thumping them with both fists like a man driving nails with his hands, the man roared, "*This is cheese! And this one and this and this! Cheese! Cretan cheese!*"

And he laughed a great laugh, and with a fearsome knife sliced off thin, sample slivers of fine, light ivory and yellow cheese, all the while muttering to himself, "*This* is *cheese.*"

He offered the tastes to Alex, demanding, "Try it. Eat. How many *real* cheeses you want, my Cretan cousin?"

Alex ate. The goats and sheep were there - the herbs of mountain meadows - the rocks and stones - the clear springs - the earth and sky.

"*Orea, poli orea.* It is true, this is cheese."
Alex had settled for a bowling-ball size - all he could carry.
Now he was eager to share his booty and his story.

*

As he comes to the port, Alex can see Max-Pol and Michael and Kostas at their table at the Meltemi. Max-Pol is just walking away. Alex hurries to catch him, but Max-Pol is gone before Alex is within hailing distance.

"Kostas, where did Max-Pol go?"

"Going to his apartment - he say be coming back later."

Kostas introduces Alex to Michael, a strong-featured young second-generation Greek American - an attorney. He has not adopted the slightly sinister-sexy look of Cretan men his age. Khaki shorts and a white button-down shirt and tassled brown loafers do not exude the same message as Levis and black leather jackets and boots.

Kostas notices that Michael is in good spirits. "*Ola kalah?* OK?"

Michael says, "I'm feeling much better now. I still have a hard time with my feelings. Dr. Millay was really kind. I lost it while we were having coffee. Like getting hit with a brick out of nowhere. And he saw it and he was there - right there. Doctors don't always share their personal lives. But when he found out about the death of my wife, he told me about his own experience. Knowing someone else has been where I am helps."

Alex is in the middle of slicing cheese. He stops, wrinkling his brow. "What experience was that?"

"His wife died suddenly - three years ago - cancer. She was a doctor too. And they had been married only a short time. Even worse, when she died, she was pregnant. He had a lot to say about all the stages of grief he went through. He was really very helpful. It was an amazing combination of professional advice and personal experience."

Alex and Kostas looked at each other, eyebrows raised in mutual wordless astonishment. Friends don't tell each other everything.

BEYOND SORROW

In his apartment, Max-Pol lay down on his bed on his back and stared up at the plastered ceiling and into his past. The tears flowed, spilling down his cheeks and on down the sides of his head.

He wasn't surprised that he had responded so automatically to young Michael's pain. But he had not been prepared to have his own private grief come welling up inside him again so suddenly.

Over the last year, he had gradually resumed being able to talk to others about death without losing control of his own emotions. But not this morning. It was because he was not in the formal setting of a doctor's office. And it was a function of time and distance. He had not talked about his wife for months. It had been almost a year since the floodgates of his feelings had failed him.

Now the hurting is back. He has been in this condition often enough to know how it will come and how it will go. He tells himself what he would tell someone else in his place, *Let the grief run its course. Let the sorrow happen. Cry until crying is done. Get it out. Then lie down in a quiet place, close your eyes, and let yourself watch the reruns of the films of your memory. Let it be.*

Max-Pol knows to allow this turn of the wheel of grief. In time, relief and calm will return. He will get up. Wash his face. Take a deep breath. And go on. He has before. He will again.

Later, he walks out on his porch and looks down through the arbor vines to see if Alex and Kostas and Michael are still at the Meltemi. They are. He doesn't want to join them. Too awkward. What would he say? What could they say? This is not a time for words.

Surely Michael will have told them about their conversation. Max-Pol wishes he had asked Michael to keep what was said in confidence. But he hadn't - probably unconsciously wanting Alex and Kostas to know. Like Alex, with some parts of his life, Max-Pol both does and does not want to talk about his past, especially this part. He wants Alex to know, but he doesn't want to tell him directly.

One reason Max-Pol has come to Crete is to escape from the category well-meaning friends have put him in: "young-doctor-Millay-whose-pregnant-wife-died-isn't-it-a-shame." Their intentions were honorable and sincere. Even so, they had no idea how their insistent sympathy kept him chained to his anguish.

Besides. Nobody knew the whole story anyway - how much an enigmatic nightmare those three years had been - how confusing and unresolved it remains in his mind, despite all his efforts to live beyond it.

For an outsider, the situation seemed straight-forward. For him, it would remain a permanent conundrum. Some parts of a human being, when damaged, cannot be fixed. The damage is lived with.

Now what to do? How to talk about all this with Alex and Kostas?

The subject will remain an unspoken awkwardness between him and his cousins until something is said. But not today. *Avrio* - tomorrow. The upcoming adventure with Alex might give them a chance to talk.

Rodopos

Alex has a genius for making friends who, in turn, want to introduce him to their friends. His personality is an oasis of enthusiasm in the middle of the desert of daily dullness.

On one of his snooping, wandering walks through the back streets of Hania, he stopped into the smallest and oldest church of the city to admire its icons. He sought the parish priest to get some explanations of the paintings. And met Father John, who, coincidentally, was a Welsh Greek who had studied at Cambridge.

"Cambridge! Well, then."

A five-minute visit became a two-hour lunch. Father John brought along to the meal his closest colleague, Father Anthony, who is the parish priest in the village of Rodopos, and one thing led to another. It is the story of Alex's life - it could be chiseled on his tombstone:

"For him, one thing always led to another."

And now Alex and Max-Pol and Kostas are all invited to attend Sunday service in the village church, and to get a tour of the Rodopos peninsula. Afterward, there will be lunch with Father Anthony and his family, joined by Father John and his family and any other family that happens by. Invitations to such impromptu feasts are typical of the seasonal run-up to Easter in Crete.

*

The Rodopos peninsula is one of the two long horns jutting north into the Aegean Sea from Crete's western end. Twenty kilometers long, with peaks up to eight hundred meters high, it is not an incidental piece of topography. It forms one side of the Bay of Kissamos, and is so commanding in height it almost cuts off the far west from the rest of Crete. Once, millions of years ago, it was a separate island in its own right. There are rocks and fossils here not found on the lowlands on either side. Its high places are frequently above the cloud and fog banks that form down closer to the sea, giving the Rodopos highlands an aura of mystery.

On the other hand, olive groves, orchards, and vegetable farms fill the peninsula's lower valleys all the way up to the centrally situated village. As the land rises beyond the village, the vineyards take over in the rocky, less arable soil of the shallow gorges. Farther on, the peninsula is so high and barren and rocky that its thin pasturage is given over entirely to sheep and goats. Herds of the long-haired traditional breeds roam the treeless landscape. Snow is not unknown here in winter. And wild orchids bloom in the areas around its springs in summer. Altogether a startling, enchanting landscape.

The village of Rodopos is the focus of life for about a thousand people who still carry on a more or less traditional way of life. It seems like a long way from anywhere, and in its churchyard is a surprising reference to the length of Rodopos's place in history. Here stands a round marble monument that looks like nothing so much as the stump of a weathered gray telephone pole. It bears a faded Latin inscription. A modern marble tablet explains that this memorial marks the completion, in 112 A.D., of a road built in the reign of the Roman emperor Trajan between this village and the temple of Diktyna - goddess of nets - at the far end of the peninsula. The road was paid for from donations to the temple. The same roadway is still in use.

When asked about the marker, the villagers reply offhandedly, "Oh, that." The church gardener usually hangs his coat and hat on this, one of the smallest of Trajan's many columns, while he works.

In modern history, Rodopos is famous for its heavy red wine, its wildflower honey, its part in the resistance to the German occupation, and for the several members of one of its families active in Cretan politics. A bronze bust of the patriarch, Polychronis Polychronidis, looks sternly across the village square opposite the kafenion - as craggy in his face as the hillsides around him. All of the life that survives and thrives here is fiercely resilient. It must be.

In the spirit of his cheese experience of yesterday, Alex points around him and shouts, "Now this, *this* is Crete."

*

The church service is in progress when the visitors arrive. Not until they find their standing places and begin to look around do they notice that three of the five men leading the liturgical chanting of the service are in army uniform. Not just army. The elite of the army. Greek Special Forces from the paratroops battalion stationed at Maleme.

The young men obviously know the service. They sing with passionate authority. With the addition of the deeper voices of two older men and the mellow baritone of the priest, the service is surprisingly beautiful - not what you'd expect in a remote village church. St. John Chrysostom would be pleased to know his liturgy survives in such a place and is well served and well sung after more than sixteen hundred years.

The church itself is plain - a working church for a living community, not a tourist attraction. In contrast with the high elegance of the service, there is a comfortable informality in the casual coming and going of the villagers during the ceremony. It is not required that one stay all the way through - only that one should pay one's respects for some time during the service.

After receiving the blessed bread from the hands of its priest, Father Anthony, the small congregation greets visitors warmly, as if they were an early-arriving contingent of the Diaspora come home for Easter. Afterward, the men of the village move more or less en masse to the kafenion across the street for tsikoudia and coffee and talk. The women return home to prepare lunch.

Max-Pol wants to know about the participation of the soldiers.

They speak English and are surprised that he asks. All three are twenty and have had two years at technical universities. Yes, they are Special Forces paratroopers - commando-trained - the first to go if there is war with the Turks. But they are citizen-soldiers, with an emphasis on the citizen. Every Greek man must serve two years. Service is an obligation of citizenship, rarely a profession.

These young men are from east Crete. They've grown up assisting in the service in their village churches, and they like being off base and back in a village like home. So - they volunteer. Their commanding officer is also a singer and feels the same way about his roots. He would have come along with them today except his wife is expecting a baby this weekend. Mixing church and state and armed forces and family -

it is and always has been the Cretan way. About such things they have no doubts whatsoever. To keep these traditions they will sacrifice their lives - or take yours.

*

Since lunch would not be served until two o'clock, excursions were organized. Kostas and the soldiers went off in a pickup truck, out to the far end of the peninsula to see where the Germans had built emplacements for their coastal artillery during the war.

The two priests and four of their children went to pick wildflowers in the hills above the village. The women were glad to have the kitchen to themselves.

Alex wanted to wander around the village and look at donkeys and donkey saddles. He has a fondness for donkeys, having tended and worked them when he was a child. The personalities of donkeys appeal to him. They are the most bloody-minded of creatures. It has been a long time since a donkey was seen in the streets of Hania. And while some are still in active use here in Rodopos, their days are as numbered as those of the older generation of villagers who keep them.

Max-Pol went along with Alex.

"Well, then," began Alex. "The donkey - the *gaidouri*, or *gaidoura*, if female - is called the Cretan Volkswagen. It will carry almost anything almost anywhere - twice its own weight is common. It is very tough, very easy to keep, usually gentle, and lives a long time. And look, here is the very creature."

Tied to a tree on the far side of a ditch, a small, slatternly lady donkey solemnly ate grass, paying no attention to her audience. Alex continued, "Donkeys don't 'do' anything to entertain you, and they do not demand attention or affection. They are a beast of burden. They are a live-and-let-live animal. You don't bother them - they don't bother you. They work very hard with very little complaint for a very long time. An admirable creature."

Alex and Max-Pol crossed the ditch, inspected the unpretentious gray-brown animal, stroked its back, and petted its head. The donkey ignored them.

Alex observed, "Odd that such a small member of the horse family should have such a large head in proportion to the rest of its body. You wouldn't call them handsome, nor is their singing beautiful." Unfazed by insult and uninterested in company, the donkey went on single-mindedly eating grass. Live and let live.

Getting no response from the donkey, Alex and Max-Pol ambled along a dirt track, out toward the edge of Rodopos where the vineyards began. As one more sure sign of spring, the vines had been trimmed and the trimmings stacked for burning. Sheep were near the vineyards, browsing on the lush, flowery undergrowth around the trunks of the vines. The soft tones of the bells around their necks punctuated the silent feeding of the sheep. *Bong, bung, bingle bingle, bang, bong-bong, bunk, bunk.* The bells were a collective musical instrument, and some shepherds still bought them in tuned sets for the pleasure of the distant harmony.

The two men sat down on a stone wall. Looking, breathing, listening - consuming the ageless tranquility of the scene before them.

LAURA

"Her name was Laura."

Without looking at Alex, Max-Pol began, as if continuing an unspoken conversation. "Laura Kohara, a third-generation Japanese American, raised in Hawaii. She came to college and medical school on the mainland to get away from all that 'aloha' mentality. When we met I was a senior resident and she was an intern. It began as a teacher-student relationship."

Alex said nothing. The bells of the sheep alone broke the silence.

"Then came friendship - then affection - then desire and passion, and a complicated attachment during tense times in both our lives. Residency and early years of medical practice are spent on the edge of madness - the stress is almost unbearable. It slams people together. We satisfied some deep needs for each other, but we also stirred up messy stuff she had been carrying for a long time. We fought. My God, did we fight! I was a punching bag for some nasty experiences she had had with her father and brothers. And I blamed her for derailing my career.

"She was the woman I wanted to fit into my idealized notion of wife-and-mother-and-companion. I was the man she wanted to both love and get even with. The odds were against us. Way, way against us. Still, we married, as if marriage would dissolve our difficulties and solve her problems and meet my needs. So stupid. We didn't want to have children right away, but we were careless and Laura got pregnant. She was sick most of the time. I was angry most of the time. Awful. And then, well, then . . ."

Max-Pol could feel the tears coming. He got up and walked off into the vineyard, hands behind his back, clinching and unclenching. Regaining his composure, he came back and sat down again. Alex had not stirred.

"The lymphoma was found too late – its symptoms were masked by the pregnancy – and – well – she was dead three months later. And the child . . . the child . . . was not viable – dead in her mother.

"If that wasn't enough, Laura died suddenly while we were on vacation on an out-of-the-way beach in Mexico. I still can't believe it, but I drove around with her body in the car, trying to find some official to give me a death certificate and papers so I could bring her across the border. What a mess that was."

Max-Pol's voice dropped to a whisper as he struggled to talk.

"The truth is, Aleko, the terrible truth is that the marriage wouldn't have lasted. She knew. I knew. From the beginning, we knew. The marriage was founded on my being a lifeboat for her in the rough seas of a stage in her life, and my wanting her to be a kind of person she was never going to be. A child would have been victimized by our animosity. We were headed for long-lasting anguish, no matter what. The last thing she said to me was that her dying was a kind of a solution for all three of us."

Max-Pol took a deep breath and began pacing back and forth in front of Alex like a defense attorney before a jury. His voice regained its strength as he moved beyond walking on the hot coals of the past.

"There's just a part of it, Aleko. Just a part. As you so often say, it is a long story – perhaps for another time – perhaps not at all. You can understand why I don't talk about it. I hate talking about it. I'm talked out – the subject is exhausted, beat to death. I hardly have feelings about it anymore.

"I have the memory of feelings, which isn't the same. I felt so awful – so goddamned guilty – so much a failure for so long. At times I really didn't want to go on living. A psychiatrist colleague and antidepressants got me through the worst. But still I really couldn't function as a family doctor.

"So. I left my practice, and did the only thing I have always known how to do well – go to school. I took a residency in radiology and buried myself in it for two years. Looking at X-rays in a dark room was a way of hiding. But that's all it was. I wasn't cut out to be a radiologist.

"So, then, Crete. Exile from my personal black hole. Being in Crete has been healing. And even though you've not known my story, you've given me great courage about getting on with life after failure. This, too, shall pass. You'll never know how much that piece of stitchery you and Kostas gave me meant to me. With all my heart I'm grateful to you."

"You think you helped kill her and the child, don't you?" said Alex. Max-Pol hung his head.
"And she was right. It was a solution for you."
"Yes."

There was no more to say. Words would not do. Alex stood up, stepped forward, and put his arms around Max-Pol in an embrace so genuinely comforting that Max-Pol felt some protection from the on-coming wave of sorrow that kept knocking him down and sucking him under. The wave didn't come this time.

Finally Alex broke the silence.
"We'll miss lunch" was all he said - or needed to say.
They walked away toward the village.

*

After a time, Alex began, "The jumwillies roar in their brabbles.
"Perspiring in dribbles and drabbles," replied Max-Pol.
Alex shot back, "Their episodes come, to not all but some."
"Far out on the sea sing the quid."

"What?" Alex demanded. "That isn't a proper limerick - it doesn't rhyme!"
"Aleko, that's what really makes it nonsense, don't you see."
"My dear Max-Pol, I, as the Lord of Learical Poetry and King of the Jumwillies, make the rules, and I say it must be a limerickal rhyme or it is out of order. You risk being demoted in rank, sir. Come now, have some respect for poetry. None of this blank-verse folderol. Let us begin again.

"A jumwillie living in Crete."
Max-Pol smiled and offered, "Lost track of his mind in the street."
Alex added, "An X-ray revealed, his brain was congealed."

And Max-Pol finished with, "So he sliced it and sold it for meat."

"Much better, sir - not great, but much better."

Alex put his arm on Max-Pol's shoulder, as if wanting support on the rough going in the stony road, but in fact extending his affection and compassion for his young companion.

If he had had a son, well, then . . .

Lunch was served out of doors on tables set up on the sunny south side of the priest's home. What was supposed to be a simple Lenten meal turned into a preview of the Paschal banquet. The table was splendidly arrayed with dishes of wild greens, several kinds and sizes of beans, rice pilaf, crimson beets, red tomatoes, and a purple cabbage salad. Bouquets of fragrant purple freesias crowned the display of food. A feast for the eye and nose as well as the stomach.

Twenty people crowded around to eat. Alex and Max-Pol and Kostas, three paratroopers, two priests, and their wives and children. Several neighbors from houses on either side came and went, bringing wine, oranges, lemons, bread, and olives.

Shouting, laughing, arguing, and passing food, the guests lingered over the table well into the afternoon. The paratroopers and the priests sang Cretan mountain songs. Tangerines and tsikudia were passed to finish the lunch. As a finale, Kostas told the latest Cretan donkey joke in a mix of Greek and English:

"This mans have wife, you know, and have also big gaidouri. Wife is be trouble - is hard woman. One day, wife is yelling - beating husband with the stick and is beating donkey - she says them they no good. Gaidouri is kick woman and she be dead. Same man is be marry another woman - hard woman also. She is also beating man and gaidouri with stick, yelling this and this and this. Gaidouri is kick woman dead. So. At the church for liturgy for wife, man is see other men talking with his brother. He ask his brother, what they say you? Brother say, they all have wifes. They want to buy your donkey."

The men howled with laughter, pounding the table and toasting one another with their tsikudia glasses. The women gave each other knowing looks and got up to clear the dishes. The lunch was over.

But the entertainment was not. A neighbor's sow was ready for breeding. Barbara was her name. The boar, Hercules, was shoving against the fence between him and his intended, grunting rhythmically like a pile driver.

The men went over to see the fracas. The gate was opened and the circus was on. Two three-hundred-pound pigs, grunting, biting, squealing and squalling, and slobbering up a froth. Shouts of encouragement from the men. The boar finally cornered the sow against the back wall of the pigsty and did what he came to do. Much applause all around. Hercules fell over in the mud and lay there - whether from ecstasy or exhaustion it cannot be said. Barbara ate the slopped-up remains of the grand lunch, as if nothing unusual had happened. Just another day in the pigsty.

Alex said to Max-Pol as they walked out to their car, "You will not find this place or this entertainment listed in the *Michelin Guide*. Nonetheless, I give it three stars for the food and the ambiance."

"And five stars for the company," said Max-Pol, laying his arm around Alex's shoulders, "five stars."

ALICE

Before leaving for Rodopos, Max-Pol had sent the Gypsy rug to Alice, along with a letter telling its story. He also told her about the impact of Edward Lear's book. Not only had he and Alex adopted each other as possible cousins because of it, but the nonsense poetry style of Lear had become a private communication between them – a way to acknowledge complicated feelings with a light heart. He included sample verses, especially those about the Jumwillies, a name they had adopted for themselves when they were on an adventure outside the boundaries of common sense. He knew she, too, was a Jumwillie.

As for the photograph of the iris of her eye, Max-Pol had it professionally photographed, so that he might carry a copy of it around in his wallet. Then he took a photograph of his open wallet, with the eye looking out of the inside plastic window. He would send the photograph to her without comment. With Alice he was learning he didn't have to explain everything.

Along with the rug and the wallet photo and letter, Max-Pol added a brief note – an afterthought – saying he was thinking of traveling. He might be in Paris and London. Perhaps they could meet again?
Max-Pol was fishing.
He simply wanted to see Alice again, no matter how briefly.
He could not say that straight out.
He was uncertain of her response.

So, a trial balloon.

*

Only four days went by before her reply came. A shiny black folder – sealed with tape. And an ivory stationery envelope, marked "please open first." Inside, this letter:

Max-Pol, dear Max-Pol:

The Gypsy queen sits on her magic carpet and exorcises your pen. (You must have guessed by now that I have it.)

From a book of spells, rites, and ceremonies: "Drive all illusion from this pen. Direct the creature in the ink to perform its dances truly. In the name of She who created All. In the name of Him who directs All. In the name of That which taketh All away."

Pilar and Hypatia and Marie-Pascal and Alice think maybe we would like to see you again. May is best. Early. London better than Paris. With all my heart I think the meeting should be brief. Let's say an hour. That may be enough. Trust me. I fear illusions created in the last few months may not stand up to reality.

In the spirit of the spell cast on your pen, I will tell you some truths now. I have felt a little guilty for not clearing these things up before.

Of course, I am not a nun. You must know that by now. Others at that conference mistook me for a nun, so I suppose you may have as well. I've liked thinking you even once imagined that I might be. Sister Alice now tells all, Just in case some doubt lingers: on the way to that conference most of my luggage was stolen from my unlocked car while it was on the ferry. All I had to wear was uniforms from my rowing crew and the clothes I could buy at a crossroads discount store. It gave me a severe appearance, I admit, but the simplicity appealed to me. And I was feeling nunnish.

My "real" name is Allyson Octavia Riley. That's what's on my driver's license and birth certificate. The old dear who was the conference registrar somehow turned it into Alice O'Really on my name tag. A wonderful name, don't you think? I think our most real names are those we give ourselves - and they can change over time as we change. "Alice O'Really" was like an unexpected birthday present. I have also used Elspeth Mucklebackit on occasion, just to name one more me you've not met yet.

(Do you have any secret names?)

Strictly speaking I'm not hearing impaired, though I have minimal hearing in my left ear from birth, which means I've always tended to look closely at people's faces when they talk and have developed a certain ability to lip-read. When I have a case of serous otitis, as I did when we met, I might as well be deaf. You know how that works. Major head cold and a long plane ride from New York. Ear infection. And cement head. Drugs for pain and sleep and infection made me a little more loopy than usual. In addition, my physician told me not to use my voice for two weeks because I might become permanently hoarse. So I fall into being a semi-deaf mute out of self-protection, I suppose because I'm tired of explaining, but I'm also intrigued with how people deal with me like that.

Now I will say these complicated things as simply as I can:
I've had some bad relationships with men. Not all, just some.
But especially doctors. My father was a doctor. And so forth.
I don't trust men. I avoid men. Well, not all, just some.
But here is the last truth: I wish otherwise.
I have some wishes, too, you see - we never talked about mine.
(This next sentence makes me anxious.)
Whatever has come between the two of us makes me very happy.
It's true, I also needed a Witness. I just didn't know a name for what I needed, and you gave me that. I'm very afraid of losing what we have by letting it become the same old thing that always seems to have to happen between men and women. Same old won't work for me.

Whenever we meet again, please, please remember these things about me.
You must.
There. That's a lot more than I intended revealing when I started writing. Maybe the spell on the pen and ink worked. The enclosed is to be placed alongside your front door. It is a sign of the protection of the Gypsies.
From one Gypsy to another.

The shiny black folder held a piece of cardboard, to which was attached a single piece of fine white silk. On it was the full print of a human hand - in bright blue ink. A woman's hand - small, slender. A left hand. Hers? The hand of the Gypsy queen?

Max-Pol leaned back in his chair. Involuntarily, he took a deep breath. He had hardly breathed while he read the letter. She had put down her own masks, and put aside the masks he had given her as well. As directly as she had approached him that day on the porch last summer. For the first time, she had spoken to him without contrivances.

Not as Witness or nun - no games. Woman.

Caution lights flashed in Max-Pol's mental control room.

Another woman who had deep-seated problems with men. He didn't want to know about that. He could feel his enthusiasm for a meeting draining away. He smelled trouble. He felt as if he were standing at a crossroads with a map that didn't describe the territory around him.

He was "here" - but where was "here"?

In a funk now, Max-Pol looked again at the blue hand on silk.

Sign of Gypsy protection or Gypsy curse?

He did not put the handprint by his front door. He put it and the letter in the black folder and put the folder in with the rest of the museum of Alice/Pilar/Hypatia/Marie-Pascal/Allyson and, what was that other one? Elspeth Mucklebackit.

For the first time since this correspondence began, Max-Pol was in no hurry to reply. Let it sit. After Easter he would think of what to do next.

MISFORTUNE

As it happened, Max-Pol spent Easter Sunday in bed.

A hospital bed. The top of his head wrapped in gauze, his right jaw and lower lip bandaged, his left arm in a cast and sling, his right leg up on a pillow, and both hands bandaged. Not the culmination of Holy Week he had anticipated.

Easter Week in Crete is *big*. It begins with *Megali Dheftera* - Big Monday, followed by *Megali Triti* - Big Tuesday, and on through Big Wednesday and Big Thursday and Great Big Good Friday, Big Saturday, and Holy Easter Sunday.

Services in the churches seem nonstop. Fasting is intensified. The relatives arrive. The lambs are selected. Passion is in the air. Everything shuts down on Good Friday except the churches. The whole of the culture is poised on the edge of the fulfillment of Great Expectations. Rational thinking is suspended. The penultimate paschal moment comes at midnight on Saturday - the last liturgical expression before the great feast.

As the final minutes of Saturday tick away, the priests and parishioners move outside, leaving the church dark and empty. At the stroke of midnight, it is announced by all to the wide world with a great collective shout:

"Christos ahnesti!" - Christ is risen!

"Alithos ahnesti!" - He is risen indeed! And at this moment, the flame from a single candle is passed to the candles held by the congregation, and moving, living light fills the night.

In Crete, it has long been a tradition for men to fire their guns in the air at this same moment - as a gesture of Cretan freedom parallel to the freeing of the souls of men. Though in some mountain villages this custom is yet maintained, in many places fireworks have replaced guns. Too many bullets that went up in joy came back down in calamity.

It is this phase of the Easter celebration that was Max-Pol's undoing.

Alex and Kostas had wanted to go somewhere special for the Saturday night service - somewhere both beautiful and historic. And also someplace where it would be safe to blow off the substantial store of fireworks Kostas had been saving for just such an occasion. "Is be for Jesus, these *pyrotechnima*." He means no joke. He's quite serious. It's an occasion for expansive, explosive joy.

The choice was the Monastery of the Virgin at Gonia - formally called the "Holy Monastery of *Hyperaghia*, Mother of God, The Guide Called Lady of Gonia," on the coast west of Hania, just beyond the village of Kolymbari on a splendid site above the sea. The monks came here to the Rodopos peninsula in the ninth century.

The present monastery was completed in 1634. It was here on June 23, 1645, that a Turkish force of 100 warships and 350 transport ships carrying 50,000 men landed to take control of the lives of Cretans for the next 253 years. The monastery still displays in its east wall a cannonball fired by the Turkish artillery.

And it is on the shore of this same bay that the invading Germans came out of the sky in parachutes on May 20, 1941. After the war, the caskets holding remains of German soldiers were stacked in the monastery courtyard awaiting final burial.

Deep history is here. Much blood has been spilled in this neighborhood. In good times and bad the Orthodox Cretan spirit has been kept alive here. Both the freedom to worship and the freedom to fire one's weapons are serious business for the monks of the Monastery of Gonia and those who come to celebrate its history.

Not only do hundreds of people come for the Saturday night worship service, but many bring fireworks to shoot off over the sea at midnight. A most joyful, unorganized affair. And very dangerous.

Max-Pol, Alex, and Kostas and his entourage of male relatives left the service a little before midnight and went down to the sea wall below the monastery. A Cretan specialty is to tie a string of firecrackers to a rocket, twist the fuses together, and send the exploding chain spewing into the sky out over the sea.

As the monastery bells pealed midnight, the pyrotechnicians went to work. Roman candles, spinners, small bombs, screamers, and one rocket the size of a bedpost with six feet of firecrackers attached. The rocket went up, but not in the intended direction. Instead of going out over the sea, it went straight up. And was coming straight back down - into the mass of people and unexploded fireworks. A cry of warning, and people stampeded for safety.

Max-Pol only remembered losing his footing and falling backward over the bank toward the sea-slammed rocks below. The rest of the story was pieced together for him over several days. He had fallen about eight feet onto sharp rocks just as a wave hit. He was rolled by the wave, sucked back along the rocks, rolled again across the rocks, and dragged back again toward the sea.

Kostas and Michael had gone to his rescue. Even Alex had clambered down the bank and out onto the rocks to help. Max-Pol was limp when they pulled him out of the water and up higher onto the rocks. They thought he was dead. But when they turned him over, he began coughing water and breathing on his own.

By the time they carried him safely out of reach of the waves, he was unconscious. By flashlight, his rescuers saw he was bleeding badly. They feared he might die. Many hands helped carry Max-Pol up to the monastery, in through a back door, and on into the dining room, where he was laid out on a table. Kitchen towels were used to staunch the blood flow, and three doctors were called out of the congregation assembled for the service.

On examination, the doctors determined that Max-Pol's injuries were not life-threatening. He was revived, stabilized, cleaned up, and wrapped in blankets until an ambulance could come.

When all got sorted out at the hospital emergency room, Max-Pol's damage list included a deep laceration from the top of his right eyebrow well into his scalp. His right ear, right cheek, lower lip, and chin all were cut severely enough to require some stitching, as were both hands in several places. He had bitten his tongue deeply and chipped both upper and lower front teeth. A bone in his left wrist was fractured, and there was some blunt tissue damage to his right thigh and knee - more X-rays would be needed.

The rest of him was bruised and sore from being rolled across the rocks by the waves. Quite a beating. But the injuries are not serious. He will heal and heal quickly. As soon as he's sure about the right leg, Max-Pol will be ambulatory - two or three days more in hospital should do it.

Megalo Pascha, he said to himself. *Big Happy Easter.*

Baptism

"Yassas (Hello)."

Max-Pol has visitors.

Alex, Kostas, and Michael. Heroes. They saved his life. If he had been sucked into the sea once more, he wouldn't be here now. And they, too, took a beating. All three are plastered about with bandages, mostly on hands and knees for cuts made by the sharp rocks.

They don't look so good either. They were up all night. Having been patched up, assured that Max-Pol would be all right, and sent home, they have changed clothes, cleaned up, had coffee, and come right back. They have been patiently waiting until Max-Pol is awake because they want to see with their own eyes that their friend is alive and not permanently injured.

They come now more like three little boys than heroic men.

They are grinning. Not smiling. Grinning. A smile can be placed on your face by your brain - "a smile for the camera" - and taken off. But a grin is forced upon you by deep feelings shoving their way up and out onto your face from your heart. You really cannot not grin when the urge is on you.

The reason for the grins is not just the obvious one: that Max-Pol is alive and will be all right. The grins are about something primitive being satisfied. Because of their injuries, the blood of Max-Pol and Alex and Kostas has been mixed - and mixed in circumstances of real danger.

"We see death together," says Kostas. "Death." He has tears in his eyes as he speaks. Blood brothers now, not just casual cousins.

Not only has their blood been mixed, Max-Pol has been baptized.

Not once, but three times. According to the Orthodox tradition, in an emergency situation a layman can baptize someone without benefit of water, oil, or priest. This is more likely to be done to an endangered infant, but as long as it is not done against the will of the person, it is acceptable for adults as well. Alex knew the tradition. And when he thought Max-Pol might die, he baptized him, in the name of the

Father, the Son, the Holy Ghost, and all the Cretans who ever lived.

"Please, God, don't let him die," he begged as he wept.

Kostas, in the meantime, had pulled one of the monks out of the service to come and baptize Max-Pol for the same reasons. And when the monk came, Alex said nothing - here was the real thing. Let it be done right. The monk wasn't sure that Max-Pol was conscious of what was going on or if Max-Pol agreed to the ritual. If not, it could invalidate the baptism, but one look at the determination on the faces of Kostas and Alex and he put his doubts aside, and went on with the formal words and acts.

Kostas rode with the ambulance on the way to the hospital, and when Max-Pol regained consciousness Kostas asked him if he would mind being baptized. Max-Pol said what Kostas thought was "OK." So, just to be really sure, Kostas baptized him for the third time that night. Or, to be accurate, that morning - for all this had taken place in the early darkness of Easter Sunday morning.

Max-Pol remembered none of this. But he would never tell them that. His being a blooded and baptized Cretan was certainly a working hypothesis, and it had come to a most satisfactory working conclusion. He wondered if he had been secretly given a Cretan name in the process. As to the praxis - Max-Pol might have to speak with a priest. Someday.

In later years, Max-Pol would explain that he got the scar on his head when he died and was resurrected on Easter morning, and was baptized three times. He always followed that statement by grinning and saying, "But, as my cousin Aleko always says - that's a long story for another time."

HANIA

Alone, Max-Pol lay in his hospital bed balancing his accounts.

He had almost died - but his friends had saved him.

He had lost a lot of blood - but he had blood brothers now.

He had taken a beating - but everything would heal.

He had missed the Easter lamb fest - but a lamb would be cooked specially for him when he felt like it - compliments of the Amnesia Cafe.

He had been baptized without knowing, but with the most honorable intentions. If it made him more Cretan in the eyes of his friends, what harm?

He is in no shape for a boat-and-train trip from Crete to France - but he will remain in Crete at the best time of year.

And now, if he needs one, he has an excuse not to see Alice-and-her-friends. He could say he is going straight back to Seattle to get a thorough medical exam.

He could do that. But he will not. He will do both. To London for matters of the heart. And on to Seattle for the sake of his body.

*

Waking late in the night - feeling much improved - Max-Pol turned on his bedlight, fumbled around in the drawer of his nightstand, and found his wallet. He opened it. Her eye looked back at him.

Yes. Why not?

*

The next two weeks went quickly by.

Max-Pol was out of the hospital and healing rapidly.

He willed his healing, repressing lingering pain. He limped around using one of Alex's canes, not because he really needed a cane but because Alex insisted, and it pleased Max-Pol to have it. As they lurched around in unison, Max-Pol thought it really was too bad that they could not tap-dance. They could probably collect a pile of coins busking in the streets of Hania. "A Gypsy and His Dancing Bear."

Alex was also in good spirits, despite his family not coming for Easter. Perhaps they would come in September, the time of harvesting grapes and making wine. In the meantime, Alex made plans to go to Oxford.

Kostas' son had come from France for Easter. A quiet, tall, intelligent young man who seemed intrigued by his growing awareness of his own Greekness. And now he had new obligations of special kinship because his blood had been mixed with the blood of all those who helped rescue Max-Pol. He, too, wore badges of bandages. Kostas was proud of him. Out of sorrow for past sins and failures, much joy has come. With tears in his eyes he told his cousins, "Is be good now for us, you know? Finally, is be good."

*

The promises of return made parting easier for Max-Pol and Alex and Kostas. They agreed not to make a fuss about leaving. A feast would be saved for their reunion. Alex invited Max-Pol to spend a few days with him in Oxford on his way back to the States. Accepted.

And the next morning, Alex was away on the early plane for Athens and London, then on to Oxford. He left his precious leather suitcases with Kostas with an admonition: "Keep my chair at the Meltemi - I will not be gone long."

A note had been slipped under Max-Pol's door:

> There once was a man named Millay
> From the land where the antelopes play
> To the sea he did blunder, his flesh rent asunder
> But he's much better now, hip hooray!

> I know it makes too much sense, but the rhyme is not half bad.

> Your cousin, Alexandros Evangelou Xenopouloudakis
> High Lord of the Spherical Learical League
> King of the Jumwillies"
> - X -

Max-Pol sent an express letter to Alice, asking her to meet him in London under the main train announcement board at Waterloo Station on Wednesday, the first day of May, at noon. He also explained about his accident and his condition and his plans. He did not want to use their hour together for a medical report.

She replied quickly. The quality of the reply both puzzled and pleased Max-Pol. Yes. She would be there. If she could. If she could not, it was because she had doubts she could not overcome. Her continued caution seemed a good omen to Max-Pol. Her caution matched his. "Do no harm."

As a final thought, Max-Pol called Alex in Oxford by phone:
"I need a peculiar favor, Aleko."
"And I am an expert at peculiar favors, Max-Pol. Ask."
"It's a little crazy, but I want you to meet me at Waterloo Station, on May 1, at noon. Actually I don't want you to meet me. I want you to watch me meet a woman there. That's all I want - you to watch without being seen. I want you to see her and to see us together and tell me what you observe. It's too complicated to tell you on the phone. I'll give you all the details by express mail. Trust me. Will you come?"

"Ah, indeed! You want a spy?" asked Alex. "Yes! I am your man."

ALICE LEAVES FOR WATERLOO

West of Paris, in the broad lower valley of the river Seine, the first light of morning sun has just gilded the rooftops of the village of Giverny. Alice hands the key to her room to Madame Fleury, her landlady.

"Will Mademoiselle Riley return today?"

"Yes, I'll be back this evening."

A taxi waits at the gate, engine running, the driver holding the door open. But Alice is not in a hurry. When she played her watching-and-following-people game in Paris, she noticed how people walked while shopping or while visiting art museums - wandering, pausing, looking - casually and comfortably moving about. It is the pace used when you wish to *be* somewhere, unlike the pace used when you want to *go* somewhere.

With varying degrees of success she has been trying to move through the world in this way - as if shopping in a great art museum. Slowly. Slowly. Without a mindless rush to a destination, in the graceful way a dancer walks out onto the floor before the music begins. This has not been easy. But Alice does not do easy.

She came to Giverny to live and move about in this way for a season. In her journal there is a list of experiences she wants to have "someday." One item is "To watch spring come to Monet's gardens at Giverny." That wish has been on the list for five years, and has stayed on the list through many revisions. A friend who manages an arboretum told her she would need several weeks in Giverny at least - from late March into early May.

In anticipation, she came out from Paris on a snowy day in February to look over the fence into the closed garden - to see its dormant state - before the transcendence of spring over winter began. She came again in early March to arrange for rooms nearby, and to look over the fence at the formal declaration of spring made by the freshly flowering trees. When the gardens opened on April 1, she was first in line. Like Sanaa approaching the hot spring, Alice eased slowly into the garden, imagining herself a personal guest of Monsieur Monet. Such a grand

258

moment! The long lines of plumed iris seemed like troops assembled for royal review.

She arranged her schedule to spend weekdays in Giverny and weekends in Paris, coming out on Monday evening and returning on Friday afternoon. In doing so, she has avoided the weekend bus tour crowds at Giverny and has had the quietest times in Paris to enjoy the city.

Alice is reluctant to leave in midweek, even for a few hours. The gardens change daily, like a slowly turning floral kaleidoscope. So she will not rush away. She will instruct the taxi driver to take the long way to the station - along the lane that divides the upper and lower gardens. She will ask him to stop and wait while she looks over the fence toward the Japanese bridge arching over the lily ponds. The iris spearing up along the edge of the water now are blue: infinite blue, milk-white blue, and blue that is silvery, blue-violet, azure blue, blue ranging from the pale dusty hue of cue-tip chalk to the dark indigo of deep water, and the blues that have no name.

When Alice shopped in Paris for her spring clothes, she found a silk dress in a blue floral print so perfect that she imagined if she went and sat among the irises, she would disappear into the foliage as if wearing camouflage designed by Monet himself.

She is traveling in this dress today. Her only accessory is a light cashmere shawl matching the flash of yellow-gold in the throats of irises. Monet painted the walls of his dining room in this color. Someday, Alice intends to paint her own dining room in this same lush yellow.

Alice will ride the local train into Paris to the Gare St. Lazare. There, she will take time to stand exactly where Monet painted the interior of the station during the arrival of the Normandy trains. And she will wonder at the eyes and mind it took to see and paint the raw moving power of steam and steel - the same eyes and mind that saw and painted the unmoving stillness of iris and water lilies.

Then she will shift into her gear for getting somewhere in a hurry, moving quickly and purposefully to catch a taxi to the Gare du Nord for the Chunnel train. She is going to London. She intends to be there for only a couple of hours at most before catching a returning train.

More than once she will laugh to herself at the quirkiness of what she is doing. But she will not laugh at the thought of why: Max-Pol.

When she volunteered to be his Witness, she had not foreseen how complex the experience would become. Most of all, she had not realized how much she wanted a Witness of her own. That was a surprise.

To see him again face-to-face, even for an hour, puts the Witness relationship at risk. She fears spoiling a fine thing - for him or for her. Especially since she has so carefully managed what he knows about her. He has not seen her since she playfully, perhaps foolishly, let him think she was speech and hearing impaired. He knows the truth now, but how will he react to the un-cloistered woman who can speak and hear perfectly well?

Still, come what may. She is going.
It is plain and simple: She really wants to see him again.
More importantly, she really wants *him* to see *her*.
She admits that.
Yet, no matter what, she promises herself not to change her mind and stay beyond the agreed-upon hour. Thanks to the Chunnel train, she can treat London as a day-trip excursion from Giverny. She will arrive just before noon and return by evening.

Alice walks to the waiting taxi.
"Max-Pol Millay, here I come."
Would she go if she knew she would not return alone?

MAX-POL ON THE WAY TO WATERLOO

On this same morning of the first day of May, Max-Pol is sitting on a bench in St. James's Park in London, watching tourists watch a brigade of Royal Horse Guards assemble for parade.

Someone watching Max-Pol watching tourists watch the Royal Horse Guards would notice that Max-Pol is also watching the time. Every few minutes he checks his wristwatch.

An hour from now Max-Pol must be at Waterloo Station, which is ten blocks away - a fifteen-minute walk. Already, a good part of his morning has been given over to the kind of walking that becomes aimless as the walker realizes he has set out far too early.

Max-Pol has not lost his way. He has an innate sense of direction, enabling him to progress consistently south from his hotel toward Waterloo. But if asked, he probably could not tell you where he has been or what he has seen along the way. His automatic pilot has directed his steps.

Max-Pol is so lost in his mental labyrinth that he does not notice when the tourist hordes and the Royal Horse Guards and band move off down the street. His attention is focused on the parade of thoughts in his mind. He had meant to do this thinking on a slow sea voyage, but because of his Easter disaster, his hope of coming to England by ship and train from Crete was scuttled. Staying in Crete until the last minute, he flew to London yesterday and treated himself to a night at Claridge's. Despite the comfort of the hotel's old-fashioned luxury, he hardly slept.

The tension in Max-Pol's mind is between excitement and apprehension. Unbridled enthusiasm is restrained by defensive caution - as the rising flow of a river might be held in check by an incoming tide. What began as a trickle of anxious thought when he left Crete yesterday has now reached a near-flood stage of apprehension by midmorning. His mental sentences all begin with words like *What if . . .?* and *Suppose that . . .* and *Maybe we will . . .*

Max-Pol laughs and says aloud, "Aleko, where are you? I have a problem of too many working hypotheses."

He recalls the early days of his medical training - when he had so many theoretical ideas and so little practical experience that every patient's symptoms seemed to suggest half the known illnesses in the book. Then, as now, he was afraid he would cause more damage than cure if his diagnosis was ill-conceived.

"Think," he says aloud.

At this moment, somewhere not very far away, coming to meet him from he-knows-not-exactly-where is a person. A woman who, for her own reasons, has used several creatively conceived names in her relationship with him. And he isn't sure what to call her when he meets her at Waterloo.

Furthermore, she has served as a serious and faithful Witness to the life expressed in his Cretan Chronicles. Never has she questioned what he has or has not written. Furthermore, she has responded with the display of an imaginative mind of her own. And she has asked in her own roundabout way that he become a Witness to her life and thought. And she has told him more about herself than he expected.

Think, Max-Pol, think.

At his request, she has agreed to meet him for an hour to give him a better sense of her - like getting a booster shot to keep some process active. His idea, not hers.

But this meeting invitation is suspect. They could have talked on the phone - had dinner in Paris - met when both were back in the States. But, instead, there is this meeting right out of a movie - on the first of May in London at Waterloo Station, with Alex lurking in the background.

"Waterloo," says Max-Pol aloud. "Waterloo." He laughs.

There is no way around another truth: Max-Pol has always been good at romance. Too good. But, as with someone who finds he's a natural at bowling but now avoids the game, Max-Pol's experience has made him wary of romance. He believes that the best parts of romance are the anticipation of its happening and the memories after it's gone. The in-between reality, for Max-Pol, is like bowling: violent fun, furiously knocking pins down, and then the game is over and what are you left with?

A score.

So. Here it is, spring. May. A lovely day in London town. And the one real female relationship he has had in the last year is with his enigmatic Witness. Another truth: He is lonely. He does not want to be. But he is. And what he has done is to half-consciously project the possibility of romance onto this meeting. Bowling, again.

No. Forget it.

What he really wants to do - intends to do - is to find just enough reasons to continue the relationship as it is - to keep it alive and healthy. For once in his life, leave well enough alone.

Max-Pol congratulates himself on having asked Alex to be a part, albeit a silent one, of this reunion with her. Just knowing he will be there to witness the meeting will keep things straight. Max-Pol is eager to have an opportunity to sort out his reactions later with someone whose judgment he trusts and whose wisdom he respects:

Aleko will know what to do.

Max-Pol now recites to himself the principles that have often kept him from making hasty decisions in medicine: *Primum non nocere - first, do no harm. Second, get more information - as much as you can.*

He checks his watch again. Almost time. He rises and walks down Horse Guards Road at a lively pace. Crossing Westminster Bridge, he slows and stops - to look up and down the river, and to admire the Houses of Parliament, whose clock displays ten minutes before twelve.

He begins walking again, with a calm, purposeful stride. He is, as his father used to say, "Hell bent but in no big hurry."

Max-Pol will be standing under the Waterloo Station clock just as Big Ben strikes the first deep notes announcing noon. In the back of his mind is the nagging fear that Alice will not be there.

ALEX PREPARES FOR WATERLOO

In another part of London, on this same May morning, Alex Evans is at No. 15 Savile Row, the venerable sartorial emporium of Henry Poole & Company. He is fidgeting while standing on a low riser before a full-length, three-winged mirror and good-naturedly harassing the tailor, who is crouched on the floor, fussing over the length of the right leg of Alex's trousers.

"Give up, Percival," he barks, "and have done with it."

Always it is this way. The tailor thinks his skill can conceal and compensate for the unmatched lengths of Alex's legs. Alex does not agree. He does not care about camouflage. But he admires the tailor's tenacity under harassing fire.

Alex came down from Oxford on Monday and has stayed at Brown's Hotel for two nights. This fitting is the end-stage of his annual spring outfitting in new clothes: socks, underwear, shirts, and suit. He calls it "the time to be reupholstered."

"Why," he demands, "should old men wear old clothes until they die and only then get a new suit in which to be buried? What good is that? What do the worms care about fashion and fit?"

It is his firm conviction that old people need new clothes far more than little children do. Little children do not know they will die.

Every year, Alex follows his well-established custom. If he is not dead by February, he orders a new suit to be alive in. Not off the rack - a bespoke suit. He wishes to enjoy choosing the fabric and style as well as wearing it. Though he grumbles, he in fact looks forward to being fussed over by the tailor. He has very few justifiable extravagances left to him. The annual suit is one.

But the matter goes deeper.

It has to do with Easter. From childhood he can remember getting new clothes just before the holy week. When young and poor, these were his only new clothes of the entire year. His annual re-suiting continues to be a small gesture of personal resurrection - a nostalgic display in keeping with his cultural roots.

Moreover, this ritual out of his Greek past helps ease the seemingly unresolvable conflict between wanting to put Crete out of his life forever and wanting to return forever. His unexpected sojourn in Crete these past months has gone a long way toward settling that account.

Since his measurements were on file at Henry Poole & Company, he called ahead in February with his order. And though his timing was thrown off by being in Crete, this final fitting at the beginning of May would do.

This year he felt the need of something a bit Churchillian in style. A softly tailored suit made of rich brown, lightweight worsted wool with white pinstripes four inches apart. Dark green, silk lining. Single-breasted, however. Made to be worn open, with vest and pocket watch exposed. The tailor knew exactly what he wanted. Of course. Poole's still had Churchill's measurements and style and fabric choices on file.

Fully kitted out, Alex straightens up like a guardsman and turns from side to side as he and the tailor survey the three of him in the mirrors.

Pin-striped brown suit: handsome. Pale pink shirt: lively. Black silk tie: like the perfect touch of accentuating black found in old Japanese prints. Watch and chain: dignified - stately touch.

Alex smiles at himself: the Right Honorable Alexandros Evangelou Xenopouloudakis, Knight of the Order of Cretan Cleverness, Beylerbey of Iraklion, Pasha of the Port of Hania, Lord of the Spherical Learical League, and King of the Jumwillies. *Ta-tah!*

He strikes a pose - warmly glowering into the three mirrors.

Churchill never looked this good. All Alex needs is a cigar.

He decides to wear the suit. He has an appointment to keep, and the fitting has taken more time than he thought. Today he is in the secret service, playing spy. The explanations in the letter Max-Pol sent were vague. Amazing that she uses so many names, this mysterious woman.

The tailor sees that Alex and his valise and cane are hustled out and stuffed into a taxi. As the car rolls away toward Waterloo Station, Alex flashes a Churchillian two-fingered V-for-Victory sign at the tailor and shouts, "Onward!" at the driver.

WATERLOO

Alex Evans has not worked undercover since 1941. Not since the days of the Resistance in Crete. To observe someone without being seen – dangerous business. Very dangerous business. Twice he had been shot at by German soldiers. The memories of those times stirred his blood, busied his mind, inflated his fantasies, and invaded his dreams. Absurd. The devious mentality required of him for espionage had been shelved fifty years ago. Deadly serious, then. Lives at stake. Never again.

But today's game seems harmless – a little skulduggery on behalf of romance. A lovely, loony assignment. Surely it is innocent enough merely to watch from a distance while two people talk, particularly if the spy cannot overhear what they are saying. Whatever he does, however it goes, no harm can come of this reconnaissance. Lives are not at stake now. Nobody will get hurt. So Alex thinks.

*

Tuesday. Waterloo Station.

Always a man to carry out his assignment thoroughly, Alex has come down from Oxford a day early to scout the terrain – to sort out exactly how to both see and not be seen.

At noon he stands under the main train announcement board, checking his pocket watch against the official railroad time displayed on the board. Seventeen seconds off.

Alex surveys in all directions. His quarries will meet *here* – and then go – *where*? "We'll sit close to where we meet" was all Max-Pol told him. The nearest place for them to sit is at one of those tables outside that coffee bar. *Over there*, then. Where should he be? Difficult place for hiding. Puzzle.

Mr. Sherlock Holmes would have used a disguise – wander about as a lady traveler, perhaps. Ha. Alex imagines himself as an old, limping woman, six feet tall, with a white mustache. Like hiding a bull in a ballgown. Scarcely a proper disguise. Getting the dress might be amusing though. He has never worn a dress in his life – not even a kilt. How about a kilt? No. Priest's cassock? No. Sheik's robes? No. Nun's habit? Ha. One of those black garments Muslim women wear that cover all but the eyes. What do they call them? Burka or chador? His mind runs wildly astray. Enough, enough. No disguises.

Look around again. Next to the coffee bar is a fast-food restaurant. Look up. Two glassed-in, bow windows. Promising. An upstairs dining area? *Yes.*

The moment he sits down at the table in the jutting bay of the window, Alex knows he's found his lair - it seems designed for his purpose. Brilliant. He has an overview of the vast Waterloo waiting room in all directions. He will be able to see Max-Pol and his lady coming and going, and he can look down on them while they talk. With this seat by the glass, he can be a few yards away and still be out of sight. The reflective quality of the glass will serve as a virtual one-way mirror. Furthermore, the restaurant is not busy at this hour of the day - no customers on this upper floor. Come early, get the window seat and wait. Mr. Holmes would approve. *Brilliant.*

Silly, all this. But Max-Pol asked him to do it, and asked him to wait for more information until after the encounter. Max-Pol must have good reasons for not telling him more. Trust him. In time it surely will make sense. What harm can come of a bit of well-meaning espionage?

*

Wednesday. Waterloo Station.

Alex is in place fifteen minutes before noon. His tray has been carried up for him. Burger with everything, French fries with ketchup, and a large root beer malt. Not that he actually intends eating this mucilaginous mélange - it is part of his disguise, and a way of paying fair rent on his perching place. Wait. Watch. Station time now 11:55.

In nervous absentmindedness Alex begins eating his French fries with one hand and stroking the side of his face with the other, all the while rhythmically tapping a table leg with his foot.

Max-Pol walks into Waterloo through an archway next to the coffee bar. Alex sees him from the back first. Head still lightly bandaged. Carrying Alex's cane, but not relying much on it. Max-Pol stops in front of the announcement board and turns slowly, methodically looking for the woman.

Even with the pink scars of the thrashing the waves gave him on the rocks still showing on his face, Max-Pol looks good, though a bit formal. Suit: navy blue. Shirt: white. Tie: red and blue regimental stripe. Face: tan. The combination of cane, conservative clothes, and bandages make him appear a bit like a noble-naval-officer-home-from-the-war-at-sea. Shift to black and white, change the vintage of the trains in the background, and he appears in the opening scene of a romantic film made in 1941.

Noon.

When Max-Pol suddenly stands motionless as if posing for a photograph, with a slight but barely controlled smile, Alex knows that *she* is coming into the station, making her entrance from off-screen. In the film you would see close-ups of their faces. Anticipated pleasure. Affirmative anxiety. Longing. The music rises.

The first view Alex has of Alice is from behind. Trim figure, dressed in pale blue, a golden-yellow shawl around her shoulders. Thick, wavy white hair. Alex leans forward and lifts his eyebrows. Has he been told about the white hair? Just how old is this woman?

Max-Pol and Alice move in cautious slow motion, each waiting for the other to take the lead in the dance they have come to do. Max-Pol is still smiling, but the smile has come to life. Wide and unrestrained now. She must be smiling back.

She holds out her hand, and he takes it without shaking it - holds it like an unexpected gift - delicately, as one might accept an antique teacup.

Dropping hands, they turn and walk toward the coffee bar.

When Alex sees her face, he lurches forward, then catches himself just as he is sliding off his chair.

"*Oh my God,*" he whispers. "*Oh . . . my . . . God.*"

A FACE LIKE HERS

Reality has merged into daydream. His own movie.

Alex has never seen clearly the face of the woman in his lifelong fantasy. The face of the woman who comes to him someday, recognizes him, runs to him in reunion, takes his face in her hands, and says with great tenderness something he longs to hear. He has never quite been able to hear her words. He has never been sure what she looks like either. As hard as he has tried, Alex has never been able to bring her face into focus in his mind's eye.

Until now.

Now he looks intently at the face of Alice and says aloud:
"There - there - a face just like hers."

Vertigo. So unnerved that he holds on to the table edge to keep himself steady, Alex stares at her face. Fine, unwrinkled features of youth framed by the white hair of maturity. A face animated now in laughing conversation with Max-Pol. An icon become flesh.

Alex mutters to himself, *A face just like hers.*

For half an hour Alex stares, unmoving, unthinking. He watches only Alice. Watches her every move, every gesture - trying to lock every detail into place in his memory. He is speechless before the fulfilling pleasure of seeing the vague image of his daydream come into sharply focused reality before him. Holding his face in both of his hands, his elbows on the table edge, he leans forward, hypnotized.

Once, when Alice tilts her head back and laughs, Alex is sure she is looking directly up at him, as if somehow she knows he is there. He doesn't move back from the window. He looks directly back at her. His espionage on Max-Pol's behalf is overcome by needs of his own. He wants her to see him. He feels like tapping on the glass and waving and shouting, "Yes! Look! It's me, Alex!"

Abruptly, Max-Pol and Alice push back their chairs, stand up, and walk away. Alex panics. Stands up to see better. Checks his watch. Is it time? No. Only half past twelve. They were going to talk an hour. Until one o'clock. He looks up again and sees Max-Pol and Alice going downstairs into a bar. To be in a quieter and more intimate place, no doubt. *Damn!* Can't follow now. Max-Pol said she would probably be taking the next train to Paris. Can't follow then. *Damn! Damn! Damn!* The committee of voices in his head goes into emergency session:

Pull yourself together, Alex - don't do anything stupid!
No. Turn yourself loose, Alex, go ahead and do something stupid.
Alex, Alex! Think of Max-Pol. Think of Alice. Don't mess things up.
Think of something, Alex. Do something, don't just sit there!

Yes. Yes. There is something he can do.
Do it now.
"Onward!" he shouts.

WAITING ROOM

Fifteen minutes later, breathing hard, Alex is sitting in the Eurostar waiting room, having rapidly retrieved his valise from storage, bought a first-class ticket on the Chunnel train for Paris, and passed through the customs and immigration formalities.

The last time in his life he had moved with such single-minded dispatch was the day the Germans invaded Crete - when he had gone over the back wall of the Villa Ariadne as the paratroops ran up the front driveway. Emergency then. Emergency now.

But then he knew what he was running from and why. Now he has run toward something, but what and why he cannot yet say. Alex's Committee keeps him under interrogation.

What if she doesn't come? I'll go back to Oxford.
What are you going to do when she comes in? Don't know.
What if she comes in with Max-Pol? Hide.
Just in case, hide now! Yes!

Alex moves to the far end of the waiting room, to a chair beside a pillar. He can see the waiting room entrance, but all he has to do is sit back in his chair to be hidden from view behind the pillar.

If she comes in with Max-Pol, it means their wanting to be together is
strong enough to break their agreement to spend only an hour together.
Right. It means they're going to Paris together.
And if she doesn't come, it probably means the same.
Right. They're staying in London together.
In either case, mind your own business and leave them alone.
But, but . . .
No buts. Three's a crowd, Alex.
If she comes and she's alone? What then?

A flash of pale blue and golden yellow moving through the hallway into the waiting room catches Alex's eye.

He leans forward.
Alice.
Alone.

She seems disarrayed. Not at all the confident young woman he first saw an hour ago. Her face is flushed. And she's disoriented enough to bump into an older woman ahead of her. She sits down in a seat in the most deserted part of the waiting room, drops her purse on the chair beside her, and covers her face with both hands. Weeping?

Alex's attention shifts instantly from his needs to hers. Tears draw him as smoke draws a fireman. Without considering the consequences or consulting his Committee, he rises and limps the length of the waiting room and eases into a seat opposite Alice. Sitting still, barely breathing, he waits. He wants to reach out to her to ask if she is OK or if she needs help.

Wait, Alex, wait.

Alice is recovering her composure. With a handkerchief, she wipes tears from her face. Carefully folding the handkerchief and replacing it in her purse, she pulls tissues from a package and blows her nose.

Opening her compact, she surveys her face. After lightly smoothing over the tear streaks and shiny spots on her cheeks and nose, she refreshes her lipstick and weakly smiles at herself in approval. She looks up in search of a wastebasket and tosses her used tissue into it.

Alex sits still, a little dazed. What to do? What to say? When to say it?
Wait, Alex, just wait.

Alice breathes deeply, sighs, and settles back into her chair. She lifts her head, gazing off into the distance. Some vague provocation interrupts her reverie. Slowly her eyes focus on the figure sitting just across the aisle in front of her.

(Vintage man. Cane. Handsomely dressed. Pink shirt, black silk tie, brown chalk-striped suit. Patrician face. White hair and mustache. Great bushy, black eyebrows. Eyes like caves. Smiling.)

He is looking directly at her. Alice senses she's being affectionately addressed with an embracing silence. The man's smile broadens. Well!

Surprising. Not offended. Pleased, flattered even. There's something very familiar about this man. *Do I know him?* He seems to be waiting for her recognition.

Unconsciously, Alice responds to the persuasive power of his attention - relaxes, unfolds her arms, and drops her hands, loosely clasped, into her lap. And suddenly: Click - it comes to her. She and Max-Pol have just been talking about Alex Evans. Can it possibly be?

"Alex Evans?"

Relieved, he winks at her, pulls his red rubber nose out of his pocket, sticks it on his nose, and grins. In the euphoria of her recognition, it is all he can manage. For once, Alex Evans is at a loss for words.

Alice laughs aloud. Alex Evans, who else? What to say? A customary how-de-do won't do. Remembering Max-Pol's account of the place of the nonsense poetry of Edward Lear between himself and Alex, she says, as if they, too, have been carrying on in this way:
"Well, then. Jumwillies?"
Alex laughs and replies, "Jumwillies, indeed."
Alice continues: "Surprising to find a Jumwillie here."
Delighted, Alex offers:
"Jumwillies come at the call of a tear."
She pauses, thinking, and says,
"So - Jumwillies must be nothing to fear?"
And he replies:
"They belong to the lodge of our friend, Mister Lear."

A sensate silence encloses them. Neither wants to break this delicate, intimate spell with mundane conversation. Continue. Alex raises his eyebrows, holds up two fingers - begin again:
"The Jumwillies prance about, high on the wire."
(Pause.)
"The Jumwillies dance while their lips are on fire," she replies.
(Pause.)
"The Jumwillies' toes can be used as a lyre," he says.
(Pause.)
"When all of them sing, they're the Jumwillies' choir."

They grin at each other.

This is rarified air.

Alex holds up three fingers extended in her direction, raising his eyebrows in questioning invitation. Alice's turn.

"Jumwillies, Jumwillies, all in a row."

"Jumwillies rain, Jumwillies snow."

"Jumwillies come and Jumwillies go."

"And nobody knows what the Jumwillies know."

All this without once breaking eye contact. Two people looking into the open windows of each other's private life. All this with little hesitancy. Two experienced actors saying the lines of a play with the ease of those who have confidence in themselves and each other, and the authority of those who speak lines from a script they themselves are writing and directing even as they act it into life.

Their intuitions whisper what their rational minds reject: for all their apparent differences, they may be more like one another than anyone else they know or will ever meet again. Out of this will come a relationship unlike any connection they have now or have had or will ever have again.

How far will they go in understanding this? Uncertain.

The knowing will come in seemingly minor moments. One day, for example, they will wander down a pebbly beach in Crete and find at the end of the walk that they have each picked up five small stones for keepsakes. Stones identical in size and shape: four white and one black. They will put the stones on a table in the same arrangement: in a square with one white stone in each corner and one black stone in the center.

Such a pattern has a formal name: quincunx.

Found in architecture, folk art and landscaping.

Gamblers know the pattern best.

Quincunx is the arrangement of five on cards, dice and dominoes.

"EUROSTAR TRAIN 934 FOR PARIS AT 14.23,
NOW BOARDING."

They rise at the same time.

"Where are you going?" Alice asks.

"I have a ticket to Paris," says Alex.

"Come with me, then," she says. "Come with me."

In reply, Alex makes a slight nodding bow and offers his arm. Alice takes it, and they walk down the aisle of waiting room chairs in the way guests at a fine wedding might exit a church, knowing there is a reception, with dancing to follow.

THE CHUNNEL TRAIN

The trainmaster is accommodating.

"Can't reseat you now, sir, but we're not full. Shouldn't be a problem to put you together after we're under way. Go ahead and take the seat you reserved. I'll sort it out."

Alex and Alice board the sleek silver train two cars apart. Alex is relieved. He needs time to regroup. Now what? He hates lies and liars and he hates deceit and duplicity. Not that he's led a life innocent of deception. But the older he gets the more he prides himself on achieving a reckless veracity. While he may be a master of social graces and white lies when called for, in matters of importance, candor is his stock in trade. No lies.

And even more than fooling other people, he hates fooling himself. For all that, he is lurching headlong into an undeniable opportunity to make a first-class fabulist fool of himself. Alice will ask why he's going to Paris. Immediately, he's in the cauldron.

> *Because you're the face in a dream.*
> *Oh, brilliant, just brilliant.*
> *Because I'm playing spy for Max-Pol.*
> *Right, Alex, throw the spanner right into the works.*
> *Because I'm an impulsive man who has made an ill-conceived move.*
> *Because I'm drawn to you in a powerful way and I cannot say why.*
> *I'm so confused, but I'm deliriously happy.*
> *There's the truth.*

But there is too much truth in that. And that truth may get him pity at best, and at worst, disapproval, or even contempt. Alex's Committee shouts in near unison:

> *Get off the bloody train, you fool!*

He stands, and is gently dropped right back into his seat as the train eases out of the station. Too late.

When the conductor locates him, Alex is in the bar car drinking a double gin and tonic. Bombay Sapphire gin, Schweppes Indian tonic, no lime, tall glass, one ice cube. His usual going-over-the-top-under-fire bracer.

"Got you arranged, sir, in the lady's car. Moved your kit, too." Alex reaches for his wallet. A gratuity is in order.

"No need, sir, the lady's taken care of everything."

"Well, then. Well, then."

Finishing his drink in one long swallow, Alex lurches off in the direction of the lady, who, he hopes, may take care of him as well.

Alice is riding backward in the window seat of a four-seat compartment equipped with a table. As Alex sways back and forth into the car, trying to stay in sync with the movement of the train, he slows his pace, diminishes his limp, stands a little straighter, and practices taking the initiative with his first line, *Oh you of many names, what shall I call you?* or *What would you have me call you?*

He notices Alice has gathered her hair and pinned it loosely in a casual heap on top of her head. She's also removed her shawl and is looking down, arching her neck. Lovely. What if he just eased up behind her and kissed her lightly there? Hello.

Good God, no! Calm down, easy on, Alex.

Alice looks up, sees Alex reflected in the glass of the door at the other end of the car, and waves at the reflection. Caught. Flustered at being surprised in his moment of small desire, his mind goes blank. He eases into the seat opposite Alice, fumbling around in the pockets of his mind for his notes.

But Alice takes charge of the moment.

"I can't believe it. Alexandros Evangelou Xenopouloudakis. What a coincidence! Do you know I've just seen Max-Pol Millay? We were talking about you. And here you are! What takes you to Paris?"

With her husky voice she throws coils of questions around him, charming and disarming and holding him at the same time. But her use of his Cretan name alerts the male Greekness in him and he recovers, dropping his chin onto his hands folded on top of his cane, raising his eyebrows, and dropping his voice into its richest bass register.

"You remember my full name. Not many people do. I am flattered. And I remember all the names Max-Pol says you have: A. O. Riley, Alice O'Really, Pilar Azul Pujol, Hypatia Loulaki Xetrypis, and Marie-Pascal Ramboulet. At least those. There are probably many others. But what would you have me call you? What's your name today? Who are you at this moment?"

It is Alice's turn to be charmed and disarmed.
"I knew who I was when I got up this morning. I'm not sure now."
"That's *Alice in Wonderland*."
"And that's me, I'm afraid. Alice in Wonderland."

"Well, then, I shall call you Alice, as Max-Pol does. But you didn't seem to be in Wonderland back there in the waiting room. You seemed in real distress, as if you were fleeing from an unhappy experience of some kind." Alex relaxes and sits back. He has gained the initiative. Or so he thinks.

Alice looks out the train window at the landscape shifting from suburb into the green countryside of southern England in May. She turns back to Alex with a shrewd, investigative look.

"Now I get it. Now I see. How could I have been so naive? You must have known I was meeting Max-Pol at Waterloo. And you probably know as much about me as I know about you. And Max-Pol must have put you up to this train ride. Admit it."

Alex smiles feebly. "Well, yes and no. It is true that Max-Pol asked me to meet him at the station, and true that I saw the two of you together, but, if it makes any difference, I'm sitting here entirely on my own. Max-Pol doesn't know. And . . . I know very little about you, actually. Max-Pol has been beyond discreet. Perhaps you will tell me more?"

Alice looks out the window again as she speaks:
"All right. But I don't want to talk about Max-Pol. Not because I don't want to tell you - it's just that I'm too puzzled myself. Nothing bad happened at the station. That's why I was upset, I suppose. I was relieved that all went well, and I didn't say or do anything I'd regret. Being together was just right."

She turns back to Alex, tears welling in her eyes.

"I'll tell you this for certain, Alex."

"Please call me Aleko."

"All right, Aleko. As I walked away from Max-Pol I was nonplussed.

"If he had called out to me - if he'd said something stupidly romantic like 'Don't leave me,' or 'Wait, I'm coming with you,' or even, God forbid, 'I love you,' I would have kept going and never looked back. Never.

"But it's what he didn't do that confused me. He said none of that. He let me go. So simply - 'Thank you so much for coming. Let's continue - Witness for Witness. Goodbye, for now.' That's all. I've never been that close to a man who didn't want something more."

"Perhaps he did not find in you this time what he found the first time, or what he has imagined you to be since?"

"No, I know rejection. We're still connected."

"So you're even more attached to him because . . ."

"I don't know. I just don't know."

"But you don't want some consequences of attachment, right?"

"Right."

"Love."

"No, no. Not love. Don't even use that word, Aleko."

"Forgive me if I have assumed too much. I know there are many ways to be attached. Forgive my limited choice."

Alice takes her handkerchief out of her purse, blots her tears, carefully refolds the handkerchief, and places it on the table. She looks out the window, then back at Alex. It's hard to stay crosswise with this man.

Alex offers a line in keeping with the rituals of their club:

"Jumwillies often read each other's minds."

"Jumwillies get caught in each other's binds," says Alice.

"A Jumwillie jumps at whatever she finds."

"And Jumwillie jam comes in different kinds."

Alex and Alice sit motionless - eyes locked again. Both knowing that this level of eye contact between two people is uncommon, usually uncomfortable, but in this case they are both doing exactly what they want to do: to see each other and be seen - without evasion.

Alice folds her hands together on the table before her. At that moment, the train enters the long tunnel beneath the sea and rushes into darkness. The light inside the train dims. Alex reaches out and places his hand on Alice's hands. In comfort or affection, Alice cannot say. He doesn't pat her hand, or squeeze it. His hand is simply, unambiguously there on hers.

She does not move her hand.

*

In the timeless twenty minutes in the Chunnel, Alice sits still. In the dimness, she feels her skin flush. She remembers the afternoon in the hot spring at Arima. If she still had the invisible ink on her skin, Alex would see the Japanese poetry when the train flashes back into daylight.

Just before that moment, Alex removes his hand, picks up Alice's handkerchief, and puts it in his coat pocket. The gesture reminds Alice of the time she took Max-Pol's fountain pen. She understands this claiming of a keepsake that connects and seals relationship. She says nothing. He knows. She knows. Done.

*

"Do you know that I also use the name Sanaa?" Alice asks.

"No, but I would like to know under what circumstances."

Alice laughed. "Well, Mr. Xenopouloudakis, Max-Pol says you like long stories, and I will tell you one if you are interested."

Alex said, "My time is yours."

"I know a limerick about time," says Alice.

> *There was a magician from Wight,*
> *Who could travel much faster than light.*
> *She started one day, in a relative way,*
> *And came back on the previous night.*

Just Before Paris

The Eurostar reached its maximum speed crossing Normandy. More than 300 kilometers an hour. For most passengers it is hard not to notice the fast-forward quality of the experience. Like being in a jet airplane at the moment of runway liftoff. But the train stays on the ground. Disconcerting.

But not to Alex and Alice. Sitting in the same car with them, you might notice they were entirely focused on one another, oblivious of the speed and scenery, talking like two old friends on a park bench.

"So there you have it, Aleko. The story of Sanaa and the invisible tattoo."

"About this invisible tattoo . . ."

"Yes?"

"I must say it's a singularly erotic image."

"Yes?"

"When will you have it done?"

Alice looked at Alex over the top of her glasses. Interesting. He had not asked "if" but "when." As if he took it for granted that she was quite capable of doing it.

"First, I'd have to persuade the Japanese master, Morioka, to accept me as a client. Then he would have to believe I'm serious enough to carry it through. And I would have to move to Kyoto. It means three years of weekly sessions to finish. And the Japanese technique is very painful. I've seen it done. The color is pushed in slowly by hand with multi-tipped steel tools, not done quickly with a Western-style single-needle, electric machine. It's expensive too."

"So?" Alex raised his eyebrows.

"The philosopher, Fabuliste Curnonsky, says of such exotic enterprises that they're like saddling and riding a zebra. If you're determined, it can be done. Others have done it. But whether it's really worth all that trouble to you and the zebra is the question."

She paused. "But, I suppose . . . if the right zebra came along . . ."

"Ha. Very good. The right zebra."

"So far," said Alice, "my experience with zebras has been limited."

"I have a tattoo," said Alex.

"You? Where? Why? Don't tell me it's a long story for another time."

"Yes, me. The tattoo is on the stern part of my anatomy. A remnant of group exuberance in my university days. The members of my rowing club all got them."

"Go on. What's the tattoo?"

"A blue frog."

"Just a blue frog, that's all?"

"Some aspects of its anatomy are biologically incorrect and over-ambitious."

Alice looked at him over the top of her glasses again.

"You mean to tell me it's an amphibian with an erect human penis? In plain English, you have a frog with a hard-on tattooed on your butt?"

"Well, actually, yes, I suppose you could say that."

"Ha. Aleko, how charming. How big is it? I want to see it."

"No, never." Alex blushed.

"Aleko, you're embarrassed."

"Not embarrassed, just a bit titillated, if you want to know the truth.

"It's been a long time since a beautiful young woman has asked to see my naked behind. Such requests were part of our hopes when we had the tattoos done, of course, but it never happened, at least not to me. We once mooned another rowing club when we won a race, but I don't think they noticed the details of our tattoos.

"You are the first woman to ask to see the frog, if you want to know the truth. And I also wonder what it looks like - if it has changed over time. I myself have not seen it for many years. I forget it's there."

"Promise to show me. If you don't, I'll secretly stick a sign on the back of your coat saying, 'Ask to see the frog on my butt.'"

"You wouldn't. Yes, you would. Well, then. Sometime.

THE
JUMWILLIES' FIGHT SONG

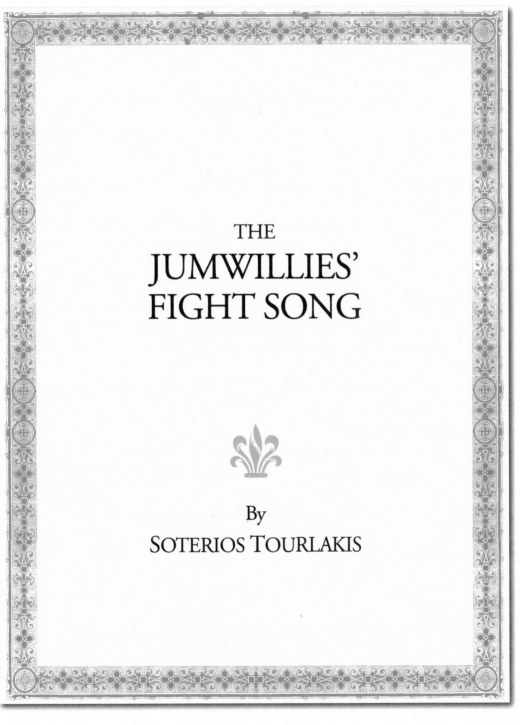

By

SOTERIOS TOURLAKIS

The Jumwillies' Fight Song

285

Jum-wil-lies, Jum-wil-lies, all in a row. Jum-wil-lies rain, and Jum-wil-lies snow.

mp

Jum-wil-lies come and Jum-wil-lies go, and no-bod-y knows what the Jum-wil-lies know.

poco cresc.   *mf*

Boom - bah, boom - bah, boom - bah, boom! Jum-wil-lies fight, and Jum-wil-lies zoom!

poco cresc.   *f*

ff

PART TWO

Ariadne
and the Jumwillies

Including

The Illustrations of Louka Mahdis

The Music of Soterios Tourlakis

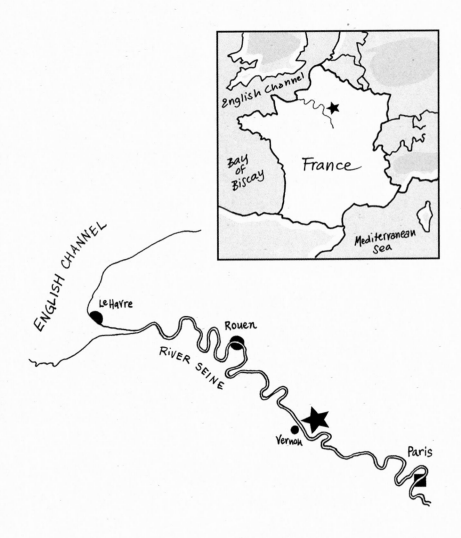

WEDNESDAY, MAY 1

Click . . . click . . . click . . .

If I make it up, can I live it down?

Alex shuttled amber beads along the cord in his hands, as if each bead of his *komboloi* were a hypothesis in an equation he was working on the blackboard of his mind. He was considering truth and fiction and Alice.

Click . . .

Never lie, but do tell the truth that is useful for the time being.

Click . . .

Do not answer questions that are not asked.

"And never, never assume you can read anybody's mind," Alex said aloud, "especially not the mind of Alice."

Click . . .

*

Twilight. Alex stood on the balcony of his second-floor room overlooking the village of Giverny. Beyond the village, poplar trees, tall and slender, marked the course of the River Epte as it wandered its small way across multi-greened meadows to merge with the Seine shoving westward along the distant chalk cliffs, toward the sea at Le Havre.

When this day began he had expected to spend the evening at his favorite London roast beef restaurant, learning all about Alice from Max-Pol. Tomorrow, they would have gone up to Oxford and set out for a few days together into the countryside on his canal boat. Instead, here he was in France, in Giverny, about to have dinner with Alice, about to discover her in person.

And tomorrow?

About tomorrow he is uncertain.

But Alex likes uncertainty - it is the source of surprise.

Click . . . Click . . . Click.

The first question Alice had posed when the Eurostar came out of the Chunnel into Normandy was the same question he had been turning over in his mind, What about Max-Pol? He said he was going to meet you later.

"I can call him now from the train and tell him I followed you to Paris on impulse. And that I will catch the train back in time for a late dinner or an early breakfast."

"Call him, then," said Alice. "There's a phone in the vestibule."

Max-Pol was not at his hotel, but Alex left the message, adding that he would call again at seven. As he returned to his seat, Alice said, "I forgot to tell you that I'm not going to stay in Paris. I'm going on to Giverny. I've been staying there this spring to watch Monet's garden bloom."

"I would like to see that garden," said Alex.

"Then you must come with me," said Alice.

"Now? Today?"

"Why not?"

"What about Max-Pol?"

"Call him again. Tell him I want you to come to Giverny with me to see Monet's garden. You can be back in London for lunch with him tomorrow. He'll understand. And the more time we spend together, the more you will have to tell Max-Pol about me. And the more I will know about you. And the more you can tell me about Max-Pol. Everybody's gain, yes?"

"Yes, when you put it that way," said Alex.

*

When Alex called at seven, the concierge read him a message from Max-Pol:

> *Glad you are with Alice. This works out best for me. I'm really not feeling well enough to go boating. It seems prudent to go on to Seattle now and get a thorough physical examination. I will return as soon as possible. No more than two weeks. Then we can cruise and talk as long as we please. Will be in touch soon. Warmest regards to you and Alice - Max-Pol.*

"Well, then," said Alex. "Well, then."

He had Alice all to himself.

*

Early evening in Giverny.

In the drippy aftermath of a sudden rain shower, Alex stood under his landlady's pink umbrella at the corner of Rue du Colombier and Rue Claude Monet, waiting for Alice. He was, as always, early. She had left him at the *Chambres d'Hôtes Boscher,* saying she would return for him at eight. But he was too restless to wait for her. Alice would have to pass this intersection.

At first glance, the only person in sight was an older woman, dressed in black, folded into herself, sitting on a bench near Les Agapanthes, a restaurant a few doors down the street in the direction of the church. Looking the other way, toward Monet's house and garden, the street was quite empty.

"Aleko."

Startled, Alex turned toward the sound of the familiar voice, but saw only the old lady on the bench. "Alice? Alice? Where are you?"

"Here."

Slowly, the "old lady" stood up. Then, with a few swift motions she slipped out of her black raincoat, revealing a light blue dress; she drew her black shawl from around her head, down across her shoulders, shook her long white hair loose, removed her dark glasses, turned toward Alex and grinned.

Alice.

Too surprised and too pleased to speak, Alex could only walk toward her, laughing. She took his arm and guided him toward the restaurant door.

*

"Before we talk about anything else," said Alex, "I can report that I have been in contact with Max-Pol, who thinks it is fine that we are together because he feels he should go straight away to the States to have a physical checkup. He will return in two weeks if all goes well. So, there you have it. I have no place to be but here. That being settled, the first thing I want to know is how you recognized me so quickly at Waterloo Station."

"Oh, that's easy. Max-Pol has been writing to me for months, describing you and Crete and your adventures together. His picture of you was very vivid. I think I would recognize you anywhere. When we were together at Waterloo, I asked Max-Pol to tell me more about you. Among other things, he said you were in London, and not far away, because he was to meet you later. Since you seem to dress according to your environment, he was eager to see you in your London costume. One of the last things I said to him was to tell you hello and say that I hoped to meet you someday in person. So, you see, you were *already* on my mind.

"Besides, Aleko, I recognized you because I *wanted* to see you. I wanted to talk to you about Max-Pol. When I looked up and saw you there it was as if I had conjured you up. I *wanted* it to be you. So it *had* to be you.

"You must have similar experiences. You're thinking of someone and they call you on the phone at that very moment. Or you dream about someone you haven't seen for a long time, and you run into them unexpectedly the next day. I don't pretend to understand why this happens. Coincidence? Magic? ESP? Who can say? But it *does* happen. It *did* happen. *Here you are.*

"I admit I was as surprised as you were when I said 'Jumwillies,' but I know all about the Spherical Learical League, and since I also like limericks, I've played a silent hand in the nonsense game between you. It's all really quite obvious when you look at it my way, don't you agree? Our meeting was *required* by our mutual circumstances."

"Well, then," said Alex. "A fairy godmother's command performance. A working hypothesis, at least. You wished me there, and there I was. Do your wishes always come true?"

"You'd be surprised how often," said Alice, "but then I'm careful what I wish for. And I work for my wishes. The truth is, Aleko, if you hadn't come to find me, I would have come to find you."

"Consider us found, then," said Alex, "The Jumwillies are in session."

GIVERNY

In early April of 1883, Claude Monet was both discouraged and desperate. By his own estimation the most recent exhibition of his paintings in Paris had been a fiasco. Neither the public nor the critics cared for his work. No sales. No income. He was broke. His debts were mounting. The lease on his house in the village of Poissy expired in two weeks. Even if he had the money to renew the lease, he found his surroundings uninspiring. Monet had to move.

Furthermore, at age forty-three, he was now responsible for a family of ten. Monet's former patron and friend, Ernest Hoschede, had gone bankrupt and fled all his responsibilities. Ernest's wife, Alice, and her six children moved in with the Monets and their two sons. When Monet's wife, Camille, died, Alice and her children remained with Monet.

They had nowhere else to go.

Somewhere along the way, an abiding bond formed between Claude Monet and Alice Hoschede. Though they could not marry until her husband died years later, they and their eight children became a family. The family needed a home. And the painter needed inspiration.

Moving was required.

Searching further west in the Seine valley, Monet found a house to rent in the village of Giverny. A large, two-story structure whose outer walls were pink, with trim painted leafy green. The colors reflected those of the blooming apple trees in the orchard behind the house. It was called "Le Pressoir" - the cider press house.

It took Monet ten days to transport his family and possessions downriver from Poissy by boat. The success of the move was not immediately apparent to him. It seemed more like exile. He wrote his dealer, Durand-Ruel, in early June to say: *"I think I've made a terrible mistake in settling down so far away. I'm totally disheartened."*

Giverny was about forty-five miles northwest of Paris, reached by taking a train from the Gare St. Lazare to Vernon, and then crossing the Seine and traveling the last three miles on foot or by pony trap.

The hamlet was small in size and rural in character, almost as far from Paris in history as in miles. Largely unchanged since the Middle Ages, Giverny had two streets of low, stone houses with slate and thatched roofs, a modest church, a tiny school, a town hall, a few taverns, two grain mills, and a blacksmith's shop. About three hundred people lived there – mostly farmers, day laborers, cowherds, and washerwomen. A long way, indeed, from the sophistication of Paris and the milieu of artists, dealers, patrons, salons and ateliers essential to the success of a painter.

And yet, Monet lived in Giverny for the last forty-three years of his life. He built three studios there and turned his land into a garden that served as inspiration for many of his masterpieces. In accord with his wishes, he and most of his family are buried in a single tomb in the churchyard a short way up the road from his home. His house and garden continue to inspire. Restored, they attract hundreds of thousands of visitors from all over the world.

Those who are in Giverny when most tourists are not – in early mornings or late evenings – or between October and April when the gardens are closed – will feel themselves inside Monet's paintings as they wander about. Despite the automobile and electricity, the village and its environment are much the same – at another place in time.

This is *la France profonde* – deepest France. The fields, the chalk hills, the streams and rivers, the farms, and the quiet remain.

Those who venture out at dawn will find what Monet found when he settled here in 1883 and walked out into the morning, year after year, to paint the light as it fell on stacks of grain and poplar trees and flowers and water. For all the changes time brings, there is still something in the air that can be seen and felt if sought – an immediate, indelible *impression*. That's how Monet felt about it.

That is what he painted.

Morning mist over the valley
Sun slowly emerging - colors, shadows
in the distance all is soft and faint
soft peach light going green

BLANCHE

In a photograph taken in the summer of 1915, Monet sits on a stool under a large umbrella by the pond in his lower garden. On the canvas in front of him is one of his paintings of water lilies. Standing close by Monet, with her back turned to the camera, is a woman in a long white dress and straw hat. She is leaning forward, focused on Monet and his work. Georges Clemenceau, the prime minister of France and friend of Monet, called her the painter's "angel."

Blanche Hoschede-Monet played many parts in the public drama that is the life of Claude Monet. Historians summarize her roles as step-daughter, pupil, model, daughter-in-law, and nurse/companion.

When Alice Hoschede and Claude Monet merged households, Blanche was eleven. She soon became his favorite child. Only she of all the eight children wanted to be a painter. For the rest of his life, she was the only person Monet truly welcomed as a painting companion, pupil, and assistant. Her work parallels his in content; she painted where he painted. Her canvases were included in exhibitions in Paris, and she continued painting after she married her stepbrother, Monet's favorite son, Jean, and moved to Rouen.

When her mother died in 1911, Blanche and Jean moved back to Giverny to look after Monet. Jean died three years later. Blanche and Monet were alone together. On the surface it might appear a bleak circumstance. All the rest of the once large and lively family were dead or departed. Monet was old, depressed, ill, and nearly blind from cataracts. Blanche was a childless widow living on the charity of her stepfather. Moreover, it was 1914 and the Great War was so close by that cannons could be heard firing east of Giverny. A bad time.

Yet, in the next twelve years Monet regained his sight, built a new studio, painted masterpieces (the great water lily series) and was recognized as a national treasure of France. Visitors noted a sense of contentment, even happiness.

Why? Blanche. More than any other reason: Blanche.

She infused his life with hers. She managed the affairs of the house and gardens, nursed him in ill health, and served as his hostess and secretary. As a colleague, she understood his judgment of his own work, and even helped him slash and burn many paintings he considered failures.

And there was more.

The rarest kind of love. Multi-faceted and multi-dimensional. Their affection for one another moved through countless stages and forms as their lives and family history changed and unraveled. They knew each other as few people do. And in the end, when they were alone, they were everything to each other.

Everything is possible.

Corner at Rue De La Dime looking towards Les Agapanthes

LES AGAPANTHES

At the restaurant the waiter came with the menus, but Alex waved them away, explaining that he and Alice wished to be treated as guests of the house. "Surprise us and please us," said Alex, smiling, "and I will surprise and please you if you do well by us."

Alice and the waiter exchanged amused glances. The waiter shrugged and removed the menus. Alice, a regular at Les Agapanthes, had called ahead to arrange the meal, but if it made Alex happy to play the host, then Alice and the waiter could play their parts as well. The waiter was free to bring what Alice had already ordered, and he would get both the credit and the tip.

She wanted to make Alex happy.

This feeling surprised her. Pleasing men was not something she usually considered when dealing with them, and this gesture of affectionate indulgence was unfamiliar territory. She felt her skin flush. *Change the subject,* she thought.

When the waiter bustled away, Alice began directly. "Let me get this straight, Aleko. You said Max-Pol told you very little about me."

"Believe me. He said he had a very unusual relationship with a very unusual woman who went by many names, which he listed for me; that he was meeting her at Waterloo station at noon on May 1 for an hour; that he wanted me to unobtrusively observe the two of you together; and that he would explain everything later. I assure you that he did not ask me to follow you to Giverny. I insist that I am here entirely on my own."

Alice replied by sitting very still and saying nothing. The Mona Lisa pose. It was her way of drawing people out. But Alex was not fooled. He, too, could sit still and silent. He was thinking to himself, *But, somehow, I know a great deal about you. I cannot say how, but I know.*

Intuition mixed with desire is a heady draught.

(Pause.)

Finally, Alex took the initiative: "What do *you* know about *me*?"

"I know only as much as Max-Pol has told me. He's been writing a long journal. Not about himself. Mostly about you and Crete. He calls it his Cretan Chronicles. He's been sending installments to me since last fall. I thought about giving it to you to read. I really don't think he would mind, but on the other hand I don't want to break faith with him. I should ask him first. And I will. I'd like to know your reaction to what he's written. I wonder how much is you and how much is him."

"Well, then," said Alex, lifting his eyebrows. "Cretan Chronicles? He has never mentioned any writing to me. I have not seen him taking notes. He never uses a camera either. Is he writing fact or fiction?"

"I don't know," said Alice, "and haven't asked. But there must be a lot of truth, because I recognized you in London. I've never seen a photograph of you, but Max-Pol's descriptions of you were so real it was as if you had walked out of his Chronicles into my life. I readily call you 'Aleko' because he does. I *do* know a great deal about you, but *all* through the mind of Max-Pol."

"He is a physician. Certainly fact oriented. An honorable man. I trust him," said Alex. "I wonder that you have doubts about what he has written to you. I thought you knew him fairly well."

"Ha! This is a delicious puzzle, Aleko. It's not that I have doubts - it's just that I don't know - being doubtful and being uncertain are not the same.

"I met him briefly last summer by accident, in somewhat peculiar circumstances. For a while he actually thought I was a nun, and I admit I helped him think so. That's a funny story I should tell you sometime. Anyhow, the next time we met was yesterday at Waterloo. In between, he sent me his Chronicles and I've responded in my own obtuse way by sending accounts and artifacts out of my own life.

"We've not had a correspondence so much as a mutual show-and-tell experience. We haven't talked *to* each other but *in front of* each other, albeit at a long distance. We are *Witnesses* to each other's lives. That's Max-Pol's word: *Witness*. I am his Witness."

Alex raised his eyebrows again. "Now that is a curious notion. Witness. In order to be a *Witness,* must you deliberately avoid being together? To know only what you choose to tell each other by mail - not to be an *eye*-witness?" asked Alex.

"It would seem like that in a way. Though I think this is only a beginning stage of what Max-Pol means by Witness. At least I hope there's more. I would, for example, like to go along on some of your adventures together in Crete. I don't know what he thinks or feels or wants - just where he's been, what he's seen, who he's met. I admit I've tried looking between and above and below the lines. But the truth is, Aleko, you know far more about Max-Pol than I do. You have actually been his Witness without realizing it. I wish I knew what you know."

"Well, then," said Alex, "I will tell you what I know about Max-Pol on the condition that you tell me what I want to know about you."

Alice usually avoided interrogation, especially by men. But she did want to hear Alex talk about Max-Pol. Even more, she wanted Alex to know more about her.

"OK, deal. But I want to think about this. Give me some time. I want your impressions of Max-Pol, but I'm not sure what I want you to know about me. Tomorrow."

Just then the waiter came with a carafe of white wine, a basket of warm rolls, and a small plate almost covered with a slab of yellow butter.
"These," he said, "are all local - from Giverny."

Alex began to discourse at length about landscapes and food and cultural migration. It was his way of respecting Alice's promise of self-revelation tomorrow. Alice was fully aware that her privacy was being respected - just for the time being. She was glad to let Alex talk. It gave her time to appraise and appreciate him.

She wondered to herself, *Aleko, what did you look like when you were forty? Very Greek, I suppose. Black hair, black moustache, and those great black eyebrows. How deadly handsome you must have been. How enchanting your manners and conversation. How many women said Yes to you? How many women still do? Were you a frog before you became a prince, or a prince who turns into a frog at the end? If I didn't know what Max-Pol wrote me about you, would I feel . . . what? Afraid? Flattered? Would I care? Probably not.*

*

Who are you? is a companion to the unspoken question, *Who do I want to be when I am with you?* A delicate collaboration is required of those who wish to successfully ask and answer those questions. There is no objectively accurate answer to the inquiries – only an unspoken collusion to reveal what increases the bonds between.

Alex and Alice ended this first evening in Giverny together intent on allowing the answers to those questions to bring them nearer. They had found each other. She had pleased him as he had pleased her. He would stay a few days.

It was just as well.

If Alex had left for London, Alice would have gone with him.

road corner ivy-covered house

wonderful tree

one window

61- the alley w/poppies

LES AGAPANTUS

View across cemetery, church and
Seine river valley

around the church wall
11th century

Path leading down to the
Monet family memorial -
Simple plaques attest to the
fact that Claude Monet is
buried here. Jean, Michel,
Gabrielle, Alice and Blanche

Abloom with pansies, tulips and
other flowers, all in violet, and
Rosemary bushes

Geraniums

Church Steeple
Against Stormy Sky

THURSDAY, MAY 2

Morning. Just after sunrise.

In the cemetery above the village church, Alice is waiting and watching. Last night she and Alex agreed to meet at the Monet family grave at 6:30, but Alice has arrived early so as to discern what Alex's mood might be from the way he walks to meet her.

Here he comes: Hatless. Without his cane. Swinging his arms. Walking with a steady rhythm - 1,2,3,4 - a 4/4 beat. Whistling a marching tune as he comes. And Alex knows Alice is watching. For from his window he saw her go by in her little-old-lady-in-black outfit. As anticipated.

He had considered coming even earlier to watch her watch him, but that would begin a contest he probably could not win or would not even want to. Why get lost in a mental maze over this? The matter is simple. If she wants to know his mood by watching him come, then he will demonstrate.

Just before walking out the door of his lodgings, he looked in the vestibule mirror and thought, *I am alive. All is well. A world-class rally driver is in the driver's seat of my old bus this morning. Onward!* And, hanging his cane on a hook beside the mirror, Alex marched out the door, down the path, and up the street.

Alex's March

Let us make a game of it, thought Alex, and he marched right on past the Monet family grave and out of Alice's view. Alice laughed, and walked quickly around the far end of the church to intercept him. She came to the street. No Alex. She walked past the church toward the Monet family grave and looked up into the cemetery. Alex was standing where she had been moments before. Anticipating Alice's move, he had gone three steps past the church, then turned and scrambled up the steps and around the church into the cemetery while Alice was going the other way. Alice laughed again.

"Wily, aren't you? Pretty good at hide-and-seek."

"You are late," he said. "I have been here for hours."

The two stood and looked at each other with amused satisfaction. An essential unspoken test had been set and passed:

Want to play? Yes! Let's play.

"Since you are in a sporty mood, Mr. Xenopouloudakis, how about a game of Left/Right/Surprise? It's a perfect morning and a perfect place," said Alice.

"I am your man. I like games. Explain, please."

"Here's the way it works," said Alice. "We begin walking in any direction. At the first intersection, we turn left and continue. At the next intersection, we turn right, and so on. If we come to a dead end or an illegal turn onto private property, we reverse our course and go back and pick up the game again at the next intersection. It's a way of seeing what you might never have seen otherwise."

"I like it. Lead on," said Alex.

"There's one more thing - a complication to make the game work on more levels than one. Between turnings, one person must give the other person an answer to a question *not* asked. It's a way of sharing *clean* secrets instead of *dirty* ones. Most of us know amazing things we are never asked about."

"But I have a lifelong policy of not answering unasked questions."

"You will just have to suspend your policy, then, or I won't play."

Before he could argue the point, Alice plunged on.

"There are two minor conditions: the person not talking is in charge and has the option of skipping one turning if it comes before an interesting answer is finished. If the person talking gets cut short, it's because the answer wasn't interesting or the answer opened up too large an area of discussion and can be continued later. Flexibility is important. OK with you?"

"Yes," said Alex, "This could be a game without end."

"So?"

Face-to-face they stood in the morning sun, each simply enjoying the existence of the other and the prospect of the game. Without taking her gaze away from Alex, Alice lifted the black shawl off her head and wrapped it around her shoulders. Shaking her long white hair loose, she took Alex's arm in hers, pointed at a lane across the way, and said, "Let's go that way. And since I'm in charge, Aleko, you have to go first and answer a question I didn't ask. Begin."

"Well, then," said Alex, "here it is - the first thing that comes to my mind:

> So she went into the garden to cut a cabbage-leaf, to make an apple-pie; and at the same time a great she-bear coming up the street, pops its head into the shop. 'What! no soap?' So he died, and she very imprudently married the barber; and there were present the Picninnies, and the Joblillies, and the Garyulies, and the grand Panjandrum himself, with the little round button at top; and they all fell to playing the game of catch as catch can, till the gun powder ran out at the heels of their boots.

"That," said Alex, "is a mnemonic device invented in 1755 by a director to test the memory of the actor Charles Macklin. I memorized it in two minutes in my university days to win a bet. It is nonsense, of course. But I am a nonsense aficionado.

"It is also part of the answer to the question, What is going on in my mind when I am alone? I am not always doing serious business with myself, you see. Sometimes I am saying this mind-emptying mantra. 'So she went into the garden . . .' as a way of priming my mental pump, using nonsense to lead me to sense."

"Remarkable. Turn left," said Alice, as they came to another lane.

"Give me an answer," said Alex.

"I've got a good one:

> Maria del Pilar Teresa Manuela Caietana Margerita Leonora

Sebastiana Barbara Ana Joaquina Francisca de Paola Francisca de Asis Francisca de Sales Javiera Andrea Abelina Sinforosa Benita Bernarda Petronila de Alcantara Dominga Micaela Rafaela Gabriela Venancia Idylla Fernanda Bibiana Vicenta Catalina.

"Those are all the Christian names of the thirteenth Duchess of Alba, who was Goya's lover, patron, and model. I memorized them when I was in college in Spain and was bored in a history class. I have answered the question, What are the names of a person who has more names than I do? Now it's your turn."

"Excellent! Turn right," said Alex, as they came to the next street.

Despite the purpose of the Left/Right/Surprise game, they were neither paying close attention to the unexpected surroundings their route offered them, nor to the off-the-wall first answers.

Both Alex and Alice were absorbed in the nearness of being arm-in-arm. Both were thinking more about the questions they really wanted to ask than the answers they were giving. So far the answers had been interesting, but mostly a way of avoiding serious matters. The constraints of the game had become provocations. The answers stimulated unspoken questions:

Alice: *What else does he really think about when he's alone?*
Alex: *Would she like it if I gave her a name of my own?*

"Your turn," said Alice. "Give me something short."

"That is easy. I give you attosecond - a billionth of a billionth of a second. That is the answer to the question, What is the shortest measurable length of time?"

"I don't want to quibble," said Alice, "but in theory there's actually a smaller measurement - Planck time - ten to the power of minus 43. You are behind in your information."

"I must be," said Alex, looking at Alice in amazement, "but that is an answer to another question. I must say I am impressed with your knowledge of science."

"That's the real point of the game - to surprise each other. Now it's my turn, and I will, I hope, surprise you. I'll give you answers to five questions because they're short: Cello. Jacqueline du Pré. Bach's Suite for Solo Cello No.1 in G major. *The Countess of Stanlein*, by Antonio Stradivari, 1707. And, final answer, Tomorrow night."

"And the questions, please."

"The questions are, Do I play a musical instrument? Who is my favorite cellist? What is my favorite cello music? If I could play any cello in the world, which one would I play? When will I play my cello for you?"

"Wonderful! I am indeed surprised," said Alex, as they came to a five-way intersection. "Which way?"

"Let's turn just a little left," said Alice, "the road up the hill. Give me another answer."

"I offer you five short answers that fit right in with yours: Tomorrow night, May 3. Nine o'clock. Venus. West-northwest at dusk. About forty-four million miles. And the questions are, When is the next full moon? At what time does it rise? What planet can be seen as the evening star? Where will it be? How far away will it be?"

They came to an intersecting lane, but Alice said, "Keep talking."

"So there you have it," said Alex, stopping and turning to Alice. "Tomorrow night by the light of Venus and the full moon, you will play your cello for me. Where will the performance be?"

"I would have said in Monet's garden. They let me do it once. But . . . maybe . . . ," said Alice, looking around her at the open fields above Giverny, "let's come up here. We can see everything in the moonlight - the village, the garden, the meadows, and the Seine - from where Monet often painted the view."

"Perfect," said Alex.

"And I think we've come to an end to the game of Left/Right/Surprise for now. I know we've walked about as far as is easy for you. You didn't bring your cane either. I sensed you limping a little as we came up the hill. You're in pain, don't deny it."

Alex sighed and smiled. "And I will be just as candid and say that in being with you I was not mindful of my old leg, but now that you mention it, yes, it hurts. Your paying such close attention to my welfare is a lovely gift. And the game and the answers you have given to unasked questions are likewise gifts. I have all the presents I can carry for now. Come. I will buy you coffee and a calvados."

Alice took him by the arm, and they strolled down the lane. Alex began whistling his marching song. In her head Alice's tune began playing: the "Cuckoo Not Song."

She stopped and turned to Alex. "Whistle that again."

As he whistled, she hummed to herself. *Surprise.* The tune in her head fit Alex's tune - a perfect counterpoint.

"One more time," she said, "and listen while I sing along."

He whistled. She sang.

When their music ended, they stood looking at one another in amazement - as they would many times yet to come.

*

The moment was too fine to spoil with explanations. Alice took Alex's arm once again, pulled him close to her to offer support on the cobbled path. And slowly, with an awkwardly syncopated rhythm, they lurched on down the hill, Alex whistling, Alice singing, like two drunks inebriated with the sweet wine of joy.

Alex and Alice

BIRD-WATCHING

"Would you like to see more of Monet's studio?" asked Alice.

Alex looked down Rue Monet and saw the parking lot full of buses and the long lines of people waiting to get into the grounds of the Claude Monet Foundation. "To be honest I do not relish standing in line or coping with the crowds. But what did you mean by 'more' of Monet's studio? I have not seen *any* of his studio."

"Oh yes you have," said Alice, swinging her arms in all directions. His studio was this world out here - all these fields and houses and trees. He painted more of this than he painted in his garden. Those buildings inside the walls were where he tidied things up or stretched canvases or displayed paintings for visitors.

"His *real* work was out here in the real world. We're not going inside the walls today. We'll go tomorrow, early, when we can be first in line. Today I'll take you to a part of Monet's world few people know about. I think of it as going bird-watching."

"I am not an avian voyeur," said Alex, gruffly.

"Trust me. Wait here. I need to get my equipment. I'll be right back."

Alex sat down on the bench in front of Les Agapanthes and watched the flow of tourist traffic become a traffic jam. He pulled his komboloi from his pocket.

Click . . . Click . . . Click . . .

Alice returned wearing a sun hat, fisherman's vest, khaki shorts, and brown, rubber workman's boots. She was carrying a canvas bag and a green, three-legged ladder. "This," she said, "is a lightweight, fruit-picker's ladder. I got it in Vernon and talked a taxi driver into carrying it on top of his car. And in this bag I have binoculars, my sketchbook and watercolors, and a collapsible stool. Come on. The birds are out."

She led him down a side street, across a paved road and parking lot, and around the back side of Monet's lower garden, where there was a dirt path. They walked along between a high wire fence and the Ru, a small tributary of the River Epte, until they came to where part of the flow was diverted into the garden. Alice set up her ladder and stool, got out her binoculars and climbed up the ladder until she could rest her arms on the top rung. She peered into Monet's garden.

"A great day for bird-watching," she said.

"I do not see or hear many birds," said Alex.

"That's because you're looking for small flying, feathered things that sing. I'm really looking at the amazing variety of people and the peculiar things they do, the noises they make, and their plumage. My outfit is a cover for watching people, don't you see?"

"Of course," he said. "When I took Max-Pol to Knossos, I had him stand outside and look at the people on the inside."

"I know," said Alice. "He told me. In his Chronicles. That's why I brought you here. I got the idea from *you*."

Once again they looked at each other in pleased amazement.

Alice climbed down the ladder.

"Now you must practice what you preach. Go on up. I'll hand you the binoculars when you're ready." Alex climbed the ladder and looked over, into the garden.

"Tell me what you see," said Alice.

"A small covey of Japanese finches perched on a bench; A Nordic stork and his rosy-cheeked mate; a slow-moving mass of straw-headed American parrots; a flock of French parakeets in adolescent plumage; pairs of migratory mavens; several double-breasted English matrons; and probably a turkey or two. Without the binoculars I see masses of moving color. No drab plumage in this garden.

"You know," Alex went on, "it would be easy to be cynical about these tourists. But they are no more and no less part of the human comedy than I. It is just like the scene at Knossos, though there the birds have less gaudy plumage.

"I like seeing these northern varieties. To their credit, they have gone to some trouble to come a long way to see this living memorial of a life. They are not shopping. Nothing in the garden is for sale. But they are looking for something. They want to be in the presence of something beautiful. When I look closely through the binoculars I see a handsome Japanese couple - she is in traditional dress - a kimono the color of the iris - Monet would like that."

"Come down and let me have a look," said Alice.

Presently, Alice put down the binoculars and started to speak to Alex, but he was not there. He had taken her stool, walked off a ways, and sat looking out over the fields toward the Seine. She watched him through her binoculars. *A double-breasted great owl. Still dressed in his London suit and tie.*

He was playing with his string of amber beads, and talking to himself.

What's going on in his mind? she wondered.

*

This is all very well, I suppose, but I am not so interested in Monet or his garden. I want to know about Alice. I want her to know about me - not through Max-Pol - through me. I shall just tell her then.

"Aleko?" Alice had walked quietly up behind him.

"Talk to me," she said, "just talk to me - about anything. Answer questions I haven't asked."

KOMBOLOI

Time suspended. A condition for which there is no scientific name. When two people are not yet comfortable with sharing intimate thoughts and not yet trusting the slack water of complete silence, they will maintain time in abeyance by weaving a thin veil between them with long threads of conversation.

Meanwhile, they consider and measure one another. Thus time is suspended, hours condensed into the present moment. Only their intuition passes back and forth through the veil they construct between themselves.

A veil that conceals may also be seen as a net that captures.

*

How can I keep you sitting there for the rest of the afternoon? I just want to look at you, enjoy you, be with you, thought Alex. If talking to her would keep her there, then he would talk to her at length.

"Very well, then, I will answer an unasked question," he said. "It is a very long answer, but it is my way of revealing some things about me that I want you to know. I have lived a life of the mind, and if we are to be friends, then sharing my intellectual interests is part of the price you must pay for my companionship. Agreed?"

"Agreed," said Alice.

"You see me playing with a string of beads, especially when I am alone. If Max-Pol has been writing to you about me, then you must already know something about these komboloi."

"Yes, he said you gave yours to him."

"Then you know how important that set of komboloi are to me. They are more than beads. They are history. Personal history, to be sure, but religious and cultural history as well. As with all history, there are many versions. I will give you mine. Do you like history?"

Alice stretched out on the grass in front of him, leaning on her elbow, head resting in the palm of her hand. "I do. Go on," she said.

"We will start with the prophet, Muhammad, sixth century of the modern era. Allah, it is believed, provided the Koran, in which man is directed to pray ninety-nine short prayers five times a day. Each prayer represents an attribute of Allah. How could a Muslim remember and keep track of these ninety-nine prayers? One idea was to have ninety-nine beans in one pocket, and transfer one bean at a time to another pocket. But the beans might be dropped. Or eaten. Problem.

"Mohammed went one step further and suggested that a hole be pierced in each bean, and that a string be passed through them to keep them together - each one separated by a knot, to keep the beans in place. *Kombos* means knot. As each bead was moved through the fingers, one of the ninety-nine prayers would be said. So the *masbaha* came into being - the Arabic word for the string of beads. It means simply, I recite."

*

Alice listened to Alex with half her mind. With the other half she thought to herself, *Here is one of the most attractive and interesting men I have ever met. If I were a cat I would be in his lap purring.*

He spoke with a deep, soft, melodious voice that fell on her like caresses. Though Alex was giving her information, the tones and in-flection of his voice felt like affection. And he meant it to be that way, weaving veil and net together.

Whatever each would remember about this afternoon encounter, they both would always think of it as an event of courtship - an invitation offered and accepted, however unspoken.

But courtship for what kind of love? Certainly not the usual. No. Something else. A courtship to find out what might come between them and what might not, never mind what name it would be given in the end.

Meanwhile, they sat, contented, in the temple of time suspended.

*

Alex paused. Studied Alice. Raised his eyebrows. Continued.

"The masbaha quickly evolved into the form that is most commonly used to this day. Ninety-nine wooden beads, with a small knot between each one, and a bigger bead of a different shape holding the two ends of the string together. This big one marked the beginning and ending of the cycle and was named the Allah bead.

"Over the years many different materials have been used: olive pits, cherry stones, seeds, coral, amber, ivory, shell, bone, and so on, but devout Muslims insist that the material should come from a living source - meaning no gold or silver or precious stones. Wood is still preferred because it is light in weight, inexpensive, and is enhanced with use, you see?"

"Yes," she said, returning his affection. "Yes."

"In time an additional masbaha came into use - one with thirty-three beads. The believer chooses three of the attributes of Allah and recites the corresponding prayers thirty-three times. For example, *Allahakbar* - God is great; *SophanAllah* - Allah is the creator; *ElhamdAllah* - Praise be to Allah."

"Praise be to Allah," said Alice, gently.

"Praise be to Allah," echoed Alex.

And praise be to you and me and this day, he thought.

*

"There are some minor details as to how the two strings of beads are strung and divided, but there you have the basics. The faithful Muslim wears the string of ninety-nine beads around his neck, under his clothes. The shorter strand of thirty-three is carried in the hands or wrapped around the wrist. About a third of the world's population has a set of these beads and uses them when praying to Allah, five times a day."

*

Alice had closed her eyes. Alex noticed.

"Are you still with me?" he asked.

"Yes, Aleko, I'm still with you," said Alice. "Very much with you."

"As an aside, I should point out that both Buddhists and Hindus use a similar string of beads for similar purposes, though theirs have one hundred and eight beads.

"The Hindus' set is oldest - from 1500 B.C. or before - used to remember the Vedas, but I know least about this aspect of Hinduism.

"The Buddhist string of prayer beads is also ancient – in use shortly after the Buddha appeared in 560 B.C. Still, there is no great mystery here. The beads are a sensible device to aid memory. This is important. They are not in themselves sacred, but are a way to help the believer keep track of sacred thoughts and acts and prayers."

"Next, the Roman Catholics enter the picture. The Christian Crusades began in the eleventh century – 1096 – and went on for the next four hundred years. At some time in those centuries, the Christians picked up the idea of prayer beads from the Muslim East and brought the idea back to the Christian West.

"The Roman rosary is made up of fifty-nine beads, divided into five sections of eleven beads (ten Hail Marys followed by one Our Father). At the end there is an image of the Virgin Mary or Christ. After that is a single cord with five beads on it (one for the Lord's Prayer, three for the Holy Trinity, one for a long prayer to the Virgin Mary) and at the end, a crucifix."

*

Alice lay down on her back, eyes still closed.

"Am I boring you?" asked Alex.

"No," said Alice, "Your voice becomes more like a song than a soliloquy at times – almost a lullaby. Go on."

*

"The Muslims had their string of beads, and the Roman Catholics had their string of beads. The Cretans had none. But beads were on the way. First, a band of Arab pirates came from Spain by way of Alexandria, and they managed to found what is now called Iraklion – al Khandak, they called it – and they managed to control central Crete for a century. The Arabs were Muslims, of course, praying five times a day, using beads.

"The Cretans noticed.

"The Fourth Crusade brought an end to the Byzantine Empire, when Western Catholics conquered Constantinople in 1204. Prince Boniface, the leader of the Crusade, was given the island of Crete as a spoil of war, and he in turn ceded the island to the Venetians, who controlled the island for the next five hundred years. They were Roman

Catholics, who brought with them, among other cultural traits, their own prayer beads - the rosary.

"Again, the Cretans noticed."

*

And Alex noticed Alice, lying there before him, eyes closed, arms and hair spread out on the long grass, breathing like one in the first wave of sleep. She had kicked off her boots and removed her socks, and her shorts had rumpled up, exposing her slender brown legs from thigh to toe. For a moment Alex imagined her naked. Hardly breathing himself, he stopped talking.

Alice opened one eye. "And?" she asked.

"Where was I? Oh, yes. In 1648 the Ottoman Turks invaded Crete, and by 1715, the end of the twenty-one-year siege of Iraklion, they were the ruling power - for the next one hundred and eighty-three years, until they were expelled in 1898 and Crete became independent. The Turks were Muslims, and had brought their prayer beads along.

"Once more the Cretans noticed."

"The Cretans are always *noticing* things," said Alice, sitting up.

"Yes, but now here is the vague part of the story. The Cretans became used to the idea that people in power had special beads, and that these beads were in turn connected to a higher power - Allah - God. Perhaps to associate themselves with power - or, even more likely, given the Cretan personality, to taunt those in power - the Cretans began to carry beads of their own. Not beads designed by religious authority, but by each man as it pleased him. Beads that were *loose* on the string, not tied with knots. Beads that could be *played* with. This is very important to remember: The Cretan beads were not for prayer but for play.

"To this day there are no knots in Cretan komboloi, and there is no established number or size or material or use for the Cretan beads. I have seen strings of seven, all the way up to thirty-five. I have seen the most beautiful precious amber, but also practical stainless steel.

"This komboloi has become a Cretan man's constant companion. Used for mindless amusement, social commentary, expression of moods, and even as a weapon. I saw a Cretan truck driver protect himself from three young drunks by slashing at them with his stainless steel komboloi.

"You can tell a great deal about what is going on in a Cretan man's mind by watching what he does with his komboloi." Alex looked steadily at Alice while holding his komboloi curled in the palm of his hand, tenderly stroking each bead.

Alice noticed.

"Tourists call them worry beads or prayer beads or patience beads, which reflects the ignorance of the tourists. Komboloi are none of these. The tourists buy them for souvenirs, which is fine with the Cretans. 'Business be business,' my friend Kostas says. Every man his own master.

"More than anything else - above all - komboloi are the passport of a free and independent man. A Cretan man. A man like me."

"A man like you," repeated Alice. "A man like you."

(Pause.)

Alice, Alice, Alice, he thought. Alex wanted to lie down on the grass beside her, but he could not. He could only sit there and go on with this string of words that said one thing and meant another. He knew he was babbling on.

"And so?" asked Alice.

"And so. The mainland Greeks have other stories, naturally, as they, too, use komboloi, but we Cretans are certain we invented them. I am never without mine. These, by the way, are an everyday set - inexpensive and resilient - made from forturan, an imitation amber.

"Here," he said, tossing the komboloi to Alice, "hold them, play with them." And he thought, *Hold me, play with me.*

Alice caught the beads with delight and ran them through her fingers. She touched their warm smoothness to her cheek. She felt very close to Alex. "Nice," she said. "Do women use them?"

"Traditionally, no. But modern women buy them for themselves. A dealer of komboloi told me. I have never seen a woman play with them in public. But why not? There is no rule against it. It is not illegal, immoral, or irreligious. It would only annoy men," said Alex, laughing. "But not me. It only pleases me to see them in your hands."

Alice smiled. And played with his komboloi, moving the beads slowly, tenderly through her fingers.

Click . . . Click . . . Click . . .

EYES

Moving to kneel in front of Alex, Alice slipped his komboloi into her shirt pocket, put her hands on his knees and looked up at him, holding her eyes wide open without blinking.

"Look into my eyes and don't blink." she said.

Alex did as she asked.

(Pause.)

"My turn to answer a question you haven't asked. Aleko, look closely at my left eye - look at the iris, and tell me what you see. Take your time. Slowly."

Pleased to have his face close to hers, Alex leaned forward, inches away, and stared. "I thought you had blue eyes, but up this close I see blue, green, and a rust-colored web pattern. It reminds me of what I see in high-resolution photographs of stellar explosions in outer space. And your iris seems to change a little each time the pupil opens and closes slightly."

"Good, now look at the iris of my right eye," said Alice, "and then compare what you see with what you saw in my left iris."

Alex leaned forward again, staring. "The irises are alike, but there are some differences - distinct differences. You have most unusual eyes," he said, leaning back and comparing Alice's eyes.

"Not just me," said Alice, "everyone's eyes are unusual. Nobody's eyes match. Even the pattern in each iris is unique. Let me show you yours."

Reaching into her canvas bag, Alice found her purse and took out a white device the size and shape of a television remote control. At one end was a small, convex magnifying mirror; under that, a protruding ledge, and under that, a blue button.

"Put the ledge just below your left cheekbone, look into the mirror, press the button to turn on a light, close your right eye, look at your iris, and tell me what you see."

Arranging the device as instructed, Alex stared into his own eye.

"Astonishing! I thought I had green eyes, but there are brown freckles everywhere and a dark brown ring on the edge," he said.

He switched to his right eye and was just as surprised. "It is similar . . . but yet . . . clearly quite different. I have been looking at my face in the morning mirror for a lifetime and never really noticed."

He put the device to his eyes and looked again. "I cannot believe it. In truth, I am a brown-eyed man."

"Look at me, Aleko," said Alice, sitting back down in front of him.
"Yes?"

"This exercise in science is the bare bones answer to a question you have not asked me. In fact, you are one of the few people I have ever met who didn't ask me the obvious question, What do you do? Meaning, of course, How do you make your living? Or, in a coarser way, Where do you get money, and how much? Or, in other words, What's a nice girl like you doing in a place like this, and how do you afford it?

"I know you don't know, because I know Max-Pol doesn't know. He also never asked. The point is that I *want* you to know, and I want to tell you in my own way."

"Well, then," said Alex, leaning forward, "tell me."

"I'll put it in a nutshell to begin with. Eyes - irises - are what I do. Or did, actually. For the past fifteen years of my life I've been involved in research and development of security systems based on biometric identification of the iris of the eye. If eyes - especially irises - are even more reliably unique than fingerprints, the implications for security are immense.

"Just before I finished college I was lured into a high-tech software startup company by a close friend, working for nothing but stock options. Remind me to tell you sometime of the non-love affair I had with the guy who set all this in motion. It was the most powerful relationship I ever had with a man other than my father.

"Anyhow. The company was very successful and was bought by Microsoft for a huge amount of money. I woke up one day truly rich - at least on paper. By then I was also truly bored, because for all the excitement of the wild ride the company had, my life had been lived in an isolation chamber. I had become a nun for technology.

"The work had become so valuable and so secret that we had to have a very high level of government clearance just to come to work. And work became a prison. One day, the week after I met Max-Pol, actually, I quit and hit the existential road. He still doesn't know it, but Max-Pol and I are in exactly the same place - going somewhere else - affirmative exile is what he calls it - but not sure exactly where we're going."

Alex looked steadily into her eyes again. "If you do not know where you are going, it does not make much difference where you are at the moment, does it? Here we are - in Monet's Giverny in the French countryside in high spring. That is enough for now, is it not? What more do you want?"

Alice sat very still and silent.
Too many long answers came to mind.

Alex, too, sat still and silent.
They had started to trust the silences between them.
The silences began to feel like promises.

Chemin Blanche Hoschedé-Monet
at the intersection with Rue Claude Monet

Window in sunshine
shadow of roof opposite
slowly climbs the wall

Shadow climbs roof

Rue du Columbier

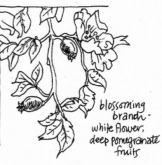

blossoming
branch-
white flower,
deep pomegranate
fruits

long Evening shadows
on Rue Claude Monet (La Terasse)

MONET

"Let us walk a little," said Alex, "I am stiff from sitting."

They strolled along the course of the River Epte, the landscape framed by a line of tall poplar trees and looking much as it did when Monet painted the scene again and again and again.

"Alice, I want to know why Monet is so important to you. His gardens interest me because I like gardening, but his paintings . . . well . . . I am not really . . . a water lily man."

As they came to the stump of a felled tree, Alice said, "Sit down, Aleko, and Professor O'Really will explain. This matter is as important to me as komboloi are to you.

Alice paced in front of Alex, speaking with intensity.

"First of all, you have seen very few of his paintings. Most likely you only know the great canvases he painted at the end of his life. But there are hundreds of others. He painted cathedrals, grainstacks, snow, bridges, meat, frost and ice, rain, wind, trains, people on picnics, seashores, railroad stations, rivers, mountains, cities, smoke - even turkeys. Very little escaped his attention or his brush. He looked. He *noticed*.

"You love ships and boats, Aleko. Not only did Monet paint ships and boats - sailboats, fishing boats, rowboats, and barges - he painted *from* boats. He built two studio-boats to use so he could be out on the water, not just painting from shore. He was first and foremost a *waterman*. He, like you, grew up in a port city - Le Havre - and all his life he returned to the sea for inspiration.

"Monet painted the world where he saw it, when he saw it.

"And that's important - when he saw it. Monet painted outside - rain, hail, sleet, snow, sun, wind, day and night. He was out there *in* it. Wet, cold, hot, dry - he was *out* there. Can you imagine the hassle of working with oil paints and canvases outside with rain pouring down when the wind was blowing? Once he painted so close to the sea in a storm that waves washed over him.

"Monet was clear about what he wanted. He was after the immediate *impression* of a scene. Not from memory or photographs – from life – from being in the middle of it, no matter what.

"Giverny was only a small part of his world. He painted in great cities: Paris, London and Venice. He painted the French Riviera, the Normandy coast, the polders of Holland, and even the mountain villages of Norway. I think I love his snow paintings most of all. *Imagine!* Painting outside in the snow! In Norway in winter! Not the usual image of Monet.

"He painted the same things over and over in series – to get at the way they changed as the light and weather changed. Monet painted *moments*. And all his moments have a quality of calm about them. It's not tranquility, just the magic stillness of a point in time."

Alice sat down on a bench. Facing Alex, she continued with passionate intensity in her voice. "Monet's *art* was his *life*! He learned all the formal rules of painting, and then broke them for the sake of what he saw and felt. He was a rebel in his art, willing to take the consequences of that: failure, poverty, insecurity, and infamy. He almost drowned himself once because he felt so alienated from what the world seemed to believe art had to be.

"I say again, his *life* was his *art* - his finest work.

"I'm not a painter, but I want *my* life to be my art and *my* art my life. He sold his paintings because he had to have money, but his life was never for sale. Nobody could own that but him. Do you understand?"

"Yes," said Alex softly, wishing he had a painting of this moment – *Alice, One Afternoon in May.*

Alice turned away and looked back at Monet's house and garden. She put her hand down on the bench a fraction of an inch away from Alex's hand – close enough for a spark to jump between them, but not close enough to touch.

"Yes," said Alex, "I understand now how it is with you and Monet." And to himself he said, *And I begin to understand how it is going to be with you and me.*

He did not cross the tiny space between their hands and place his hand on hers. He thought about it.

But he did not.

FRIDAY, MAY 3

Morning. Warm. Low clouds. Light rain showers off and on.

Alice sat on her folding stool under a large, lavender-blue umbrella.

She had come at 8:45 to be first in line at the entrance to Monet's estate. In her hands she held an unopened volume of the collected letters of Monet. While waiting she had intended reading and marking passages before making Alex a present of the book. When they parted the night before, she told him she needed time to practice her cello in the morning and, since the gardens did not open until 10:00, she would meet him at the entrance just before then.

She looked at her watch: 9:45. She looked down the Rue Monet to see if he was coming. No Alex. *Where is he? Maybe something's gone wrong. Maybe he decided not to come. Maybe he thought the rain would postpone the opening of the garden. Maybe he's been here all along, watching me.*

She scanned the parking lot, the nearby walls and fenced yards and clumps of trees - guessing where he might conceal himself. No Alex. 9:50. No Alex. 9:55. And still no Alex.

Sadness.

It began last night, when she could not fall asleep for a long time. In her mental theater the *Alex* film was playing nonstop. He and the sadness were there again when she woke at first light. What was the sadness about?

She knew, but she could not deal with it openly: No matter what happened between them, their time together would not be long. They should have met years ago. Think of what there would be to remember. Instead, there were only blank pages of what might have been.

She imagined Alex would disapprove of these thoughts. She dressed haphazardly. Coffee and croissants were left untouched on her breakfast tray. She practiced her cello but found concentrating difficult. Over and over she played variations on a theme from childhood:

Row, row, row your boat . . . Gently down the stream . . .

328

Merrily, merrily, merrily, merrily . . . Life is but a dream . . . "

The tune became a lullaby and faded into a dirge. She was almost in tears when she gave up practicing. Alice did not believe in premonitions, but when she dug deep she came to the bedrock of her sadness: Alex would die - all too soon.

She left her lodgings earlier than she needed to, as if getting there quickly would bring Alex sooner and keep him longer. Now, after an hour of sitting and waiting and worrying, she was about to give up her place in line and go looking for him. *What if . . . ?*

At just that moment a taxi sped up the road, slid to a stop, and out stepped Alex, fully equipped for foul weather: yellow raincoat, green rubber boots, and a black-and-white-striped golfing umbrella.

"Voilà!" he shouted, and stuck his red rubber nose firmly in place. Those waiting in line laughed and applauded this sudden manifestation of exuberance on a gloomy day.

Alice joined the laughter - but tears came as well - from being relieved of her fears. She touched her fingers to her lips and then to his red nose, both in blessing and to confirm that life - this day - was not a dream. *Merrily, merrily, merrily . . .*

*

"I have made a raid on the shops of Vernon, thanks to this grand prix taxi driver," declared Alex. "I admit my attire would not pass without notice in some conservative circles, but it seems just right for a rainy-day stroll in the gardens of Monet. An item for bird-watchers: A yellow-bellied wading booby in full spring plumage. Ha! What do you think?" he asked, turning about.

"Bravo! Well done." said Alice, applauding. "But come on - the gates are opening. We have to move quickly because I've made special arrangements, and we have to stay ahead of the crowd."

They passed through the foyer and down a short passageway into Monet's last and largest studio. Alex stopped. He was unprepared for the size of the space, and surprised at how much it had been restored to appear the way it was in Monet's final years. It seemed as if Monet had just stepped out for a moment and would soon return to work at his easels.

"Come on," said Alice. "We'll come back here later."

She led Alex out a side door, along a graveled path to the front steps of the porch of Monet's house, and across the porch to the front door. A sign in five languages advised that the house was closed to visitors because of weather. Alice tapped on the glass of the dark green door. A hand pulled back the lace curtain on the other side of the glass. The door opened.

"Come in quickly," said Alice. A tall, thin woman closed the door behind them and exchanged cheek-to-cheek kisses with Alice, burbling in French.

"This is my friend, Marie Claire, who is both a docent for the Claude Monet Foundation and a cellist. The house is closed on rainy days because visitors bring too much wet into the rooms. But Marie Claire and I exchange gifts. I gave her a new bow, which she cannot afford, and she gives me privileges, which money cannot buy. Today, for a little while, you and I have Monet's house to ourselves. Take your boots off, and come with me into the sunshine."

Sunshine? Puzzled, Alex shed his raingear and followed.

Monet's Yellow Dining Room

YELLOW

They stood in the doorway of a room that seemed to generate its own warm sunlight. Yellow - everywhere - yellow. Dazzling yellow. Walls and moldings, chairs and tables and tablecloth - even the ceiling - all in shades of yellow: sulfur, butter, saffron, corn, dandelion, fresh egg yolk, ocher, straw, and custard. Whatever the day might be like outside, in this dining room the sun would always be shining, by night as well as by day.

"It would be hard to be unhappy in this room," said Alex. He did not add, though he thought to himself, *But yellow is also the color of caution.*

The room was a constant in Monet's life. Though his mood was often gray or black, this room must have been redemptive. For most of forty-three years he sat down here every day in this pool of light - at 11:30 for lunch and 7:00 for dinner.

The candlelight at night must have intensified the yellows. Sometimes yellow, lemon-flavored deserts were served. It was as if Monet wanted to complete a meal by ingesting the light.

"It is like no other room I have ever been in," said Alex.

"There's more than yellow that makes it unique. Look at the art on the walls," said Alice. "Nothing by Monet or any other European painters. Only nineteenth-century Japanese prints; the same ones that hung here in Monet's day. He began collecting these prints when he was a teenager in the port of Le Havre, and added to his collection the rest of his life. His favorite artists were Hokusai and Hiroshige.

"You can't really understand or appreciate Monet's art and life if you don't know the impression Japanese art made on him. When scholars put his work side-by-side with Hokusai's and Hiroshige's, the influence is clear; the parallels of content are unambiguous. Without Japanese art, Monet would not be 'Monet.'

"Monet owned twelve of the fourteen volumes of Hokusai's *manga* - the collection of Hokusai's black-and-white drawings. And Monet's series paintings of grainstacks, poplars, and the cathedral at Rouen owed much to Hokusai's series of prints focused on a single theme.

"Monet also owned the three volumes of Hokusai's *One Hundred Views of Mount Fuji*. And he was a regular visitor to the exhibitions of Japanese art in Paris. Monet's *Grandes Decorations,* the huge water-lily pond paintings at the end of his life, must have been influenced by the large Japanese screens he saw. The Japanese certainly recognized this affinity. In the last years of Monet's life, many Japanese collectors visited him, and there are more Monets in Japanese museums than any other Western painter.

"This Japanese connection," said Alice, "is no small part of my interest in Monet. Hokusai is my favorite artist, for one thing. Hokusai used more than thirty names in his life, by the way. There is also something very personal in my feelings for one of Monet's Japanese prints. Come over here and I'll show you."

Alice led Alex to a print on the far wall. It was the portrait of an attractive young woman in traditional Japanese dress. A flowered kimono in shades of pale peach contrasting with her black hair, eyes and eyebrows. The slight smile and raised eyebrows expressed an intelligent liveliness. Instead of the idealized formality characteristic of most Japanese portraits, this was clearly a portrait from life.

"This," said Alice, "was done by Toshusai Sharaku in 1794, of the Kabuki actor, Iwai Hanshiro IV, in the role of Shigenoi, in a famous play, *Koi Nyobo Somewake Tazuna.*"

"I see," said Alex. "And, then again, I do not see. Alice, I know little about Japanese art or Kabuki. I am out of my realm of expertise, and I must admit that out of all the prints hanging on the walls of this room, this is not one I am drawn to, especially in its faded condition."

"I understand," said Alice, "but there's more to tell." She opened her purse and took out a small portfolio. "Here. Look at this," she said, holding a photograph alongside the print on the wall.

"It is almost the same - even the face," said Alex.

"This is a picture of the Kabuki actor, Iwai Hanshiro XI, made last year when he played the same role of Shigenoi in the same play. I am the photographer. He is the eleventh Kabuki actor to carry the name, because he is the direct descendant of the man in the print here on Monet's wall, who was the fourth. Quite a similarity and quite a coincidence, don't you think?"

Alex stared at the photograph. "Yes, but, this young woman – a man?"

"All roles in Kabuki are played by men. Those who play women – *onnagata* is the Japanese word – must be the most talented. And despite what you might think, most of them are not homosexual or even effeminate in real life. They are *actors*, and many can play any role – male or female, old or young. Because of this, they must know things about human beings that most people don't know. A profound understanding of human nature is their stock in trade. I admire their extraordinary talent."

Alex looked through the portfolio. "You have several photographs of this actor. Do you know him well?"

"Yes. His offstage name is Matsui Zenkichi. He's a cousin of the master of tattoo I told you about – Morioka. I was introduced to Zenkichi at a calligraphy exhibition. For both of us it was like meeting someone from another planet. But somehow . . . we just clicked.

"We sat on a bench and talked until the gallery closed. I never did see the calligraphy. We've spent a lot of time together since, and have become very close friends. Look, here's what he looks like offstage."

Alice held up a formal portrait of a handsome man in a Western suit and tie, with the same wry smile portrayed in both the Kabuki prints.

"Here's another. On his motorcycle – leather jacket and all. He has many faces in real life as well as onstage."

Lots of time together . . . very close friends, thought Alex, *close enough that Alice carries his portraits with her. Just how close?*

Monet's dining room did not seem so sunny now. It *was* possible to be unhappy in this room after all.

I am jealous, he thought, *jealous.* He thought of yellow again – the color of a third-place ribbon. Frowning, he turned away to look at other prints. He recognized Hokusai's famous *Under the Wave off Kanagawa.*

He had been at sea in such conditions. And felt at sea now.

As Alex turned away, Alice saw the troubled expression on his face. *I've hurt his feelings*, she thought, *but I've also seen his feelings*.
"Aleko."
"Yes?"

When he turned to look at her, he leaned on the back of one of the yellow chairs in a pose that almost matched a photograph of Monet in the same place. Alex was dressed in his new three-piece suit, somewhat rumpled now - which was also Monet's daily dress - even when painting.

Add a long gray beard and a fat pillow underneath the vest, and it could be Monet standing there. Solemn, dignified.

Alice wanted to assure him - to say that she and Zenkichi were friends - good friends - just *friends*. But she did not. *He's jealous,* she thought. Pleased with the discovery, she changed the subject.

"Aleko, we should see the rest of the house before the rain stops and the crowd is let in. Come on."

They walked out of the yellow sunshine of the dining room and into the moody blues of the stairway up to the second floor. Alice led him first to Monet's bedroom, furnished with a single bed, and hung with reproductions of the paintings of artists Monet admired.

Next door was the bedroom occupied first by Monet's wife, Alice, and later by Blanche. But Alex was only politely interested. Clearly his mind was not on the life of Monet, and Alice sensed it.

"It's still raining," said Alice, "let's go outside. A rainy day is perfect for the gardens, especially the water-lily pond."

Relieved to have a change of atmosphere, Alex readily agreed. They went downstairs without seeing the rest of the house. Putting on their raingear, they walked out onto the porch, raised umbrellas, and went out into the rain.

tulips in bunches.
red, pink, yellow, rose
purple and white pansies

H. slate blue roof
- pink house
  kelly green
  window shutters

- great dark
  pine trees
- light
  gravel
  walks

exploding tulips.
fully opened and
glorious in red and
yellow

path above Giverny, early morning
very soft light. silver green

Cat waits patiently to be let in
(not at Monet's house)

WET PAINT

They stood on the porch in a blustery shower of rain and wind.

The garden seemed smeared onto the background of low gray clouds.

The rain intensified the colors of the flowers and blossoming trees, and the wind waved the colors back and forth until they seemed like wet paint on a canvas. Blues and purples and whites of bearded iris, yellows and whites and oranges of tulips, all sloshed about with countless shades of green foliage.

Alex was stunned. "Now I begin to see," he said. "This is Monet's biggest canvas. If we walk down into it we might get paint on our clothes."

"Come on," said Alice, "into the painting."

As they started down the main gravel path that ran through the middle of the garden, Alice realized she couldn't walk alongside Alex because of the size of their umbrellas. She furled her own and moved close enough to get under Alex's umbrella. She put her arm around his waist. He put his arm protectively around her shoulder, and, holding each other close, they moved on into the garden.

"Wait," said Alice, and she reached out into the center of a purple iris, caught the bright yellow pollen on the end of her finger, and rubbed some on the end of her nose and then on the end of Alex's nose.

"Wet paint!"

*

Monet's water garden is reached by way of a tunnel running from one corner of the flower garden, underneath the road, and up into a green tunnel of bamboo at the end of the pond.

"This is my favorite spot," said Alice.

They stood looking across the rain-splattered pond to the green Japanese bridge. From the trellis over the bridge hung long streamers of pale violet wisteria flowers. Deep purple Japanese iris marched along the edge of the pond like spear-carriers with banners. And in the far background, weeping willows and assertive bamboo waved in the wind.

Moored to the shore in front of them was a green rowboat - a re-production of the boat used by Monet. He included the boat in his paintings, and often rowed out in it to paint or enjoy the garden from the water.

"Let's go out in the boat," said Alice.

"Is it permitted?" asked Alex.

"Who cares? If we get arrested for going rowing in Monet's boat we'll have a story to tell the rest of our lives."

"Well, then," said Alex, "Why not? We will be the owl and pussycat, sailing away in our pea-green boat. Mr. Lear would be pleased."

But the boat was chained and locked.

"We have imagined it. We would have done it, too," said Alice. "And what you can imagine is real. Picasso said that."

"As real as a dream," said Alex.

*

The rainstorm ended. The clouds began breaking up, allowing shafts of sunlight to pierce the gray mist, highlighting the garden.

Alex and Alice strolled slowly around the pond as if in a trance. No words. Caught up in beauty, and caught up in their closeness. Not needing umbrellas now, they nevertheless walked as before: Alice's arm around Alex's waist, his arm around her shoulder. It was going to be a sunny afternoon.

To hell with Kabuki actors, thought Alex.

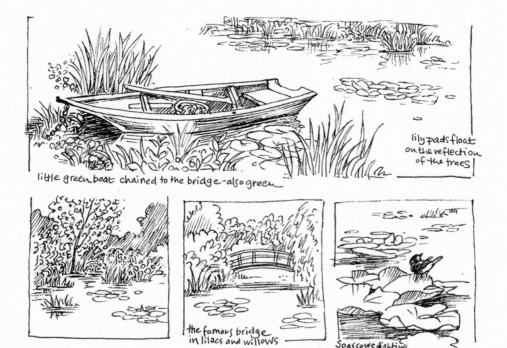

little green boat chained to the bridge - also green

lily pads float on the reflection of the trees

the famous bridge in lilacs and willows

Sparrows alighting on waterlilies

SELENE

"Shall I give you answers to more questions you have not asked?"

"Sure," said Alice, "as long as I get a turn."

Dusk. Dinner at Les Agapanthes. They had finished dessert. Espresso and cognac had just been served. It was almost time for Alice's promised cello concert.

"Do you know about Selene?" asked Alex.

"Not much. Elaborate."

"In Greek mythology, Selene is the name of the moon goddess. She was honored in three aspects: as a young maiden, a mother, and an old wise woman. Selene was associated with Hecate, who presided over the crossroads of life, and who was honored by pilgrims at places where three roads met.

"The ancient Greeks liked triads or multiples thereof - which accounts for the nine muses, whose names were Calliope, Euterpe, Erato, Polyhymnia, Clio, Melpomene, Thalia, Terpsichore, and Urania. I like things that come in threes or nines."

Alice stared at him.

"Too much information? Am I boring you again?" Alex asked.

"No, no . . . it's just that . . . I don't know how to respond. Are you sure Max-Pol hasn't told you anything about me or my letters to him?"

"I swear it," protested Alex.

"Then, once again, we have something in common. Three is my favorite number. I collect things that come in threes - gods and goddesses, sayings, proverbs, names of queens and on and on. I collect them like trading cards. I can give you pages of notes and scrapbooks of pictures. I even write three-line aphorisms under a pseudonym. And now you tell me *you* like things that come in threes. I'm not superstitious, and I don't believe in fate, but you must agree these coincidences between us are . . . are . . ."

"The way it is," said Alex, solemnly.

"Yes," said Alice. "The way it is."

"Well, then," said Alex, "as a remembrance of this moment of discovery, I will give you a triad you do not have. I wrote it down this afternoon while sitting in the sunshine beside Monet's grave. As you see, I used the back of the ticket to his garden."

Alex took his wallet out of the breast pocket of his jacket, removed the ticket, and handed it to Alice. She read aloud:

> *Life is a near-death experience.*
> *Life is the leading cause of death.*
> *Life cannot be saved, only used up.*

"May I keep it?" she asked. "I'll give you my ticket if you like."

"Only if you write three lines on it for me," said Alex.

"Done. But I'll have to think about just the right lines."

*

"Stay here and have another cognac while I get my cello," said Alice, rising to go. "Wait," she said, sitting down again, "I just thought of what to write on my ticket for you. These three lines are pinned to the wall above my bed in Paris. They are the words of Fabuliste Curnonsky."

Taking out her ticket and pen, she put down the lines, handed the ticket to Alex, and went to get her cello.

> *Romance is easy. Love is hard.*
> *Sex can be safe. Love is always dangerous.*
> *You need not fear men or women -*
> *only the ones you know well.*

Now what am I supposed to make of that? Alex wondered.

He took his komboloi out of his jacket pocket. Click . . . Click . . . Click . . . He asked the waiter for another cognac. Before he could sort out his thoughts, Alice returned, carrying two folding stools in one hand and a long, black leather bag, slung by its strap over one shoulder.

"Where is your cello?" asked Alex.

"Here," she said, holding out the bag. "I know it looks like a sack of tent poles, but it really is my cello. Open the bag and take it out. You won't hurt it."

The bag - a squarish, black nylon tube - was four feet long and about nine inches square, and weighed about eight pounds. Carefully, Alex unzipped the bag and took out what seemed to be just the working parts of a cello - wooden neck and lower frame with strings, but without the full body.

"Here, I'll show you," said Alice. She released the endpin at the bottom and slid it out; then, resting the cello on the floor on the endpin, she unfolded two smooth wooden forms - one from each side near the bottom.

"These fit at the same place between your legs where the body of the cello would rest."

And, unfolding two shorter forms from the upper neck, she explained, "These are the minimal shapes for the top of the body for chest support. Everything else is the same: strings, maple neck, and ebony keyboard. It's Japanese - made by Yamaha - and called the Silent Compact Cello - a Zen cello - minimal essentials."

"It looks more like a giant praying mantis," said Alex.

"But it does the job. Look."

Alice held the cello in the standard playing position. "Everywhere I need to touch or hold a cello, it's there."

"But how can you hear it?" asked Alex.

"Two ways. Listen."

She took her bow out of the bag, tightened it, and drew the bow across the strings, making just enough sound for Alex to hear.

"Now, try these." She handed Alex a delicate pair of earphones, which she plugged into a small connector on the back of the neck. She pushed a switch and said, "Now listen."

Alex put the earphones in place, and this time, when Alice drew her bow across the strings Alex heard a full cello sound.

"Well, well - *yes!*" He exclaimed. "Do it again."

Alice played the beginning of "Row, Row, Row Your Boat." Alex laughed, took the earphones out of his ears, and asked, "How does it work?"

"Two AA batteries, Piezo electric pickup, tiny amplifier, built-in reverb, line in for tapes or CDs, line out for auxiliary amplifier. Maximum tech," said Alice.

"Most of all, it's lightweight and easy to carry. I can take it everywhere, which solves a big problem. And I can play it anywhere, and practice without disturbing anyone."

"I am very impressed," said Alex.

"I do have a cello with full body, but it's also a high-tech instrument. Purists would not approve, but then, cellos have always evolved. Mine is made of carbon fiber, with small modifications in shape to make it fit the body more comfortably. I never get sore shoulders while playing it, and I don't worry about it being damaged. The maker even left one outside in the rain and sun for a week without any harm coming to it.

"I'm not attracted to the cult of worship that surrounds the old wooden cellos. They're beautiful, no mistake about it, and in the hands of a great musician, they make magnificent sounds. But I'm an amateur, not a professional. I'm a player, not an antique dealer. And I don't need to impress anyone with something I paid a lot of money for but can't justify.

"And - I don't want to play with a group. I play for me. Playing cello is about the music, which is inside my mind and soul more than it is in an instrument. It's not the usual way with a cello, but it's my way."

"It serves you like my komboloi serve me," said Alex.

"I like that. Yes. My cello is a companion. And it's like your string of beads in that, when I play, I get lost in what I'm doing. Sometimes I don't know if the music is inside me or if I am inside the music."

Alex pulled out his pocket watch, flipped open its cover, and held the face up for Alice to see. "Time. The moon is rising. Take me into your music with you."

*

"My turn," said Alice, as they walked up the lane climbing the hillside above Giverny. "I'll answer a question you have not asked me. In fact, in the spirit of our conversation, I'll give you three answers.

"First, I wanted a passport into the world of music and musicians and the part music plays in human history. I wanted to be able to read the code - to make sense of those black marks - to know the language. And you need an instrument to play the code on.

"Second, and this is a little odd, I admit: I wanted a large instrument – not a bass, but something with substantial presence – more than a piece of equipment – an instrument with 'otherness' about it. Something big enough to fight back. Do you understand?"

"Yes," said Alex. "Like choosing a horse instead of a puppy dog."

"Ha. Yes. And the last answer is: because the cello is the instrument that mimics the human voice most closely. It has the same register and same melodic qualities. Sometimes the cello is my voice, and sometimes I can sing with it – even manage harmony."

"What will you play for me?"

"Variations on children's songs – you'll recognize them. Keep in mind I've been playing only three years. The first thing I learned to play was "Twinkle, Twinkle, Little Star," and I always begin with that when I practice. And then the easiest parts of Bach's suites for solo cello. And from there, improvisations on themes you may or may not know."

"I will appreciate your performance whatever you play," said Alex.

"This is *not* a performance, Aleko. I am *not* a performer. But I'm not apologizing. I'll play what I play when I'm alone. You will be there. The first to be there, I might add. And that's all you have to do: Be there. Max-Pol would say, Be my Witness. If you applaud, I'll know you're trying to be a polite audience. Don't patronize me. I don't play that well. Just *be* there."

"Agreed," said Alex, and they walked on.

*

The hillside behind and above the village of Giverny looks much the same as in Monet's day: sloping pasture land that ends in a line of trees, which in turn give way to more pasture. After six o'clock the village below is already quiet and calm. Nothing speaks its fame. At nightfall the village life turns inward and people go to bed early.

This night was damply clear, with smells intensified by the passing afternoon rain: the odor of wet cow manure mixed with the perfume of the fruit-tree blossoms mixed with the new green fragrance of trampled grass mixed with the aroma of freshly plowed earth. Spring. May.

Alex and Alice settled in on a level place where three lanes came together. He sat on his stool just behind her. While she was tuning, he realized he could hear the sound well enough in the stillness to forego earphones. He did not need a wire to connect him to Alice or the music.

In the western sky, there was Venus.

In the eastern sky, the light of the moon spilled down over the hills.

Alice began to play: Twinkle, twinkle, little star; how I wonder . . . Frere Jacques . . . Baa, baa, black sheep . . . Rockabye baby . . . Brahms's lullaby . . . and "Send In the Clowns" from Sondheim's *A Little Night Music*.

Each one blending into another, with variations and combinations. Simplicity became complexity and came back to simplicity again. Alex recognized the beginning of Bach's first cello suite, but after that he was lost, caught up in the voice of the cello that came to him like someone singing far, far away.

When the full moonlight reached them, Alex suddenly remembered moonlight flooding his room in a hospital in Cairo long ago. He closed his eyes. The heat of the Egyptian night. The pain from his ravaged leg. The stench of infected flesh. The loneliness. The dread. That was the night he wanted to die; the night he would have killed himself if he'd had the means.

He looked around at the valley of the Seine and Giverny and Alice.

And I would have missed this, he thought. *I would have missed this*. With tears in his eyes, he looked up to see Alice sitting still in the moonlight - moonlight bright enough to cast her shadow across his lap.

She was looking over her shoulder at him. He wanted to reach out and take her in his arms. He wanted to say something so memorable she would never forget it. He wanted to frame this moment and hang it on the wall of his mind beside the picture of that night in Cairo.

But she turned away and began playing her "Cuckoo Not" tune. Alex stood up behind her, put his hand lightly on the nape of her neck, and hummed his marching tune as she played. The three of them sang together - Alex, Alice, and the cello.

To hell with Kabuki actors, Alex thought, and began to laugh in that curiously contagious way that makes others laugh, even when they don't know what about. Alice didn't ask. It didn't matter. She felt like laughing. They laughed on.

Finally, Alice stood up, leaned her cello against the stool, took a deep breath, held out her arms to Alex, and said, "Aleko, shall we dance?"
Alex held out his arms.
And carefully, slowly, holding one another at a delicate distance, they turned around and around and around in the light of the moon, saying nothing, and yet saying everything that need be said.

*

Later, at midnight, Alex, sleepless, got up from his bed, wrapped a blanket around his shoulders, and went out onto the balcony of his room to stand in the moonlight. He thought of Alice, asleep in her bed not far away.
Sweet dreams, he thought.

At the same time, Alice, equally sleepless, was sitting up in her bed thinking of Alex and the events of the evening. She sang softly to herself as she lay back on her pillow, *Merrily, merrily, merrily, merrily . . . life is but a dream.*
Slowly she rowed off down the river of contented sleep.

OSCAR

"Oscar?"

Monet was christened Oscar-Claude. Only Blanche ever called him Oscar. And only when they were alone together. It pleased Monet.

Blanche, in her nightgown, whispered from the doorway:

"Oscar?"

"Ah, dear one. I am not asleep," said Monet.

"A good day?"

"The best of days. I never thought such days would come again. Only the darkness and the need for sleep kept me from painting on. In the life after this one there will always be light, and I will always feel like painting, and the painting will always go well. That is all I would require of heaven."

"And your eyes?"

"Clear sight and no pain."

"Good night, dear Oscar."

"I am not sleepy. Come, Blanche."

Blanche crossed the darkness to sit on the side of Monet's bed. Tenderly she placed her hands across his eyes. "If I were an angel, I would make sure you would see clearly as long as you live," she said.

Monet took her hands in his. "You are my angel. My guardian angel. If not for you I would be a blind and dying old man whose art would be ashes. As it is, I am so alive. I *want* to be alive. And I paint with all the passion I ever had. Because of you these years are the grand dessert of my life. A dessert flambé."

He gently pulled her toward him and took her in his arms.

SATURDAY, MAY 4

"Damn! . . . these socks are still wet . . . and shorts . . . and shirt . . ."

Alex grumbled around in his bathroom in the half-light of early morning. When he left Oxford he had packed light, expecting to return the next day. One night away had become four. Having only two sets of clothes meant he had to wash out one set of underwear every night and then supervise the maid's ironing of his shirt every morning. He was fussy about his shirt. The maid was not. Grumble, grumble.

Sleep had been shallow and short. He had a headache. And his leg was stiff and swollen from all the walking he had been doing. The hot water was exhausted in the middle of his shower. Forget shaving. Reluctantly, he put on yesterday's socks and shorts and shirt, and the rumpled jacket and slacks he had not bothered to hang up the night before.

"Damn! Damn! Damn!"

He stared at his woebegone face in the bathroom mirror. *Looks like I have been sitting up three nights on a Balkan train*, he thought. Bloodshot eyes, stubbled cheeks and chin, uncombed hair. "You are old and ugly," he said to the person in the mirror. "And even worse, you are making a fool of yourself."

All the circumstances of the morning were inconveniences that Alex would ordinarily dismiss and quickly overcome. Except for the part about feeling old and ugly and foolish.

There is the real problem, he thought, *I do not want to be old and ugly and foolish. I want to be young and handsome and wise - no, not wise, clever. If Alice and I were only the same age . . . any age would do . . .*

He felt himself far out on an emotional limb that was about to break. The words of the lullaby Alice played the night before came to him: *When the bough breaks, the cradle will fall, and down will come baby, cradle and all.*

Aloud, he muttered, "I should not have come. I should not have stayed. And if I have any sense, I will leave on the next train. God damn it! How could I have got myself into this mess?"

Tap, tap, tap - a cautious knocking at his door.

"What now?" he shouted, as he flung the door open.

The chambermaid retreated fearfully down the hall, whispering that breakfast was served in the garden and that a lady was waiting for him. Alex slammed the door.

"I DO NOT WANT BREAKFAST IN THE GARDEN!" he shouted. "I DO NOT WANT BREAKFAST WITH THE LADY. ALL I WANT . . . I WANT . . . GOD DAMN IT! I CANNOT HAVE WHAT I WANT!" He knocked over a chair, then kicked the chair for good measure.

The sound of Alex's rage carried out onto the garden terrace below, where Alice sat waiting in the sunshine. She heard every word. She got up, walked around the corner of the building, stood underneath Alex's room, and shouted,

"I DON'T CARE WHAT YOU WANT OR DON'T WANT. I WANT TO HAVE BREAKFAST WITH YOU. STOP SHOUT-ING AND COME DOWN HERE NOW, OR I WILL COME UP AFTER YOU! AND IF YOU DON'T COME OUT, I WILL CALL THE POLICE AND THE FIRE DEPARTMENT!"

(Silence.)

"DID YOU HEAR ME, ALEKO?"

Stunned by Alice's assault, Alex came out on his balcony and looked down to see if she was making fun of him or was seriously annoyed. Alice was not smiling. She was momentarily nonplussed. Because she didn't know which surprised her more: her spontaneous maternal reac-tion to Alex's anger or his disheveled appearance.

"Oh," she said.

Taking a deep breath, Alex said, "I am coming," and turned back into his room. Pausing to wash his hands and comb his hair, he looked at himself one more time in the mirror. *When the bough breaks . . .*, he thought.

On the sunlit terrace, breakfast waited: served on a Monet-yellow tablecloth, with yellow-and-blue plates and cups and saucers (reproductions of Monet's tableware), and two silver jugs of hot coffee and hot milk; a crystal pitcher of fresh orange juice; a basket of warm croissants and brioches; a generous slab of pale yellow butter; pots of fruit jam and amber honey; little squares of dark chocolate; and small tumblers of calvados.

Add a vase of purple iris, the singing of birds, the green of spring in May, and the view over the fields to the Seine. Glorious. An utterly utopian breakfast.

None of this registered with Alice or Alex.

They sat glaring at one another.

"What the *hell* is going on?" demanded Alice. "What's wrong?"

Alex hung his head, stroked the side of his face, and muttered.

"I had a . . . a sleepless night . . . I feel . . . I think I . . . I do not know . . . what to say . . . except to say . . . I am sorry . . . I have fouled the morning . . . I apologize for . . . for . . . I do not know . . ."

He broke off in midsentence, waved his arms in frustration, turned his head away and was silent - a man surrendering to the clutches of emotional quicksand. He hung his head again and closed his eyes.

Alice reached out and took both his hands in hers.

"Aleko . . . oh dear Aleko . . ." she said, tenderly.

(Silence.)

"I have a suggestion," said Alice. "Let's rent a car and get away from Giverny. We could go down the river to Rouen to see the cathedral. Monet painted the façade thirty times, and one of those paintings is in the museum there. The place where Joan of Arc was burned at the stake is there too.

"And, if I may say so, your clothes are the worse for wear. Would you let me take you shopping? That would be fun. And you could buy me a hat. I like hats, and I would like to have a springtime straw hat - one you choose for me."

Alex was unmoved. He looked up at Alice without expression.

"And *eat,* Aleko. We'll go to the Normandy coast and *eat.* Scallops, oysters, lobsters, shrimp, and mussels. Salt-marsh lamb and cassoulet. Cheese: Camembert, Brillat-Savarin, Neufchâtel. Pear and apple cider, aged calvados. And butter and cream with everything. We could feast until we burst, Aleko."

Alex relaxed. Eating appealed to him.

"And then we could see all the places on the coast where Monet painted; drive on down to Bayeux to see the tapestry, and take a look at the D-day beaches, the monuments and cemeteries, and then drive the back roads across the countryside on the way to Giverny. What do you say?"

"Let me first ask you a question," said Alex. "What would you have done this week and next if I had not been here?"

His question surprised her. She thought she had distracted him - that he was pleased with her excursion plans.

Releasing his hands, she sat back in her chair, thinking.

"Well . . . this was to be my last week in Giverny," she said.

"I suppose that . . . I would have spent time packing up my things to leave. I might have gone down to Rouen and Le Havre one day. I would have stayed here through Monday. That's the day Monet's gardens are closed to all except a limited number of painters, and I have a place reserved.

Alex raised his eyebrows. "And you would . . . ?"

"Paint. I've been taking watercolor lessons. I paint postcard-sized miniatures in a pseudo-impressionistic style. I draw better than I paint, but I confess I've kept it up mostly as an excuse to be in the gardens on Mondays. And, I suppose I would have left for Paris on Monday afternoon."

"And then?" asked Alex.

"Back to the States. This winter-in-Europe experience is over. The tourist travel season is not a time to be in Paris or anywhere else in Europe, for that matter. It's time to go."

"And where will you go - and when?" asked Alex.

"To Seattle for a while. I have roots there. I'm not in a hurry. But sometime soon. Why do you want to know all this, Aleko?"

(Silence.)

"Alice, I will not go with you around Normandy. For one thing, a holiday weekend in May will attract hordes of English from across the Channel. And then, to be candid, I am not interested in seeing the places where Monet painted. None of the sites will be as they were. Cathedrals bore and depress me. I do not care for Joan of Arc. Teenage girls who claim to speak with God and his angels are dangerously mad. And, finally, I do not want to see the invasion beaches and cemeteries. I have friends who died on those beaches. Being there would depress me. No. I will not come."

"Aleko, I . . .," began Alice, but he interrupted her.

"Let me finish. I also have a proposal. You know that I came with you as a spontaneous gesture. I do not regret that I came. It is important to me to be able to do such things. It keeps me from accepting the padded cell of old age. But it is also important to me to have time to consider what I have done these past few days.

"If I may be frank, I do not want to spoil what has obviously come between us. A little time to myself on my own turf would be useful. Therefore . . . I do not want to go on the trip you suggest, and I do not want to hang around here or get in the way of your bringing this important episode of your life to a comfortable close. I want to go back to Oxford."

"Aleko, I . . .," Alice began again, but Alex put a finger to his lips and said, "Wait, I am not quite finished."

"Listen. Consider. My canal boat waits in the boatyard in Oxford. Repaired, cleaned, serviced, and provisioned. Ready. I would have spent this week on the canals of Oxfordshire with Max-Pol, but he is in Seattle and I am here and he will not be back for a week or ten days. Therefore, I propose that *you* come to Oxford. Soon. Travel with me on my boat for a few days. That would please me. That . . . *that* . . . is *exactly* what I want. What do you say?"

Alice had sensed an invitation was coming before he asked. In fact, she would have invited herself if he had not. But she wanted him to ask her. She smiled and, avoiding all the small talk of the details of her coming such as When? Where? What time? What clothes? she went directly to the only answer Alex wanted to hear:

"I'll be there Wednesday morning, if that's not too late."

As if touched by the wand of a fairy godmother, Alex relaxed, laughed, stretched his arms over his head, yawned and, as if this was the way the morning had been all along, said, "Please pass the croissants."

Alice looked at Alex with approval. She liked seeing the scruffy and moody side of him. Even his anger brought her closer to him. She wondered what other sides of Alex she would see when they were alone on his boat together.

AWAY

"Then that's that," said Alice, after breakfast. She rose to leave.

"See you in Oxford."

She took Alex's hand, pressed it to her cheek, and went away.

Goodbyes are tedious. Goodbyes are awkward. Goodbyes often drain away the joy of having been together. Alex and Alice were in agreement about goodbyes. No standing around and making small talk for two people who knew exactly what they were going to do next and were ready to do it.

"Right," said Alex, who went back to his room with marching music playing on the parade ground of his mind. Restarting his day, he showered, shaved, and put on his now-dry socks and shorts. The maid had hung his newly pressed shirt in the sunshine in the balcony door.

Dressed, he considered himself in the mirror. He looked good. He smelled good. Life was good. As he packed his suitcase, he reviewed the events of the past week as they arrayed themselves before him. He was whistling as he went out the door of his lodgings:

He was quickly under way: taxi to Vernon, train to the Gare St. Lazare in Paris, taxi to Gare du Nord, and the Eurostar through the Chunnel to London. He would be in Oxford by afternoon.

"Onward!"

*

Seated across from Alex on the Eurostar was an elegant man. Well dressed, hair graying at the temples, patrician features, healthy and trim. Not far over fifty years old. He was looking out the train window, while talking and laughing softly to himself.

In appraising his seatmate, Alex noticed the small pin in his lapel: dark-green enamel with a white edelweiss flower in the center. An intriguing clue - a flower of the high mountains. Swiss? German? Austrian? Still laughing, the man turned to Alex and said, "Forgive me. The cup of my joy is running over. I am a very happy man. May I tell you why?"

"Please," said Alex.

"I am in love. For the first time in many, many years. Foolish love. A young man's love. I am on my way to London to propose marriage."

"Congratulations. May your joy continue," said Alex, extending his hand. "I am Alex Evans." Firmly, warmly, the man shook Alex's hand.

"Permit me to introduce myself," he said. "My name is Hans Dieter von Galen. Before I give you my card, you must promise to call me Hans."

Alex took the card and read:

Hans Dieter von Galen
Generalmajor
Befehhishaber Wehrbereich VI (Bayern)
Kommandeur 1.Gebirgsdivision

In the left-hand corner, the green oval with the edelweiss; in the right-hand corner, a black, red, and yellow emblem; a medieval eagle in the center. The surprise showed on Alex's face. He understood what the card meant.

"General," he said.

"Hans, please. While it is true that I am the commanding officer of the First Mountain Division of the German Army, stationed in Bavaria, it is far, far more important that I am simply a man in love about to propose marriage. You *must* call me Hans."

Alex wanted to respond with his own calling card. But which one? He had several, each for specific occasions: a plain social one, a business card with all his addresses and numbers, a card in Greek, even a blank card. He chose to keep his introduction simple, but still declare a little of himself to this German general. "You must call me Alex," he said, extending his card.

ALEX EVANS
(Alexandros Evangelou Xenopouloudakis)

As he read Alex's card, Hans's mood sobered.
"You are Greek then?" he asked.
"Greek. Cretan, actually," said Alex.

Hans sat back in his seat, suddenly solemn.

(Silence.)

"I have been in Crete recently," said Hans. "My father is buried there. In the cemetery at Maleme on the west end of the island. He was a paratrooper who dropped behind the lines at Iraklion and was killed the first day of the invasion - very close to the Minoan ruins at Knossos. I never knew him, of course."
"Well, then," said Alex. "I was at Knossos . . . that same day."

(Silence.)

"Really? You don't look old enough," said Hans.
"I was born in 1915. I am eighty," replied Alex.
"Hard to believe. If you were in Crete in 1941, then you must have a story of your own," said Hans.
"Yes. It is a long story, but I should tell you," said Alex.

And for the next two hours Hans listened as Alex told him about Crete, Pendlebury, the day of the invasion, the retreat over the mountains, his life for the next fifty years, and his own recent visit to the cemetery at Maleme on the anniversary of the Battle of Crete.

"Hard to believe," said Hans. "I was there at the same anniversary celebration."

The Eurostar suddenly entered the darkness of the Chunnel. Neither man spoke until the train roared back into daylight.

"My uncle - my father's brother - was also in Crete in 1941, and was there until the bitter end in 1945," said Hans. "He survived, was repatriated to Germany, and lived a long life. He never spoke about the war, but family rumors said he had fallen in love with a Cretan woman and fathered at least one child. I would not be surprised. It was a common story - more common than the Cretans or Germans want to admit.

"Whatever happened, he never went back, never spoke of the war, and took his secrets to his grave. I sometimes wonder if I have family there - a half-cousin perhaps - but I have never looked into it."

"What a world," said Alex. "Your father and I were probably not far from one another on that terrible day. We might have tried to kill each other had we met. And, after all these years, you and I meet on a high-speed train bound for England, having a civil conversation about love.

"Well, let the past be. That was then. This is now. And that is that. For me, I am only interested in the present and the future. You must tell me about your bride-to-be. I like love stories."

"Her name is Winifred Lightfoot MacLeod. Very, very English. I met her when I was stationed in Washington at the Pentagon as a liaison officer for NATO operations. Her husband, a colonel in the Queen's Own Highlanders, was also at the Pentagon for NATO. My wife and I became social friends with Winifred and her husband.

"One night at a military ball, Winifred and I danced together. And we both recognized a soul-stirring attraction. But I was a gentleman and an officer, and she was a lady and an officer's wife, and, well, we did not act in any way on what we felt. Yet, we knew. Do you know that feeling?"

"Yes," said Alex, "yes, I do."

"We were already married, and while neither marriage was satisfying, we were loyal to our vows and our children. We kept what we knew to ourselves. Last year my wife died of breast cancer, and Winifred's husband died of a heart attack. To make a long story short, we reached out to each other and were drawn together like magnets suddenly released from the forces that held them apart. And so . . . well . . . and so!

"Nine months ago I was a widower, a year from retirement, with an unknown future. And now, my world is turned upside down by love. She returns my enthusiasm. She awaits my arrival at Waterloo Station.

"All my life I have done the rational, correct German thing. But the rules of war are not the rules of love. And today, I will run from the train, pick up the lady in my arms, whirl her about, kiss her, set her down, fall to one knee and, with ring in hand, and propose marriage."

"Lovely. I would like to see that," said Alex.

"And you shall. You are invited to be the witness to my proposal."
Alex laughed. "I accept with greatest pleasure. I seem to have developed a talent for being a witness."

He considered Hans's surprise that love should waltz in the door at his age. Would Hans think love possible at eighty? Or the real question, Would Alex think love possible at eighty? Or Alice?

He had not mentioned Alice. He wanted to. But he could not. His thinking changed shape like clouds from one minute to the next. He could not say he was in love. He could not say Alice was in love with him. This was not romance and not an affair. Something else.

But, I am a man. She is a woman, said Alex to himself, *and something is going on. Why can I not call it love? What am I afraid of?*

*

Hans von Galen did run to meet his Winifred.

Dressed like a bride in a frilly white dress and white flowered hat, and carrying a scarf full of flower petals, she flung the petals in the air as she flung herself into the arms of her Hans, who picked her up and swung her around and around, kissing her face and lips and babbling his affection in German and English.

And she *was* lovely indeed.

Setting her down carefully, Hans dropped to one knee and opened his hand to show the ring he had been clutching for hours. But before he could ask, Winifred gave him the answer, which she had been clutching in her heart.

"Yes, yes! I will, I do, I do, I do!" she shouted, and threw her arms down around his neck with such abandon that Hans sat down on the station floor with Winifred in his lap.

Applause burst from the crowd of passersby who had been attracted to this glorious reunion of lovers. A passing Anglican priest said, "I pronounce you husband and wife," and made sign of blessing over them. The crowd applauded again and helped the couple to their feet.

"Winifred," said Hans, "I want to introduce you to our chief witness, my new friend, Mr. Alex Evans."

But Alex was not there. Their happiness was more than he could bear. *Joy to your hearts, and long life,* he had thought, as they sat there in a laughing heap. And in sadness, he had walked swiftly away into the crowd.

As he passed underneath the Waterloo Station clock he paused, realizing he had first seen Alice here. Four days ago. Only four days. It seemed more like a year and four days ago. She had been standing exactly here. With Max-Pol.

Feeling old and lonely and foolish, Alex limped slowly toward the exit, head down, shoulders slumped. He caught sight of himself reflected in a coffee shop window.

My God, he thought, *this will not do. A Cretan man does not run away from a fight or a party or love. Get a grip on, Alex!*

He straightened up, took a deep breath, and walked out of Waterloo Station humming his marching song.

Sunday, May 5

Aleko was right, thought Alice.

Unprepared for the flashes of anger or his refusal of her travel suggestion, disappointed at his wanting to leave, elated at his invitation, and then taken aback by his decision to leave immediately, Alice had walked away from breakfast in a daze. Now what?

He was right though, she thought. *These four days have been intense. Some space between us . . . a good thing. And a change of scenery still a good idea.*

In the few minutes after leaving Alex, her mood shifted from confused to focused. *Rouen*, she thought, and an hour later she was on the train.

As Alex had predicted, the English invaded Normandy for the holiday weekend. The coming Wednesday, May 8, was VE-day. Crowds had come early, to get ahead of the even bigger crowds that would arrive midweek to tour the invasion beaches and visit cemeteries. In Rouen the square in front of the Cathedral of Notre Dame was clotted with people grouped around tour guides busily delivering truths and fictions:

> *"And this, ladies and gentlemen, is exactly the spot where Madame Bovary and Leon came out of the cathedral and got in the closed carriage to ride madly around Rouen making love. The exact spot."*

The façade of the cathedral was, as Alex had predicted, not as Monet had seen it. Blotched - with sections of stone scrubbed white alongside sections grimed with age, and the great towers concealed by the cranes and scaffolding and tarps of ongoing restoration efforts. It seemed like one more construction site rather than a great historical monument. Nevertheless, Alice was not disappointed. She was there to experience something invisible.

*

In February of 1892 Monet came to Rouen, acquired use of space in an apartment one floor above the street, and stayed until mid-April, painting the west façade of the Cathedral of Notre Dame. He came again the following February and stayed another two months. He had no interest in the cathedral in its religious context. As far as anyone knows, he never went inside. He came to paint, as he put it, *"what exists between the subject and me."*

More than thirty paintings came of this campaign. The cathedral appears like a craggy, weathered cliff at different times of day in different weather. Only when the paintings are seen side-by-side together is it clear that Monet meant exactly what he said. His painting was not about the cathedral but about impressions of light and color. Moments.

Monet came alone on these painting adventures, and he did not return home until he accomplished the task he set for himself.

There were other series of paintings in progress in the same years. Grainstacks in the field across from his house in Giverny; poplar trees lining the banks of the Epte; and the ice and snow in the Seine valley during the exceptionally cold winter of 1893. These subjects fit tidily into the category of plein air painting and were of no surprise to Monet's dealer and patrons. But the same façade of the same cathedral over and over? Two years in a row? Why?

His wife was unhappy with his absence. His dealer thought paintings of a cathedral would not sell. When word reached his critics, they thought he was wasting his time in Rouen.

Even Monet had his doubts. Letters written to his wife, Alice, reflect his frustration, dissatisfaction and despair. He was exhausted by the hard work - even defeated at times. Whatever the art world might think of him, Monet's self-appraisal as a painter was negative.

"Hard as I work, I am not getting anywhere . . . I was right to be unhappy last year; it's horrible, and what I am doing this time is bad, too, it's just bad in a different way . . . I am worn out."

He went on to say, regarding his growing fame: *"Heavens, they really don't know much, the people who think me a master. [I have] great intentions, but that's all."*

In another letter he expressed his anguish in these words: "*I shall never manage anything good; it's an obstinate overlay of colors, but painting it is not."* Still, he kept on all those years, reaching for something always beyond his accomplishment.

Why was Monet in Rouen? Why the cathedral? Why keep at something so frustrating? He never said. The paintings are the only answer we have. The art world received them with astonishment. Monet's dealer was pleased after all – the cathedral paintings sold at good prices. Even Monet overcame his dark mood about the experience to say, *"I am less unhappy than I was last year, and I think some of my 'Cathedrales' will do."*

*

Alice admired and envied Monet his clarity of purpose no matter how hard it was to maintain at times. He really was an artist in all the finest senses of the word. While success in the marketplace was welcome, he did not paint for the marketplace. He painted for himself, accepting all the risks of public failure. It was this single-minded tenacity of Monet's that spoke to Alice.

She wanted to stand in that space between Monet and the cathedral. Being there by herself gave her courage. If Alex had been with her and she had tried to explain why she was there, he would have asked her a question she was not ready to answer. She could hear him asking, Well, then, Alice, what is it that commands your conviction? What will *you* do at any price?

And that was exactly the question in Alice's mind.

*

She walked away from the crowds, down a narrow street in the direction of the market square where Joan of Arc had been burned at the stake. She passed a millinery shop. The window was filled with straw hats trimmed with ribbons and flowers. The door was open. She walked on. Stopped. Turned back. *A hat. I need a hat,* she thought, *a boating hat.*

Alice did not usually wear the hats prescribed by fashion. Head covering for her was a response to practical conditions - cold, sun, rain, and wind. She liked shawls or scarves over her head, a soft cloche or a beret, perhaps. But hats of the purely decorative sort seemed much too fussy.

On the other hand, she had a recurring dream in which she was making love while wearing a rather large straw hat decorated with ribbons and flowers. Riding atop a faceless partner, she bounced up and down and even waved her hat over her head, rodeo-style.

She liked those dreams. Nevertheless, they were only dreams. *But, she thought, someday - who knows? I should have a hat just in case the real opportunity comes along.*

The mistress of the millinery store was patient and persuasive. Alice came away with a wide-brimmed, yellow straw hat with long blue ribbons; a white sailor's hat; and a flat-crowned, Spanish-style riding hat in black felt.

She did not visit the site of Joan of Arc's final tribulation. Alex was right on that score as well. They were all crazy - the girl, the soldiers, the bishops, and the terrorist God they served. Satisfied with her visit with the spirit of Monet, and pleased with her new hats, Alice caught the next train back to Giverny.

MONDAY, MAY 6

Painters covet Monday mornings in May in Monet's garden. The general public is not admitted. The foundation accommodates a limited number of artists, who must apply well in advance to reserve specific painting locations. "Quiet" is the rule, and it applies even to the gardeners, who must go about their required work without distracting the painters. It is called The Sacred Day, out of ongoing reverence for the spirit of Monet.

Alice had taken watercolor lessons in Paris during the winter. She bought her supplies at Sennelier on the Quais Voltaire, a store patronized by generations of French and expatriate artists. For portability's sake, she chose a small, compact unit that just fit into one hand. It included a tiny palette of limited colors and a few sable brushes with short handles. A small sketchbook, a block of watercolor paper the size of a postcard, and a pint of distilled water completed her equipment. It was easy to carry these tools with her, and the small scale of her operation kept her painting private.

She had surprised herself with an easy revival of drawing skills not used since high school. But her paintings had nothing special about them beyond the satisfaction of playing with color. *I am not an artist,* she thought, though other painters in the garden admired what they saw when they had a passing glance at her work.

What Alice liked best was how the task of painting made her notice things she would have not seen otherwise: the details of plants, the variations in shapes, the stages of growth in a species, and, like Monet, how different the same plants looked in different weather in different light. But more often than not, like Monet, she went away failing to quite get on paper what she felt and saw in the garden. Knowing about Monet's frustrations gave her confidence to continue.

This Monday was one of those days. Restless, she was not concentrating on seeing or painting. Her mind wandered. *Where is Aleko now?*

And Max-Pol? Taking out her accumulated paintings of the last four weeks, she spread them out on the grass. "Terrible," she said aloud. Slowly, deliberately, she tore each one into pieces.

*

One spring, in the last years of his life, Monet destroyed sixty of his paintings. Sixty. He had Blanche bring them out to him somewhere in his garden. Most were painted when he was having trouble with his eyes, when he could see only a few colors. After looking at each one in critical despair, he asked Blanche to cut them out of the stretchers with a knife and slash them into pieces. Only Blanche would have helped him do such a thing.

After the canvas scraps were piled up, they were burned. Monet's dealer was horrified when he heard. But Blanche understood. She took the ashes down to the water-lily pond, rowed out in Monet's green boat, and scattered the ashes on the surface of the water, where they sank, becoming a part of the scene Monet could not get right on canvas.

*

Alice knew this story. She went back to her lodgings, asked her landlady for permission to use the trash burner behind the house, and set fire to the torn shreds of her watercolor paintings. *I'm not destroying anything,* she thought, *I'm just turning matter into energy and memory.*

The last thing she did before leaving for Paris was to take the ashes from her fire, walk down to Monet's grave, and scatter the ashes carefully around the iris and poppies growing there.

"Thanks, Oscar-Claude," she said. "Dust to dust, ashes to ashes. Around and around and around we go, and where and why we do not know."

She turned and walked away smiling, her eyes filling with tears.
She would never come back to Giverny.
She would not need to.
She would carry it with her.
Always.

steps leading up

Corner garden
& neighboring house
Rue Claude Monet

TUESDAY, MAY 7

Seattle. Morning. Warm and damp. The greenhouse of May.

If Max-Pol were a plant he would be in bloom on this day. Light-hearted, he walked through the revolving door of the outpatient clinic of the hospital into the day, released from the custody of his fears.

Now, he had one thing on his mind: coconut banana cream pie with shaved dark chocolate on top and a glass of whole milk on the side. No matter that it was ten o'clock in the morning. No matter that this was not a healthy meal. Max-Pol was feeling *good*. And the pie was just two blocks away, waiting behind the counter at Jack's Cafe.

When he was in the hospital in Hania the morning after his accident, he had daydreamed about this favorite dessert. It was his private treat when something fine had happened. It wasn't the dessert he wanted so much as the feeling of reckless optimism he connected with it. He wanted to feel good enough again to go for the coconut pie. And now, as he walked quickly down the street, he felt that good. *This might even be a two-piece-of-pie morning,* he thought.

Irrational fear had brought him back to Seattle. After meeting Alice at Waterloo Station, he had returned to his hotel and collapsed. The energy surge from excitement had drained away, and he felt awful. When he considered his condition as objectively as possible, he was worried. His lacerations were healing slowly, his hands and fractured wrist throbbed, his tongue was still slightly swollen, his front teeth hurt, and he had a persistent fever. A staph infection was a real possibility.

Going on a boat trip with Alex was out of the question - Max-Pol would be a useless burden. And he did not want to seek unfamiliar English medical help. He would not be satisfied until he had been examined by doctors he knew well, and whose professional judgment he trusted. Alex's unexpected decision to travel with Alice to France was welcome. That had made it easy for Max-Pol to go on to Seattle.

Part of his anxiety came from his lack of personal experience with being sick or injured. Apart from the usual childhood maladies of colds, measles, and mumps, Max-Pol had never been sick. And apart from the scrapes and cuts and bruises of childhood, he had never had an accident. Now, he was one of "them"- those in pain and distress. Now, he knew something that couldn't be taught in medical school.

Max-Pol's reaction to being back inside the world of medicine surprised him. He had left thinking he would never return. And now he felt at ease in the environment of doctors and nurses, eager to know what was going on and what was new. He actually felt like putting on a white coat and going to work. His desire to be useful and helpful had not been satisfied since he turned his back on medicine.

After a week of examinations, tests, and consultations, he was given the good news: His only problem was impatience with the time healing takes. Even his chipped front teeth were easily repaired. He already felt better. Time for pie.

And time for one more errand on his list. As long as he was in Seattle for a few days, he might as well try to find out more about Alice. Meeting her at Waterloo Station had blindsided him. He went to the meeting out of intense curiosity, and left out of his mind with . . . with . . . what? Max-Pol couldn't name it, but he still felt the impact of the encounter, wanted to see her again, and soon. *Chemistry and pheremones,* he said to himself.

He was pleased to know that Alex was with her, being a bridge between them. He expected Alex to tell her a great deal about him - things he could not say about himself. And Alice would do the same. When he saw them again, both would see Max-Pol Millay in a new light.

lightest - brick-face of largest building

darkest - overhanging foliage & reflection of same

Oxford

Cottage Cruisers
Moorage next to The Boatyard AND
Oxford Canal Towpath
Warm, white clouded sky, drops of rain

WEDNESDAY, MAY 8

Alice had phoned last night.

"I'll be there at noon tomorrow," said Alice.

"Excellent." said Alex. "Take a taxi to College Cruisers' moorage at Combe Road Wharf, just off Canal Street. The driver will know. It is not far from the station. Just ask for me at the wharf office."

When they hung up, Alex thought, *She will come early - she always does.* He checked his train timetables for possibilities. *If she takes the 6:37 a.m. Eurostar from Paris . . . factor in an hour's time difference . . . Waterloo at 8:46, catch the 9:15 from Paddington, and be in Oxford by 10:15. No. Too early. There is another Eurostar at 7:00 . . . and she could be here by 11:00. That is what she will do. If she took the next one at 8:13 . . . Oxford at 11:45. No. She will be on the 7:00 from Paris. And I will be at the station to meet her at 11:00. Surprise!*

*

When the 11:00 from Paddington pulled into Oxford Station, Alex was there, sitting on a bench as casually as his enthusiasm allowed. An assortment of students, tourists, and academics got off the train. No Alice. Not even Alice in disguise.

Ah, well, Alex thought. He reluctantly hailed a taxi and went sullenly back to Combe Road Wharf. So much for surprises. *Maybe she changed her mind,* he thought, *or there was a train wreck. Or . . . she has already come - really early?*

On the way down to his boat, Alex stopped at the moorage office.

"Has anyone been asking for me?"

"No. There's a lady waiting for you," said the wharf master, grinning, "but she didn't actually ask for you."

"Where is she?"

"Over there, sitting in the stern of your boat. She walked through the yard and went aboard without saying anything to anybody. I assume you know her?"

Looking out the window and down the dock, he saw her. Alice. Curled up in a chair, eyes closed, face turned to the morning sun. Damn! She had out-foxed him. He walked quietly down the dock, half annoyed, half overjoyed.

"You are early," Alex said, whacking the side of the boat hard with his cane.

Startled, Alice sat up and laughed. "And you went to meet my train."

"Never mind. How did you know this was my boat?"

"How could it not be? A boat named *Ariadne*, flying a Greek flag? Whatever, here I am. And if you will confess that you were so glad I was coming you went to meet an early train because you thought I would come early, then I will confess that I was so glad to be coming that I caught the first train from Paris, got here at 10:15, and was up there at the corner sitting in The Old Bookbinders Ale House composing my mind when I saw you go by in the taxi."

"All right, I confess." said Alex, "But we will drive each other crazy if we keep trying to read each other's mind."

"Yes . . . but think what we prove by this anticipation game. It's clear, isn't it? I missed you Aleko. You missed me."

"Yes," said Alex, "there is that."

*

"Let's play show-and-tell," said Alice.

"Look. Here's my new hat. My boating hat. You bought it for me - or would have bought it for me if you had been with me in Rouen on Saturday. Monet's colors."

She held out the yellow straw hat with the pale blue ribbons for Alex's inspection before placing it on her head at a jaunty angle.

"Lovely," said Alex. "I certainly would have bought it for you. Let me pay you for it so that I can say it really was my gift."

"The price might be high," Alice replied.

"Name it."

"Not now - later - at the right time, and cash won't count."

"Are you going to begin the trip by teasing me?"

"Yes. There's a time for everything, Aleko. Be patient. And in the meantime, make me welcome, Captain. Show me your ship."

Most English canal boats are long and narrow, defined by the width and length of canal locks, and the clearance under bridges and inside tunnels. Seventy feet long by seven feet wide by seven feet above the waterline is theoretically the maximum space available, but most boats must be more realistically designed to allow for the deterioration of the canal infrastructure. Because they are no longer used for commercial purposes, the canals are in disrepair. Thus, the *Ariadne* is fifty-seven feet long, six feet ten inches wide, and six feet above the waterline and will fit almost anywhere on the canal.

The traditional narrowboat used for pleasure has evolved into a floating Gypsy wagon, a product of English nostalgia at its most excessive. Elaborate woodwork inside and out; every surfaced decorated with curling designs or flowers or scenes of water life. Polished brass, braided lines, and pots of geraniums prevail. And down below, the essences of British middle-class, cluttered hominess: chintz curtains, handmade rugs, displays of china and knickknacks. There are annual contests to establish which boater has pushed quaintness to its limits.

Alex does not compete.

While the *Ariadne* is traditional in shape, it is without external embellishment. Black hull, dark green topside, and plain black working gear. No brass, no chrome, no geraniums. Quaint, it is not. This austere but traditional exterior suggests the thoroughly modern fittings and machinery inside the boat.

Designed for efficiency and ease of maintenance by Alex, the interior is surprisingly sleek - crafted of stainless steel, oiled teak, molded Corian, and leather. The floors are industrial-grade cork and rubber. Clever use of space allows for three sleeping berths, two bathrooms with showers, a galley, and a combination sitting room/dining area. A brown, saddle-leather easy chair, small woodstove, and well-stocked bookshelves are the only signs of hominess.

The operating equipment includes an efficient diesel engine, bow thrusters, power steering, and electronic controls. All in all, the *Ariadne* is relatively easy for one man to operate and maintain.

Alice was impressed. The *Ariadne* was not an old man's lair.

"I will give you answers to questions you are not asking," said Alex.

"I once was a married man, living in Oxford with a wife and twin daughters. That major episode of my life ended when the twins grew up and moved away to Australia, and my wife, Gwyneth, died a year later. I will not elaborate the details now. The point is that I was free to choose how I would go on living. What now? I wondered. I watched my peers in similar circumstances. They became caretakers of a museum of their past. Sooner or later they sold off the artifacts and moved into a small apartment, took long walks and waited for old age to come and cart them away to a retirement home, or waited for death to box them up for the cemetery. I am not skilled at waiting. I decided old age and death would have to chase me down.

"So, I ran away to sea, like many a Greek before me. In my case the nearby canals and rivers of England were sea enough. I hired a narrow-boat until I was certain I liked the reality and not just the idea. Then I sold my house, car, and most of my possessions, and plunged into the canal way of life. Twenty years now. In the early years I traveled most of the waterways of England. In winter I moored up and went to Spain, Morocco, Mexico - anyplace warm.

"Between my wife's inheritance and my own good fortune with investments I am financially secure. I could go and live almost anywhere. And three years ago I considered moving ashore. Perhaps Spain, the French Rivera, or even Crete. But I like this waterborne life. I like the freedom of moving around, like a turtle with his shell. And I like the companionable eccentricity of those who have chosen the water as a way of life in this floating village.

"But. There is a difficulty. These are awkward craft. It is not easy handling one of them alone, even if you are young and fit. On the other hand, that means one must continually reach out for new and younger friends who can come along for the ride and learn the ropes.

"I needed a certain kind of boat - one that would both keep me afloat and make company comfortable. So here you have it: the *Ariadne*. Designing it, having it built and fitted out took two interesting years. It is unique. And since word gets around in the canal-boat community, I always have visitors; and visitors lead to new friendships, and new friendships lead to new adventures. Old age and death still do not know where I am most of the time.

"There is more to tell and more to show you, but first we must move to my permanent moorage, not far up the canal. I will need your help, and the best way for you to help is to pretend you are stupid, but willing to do just what I say and no more. Later I will give you a manual to read about boat handling and canal operation and all the rest. You will quickly get the hang of it. Agreed?"

"Aye, aye, my captain," said Alice.

"First order: you will sit here in the sun. I will go below and change clothes."

Well, well, thought Alice, when he returned. Here was an Alex she had not seen or even imagined. Green baseball hat, sunglasses, long-sleeved white sweatshirt, and faded blue jeans, with sockless feet in oil-tanned boating shoes.

"Ready, Mate?" he asked.

"Should I change, too?"

"No, just go forward through the boat to the bow and, when I tell you, take the line off the cleat and toss it onto the shore."

"And then?"

"That is all for now. Just stand up there looking beautiful and enjoy the ride. You will be my figurehead and stir up gossip all the way up to the mooring."

"Shall I go bare-breasted and lean into the wind?"

You probably would, thought Alex. "Not today. Some other time."

All business now, he switched on the engine, tossed the aft line ashore, engaged the forward bow thruster and shouted, "Cast off." And slowly, grandly, the *Ariadne* eased away from the bank, outward bound, Captain Xenopouloudakis at the helm. First Mate Alice at the bow.

Alice looked back at him, feeling the distance between them grow very small. She took off her shoes and hat, turned her face into the breeze, and waved like a beauty pageant queen at everyone she saw on shore or on other canal boats.

Let the gossip begin, she thought.

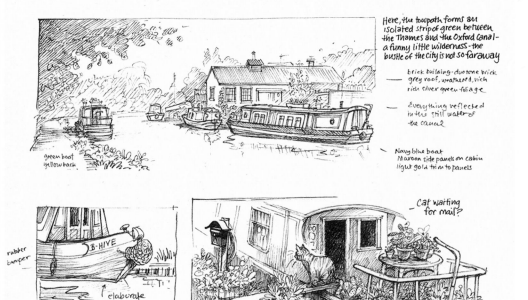

Here, the towpath forms an isolated strip of green between the Thames and the Oxford Canal - a funny little wilderness - the bustle of the city is not so far away

brick building - duo tone brick grey roof, weathered, rich rich silver green foliage

Everything reflected in the still water of the canal

green boat yellow back

Navy blue boat Maroon side panels on cabin light gold trim to panels

rubber bumper

B-HIVE

↑ elaborate braided-rope bumpers

- Boats here are lovingly polished and kept up. Many have someone living aboard

- Cat waiting for mail?

- Permanent moorings have gardens, mailboxes, and charming walkways, garden hoses & electrical hookups

MECONOPSIS

Slowly they cruised along a line of live-aboard boats moored more-or-less permanently along the banks of the canal like a floating Gypsy camp. Abruptly the shore became a residential community of brick houses with green lawns and flower gardens between them and the canal.

Alex called out, "See that small greenhouse just ahead? My moorage is right in front of it. When we drift up to the bank, hop ashore and get the line there and jump back on and put the loop over that same cleat, and I will take it from there."

Alice did as she was asked, nimbly and efficiently.

Alex noticed.

Pleased with his crew, he busied himself securing the stern of the boat, shutting down the engine, and swinging out the gangway.

Alice's eyes were drawn to the small greenhouse and the rocky ledges in front of it. The beds were filled with tall flowers of the most intense shades of blue she had ever seen. *Poppies?* she wondered. *But poppies aren't blue.*

"Aleko, is all this yours?" Alice asked.

"Yes and no. The greenhouse part is mine in a way," he said. "A dear friend and colleague, now deceased, gave me the use of it and the moorage when he became bedridden. He and I shared an interest in bonsai and exotic plants. When he died, his widow, who remained in the house, asked me to stay on. When she died, their daughter moved into the house, and she insisted the greenhouse and moorage had really become mine. She and her husband look after the greenhouse and plants when I am away, and I take them on trips on the canal when I am here. It is a fine arrangement.

"Someday I shall have a much larger greenhouse of my own and get serious about plant propagation. Forgive the long answer to your question. But I have to tell you all that so you will understand that it is both *mine* and *not mine*. I can say that about much that I care for."

"Aleko, don't apologize. I like your long answers. I like knowing anything and everything about you," said Alice. "I suppose those blue flowers have their own story?"

"Yes. *Meconopsis* is the genus name for Himalayan poppies. The seven species here were originally collected from the wild in Nepal, Tibet, Sikkim, and the Shan province of western China by botanical adventurers in the late nineteenth century. The plants were brought to the gardens in Kew.

"Their blues are unmatched in the flower kingdom. I raise them because they remind me of the skies of Crete and the blue in the Greek flag. They are temperamental - the very devil to raise - but somehow I have found the right mix of soil and drainage and light. You can see they are at home now, here in this small corner of England."

He cupped a pale, lavender-blue flower in his hands and bent it toward Alice so she could see the yellow-orange pollen. Alice touched a finger to the pollen and smeared it on the end of Alex's nose.

"Wet paint," she said, and laughed. And for a moment they were back in Monet's garden in the rain.

(Silence.)

"Well, then. *Meconopsis latifolia, aculeata, horridula, grandis, betonicifolia,* and *sheldonii* are their formal names. Technically speaking, the latter is a hybrid of those two next to it. One of the hardest things about growing them is the discipline required the first year, when they begin to flower.

"You must forego the pleasure of seeing them bloom and cut all the buds off. They will usually not last another year if you do not. But if you can bring it upon yourself to do the pruning, then the next year they will be strong, and they will reliably flower for several years to come.

"Alas, as I remind you, I am not a patient man, and the older I get the less patient I am. These *Meconopses* teach me patience. They give me something to look forward to if I can only postpone gratification. I collect the seeds and plant them, knowing it will be two seasons before I see flowers. This is the first year the *sheldonii* have bloomed. As promised, I am here to witness their flowering. Poppies have taught me to wait."

Alice was not listening.

She was looking through the windows of the greenhouse to the rows of bonsai displayed on the wooden benches inside.

Alex noticed.

"Ah. Come see my bonsai," he said, and walked around the end of the greenhouse and opened the door for Alice.

"*Ginkgo biloba,*" said Alice, pointing at the first miniature tree she saw, "and that's *Salix babylonica* - weeping willow, and next to it in bloom is *Cydonia oblonga* - quince." Alice smiled at Alex's expression of surprise.

"I could go on," she said. "I think I know most of them, which means that I recognize how superb a collection of trees you have."

"How . . . ?"

"As you often say, Aleko, it's a long story for another time. But for now I'll simply tell you that the main reason for my interest in all things Japanese is because I am one-quarter Japanese. I know - it doesn't show. My mother was half, though you would never know it from looking at her either. Her mother came from Japan when she was very young.

"Her father's father - my great-grandfather - had a famous collection of bonsai, which still exists in Kyoto in the care of distant members of the family. Every time I go to Japan I spend time in that bonsai garden. I know a lot about bonsai, in part because I have a good friend who is himself a master of bonsai, with an important collection of his own."

Alex frowned. "Not the Kabuki actor?"

"Yes," said Alice, "Matsui Zenkichi."

Damn! thought Alex.

"Well then," he said abruptly. "There is much to do before going on up the canal. Come back to the boat, and I will get you settled and give you some homework, while I go for the supplies I have ordered."

He gestured toward the door, and Alice went out without protest, once again thinking, *He really is jealous.*

"Come on," said Alex, "Let us get on with it."

Yes, she thought, *let's get on with it.*

And they went aboard the *Ariadne*.

WONKO

Hooot, hooot, hooot, hooot.

In the early afternoon of this perfectly clear day, the mellow moan of a foghorn rolled down the canal. Four short blasts, the inland waterways alarm signal for "I am unable to maneuver." Alex moved quickly toward the cockpit to deal with oncoming danger.

Hooot, hooot, hooot, hooot, followed by a loud, deep, gravelly shout: "Helloooo, *Ariadne!* Aleko, you crusty old Greek sod! Come out and fight!"

"Oh, dear God, it is him," said Alex.

"Who?" asked Alice.

"Wonko the Weird. Come see for yourself," said Alex.

They hurried out on deck. "Hang on, he will probably bang into us."

Drifting alongside was an all-black barge, a pirate's pennant fluttering from its prow. At the wheel in the stern stood a large, roundish man with a roundish, bewhiskered face, steering the boat with his roundish belly against the tiller. On his head was a Viking helmet. In one hand an old-fashioned brass foghorn, and in the other a pint of beer.

Hooot, Hooot, Hooot, Hooot!

"Stop it, you bloody crank! People will think there really is an emergency," shouted Alex, as he tossed out a line and dropped a protecting fender overboard just in time. BANG!

"It's always an emergency when I am around, Aleko!" bellowed Wonko. Spying Alice, he lowered his voice, "Aha, you've caught another fair bird in your silky net. Madame, *you* are in *dangerous* hands!"

"Dangerous hands are the kind I like best," replied Alice.

"Oho - a lively one with a tarty tongue - the kind I like best. Welcome to our floating zoo, Madame."

Wonko, behave yourself. This is my dear friend, Alice," said Alex.

"Ah, they're all your dear friends, these migratory birds perched on your deck. And I must say you attract the most exotic species," said Wonko, bowing in the direction of Alice.

"Madame, we must talk. I, Wonko the Sane, will be honored to accept your company as soon as possible in my office at The Constipated Duck. Do come alone. We shall lift a pint or two or three and speak of the sordid affairs of Aleko the Lion, and you will tell me the story of your lovely life, and I will induct you into the Pantheon of the Goddesses of the River. Ah, Madame, do not refuse this chance of a lifetime! And now, Away!"

Half drowned in the waterfall of words poured over them, Alex and Alice could not reply before Wonko had tossed back the mooring line, gunned his engine, picked up the foghorn. *Hoot, Hoot, Hoooot, Hoooooooooot*, he blasted, as he steered away up the canal.

"He makes a lot of noise, but it's an act, isn't it? For all his bombast, I like him. There's more to him than meets the eye," said Alice. "By the way, which is it – Wonko the Sane, or Wonko the Weird?"

"That depends on your point of view, but I think both. Most of the time he is a one-man carnival. Some think he is a nut case. Some think him dodgy. Some even think his act is a cover for criminal activity. Who knows? I can tell you Wonko stories for hours. And he will tell you Wonko stories for days.

"His tales of military combat will go on as long as you will buy him ale. The last time I saw him, the two of us started with gin at six o'clock and were still there at closing time, with half the pub sitting around us completely caught up in Wonko's exploits at the siege of Khartoum. A wonderfully outrageous evening."

"Why outrageous?" asked Alice.

"So far as I know, he has never served in the British military. On top of that, the siege of Khartoum took place in 1885. Still, most of us would have testified in court that Wonko *must* have been there. Brilliant! He knows his military history. He is not as barmy as he pretends to be.

"In fact, I have also thought he was playing at being Wonko. Behind the public performance, something else is going on. I have never caught him out, mind you – but I am also certain that he is more than meets the eye. Yet, I must say I really do not want to know all the rest of his story because I like what I know, and do not want to spoil it with too many facts. He is one of those salt-and-vinegar characters who keep life from being drab and boring."

"That's for sure," said Alice. "Whatever he is, I'd like to see more of him."

"No doubt you will. He is always on the canal somewhere. We will accept his invitation. In his own roundabout way he has just invited us to have an ale with him at his favorite pub, The Boat, in Thrupp, where we will moor tomorrow night."

"I thought he said The Constipated Duck," said Alice.

"He is always giving the pub another name because he thinks The Boat is so mundane. He makes up a new name for it every time I see him. The King's Drawers, The Deviant Swan, The Ass of the Ostrich, and The Sour Grapes are a few I can recall. He has a permanent moorage in Thrupp, and is in The Boat so often he calls it his office. The owners do not mind because he draws business. Wonko is their comedian-in-residence.

"The last time I was there he got into a jumping contest with a rugby team, and jumped so high he hit the low ceiling, leaving his Viking helmet stuck in the rafters. He was still on his feet at evening's end, though several of the heartiest rugby players had to be carried out dead drunk. He is tough. They made him an honorary member of the team.

He also plays bagpipes and fiddle, and builds medieval siege machines for melon-throwing events. As I say, the Wonko stories are endless. You will see for yourself tomorrow night."

382

EVIDENCE

After showing Alice around her cabin and giving her the Inland Waterways Manual to study, Alex went ashore with a small folding cart to retrieve supplies for the voyage.

"I will return in an hour or so. Please make yourself completely at home," he said.

Alice took him at his word.

*

Much can be learned about another person by inspecting their most private and personal spaces - bathrooms, bedrooms, desk drawers, and closets. This, of course, is usually the device of detective novels. In real life the opportunity seldom arises, even with the closest of friends.

For one thing, nice people don't snoop. And the price of snooping can be high. The possibility of learning what you had rather not know is always there. The drugs and pills and potions and salves in the medicine closet; the dreary night garments hung on the back of the bathroom door; the rich animal smell of closets with old-but-undiscarded shoes piled in the back; the cluttered chaos of drawers; collections of ratty underwear; diaries and journals; sexual aids - even pornography.

Snooping is risky business. We can know people well for a lifetime and never gain access to the backstage story of their existence. Perhaps that is just as well.

*

"Make yourself completely at home," Alex had said.

Alice did not snoop - not in the pejorative sense - she had too much respect for Alex to do that, but she did take Alex at his word and made herself at home, taking a closer look at his floating world. Before she even bothered unpacking and settling into her own space, she walked through the boat to see what it might tell her about Alex.

She had not expected the spare, monkish neatness she found everywhere she looked. Not the layers in the settling pond of a stagnant life.

No clutter, no holding on to the old and worn, no useless collections of odds and ends. No photographs or even pictures on the walls.

A monk would be happy here, she thought.

In his bathroom his dark green towels were new. Hanging behind the door was a fluffy white terry-cloth robe in mint condition. Opening the medicine cabinet over the sink, she saw only the barest necessities for personal grooming neatly set out on the shelves: a wooden-handled Kent hairbrush, a tortoiseshell comb, a silver safety razor, shaving brush, shaving soap in a wooden bowl, a bottle of *4711* after-shave lotion, one high-tech toothbrush, and a tube of mint-flavored toothpaste.

The only pharmaceuticals she found were aspirin and an unopened container of over-the-counter antihistamine. No prescription drugs. A fresh bar of soap sat unopened on the sink edge. The same *4711* brand - an astringent fragrance of limes and lemons. In the adjoining shower there was more *4711* soap, an unmarked white container that must be shampoo, and a long, wooden-handled back brush.

Alice discovered that the shower opened out on the galley on the other side, an odd but clever arrangement. She supposed it provided flexibility when several guests were aboard. The galley looked neat and efficient and clean, but she did not explore it. There would be time for that later. She turned back to consider Alex's cabin.

His clothes closet smelled of cedar. Two suits, two tweed jackets, five dress shirts - three white, two blue. Two wool plaid shirts. Five conservative striped ties, two belts, and a black wool shawl. Nothing more - not even shoes. *Where does he keep his shoes?* she wondered.

Alex's bed was in a curtained alcove in his cabin. An extra-wide bunk made up with white sheets, three plump pillows, and a blue-and-white checkered quilt. A black-and-white-striped wool blanket was folded at the foot of the bed.

This sleeping alcove had the unmistakable fresh smell of bedding that has been hung out in sunshine. Alice climbed up into the bunk and lay down.

How cozy. Wonder what he would do if he found me asleep here when he got back? Goldilocks and the one bear?

Alice got up, smoothed the pillows, and went on with her investigation. Slowly she began to understand she would find no surprises. She walked through the length of the boat without seeing anything more that tempted her prying. No locks prevented her from looking either.

Suddenly she understood. Alex had three days before she came. He had probably set the stage for her, as she herself would have done when expecting live-in company. "Well, of course," she said aloud. "He knew I'd look around. That's why he went off and left me alone to make myself at home. Wily man."

True. Six blocks away at Bunter's store, Alex stood at the counter wondering how far Alice had got in her inspection by now. He would have been disappointed if she had not taken a good look around. He had tidied up a bit before she came, but not much. What Alice would find was an essential part of his sense of self: contentment does not reside in clutter or possessions.

*

When he decided, after his wife died, to move from his home of many years, he took stock of his belongings and was dismayed by the accumulation. Going through her personal things had been hard. There was so little he wanted to keep, and yet he felt ill at ease in getting rid of anything. Deciding to decide was the barrier he had to break through.

Not wanting to be the caretaker of a museum of the past, he had given a truck-load to the Salvation Army and hired an auction house to dispose of the rest in the spirit of an estate sale. "Treat it as if both my wife and I were dead," he told the puzzled auctioneer.

He had been ruthless. His goal was to leave with two suitcases and two boxes of books. Twenty-four boxes of personal files and letters and who-knows-what had been turned over to two young men who came around in a van with a shredding machine. He kept only a small folio of essential financial records.

He leased a canal boat in a nearby marina. Early one morning he left his house without looking back. The real estate agent and his solicitor took care of the financial and legal details.

Done. It was not that Alex hated his past or was running away. The baggage of it was too heavy to carry for the rest of his days, and maintaining it left little space for the present and the future. He wanted to travel light, to live light, to be light. To let go. Everything he cared most about went with him in the form of memories, not things.

When he was having the *Ariadne* designed and built, he promised himself that he would never bring anything aboard he did not need or truly like having. Once his minimal needs were met, he vowed that for every new thing he bought an old thing must go. He had one small bookcase - mostly reference works. When he bought a new book, he read it and passed it on to the local library or to friends.

And every year he called the Salvation Army to come again. Afterward, he went out and bought new linen and new clothes and new underwear. In this spirit, he got fitted for a new suit every year and gave an old one away. It was enlightened charity. He liked thinking some needy man got some high-quality clothes in good condition because of him. Once he was pleased to see what was unmistakably his suit on a cab driver in Oxford.

On more than one occasion, he thought of his old house and life and compared it to his life on the *Ariadne*. He had pulled it off. *I am free of all that*, he thought. Recently he had read Kundera's novel, *The Unbearable Lightness of Being*. He had read it without enthusiasm and had given it away. For Alex, *being* had become both light *and* bearable. He intended keeping it that way as long as possible.

All this was one more way of fooling Death into thinking Alex Evans was alive and well. If Death should drop by the *Ariadne,* he would find no evidence that a worn-out old man lived there. For one thing, Death would notice Alice and know for certain that Alex was not available this week.

*

Alice was tempted to open a desk drawer, but stopped. She knew she would find nothing of consequence, though she would not put it past him to have left a note for her in a drawer saying something like, Nothing of interest in here. Or, The gold is in the vault. And even if there was such a note, she didn't want to find it. Opening drawers crossed a forbidden line.

What would a microscopic investigation by police turn up? she asked herself, looking around the kitchen. *What would forensic science make of samples of hair, fibers, stains, pollen, and fingerprints? Would I learn anything I want to know? No.*

Without exploring any further, she went back to her cabin and sat down on the bed. Puzzled. Had she been complimented? Or insulted? Was this an inning in a game or just Alex straight up? Or was it simply that he meant what he said - that she should make herself at home. To be at home in the most comfortable sense - no boundaries. That was probably it.

Then that's the way it's going to be, she thought. *No boundaries.*

*

When Alex came whistling back accompanied by a young man pushing the cart full of provisions, he found Alice sitting in the sunlight in the stern studiously annotating the Inland Waterways Manual.

She had changed into shorts and T-shirt. The young man carrying the groceries aboard could hardly keep his eyes off her. Distracted by her loveliness, he left without proffering his hand for the usual tip.

"You just saved me money," said Alex. "He forgot his tip."

"By the number of boxes and bags you brought back, I think I cost you money," said Alice. "What is all this?"

"I would rather surprise you day by day. But when I tell you that Bunter's store is owned and operated by a family of my countrymen and that I am a regular customer of many years, then you will guess that I have nothing but the best."

Somewhere below, a clock chimed twice - two bells of the ship's clock. "It is five o'clock now," said Alex. "The British usually have tea and biscuits or gin and tonic at this time of day, and the Greeks have *ouzo* and *mezezes* - a little taste of this and that. What will you have?"

"Greek," said Alice. "Can I help?"

"No, today you are my guest. Stay here - it is crowded in the galley."

"Aleko," Alice called, as he started down into the boat, "is it that you want to go below without me to see if I've snooped around while you were gone?"

Alex stopped halfway down the stairs to look at back at her. He raised his eyebrows. Smiled. "You do not beat around the bushes, do you?"

"You don't expect me to, do you? And by the way, did you leave a thread stuck across a drawer, or a piece of clear tape somewhere? I didn't find any."

Alex laughed. "To be honest, I thought of it. But I guessed you would be too clever for that, or else would just tell me what you had done without my asking – as is the case. I admit I tidied up a little, as I always do when I have guests aboard, but whatever you found is the way things usually are.

"I have nothing to hide from you, Alice. Nothing. And it is not an issue of trust or mistrust. I both hoped you would look around and hoped you would tell me. I could not be more pleased. You have made yourself very much at home - *that*, and *only* that, was my intention."

Satisfying silence fell between them as they considered one another. Once again they were of one mind.

"Ouzo," said Alice, breaking the spell.

"Ouzo," said Alex, "coming right up. And I warn you that I shall test you on your knowledge of the Inland Waterways Manual. Starting to-morrow you are my crew and I am a very demanding captain."

"Try me," replied Alice, "I'm ready for anything."

Anything? thought Alex, and went below.

"Anything!" shouted Alice.

*

Too tired to fix a meal on the *Ariadne* that night, they settled for fish and chips at The Anchor, a pub on the Aristotle Lane route into Port Meadow. A rowdy game of trivia led by Oxford students made an entertaining bedlam of the pub.

Walking back in silence in the early evening, Alice and Alex returned to the boat and went straight on to bed with little conversation. Each in their separate cabin and bunk, but knowing each was nearby, they were quickly and contentedly asleep, lulled by the smells and sounds and air of the spring night coming through the portholes latched open above their heads.

They were not aware of the man who came quietly along the bank and stood in the darkness by the *Ariadne*. Squatting down, he briefly peered through the portholes of the boat, and went away as quietly as he had come.

Wonko the Weird or the Sane – as the case might be.

235- Bridge over Wolvercote Lock

Thursday, May 9

Daybreak.

Alex, barefoot, in his white bathrobe, making coffee as quietly as possible in the galley, listened for signs of Alice rising. Silence. As was his habit he had lit an oil lamp, preferring its cozy warm glow to the instant artificial white light from the fluorescent fixture above the sink. He liked easing into the day instead of bringing it on all at once with a switch on the wall. He opened the skylight hatch above the galley to sample the morning air. *Dew. Going to be warm,* he thought. He yawned and stretched himself like a contented old cat.

Ding-Ding. Ding-Ding. Four bells. Six o'clock.

Alice, your time has come, he thought.

Instead of knocking on her door, Alex decided to wake her with a CD recording of the sounds of dawn coming to the Amazon jungle. The boat was wired with speakers in each cabin, controlled from a central sound system in the salon; the cries of parrots and howler monkeys, even at low volume, usually roused his guests better than a bugle call. At full blast the alarming din could raise the heaviest sleeper straight up out of the bed and out on deck in rattled disarray. Guests seldom slept in late after that.

But Alice had been awake for some time, waiting for some sign from Alex. Even so, she was not expecting the Amazon jungle cries.

When the water pump kicked on, Alex knew Alice was in the shower. Now he could use the coffee grinder and the juicer. He was just pouring fresh orange juice into glasses, when Alice ever so quietly opened the door and stood looking at him.

He knew she was there. He could smell the steam from the shower and the scent of his favorite soap drifting in through the doorway into the galley. As if unwrapping an unanticipated gift, he slowly turned toward her.

Alice in the morning.

White hair piled on top of her head, held with a tortoiseshell clip. Indigo-blue cotton kimono – a *yukata* - splashed with white Japanese calligraphy. Bare feet. Her only makeup was a touch of bright red lipstick in the middle of her lower lip, geisha-style. A large but unlit cigar was clamped between her teeth.

"Got a light, sailor?" she purred.

Alex laughed so hard he spilled orange juice on his hands and down the front of his white robe. And Alice, laughing with him, pulled a roll of paper towels off the holder and went to work dabbing up the damage.

"I brought the cigar for you, actually, but if you can surprise me with howling monkeys, then you deserve a surprise of your own," said Alice.

*

Wonko coasted silently by in his boat, moving under minimum power.

He heard the laughter from the darkened *Ariadne*.

"Well, well, well," he thought.

Engaging cruising gear, he eased the throttle forward and passed on quietly up the canal toward his moorage just beyond Thrupp.

*

When the mess had been mopped up, Alex and Alice stood looking at each other with the unfettered joy of children at play. What a way to begin the day.

Why didn't they throw their arms around one another there and then? A natural enough spontaneous gesture in the circumstances. Why not?

Perhaps it was nothing more than a restraining thread of ongoing caution - knowing that hugging in the kitchen in the half-light of early morning with only bathrobes between them might - *or might not* - lead to other gestures of delight and affection, which might - *or might not* - be reciprocated.

Even the smallest uncertainty can be the largest barrier between people - like the slender, striped pole marking a border crossing between friendly countries. Passports and formalities of some kind may still be required. One should be careful. No one wants to be turned away on the grounds of having made wrong moves at the border.

"Here," said Alex, holding out half a glass of orange juice. "Have some first aid. The coffee is ready, but it is not Greek. I hate Greek coffee. This is a blend of Ethiopian Harare and Blue Mountain from Jamaica. Do you want cream or sugar? Hot milk? Cup or mug? Cognac on the side? Croissant? Toast? Muffins?"

Alex was babbling on without waiting for answers from Alice. Not hugging her when he felt like it - not reaching out - not holding her close -had short-circuited his sensibilities. Hearing himself, he abruptly stopped talking, turned back to the sink, and began washing his hands.

Alice moved behind him, put her arms around him and hugged him. He felt her lay her head against his back.

She whispered, "Aleko, I'm really, really glad I'm here with you." And before he could react, she released him.

And saying, "I'll get dressed and be right back - let's have coffee topside," she went out of the galley and closed the door behind her.

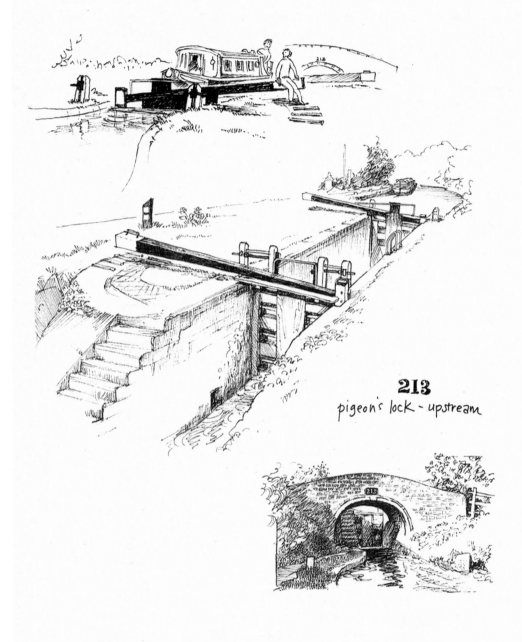

213
pigeon's lock - upstream

JAM TODAY

"Well, then," began the captain of the *Ariadne*, addressing his one-woman crew assembled before him on deck. "Today we shall travel as far as Thrupp. About three hours at normal cruising speed. No reason to rush.

"There are interesting historical sights along the way, a possible excursion ashore, fine places for a picnic, and a fusty old pub where I am a welcome guest. There are only five locks between here and Thrupp. Easy locks. You will have time to learn how to handle lines and the lock gates. I will demonstrate emergency procedures and equipment, and, if you wish, I will teach you how to handle the boat while under way."

Alice stood at mock attention and saluted.

"This evening we will moor in Thrupp and dine with our friend, Wonko, the Weird or the Sane, as the case may be. Thursdays are the locals' last night of the week because the canal tourists overrun the pub on weekends. It should be lively. What say you, Mate?"

"Aye, Captain."

"Look," said Alice, as she made a pirouette. "You haven't said anything about my outfit. What do you think?" she asked.

Alex considered her white canvas shoes, faded blue jeans, pale blue chambray shirt, and perky, white sailor's hat.

"Very practical. But . . ."

"But what?"

"I do not know where you got that hat, but it is an American-style sailor's hat, you know - not French or English - and it does not flatter you. I do not mean to insult your taste, but you asked. Why do Americans make their sailors wear such childish cupcakes on their heads? Cute. No dignity. Actually, I would rather you carry an umbrella than wear that hat. Let us buy you something more English in the ship's store in Kidlington. In the meantime, go hatless."

"Aye, aye, Captain," said Alice, saluting, and carelessly flipping her hat over her shoulder into the water, where it floated slowly away.

"Do you always follow orders so well?"

"No. But I only bought the hat to please you in the first place."

"Well, then, since you are in a mood to please me, I would like it if you let me read a paragraph to you from a favorite book of mine, *The Wind in the Willows*, by Kenneth Grahame. Do you know it?"

"Know about it, but I've never read it. Read to me."

Alex produced a small, worn paperback from his back pocket.

"Since it is an English children's book, I had never read it, either, until Wonko gave it to me last year. He said it was a book for adults, really, and that I would recognize many of the characters. Actually I find myself in all of them. The book has become very dear to me. But, I digress. Here is the paragraph – a manifesto for our adventure on the water. Rat is speaking to Mole, who is a first-time guest in Rat's boat:

> *'Believe me, my young friend, there is nothing - absolutely nothing - half so much worth doing as simply messing about in boats. Simply messing,' he went on dreamily: 'messing - about - in - boats; messing -'*
>
> *'Look ahead, Rat!' cried the Mole suddenly.*
>
> *It was too late. The boat struck the bank full tilt. The dreamer, the joyous oarsman, lay on his back at the bottom of the boat, his heels in the air.*
>
> *'- about in boats - or with boats,' the Rat went on composedly, picking himself up with a pleasant laugh. 'In or out of 'em, it doesn't matter. Nothing seems really to matter, that's the charm of it. Whether you get away, or whether you don't; whether you arrive at your destination or whether you reach somewhere else, or whether you never get anywhere at all, you're always busy, and you never do anything in particular; and when you've done it there's always something else to do, and you can do it if you like, but you'd much better not. Look here! If you've really nothing else on hand this morning, supposing we drop down the river together, and have a long day of it?'*
>
> *The Mole waggled his toes from sheer happiness, spread his chest with a sigh of full contentment, and leaned back blissfully into the soft cushions. 'What a day I'm having!' he said. 'Let us start at once!'*

"There," said Alex. "That is the heart of the matter, not mentioned in the waterways manual I gave you, but truly a waterman's manifesto."

"Lovely. May I have the book to read along the way?"

Pleased, Alex passed the book to her. "It is yours to keep."

Alice accepted the book, kissed Alex on both cheeks in thanks, and briefly closed her eyes and wrinkled her brow in thought. She smiled and looked up at Alex.

"I was thinking of a line from another children's book that speaks to adults - *Alice in Wonderland*," she said. "Another book written in Oxford, of course. There's a part where the White Queen offers Alice a job as her lady's maid. The wages are two pence a week and jam every other day.

"The Queen says she can't have any jam today. The rule is: jam tomorrow and jam yesterday, but never jam today. Alice says there must be jam today sometime. But the White Queen is insistent about the rules.

"But we, you and I, Aleko, are not bound by those rules, are we? We like jam, don't we? Then we shall have jam today. The French say, *La vie est dure sans confiture*. Life without jam is hard. The morning began with jam, as a matter of fact. Let us continue. More jam, please."

"Plat du jour, confiture," replied Alex. "Today's special: jam."

212 · cement, reeds, biker
(Old Brighton Bridge)

tree at water's edge

Nest high in the branches

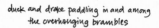

duck and drake paddling in and among
the overhanging brambles

398

Mooring just beyond Sutton's Deep · absolutely raining. soggy sheep

Stormy weather · Chisnall Lift Bridge · 193

ONWARD

Alice untied the forward mooring line. At a nod from Alex she released the line and jumped aboard. He watched her expertly coil and stow the line. *She knows more about boats than she lets on,* he thought.

And she did. Growing up in the maritime city of Seattle, she had learned to sail small boats as a child and served in the crew of her father's yawl as a teenager. She had inherited his boat after his death. Moreover, there were all those years she spent as a coxswain for eight-oared shells.

Alice was at home on the water.

She came back to sit beside Alex as he eased the *Ariadne* away from the bank. With electronic controls and bow thrusters he handled his boat by himself deftly. All he needed now was company in the cockpit.

Gesturing to the west side of the canal, he said, "All that open land over there is Port Meadow. The Thames runs along the other side of it. Remnants of Iron Age fishing camps have been found there. The meadow is mentioned in William the Conqueror's Domesday Book. Never been ploughed – always a common grazing ground for horses and cattle and sheep. Lovely place, especially in winter covered in snow. Much of what inspired *The Wind in the Willows* came from Grahame's rambles around that meadow and the river's edge when he was a schoolboy."

A passenger train suddenly shot across their view, running on the tracks between the canal and the meadow. A ripping roar and then tranquil silence again.

"It is just about here," said Alex, "where in May of 1920, Alastair, the beloved son of Kenneth Grahame, lay down in front of a speeding train a few days before his twentieth birthday. The father and son are buried together in Holywell Cemetery."

(Silence.)

"Speaking of cemeteries, just ahead, on the east side of the canal, is the suburb of Wolvercote. The cemetery there is reserved for those who were not of the Church of England, especially Roman Catholics. Under a rather plain gray slab of Cornish granite lie the remains of John Ronald Reuel Tolkein and his wife. They say it is the most visited grave in Oxford."

"Did you know him?" asked Alice.

"No, not really. I met him once or twice and saw him a number of times around Oxford, but we were not acquainted. He was a very private man. The classic, tweedy, pipe-smoking, absentminded Oxford don.

"Several times I saw him peddling along on his bicycle on the way to morning mass at St. Aloysius, and I wondered how he could be a practicing Roman Catholic and accept the prescribed dogma of the Church, while at the same time carrying on an existence in the boundless world of Middle-earth. Obviously, he found it possible. Nothing wrong with that, though it seems to have unsettled his more conservative critics.

"To answer a question you have not asked, No, I will not take you to visit Tolkein's grave. I was there once. There is nothing to see. I have lost my enthusiasm for cemeteries and do not wish to be found in one, dead or alive."

"Then what do you want done with your remains?" asked Alice.

"Well . . . If I have any say in the matter, I would like to be cremated and have my ashes shot out of a cannon into the sea. But since that is highly unlikely, I would think having my ashes scattered under some anonymous old olive tree in Crete would be appropriate."

"Aleko, there is one cemetery you might consider. How about alongside the grave of Pendlebury at Souda Bay?"

(Silence.)

Speechless, Alex stared straight ahead, avoiding a reply by making minor adjustments to the controls of the *Ariadne*.

"Pendlebury," he said, softly. "How did you know about him? I suppose Max-Pol told you. His Chronicles. I forget how much you must already know about me. It is just as well. I will not have to tell you myself."

(Silence.)

"Alongside Pendlebury at Souda Bay. I had not considered that."

The image of that cemetery came to him. He felt his eyes mist up. When he regained his composure, he turned to look at Alice, and said, with great feeling, "*Epharisto para poli*. Thank you very much for that thought."

Returning to the business of navigating the boat, he said, "We are being too solemn, Alice, and the first lock is coming up. We will tie up just this side of Wolvercote lock, and I will walk you through the drill. On the face of it, the matter is simple. But as with all things simple, there are still ways to go wrong, and each lock has its quirks requiring attention."

*

No problem, thought Alice, as they floated free of the lock and back into the canal. Alice had handled her part with proficiency, needing few words of instruction from Alex.

On they went. Through Duke's lock, negotiating Drinkwater's lift bridge, through Kidlington Green lock and Roundham lock - each passage negotiated more efficiently as captain and crew became synchronized.

Alex lectured about the Romans, the coming of coal, the building of the canals, and impact of the railroads. Alice listened and did her part at locks now without prompting or direction.

Both were aware of this easiness between them.

The silent working of the boat together had its own eloquence.

*

They tied up and walked into Kidlington to have lunch of cheese and bread and ale in the sunny courtyard of The Anchor, where Alex was welcomed by the proprietor's pretty wife with hugs and kisses and greetings in Greek. She brought food and drink before Alice had finished considering the menu, as if she already knew what Alex wanted and what Alice needed.

"She is Cypriot," said Alex. "We expatriate Greeks are all family – all cousins – *ex-adelphia* is the word."

His cousin continued to hug Alex at any opportunity.

Alice smiled feebly. She was vaguely aware of feeling jealous of all this easy hugging and kissing.

Right, she thought, *just cousins*.

*

In the early afternoon *Ariadne* drifted slowly into Thrupp, where the canal seemed more like the main street of a small village than a waterway. They tied up beyond the village at a visitors' moorage.

"We have made quick time of it," announced Alex. "Since it is early, put on your walking shoes, and we shall go across the sheep meadows and the Cherwell to the abandoned village of Hampton Gay. There are great old trees there and an ancient church. I will provide a chilled bottle of Greek wine from the volcanic soil of the island of Santorini, glasses, almonds and raisins from Crete, and a small blanket. You will be my donkey and carry the boodle. Come along. The captain is going ashore."

"Aye, aye, Captain," said Alice, saluting.

"Onward."

Boats Moored At Thrupp

HAMPTON GAY

East of the Oxford canal at Shipton, across the River Cherwell at the top
of a long rise of green meadow, is Hampton Gay, its location marked by
the spire of an old, small, and rarely used church. Most of the stones in
its cemetery are unreadable, their inscriptions smoothed away by lichen
and weather. Some of the graves bear the broken remains of unknown
victims of the great railway disaster of Christmas Eve, 1874, when a
packed train left the bridge crossing the canal and river at Shipton, and
plunged into the icy waters below.

Nearby the church are the grassy mounds of medieval house plat-
forms, all that remains of the deserted village of Hampton Gay, depopu-
lated by the Black Death in 1340. A little farther on are the ruins of a
manor house, destroyed by fire in the late nineteenth century.

Hampton Gay epitomizes melancholy beauty. Tranquil and green
- yet marked by death and darkness. The English Romantics come
to mind in such a place: Thomas Gray, William Blake, Wordsworth,
Coleridge, Keats, and Shelley. If Alex had brought a volume of their
collected poetry he would have read to Alice.

But it would be scholarly pretense on his part if he did. The English
Romantics did not, in fact, appeal to him. Especially Byron. Despite
that poet's commitment to the struggle for Greek independence, Alex
thought Byron a prime example of British upper class narcissism in
full flower. Brilliant, in a perverse way, but degenerate, and morally
corrupt.

*

Alex and Alice had rambled around the ruins of Hampton Gay, looked
in through the dirty windows of the musty church, and found a place at
the edge of the trees to sit looking out over the valley of the Cherwell.
After sharing wine and nuts and raisins, they were now lying side by
side on the blanket in the shade, eyes closed, but still awake.

Alex felt himself in a mental minefield with tripwires stretched to respond to any thoughtless move he might make. He was trying to compose a bit of idle monologue concerning literary matters. Perhaps he would throw in some thoughts about Constable's paintings of the English countryside, or perhaps some commentary on Turner's views on landscape.

But he knew he was only trying to avoid talking about the third person there on the hillside. Sooner or later they were going to talk about Max-Pol. Either Alice would ask, or else Alex would take the initiative and answer her questions before she asked. He had promised this conversation. And now was as good a time as any. But Alex was avoiding the subject.

Obeying an urge to empty his bladder, he excused himself and walked off into the trees. On the way back he stopped by the graveyard, considered the stones around him, and considered Alice lying in the sun alone on the blanket, eyes closed, body in rag-doll disarray like one dropped onto the bed of oblivion by the hand of unexpected sleep.

(Silence.)

The Committee in Alex's mind was holding a rowdy meeting:

Be a fairy-godfather, Alex. You know enough about Alice and Max-Pol to know you should push them along toward one another.
No, Alex. Mind your own business. They have enough between them already to move on their own.
Alex, Alex - look around you. Life is short. Forget about matchmaking. Enjoy whatever comes between you and Alice - today - tonight - this week. The only space between you and Alice is age. Forget age.
No, no, no, Alex. You are the agent of their fate. You are a grandfather person here. You at least can add strands to the ties between them. Years from now they will bless your memory.

But, but, but . . .

Alex, come to your senses. You do not know Alice very well, and you are projecting your needs and fantasies on her. Give it up. Do not make trouble for you or her or Max-Pol.

406

*Remember what Pendlebury did for you, Alex. Do what they can-
not do for themselves. Do what is best for them.
But, but, but - what if . . .*

In a mental muddle, Alex walked around in the cemetery, considering the graves, wondering how long he had until he would cross over
from this life to whatever came next. He recalled a line from *The Medi-
tations of Marcus Aurelius:*

*"Be not distressed, for all things are according to the nature of the
universal, and in a little time you will be no one and no where."*

"So be it," Alex said aloud, and firmly closed the door on the Committee meeting in his mind.

Suddenly, from the meadow below, a grazing cow lifted her head,
and, sounding if she had just been jabbed with a pin, lifted her head and
bellowed out of the utter cow-ness of her existence. *Moooooooo-ahh!*
Having declared herself, she went calmly back to grazing.

Awakened and alarmed by the oncoming-train sound of the cow,
Alice sat up. "Aleko? Where are you? What was that?"

"A bugle call from fate," said Alex, as he came to sit by her. "I was
thinking of Max-Pol and my promise to tell you more about him. What
would you like to know?"

*

Alice turned away to look off into the distance. She had not anticipated
this. Max-Pol was not on her mind. Most of what she wanted most to
know she would find out for herself. The time for that would come.
But Alex had taken the initiative. If he wanted to talk about Max-Pol,
so then, let him.

"I don't know where to begin," she said. "Help me out. Answer questions I haven't asked. Tell me what you will."

"Well, then," said Alex, "I will begin with something simple. With his
unusual name. It is a straightforward matter, actually, but it leads me to
an important observation about the character of Max-Pol.

"His birth certificate names him Maxwell Pollock Millay. As a child,
his mother called him, as mothers will, 'Maxie,' a name he came to hate,
as teenagers will. He shifted to the self-invented combination of his

first two names when he went off to college, as undergraduates will. Henceforth: Max-Pol. His continuing choice. He asked me to call him that, not Max and especially not ever Maxie - and so it is."

"Why is this so important?" asked Alice.

"It is a detail. And Max-Pol is ever attentive to details - in his life, and in the lives of others as well. In all things I find that he employs a remarkably observant eye. And he is not afraid of acting on the conclusions he draws from what he sees and thinks, even if the conclusions are uncommon. I suspect this is a clue to his strength as a physician."

"But he says he doesn't want to be a doctor," said Alice.

"True. That is what he *says*. However, it is my conviction that he is passing through a stage of life where one must move some distance away from one's identity in order to gain some perspective on it. If successfully negotiated, it is the passage into full maturity.

"If not, well . . . But, in time, and who can say how long, I suspect that Max-Pol will find his way back into the practice of medicine - there are many ways to do so, and many places where a man like him could be useful and content.

"He is following the path into the labyrinth of his mind, but he will find the center and come out where he went in. He thinks he is going around the world incognito. But I say he is a man masquerading as himself.

"At the heart of the matter is a term the German philosophers use for a certain kind of self-recognition. I think Heidegger used it first: *Eigentlich*. I would not use an academic term in a foreign language if there were an equivalent word in English, but there is not, and this is the word that fits the case.

"*Eigentlich* refers to the unique quality of one's essential being - what you cannot escape from about yourself - what you hold on to, despite everything - what does not fall away through whatever storms you pass through on the way of your life."

Alice stared at Alex. He was addressing her own situation exactly.

"Max-Pol is more than a trained physician. I saw this in Crete in every personal relationship he had, even when he was not identified as a doctor. There are many qualified people in the helping professions -

doctors, social workers, psychologists and so on – who do a competent job, but whose patients and clients do not seem to improve their situations.

"And then there are those whose patients and clients are more likely to get well – more likely to make progress – more likely to feel confidence in their own power to make life better for themselves. Max-Pol is one of these. In ancient times or in more primitive societies he would be recognized as a shaman – a healer. This is not a passive role. Things happen when a shaman goes to work.

"This describes Max-Pol. He pays attention to people. Good things happen. And I do not feel he will ever be happy until he has found the place in which to fully employ his gift or calling or professional skills – however you want to describe it."

Puzzled, Alice frowned.

"None of this comes through in his Chronicles and I'm not sure I have experienced it personally either," she said. "He never writes or talks about himself, and he speaks of other people as if he is only a passenger on their bus."

"Of course," said Alex. "That reflects his present condition. Max-Pol is deliberately focusing outside himself. It is his way of recovering from a personal tragedy. I will not elaborate, for fear of breaking a confidence. He will tell you in time, I expect. It is enough to say the event seriously derailed his life."

(Silence.)

Alex cleared his throat, and continued. "As to your point, it is simply his way to describe himself as going along with the plans of others, as if they had the idea first, but, in truth, he is usually the inspiration and catalyst for adventure."

"What else?" asked Alice.

"When Max-Pol had his accident at Easter – when he fell into the sea and was rolled across the rocks – I was sure he had been killed or else would die on the way to the hospital. It was a very close thing, you know. During the long hours while we waited for a verdict, I found myself doing an absurd thing: I composed a speech for his funeral. I know it sounds macabre, but one is not always in control of one's mind.

"What I have just told you about his essential self and his being a shaman is actually an excerpt from that funeral oration. What I will now tell you is yet another excerpt. It falls into the category of things only other people can relate about you. It, too, begins with a story.

"As you may know, Max-Pol had the loan of an old, blue Mercedes sedan once owned by a Greek Orthodox bishop. Our friend and cousin, Kostas, and I often rode as royalty in the back seat, never having enjoyed the services of a chauffeur.

"Max-Pol indulged us. And playing the role, he often wore a black turtleneck sweater and a black beret. He had also let his beard grow. Villagers familiar with the Bishop's old car guessed he might be a priest or a monk. And the passengers might be important officials of some kind.

"So. Villagers would cross themselves and give the car a deferential greeting. Max-Pol would smile and return their homage with a two-handed gesture that looked like he was unscrewing the lid from an invisible jar, leaving the villagers utterly nonplussed. Kostas and I were greatly entertained. And to this day, the three of us often greet one another with the jar-unscrewing blessing."

Alice laughed.

"There is one sample of Max-Pol's fine-tuned and subtle sense of humor. Never cruel. Never off-color. But always clever. The Cretans admire a clever man, so they have come to admire Max-Pol. Their response to him reminds me of their feelings about Pendlebury. Not a tourist. *One of them.*"

"Keep going," said Alice. "What else?"

"Well . . . another example of his sense of humor is his way with language. He thinks the idiotic and often useless phrases in the tourist's standard phrase book are hilarious, especially when garbled out of context. When a waiter would inquire about our order, Max would say in Greek something like, 'I would like my squid washed and ironed.' Or, 'Do you have a dentist in the kitchen? I need a laxative.' And so on."

Alice laughed.

"In time the waiters at restaurants caught on to his game, and the whole conversation between them and Max-Pol would be carried on in this ludicrous fashion. The last time we were at the *Amnesia*, when Max-Pol came through the door, a waiter called to the kitchen, 'The crazy American is here to have his oil changed.' Max-Pol replied, deadpan, without missing a beat, 'Make it twenty-weight and don't cook the French fries in it before you put it in the car like last time.'

"The staff was in hysterics. Now they do the same thing back to him in English, especially focused on the health of Max-Pol's invisible pet cow. It is an odd way to learn a language, I admit, but a fine way to make friends.

"You see, he turned his language inadequacy into theater, at his expense. When he walks into the *Amnesia,* the agenda is laughter. It is no longer a tourist taverna, it is a stage for entertainment, and everybody is in on the show. Sometimes this gets going in several languages at once - not only Greek and English, but also French, German, Dutch, whatever. And it is Max-Pol who lit the fuse.

"He would not tell you such things about himself. But as the orator at his funeral, I would leave the audience laughing, to honor his memory.

"Finally, I should tell you that Max-Pol is also a practical joker of a very high caliber. But I will save such stories for another time. It is getting late and we are due for dinner at The Boat as Wonko's guest. I would like to see Wonko and Max-Pol together. That would be fun indeed."

Interior of "The Boat"

BELLY UP IN THE BOAT

"MY WIFE IS POISONING MY FOOD!" cried a voice, just as Alex and Alice opened the pub door. A booming, soccer-yob voice from the far back of the crowded room.

"HURRAY FOR YOUR BLOODY WIFE!" shouted the rest of the patrons of the pub in return.

"Wonko and his mates," said Alex, "in full cry."

"Aleko, Aleko! Come sit, important operations are afoot!"

The large, roundish, bushy-faced man with the Viking helmet on his head held a finger to his lips, motioned Alex and Alice to chairs on either side of him, put his hammy hands on their shoulders, and pulled them closer. Whispering hoarsely, he declared, as if addressing co-conspirators, "Those idiots down at the Bird and Beanie in the cow crossing have challenged me to shanghai a crew and enter the race to relieve Khartoum - six hearties to a punt - full kit - and I need one more stalwart, such as you or your tarty-tongued lass here - to pull an oar. What say you?"

"Translate, please, Aleko," said Alice.

"The Rose and Crown, a pub in Oxford, has an annual silliness contest, in which local loonies dress in ragtag military costume and race down the River Cherwell in punts to relieve Khartoum. I should explain that Khartoum has never been relieved because the punters always end up in the water.

"They haul out on the riverbank and consume the mostly-liquid supplies for Khartoum, while Kipling's chauvinistic poems are read aloud by someone costumed as Lord Cardigan, the idiot general who ordered the Charge of the Light Brigade. It is a kind of sentimental tribute to British colonial eccentricity - a special skill of the intelligentsia of Oxford. Do not volunteer unless you like the company of the unhinged."

"BELLY UP," roared a man standing at the bar. A bulky, redheaded, redbearded and redfaced Scotsman in a wide leather belt, tartan kilt, knee hose, and sporran - with a bone-handled dirk tucked into the top of his wooly hose. The drinking garb of the outlaw Highlander looking for trouble.

"BELLY UP," shouted the bartender, pointing at Wonko.

"BEL-LY UP, BEL-LY UP, BEL-LY UP," chanted the crowd, pounding on the tables with their fists and mugs.

Wonko rose to the challenge - to hearty applause. When he got up and paraded to the bar, Alice saw that Wonko's outfit was a parody of the Scotsman's. He also wore a properly tailored kilt, but it was made of flower-print cloth, Hawaiian-style. The sporran hanging below his belly was made of skunk fur, and tucked into the top of his Day-Glo pink knee hose was a toothbrush. When he walked he made a clicking sound.

"He has got on his tap shoes," said Alex. "And, yes, he can tap dance."

"BEL-LY UP, BEL-LY UP, BEL-LY UP," chanted the crowd, as Wonko toured the room, tap dancing, with his hands clasped over his head as the champion.

"Let me explain," said Alex to Alice. "There is a red line painted on the floor in front of the bar. The two contestants stand with their toes on the line, belly-to-belly, and when the bartender rings the 'last call' bell they try to bump one another off the line."

"A YARD OR DOUBLE," shouted the Scotsman.

"A YARD OR DOUBLE IT IS," shouted Wonko.

"The challenger offers the bet. If he wins, Wonko has to buy him a yard of ale. See the tall, skinny glass tube with the bulge at the bottom - behind the bar - in that wooden rack? That holds a full thirty-six inches of ale. If the winner can not finish the ale in one long swallow, then he is obliged to pay double for it. If he wins the belly pushing and drinks the ale, then he is the king of the pub for the night. If the challenger loses the belly pushing, he must buy Wonko the drink of his choice."

Wonko stood several feet back from the red line, making faces at the challenger and the crowd. "This is part of Wonko's strategy," said Alex. "He is heavier, stronger, and cleverer than you might think. But for him it is more of a mind game than a contest of strength.

"Sometimes he marches right up to the line, gets belly-to-belly, suddenly empties his lungs at the bell, sucking his mass back, and then, taking a huge gulp of air, thrusts his belly and hips forward with all his might. I have seen him knock opponents off their feet in one thrust. He calls it 'dropping the Belly Bomb.'

"Sometimes he takes off his shirt, leers at his opponent, gyrates his hips and hairy belly around in an obscene way, which so embarrasses or amuses his opponents that they back off, laughing. Though sometimes he just stands there like a stone monument, and no opponent can budge him.

"I have seen him lose too, but I am never sure if he loses on purpose or is truly beaten. He says he does not care what happens as long as he has fun. He says always winning would be a burden. Once I saw him back down and play the coward when confronted with a huge, angry drunk. Wonko said there was no laughter in the man - not worth the trouble winning."

"BELLY UP," shouted the bartender, and the two contenders came to the line. Suddenly, Wonko took off his shirt. Painted around his navel were bright red lips. The Scotsman was too busy trying to get his own shirt off while keeping eye contact with Wonko to notice the lips. But the crowd noticed, and howled with laughter.

The barman rang the bell, and, like two walruses mating, the bellies were pressed together. Wonko leered, made kissing sounds with his lips, and began to rub his belly sensually against the belly of the Scot.

"FIGHT LIKE A MAN," the Scot roared, and in that ill-conceived moment of wasted energy, he left himself open to Wonko's Belly Bomb. As the Scot staggered back off the line, the crowd cheered and Wonko shouted, "ALE FOR ME, MILK FOR THE SCOTSMAN," and tap danced away from the bar while the crowd went wild. Even the mighty Scot was impressed, surrendering an imaginary sword to Wonko, who declined it with royal generosity.

Sitting down as if nothing had happened, Wonko became conspiratorial again, putting his arms around the shoulders of Alex and Alice and pulling them close to him once again. "Listen. You must come up to my moorage for a bit of illicit pleasure. I just happen to have, straight from the froggy sauce runners, a bottle of genuine green death. It will not, as you suppose, make you blind or crazy - unless, of course, you drink it for days at a time - but you must sample it, and I know the proper ritual. No arguments - come at ten. And now, I must away to organize my crew for the heroic assault on the wogs at Khartoum."

And with that, Wonko was up, tap dancing and roaring across the room. "MY WIFE IS SLEEPING WITH SHEEP AGAIN!"

"HOORAY FOR YOUR BLOODY WIFE," they cried in reply.

"GOODNIGHT, YOU SLOBBERING SODS," shouted Wonko, and, blowing kisses, he danced nimbly out the door.

ABSINTHE

"Are we going to Wonko's?" asked Alice as Alex opened the door of the pub for her. They walked out into the moonlight, on a night aromatic with the fecundity of oncoming summer.

"I think you should see Wonko's canal boat, hear some of his stories, and have a go at his 'green death' - absinthe. But I am well-on-weary from the day on the river and look forward to the deep sleep of the carefree. I will go to bed and you will go to Wonko's. It is quite safe. The moonlight is bright, but you can have my torch if you need it. Wonko's boat is just across the canal, beyond that little bridge.

"How will I recognize it?"

"It is the *Water Witch*. James Fenimore Cooper, the American author, used that name in his novel about William Kidd, the Scottish-born pirate, known as Captain Kidd."

"So he's a pirate?"

"No, not at all. He is, despite his public behavior, a gentleman at heart. And every carnival closes its tents for the evening. I do not think he performs for audiences of one. Wonko at his ease should be engaging company. And, if you have never had genuine French absinthe, you should at least have a taste. The ritual is a habit Wonko picked up from French Legionnaires in Tunisia. You can add it to your collection of experiential curiosities. Go ahead without me."

"All right," said Alice, "I'm game."

*

When Alice walked alongside Wonko's all-black boat, she could see through the windows into a cabin fitted out in traditional narrowboat style: warm brown wood decorated with painted scrollwork, chintz fabrics, leather-covered easy chairs, oriental rugs, and antique brass boating lamps. Cozy. Not crazy. Hardly a pirate's lair.

When she boarded at the stern, she found the cabin door latched open as if she was expected. When she knocked, a pleasant male voice called out at a civil level of sound, "Come."

418

Wonko? Someone else? Alice was uncertain.

When she walked through the door and down the short flight of steps, she found herself in a small, neat bedroom with a double berth.

"I'm in the bow," called the voice, "come on through."

Next, a small bath with a shower, then an office nook with desk, a tidy galley, and finally the main cabin, complete with a fire in a tiny stove.

Without his Viking helmet, Wonko seemed smaller. Without his Hawaiian kilt, he seemed plain. In brown corduroy pants, a khaki shirt, with a dark green wool shawl wrapped around his shoulders, he seemed tweedily domestic.

He was arranging items on the table: two glasses, spoons, a carafe of water, sugar cubes, and a tall, handblown crystal bottle containing an emerald green liquid. Absinthe.

"Ah, Alice," he said. "Welcome. I saw you coming across the canal. Alex has gone off to bed, has he? Early riser, that one. Come sit. Have you ever tasted absinthe?"

Alice was eased into the comfort of Wonko's world by his soft-spoken voice and gallant manner. It was as if he anticipated appropriate caution on her part, yet knew enough about her to presume on her own habit of not beating around the bush in social encounters.

She was pleasantly surprised. Up until now he seemed to be a master of drawing attention to himself. And now, all his attention was focused on her. She sat down.

"Are you really Wonko, or a twin brother to the wild man I saw in action at the pub?"

"Same man, different view. You saw me on stage. All my life I've had to suppress a tendency toward zaniness in favor of what was required of me in my work. I was a career officer in the U.S. Navy SEALs - special forces - serious business - not much allowance for foolishness there.

"Now that I'm retired I can do as I please. And it pleases me to play Wonko. I like being a one-man circus. And I've perfected my act: I can juggle, tap dance, sing, play several instruments including bagpipes, perform close-up card and coin tricks, and ride a unicycle. I can even eat fire and do strongman feats."

"Amazing," said Alice.

"Never do things by halves, I say. I could still blow up a bridge or kill with my bare hands, I suppose, but there's not much call for that these days, and it's not very amusing.

"Belly up! Ha. If it is entertainment you want, Wonko will gladly provide. It makes me lots of friends, provides me free food and drink in pubs because I draw business and make people laugh. It's not a bad life. I'm known and welcome wherever I go on British waterways. My audience is an altogether better class of riffraff than I dreamed of. But, as you see around you, I do not live on stage. Most actors don't. And the ones who do are insufferable."

"That's why some people call you Wonko the Sane, isn't it? You're not all weird. It's just that most people don't look at the world the way you do, but they're intrigued by the world you show them."

"I could say the same about you," said Wonko, pointing at Alice's mis-matched shoes. I saw Alex the evening before you came. He told me a little about you. That's why I came charging up that first afternoon. I wanted to see you for myself. 'Alice is different,' he said, and so you are."

"Are you just curious, or are you some kind of spy?" asked Alice.

"A spy?" said Wonko, laughing. "Actually I'm more a talent scout, looking for new recruits for circuses and mischief and raids on Khartoum. Would you like to join my Gypsy band? There's always room for one more."

Before Alice could reply, Wonko went on. "It's getting late, and we could probably talk the night away - you wouldn't want to get me started. But I promised Alex I wouldn't keep you. He has a surprise to show you tomorrow and wants to leave at first light. But stay long enough to be initiated into Wonko's World with the absinthe ritual. We'll have time to talk another time."

Alice gave Wonko her sharpest gaze.

"Are you game?" he asked.

"I'm always game," said Alice. "Always."

*

Wonko began the ritual.

"First of all, lest you be concerned, absinthe is legal in Britain and always has been, despite being banned at times elsewhere in Europe. Notwithstanding the myths about it being hallucinogenic and the cause of insanity, the truth is that it is 75 percent alcohol by volume, and if you drink enough of anything that strong your head will become a baked apple.

"I quote from Oscar Wilde, writing about absinthe. He spoke from experience I'm sure: 'The first stage is like ordinary drinking; the second, when you begin to see monstrous and cruel things; but if you can persevere you will enter in upon the third stage, where you see things that you want to see - wonderful and curious things.'

"That's why it was often called the green fairy. First taste it straight from the bottle," said Wonko, "just a sip."

He poured a small amount of the emerald green liquid into a shot glass and handed it to Alice.

"Sip, and then toss it down," he said.

Alice drank and grimaced. She first tasted bitter licorice, then her tongue and throat seemed to catch fire, and a stream of that fire burned on down her throat to hit her stomach with an electric shock.

"Whoa!" exclaimed Alice, eyes wide, her face flushing. "That's potent stuff. My eyes are watering."

"Yes, but that's not the way aficionados like Toulouse-Lautrec took it. Drinking absinthe became a ritual performance. These four lines of poetry from "Lendemain" by Charles Cros express their sentiment:

> 'Avec les fleurs, avec les femmes
> Avec l'absinthe, avec le feu
> On peu se divertir un peu,
> Jouer son rôle en quelques drames.'

With flowers and with women,
With absinthe and with fire,
We can divert ourselves a little,
Acting our parts in the play.

As he recited the poetry, Wonko poured just enough absinthe into a larger glass to cover the bottom. With silver tongs he dipped a sugar cube into the absinthe until it was soaked, and then put the sugar cube into a spoon. With a match he lit the alcohol-soaked sugar, making a ghostly blue flame. When the sugar had melted, he poured it into the bottom of the glass, stirred it into the absinthe, and slowly began dripping water from a carafe into the glass.

"This is Evian - from glacier-fed springs in France - thousands of years old. Absinthe should not be insulted with tap water."

The liquid in the glass turned a pale, opaline green. Alice had seen this color only in paintings and collections of Chinese jade. Wonko poured half the liquid into another glass and handed it to Alice.

He lifted his glass to hers, making an unspoken toast.
Alice touched her glass to Wonko's, and drank cautiously.

"Oh, this *is nice*," she said, "Exotic. Mildly erotic. I can see why it was associated with creativity. It's *liquid surprise*."
"Would you like another?" asked Wonko.
"Are you trying to loosen my morals or my tongue, Mr. Wonko?"
"Both," he said, laughing.
"Well, then," said Alice, "no more. I'm always interested in new experiences and an unfettered mind. But not tonight."

Wonko looked at Alice shrewdly.
Alice returned his look.

"Does this absinthe ritual entail any obligations?"
"Yes," said Wonko. "You'll be expected to attend future meetings of Wonko's World, and undergo the next stage of the rites."
"And Alex," said Alice. "Is he a member of Wonko's World?"
"That's a secret I cannot divulge," replied Wonko. "Ask him."

Moorage at Northbrook

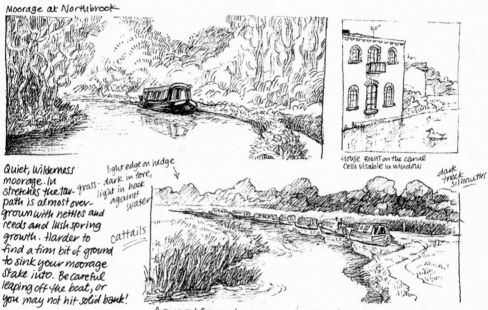

House RIGHT on the canal
Cello visable in window

Quiet, wilderness moorage. In stretches the tow-path is almost overgroun with nettles and reeds and lush spring growth. Harder to find a firm bit of ground to sink your moorage stake into. Be careful leaping off the boat, or you may not hit solid bank!

light edge on hedge
grass- dark in fore, light in back against water

cattails

dark trees silhouettes

Coming out from under 224. Langford Lane Bridge near Thrupp

Drinkwater's Lift Bridge

231

View through to
Drinkwater's lift Bridge · 231

Each bridge and lock has its own personality. I try to sketch them on the fly. It's easy to know where you are on the canal, because each bridge has a number, and each number ~~strike~~ is listed on the map. We are evidently traveling backwards upstream, ~~strikethrough~~ starting at bridge 243 and working to 188.

Shipton Weir Lock - 218

Friday, May 10

Early morning. Not quite sunrise.

Alex tapped sharply on Alice's door and went away. When she got out of bed and opened the door, she found a wooden tray on a stool. On the tray were a small glass of orange juice, a stainless steel thermos mug of coffee, two squares of dark Greek chocolate, a pitcher of steaming hot milk, a shot glass of brandy, a white linen napkin, and a note: "Jumwilly, Arise!"

In her blue-and-white, summer kimono, Alice carried the tray out onto the stern deck of the *Ariadne*. Standing barefooted on the dew-wet teak, she turned around in a circle, slowly, tasting the morning.

Stillness.

Mist on village and field and canal. Steam and smoke rising straight up from stoves on the other boats close by. Fifty feet away, at the bow of the *Ariadne,* Alice could see the top of Alex's head. With his eyes just above the hatch cover, he was watching her. He raised his eyebrows in greeting. She picked up the shot glass of brandy, lifted it in his direction, and tossed it down.

Now she is awake for sure, thought Alex, as Alice squinched her eyes and coughed. He had waited for her to appear, saw her turn slowly in the morning light, and recorded the image in his permanent file of fine moments. He thought about how astronomers described that place in the far reaches of outer space as "a continuum where conventional notions of time and place cease to exist." *Such things exist in inner space too,* he thought, looking around him, *and here is proof. The whole day will be like this. A day to remember.*

Without speaking, Alex and Alice continued looking at one another. She in the stern, he in the bow. Looking. Seeing. Thinking. Not many people are comfortable doing this. But it had become a natural part of their being together - not for lack of words, but out of caution for the confusion words can cause.

Alice poured the hot milk into her mug, dropped in the chocolate, stirred the mixture with what Alex had claimed was a "runcible spoon," and again locking her eyes with Alex's, sipped the coffee with relish.

Out of Alex's sight, Alice sat down on the stern bench and spread the linen napkin beside her onto a section of the bench wet with undisturbed dew. When the napkin had soaked up the dew, she patted her cheeks and lips with it, and then carefully folded the napkin and put it back on the tray.

Alice had read that the Gypsies believed there was magic power in the first dew of morning. If you placed your hands in fresh dew and rubbed it on your face, you would be blessed that day.

Alice was not a Gypsy and did not believe in magic. But she did believe that ritual acts focused the mind on the object of one's desire. And her desire was . . . what?

It clearly had something to do with Alex, but she could not put it into words. She wanted something. She felt she could have it, but she could not name it. Smiling, Alice picked up the tray and disappeared from sight into the cabin.

Time to get under way.

As the oncoming sunlight began moving the morning shadows and mists away from the *Ariadne*, Alex ran up the small Greek flag, moved back across the top of the boat to the cockpit in the stern, started the engine, and waited impatiently for his crew.

When Alice appeared again, she carried the damp linen napkin with her. "Aleko, look at me," she said. "I want to bless you. Don't ask me to explain."

Always glad to look at Alice up close, Alex complied.

"This napkin is wet with the first dew of morning. The Gypsies say it has magic power. I don't know about that, but what harm can it do? It at least has the fresh feel of a fine day about it. Close your eyes and be still."

Slowly, carefully, Alice touched the damp napkin to Alex's cheeks, lips, forehead, and eyes. When he opened his eyes, Alex looked at Alice and reached for words.

Careful. Let it be, is what he thought.

"Amen," is what he said.

*

The Oxford Canal between Thrupp and the Somerton Deep lock defies poetic description. Metaphors insult the reality. It is not *like something else* – it is exactly and only what it is: the English countryside in May at its oldest and best.

The canal and the river become one and drift through the Cherwell valley well away from highways and railroad and villages. A Roman packhorse path crosses a bridge along the route, willows make long green tunnels filled with birdsong, and sheep graze the open fields.

If you like the color green, then almost every hue is available for inspection – a full spectrum – spinach green, lime green, olive green, sea green, lettuce green, emerald green, and on to greens that are not or cannot be named.

Because they had left Thrupp at sunrise, Alex and Alice had the canal to themselves. For miles they moved along without speaking. There was nothing to say. It was enough to be there together, Alice sitting alongside Alex in the stern; the only sound the steady, pulsing throb of the engine.

Other canal boats began passing. Then came Shipton Weir lock, Baker's lock, Pigeon's lock, Northbrook lock, and Dashwood lock. All were negotiated with little effort or conversation.

So quickly had Alice got the hang of her tasks that an observer would think that Alex and Alice had been working canal boats as a team for a long time. They took unspoken pleasure in their synchronized moves. A tricky, silent passage completed was expressed only by a look between them. It reminded them both of rowing shells without coxswain, when the crew was in a common groove because they were of one mind.

And so the lovely day passed. Perhaps the dew was working.

Countryside, river, canal. Locks, villages, and pubs. At Lower Heyford they stopped to take on fuel at Oxfordshire Narrowboats and have a quick plowman's lunch of brown bread, blue cheese, pickles, and ale at The Three Horseshoes. But they did not linger, even when they came across friends and acquaintances of Alex. "We must move along," he said, "there is something very special to see today."

darker hedge

reddish brick

warmer, multicolor yellow + brick

Sommerton Deep Lock

distant trees, hills

Village of Sommerton visable in distance

countryside below - River Cherwell...

level of canal high above locks

LABYRINTH

In the afternoon they came to the yawning jaws of Somerton Deep lock - appropriately named - at twelve feet, the deepest on the Oxford Canal.

"Think of it as the entrance to the labyrinth of the Minotaur," said Alex. And when the gates shut behind the *Ariadne*, it did seem as if they had entered a wet, slimy cave and might sink into the earth instead of rising with the inflow of water.

Not far beyond Somerton, Alex said, "We will moor on the starboard side - along the bank just before bridge 193, which is coming up. After we moor, put on your walking shoes."

*

They set off uphill on a graveled road. Alice noticed that Alex was not carrying his usual cane. Instead, he had a gnarled old stick, longer than a standard cane.

"This is a Cretan shepherd's crook," he said, "appropriate for the surprise I have for you."

They came to a gate. "Private - Please" insisted the posted sign.

Opening the gate, Alex explained, "I have been here many times before, and I have arranged for us to be here today. The owners said they would be away in Banbury taking sheep to market, so we have the property to ourselves. Come on."

They walked along a dirt road for a way, and then turned up a path toward the edge of a small forest. At the top of the hill, they came to an open field ringed with trees.

"Behold," said Alex, "The Somerton Labyrinth."

Into the green grass of the wide field a shallow ditch seemed to have been carefully plowed in the pattern of a labyrinth. The raised green path between furrows had recently been mowed.

"I will answer your unasked questions," said Alex, "or at least the obvious ones. This labyrinth carved into the turf dates at least from the middle of the sixteenth century. And by the way, the path of the labyrinth is not in the dirt of the plowed furrow, but in the raised green grass between furrows. There are written references to this one's existence as far back as 1744, but it is surely much older."

Alice tried following the path with her eyes.

"Mesmerizing," she said.

"It is not at all unique. In Britain more than fifty have been identified, and many are still being cared for like this one. Nobody knows who the original builders were or exactly why they constructed labyrinths. Oh, the experts speculate, the scholars expound, but the mystery remains. I hope they never figure it out."

Alex and Alice stood still, considering the labyrinth.

The wind riffling through the trees made the only sound.

"Well, then. I can tell you far more than you would ever want to know about labyrinths, but we have not come for lectures. A man named Hermann Kern has written a fat book, *Through the Labyrinth*, which thoroughly covers the labyrinths of the world, complete with endless illustrations and speculations. This labyrinth is in it. The book is on the boat if you want to look through it. Labyrinths are still being constructed, by the way.

"A few facts are useful. The pattern of this labyrinth is termed Classic Cretan by the scholars because it follows the same design found in Minoan Crete, and is associated, of course, with the labyrinth of the Minotaur and the myth involving Minos, Pasiphae, Ariadne, and Theseus. Perhaps I have said enough."

"Keep going," said Alice.

"In short form, Pasiphae, the wife of the Minoan King of Crete, slept with Zeus disguised as a bull. The resulting offspring was a wild creature, half man and half bull - the Minotaur. This beast was at the center of a labyrinth. Athenian youths were sent in as sacrifices to him, but they never came out. Theseus, a handsome young Athenian prince, was about to be one of these victims, but the daughter of Minos, Ariadne, fell in love with him. She gave him a ball of twine to take with him, so that, when he found the Minotaur, he could slay it and follow the string back out of the labyrinth and into her arms.

"Theseus did these things, and fled with Ariadne. There is more to the story and there are many interpretations of the myth, but that will do for now. What happened between then and now is everybody's guess, but the labyrinth before you is one more proof that the idea and the mystery have lived on.

"Just one more thing. Most important. This is a *labyrinth*, not a maze. A labyrinth has only one path; it ultimately leads to the center - unicursal - and the same path is followed back to the same place you entered. It is a path, a way, a pilgrimage on a small scale. Labyrinths predate mazes by centuries.

"And a maze is . . . ?"

"A maze has more than one entrance, more than one path, many dead ends, and you may never find the center. Even if you do, you will not always come out where you went in. A maze is a puzzle, a game, even a competition. To this day they are very popular entertainments carved into cornfields in Britain and the United States.

"As metaphors, labyrinths and mazes represent very different views of existence. Of course, one may hold both views as parallel working hypotheses."

Before he could continue, Alice placed her finger across her lips, asking for silence.

She turned and entered the labyrinth, walking slowly, head down, stopping at times with eyes closed. The path took her close to the center and then far away and back again, around and around. When she reached the center, she sat down with her back to Alex, and was very still.

After a time, Alice stood up, turned to look at Alex, smiled, and instead of following the path around and around and back, she surprised him by walking straight toward him, stepping over the furrows and across the path to Alex. She threw her arms around his neck, hugged him, held him tight, and said, "I want to go now."

*

Alice had listened attentively when Alex explained there was only one way to the center and back. She had carefully considered the labyrinth, and walked the path with respect.

And then, she had made her own path back, not being bound by custom, tradition, or the pattern others had made.

There *was* more than one way back.

Alice's way. Straight across the pattern.

Alex understood.

He, too, never went back exactly the way he came.

He, too, found other ways.

If he had any doubts that he and Alice were kindred spirits, the doubts ceased with her leave-taking of the labyrinth, making her own straight way.

THE OWL AND THE PUSSYCAT

Night.

After returning from the labyrinth, Alex had moved the *Ariadne* back down the canal to tie up against a flowered, ferny bank, where the River Cherwell runs close by and parallel to the canal.

A wilderness moorage.

They fixed dinner together, batted limerick lines back and forth, and tried remembering all the lines to Edward Lear's poem, *The Owl and the Pussycat,* that odd couple who put to sea in a pea-green boat, and ended up dancing by the light of the moon.

*

Later, after her shower, Alice sat outside in the stern of the *Ariadne* drying her hair with a towel, and drinking in the sweet-smelling air. They had tied up so far away from the lights and sounds of civilization that they might be moored back in time as well.

It was so still and silent that Alice heard the wings of some bird as it swam through the night air. She combed out her long hair, thinking of Rapunzel and wondering how long her hair had to be before a prince could climb up it to her tower.

I'd prefer a guy smart enough to bring his own ladder, she thought.

In the last light of evening, she watched a single leaf float slowly out of the darkness and on downstream past the *Ariadne,* into the darkness again.

From a canal boat moored somewhere nearby, a bagpiper played down the curtain of night with a melancholy tune.

Suddenly, a boat rounding a bend of the canal invaded the tranquility.

A party of weekend boaters in a modern cabin cruiser were breaking custom and traveling at night. They passed too close and too fast, rocking the *Ariadne* with their bow wave.

From inside the *Ariadne*, Alice heard a muffled shout and a crash. She rushed below deck, calling, "Aleko? Aleko?"

Alex lay sprawled naked and wet on the galley floor.

He had been taking a shower, standing on one foot while washing the other, when the wave rocked the boat. Taking the curtain with him as he went, he had fallen out of the shower, grabbed for a counter as he fell, but caught hold of a dish drainer full of pots and pans and utensils instead, pulling the kitchen equipment down with him onto the floor.

"Damn, damn, damn," he moaned to Alice on her knees beside him.

He was not injured. Nothing broken or cut.

Later he would realize that the combination of warm shower, wine, and bending over to wash his feet had left him light-headed, and he couldn't react in time to the sudden rocking. Tomorrow he may laugh at the image of himself naked on the galley floor tangled up with the cutlery and pots. But for now, he was in mild shock.

"All right, I am all right," he mumbled, "help me up."

In short order Alice had helped him into his bed, dried him off with a towel, covered him with his favorite quilt, and brought him a cup of tea. Assured he was shaken up but truly all right, she went to put the galley back in order.

When she returned to check on him, Alex had rolled onto his side and appeared asleep. She stood and considered him thoughtfully. When she had dried him off, she could not help but notice the landscape of his naked body. Surprisingly lean and fit for a man his age, except for his leg and foot, which were laced with stitches from operations and scars from accidents. Alice wondered that he got about as well as he did. There must be more pain than he admitted.

She gazed at his sleeping form.

It's now or never, she thought, and went back to her room to get the penlight from beside her bed. She returned to stand beside Alex. With the penlight between her teeth, she carefully lifted the quilt off Alex's naked backside, and there it was, just as he had said: the tattoo on the left side of his butt. The size of a hand - a popeyed blue frog, rearing up on its hind legs, displaying an erect penis as large as the rest of its body.

Alice smiled. "I'll be damned," she giggled, and dropped the penlight onto the bed. "Oops."

Alex stirred. "Damn, damn, damn," he murmured.

As a mother might be drawn to comfort a child, Alice sat down on the bed with her back to the wall of the bunk and drew Alex's head and shoulders over into her lap - one arm across his chest, one hand on his cheek, and her chin resting on the top of his head. She held him close, and gently rocked back and forth.

"Oh, Aleko, Aleko - dear Aleko," she whispered.

He had not been asleep.

Annoyed by needing help, embarrassed by having his body exposed in such clumsy circumstances, and feeling foolish, weak, and lonely, he had turned to the wall in despair.

Now he was being tenderly held in Alice's arms.

Never in his life had anyone held him this way.

Never as a child. Never as a man. *Never.*

Her tenderness breached the dam of his feelings.

Alice felt tears run across her hand as she softly stroked Alex's cheek. She held him closer, her cheek on the top of his head. He was trembling.

"I am so afraid," he said.

"I know," she whispered.

"I have always been afraid," he sobbed.

"I know, I know, I know."

She held him, rocked him, and sang softly to him, until he slept.

Alice eased out from under him, tucked the quilt up around his chin, turned out the light, and went quietly back to her room. She had just turned off the light, when she heard a sound and went back to check on Alex. He had rolled over onto his side again, facing the wall.

She stood beside his bed, drawn to him, unwilling to leave him alone. She lifted the quilt and, still in her yukata, lay down beside him and pulled the quilt over her. Snuggling up against his backside, spoon fashion, she put her head against his neck and her arm over his chest.

A hand wet with tears reached for hers and held it.

"I'm here, Aleko," she whispered.

Sleep overtook them both about the same time the half-moon rose.

The Owl and the Pussycat floated away on a sea of dreams in their dark green boat.

Dew began to appear on the outside surfaces of the *Ariadne*.

In the morning when Alex awoke, Alice was not there in the bed beside him. Had he dreamed that she was? Wished that she were? Or had she really been there?

He went out on deck to find Alice sipping orange juice in the sunlight.

He did not ask.

She did not say.

217 - Horse Bridge
We didn't actually go UNDER Horse Bridge - this is where the river Cherwell joins the canal, flowing along as one stream until Shipton Weir

white railings

white edges to bottom arc

← brick

dark square, white number

dark stones against mortar

darker to top ↑

darkest= bridge arch lock shadow

210
Morning light- distinct tufts of grass

Darkest= bridge shadow on water, shadows on edges of grass

light rim along upper edge of bridge
↓

Northbrook Bridge

SATURDAY, MAY 11

"Today," said Alex, "we will go as far as King's Sutton, on the outskirts of Banbury. We will turn around at King's Sutton and begin our trip back to Oxford. Between here and King's Sutton the locks and bridges are standard -nothing complicated - though we may have to wait for traffic at times. An easy day.

At King's Sutton there is a fine view of a handsome old church with a stately spire. Very picturesque - the classic Oxfordshire village at a distance. We might have time to walk over to Adderbury Manor, the home of the Earl of Rochester, who courted his insane second wife by disguising himself as the Emperor of China.

"Along the way back, we shall choose our moorage site for tonight. Somewhere between Upper and Lower Heyford, I think. The canal will get crowded with weekend boaters, and finding a moorage at some distance from any popular pub is a good idea if we want peace and quiet."

Alice noticed that Alex was moving awkwardly. Though not really injured, no doubt he was bruised and strained from his fall. And he didn't want to talk about it. Of that, she was certain.

"Alex, I want you to know that if you need me to take the wheel for any reason, I can do it. I haven't mentioned it, but I've skippered sailboats as big as this canal boat, and was the coxswain on eights and fours for several years. I can steer."

"Really," said Alex, "perhaps it is I who should be crew. Do you know . . . "

"That you rowed for Cambridge? Yes. Max-Pol told me. And that you gave it up to go volunteer to fight in the Spanish Civil War," replied Alice.

(Pause.)

I've done it again, thought Alice.

In truth, she didn't want to talk about Max-Pol or Alex – she wanted to talk about herself – to tell Alex anything he wanted to know – but she wanted him to ask. Round and around went the game, caution blocking yearning.

Their mutual ignorance and desire hung like a Mexican piñata between them. Struck at the right time in the right way, the prizes of information would spill out delight and pleasure.

Wrongly struck – or missed – someone could get hurt.

So they began the day with minimal conversation, both of them submerged in their own thoughts, both at ease with the other's silence. It is a rare thing to spend time in close quarters with another human being without feeling obliged to talk.

If one assumes the worst, silence can be intimidating. Yet, if one assumes the best, mutual silence can be as intimate as waltzing without the need to call out steps. It usually takes a long time to discover this, yet it came quickly to Alice and Alex.

Accomplished dancers do not need to talk while dancing.

*

From beyond the bend in the canal behind them came music. Faint at first, then louder as a canal boat appeared, bearing musicians. An Irish tune was being played on two fiddles, a pennywhistle and a concertina, accompanied by a hand-drum. The musicians were gathered on the foredeck of the all-black boat. Though he had his back to them, one fiddler was wearing a familiar Viking helmet.

"Wonko," said Alex, slowing the *Ariadne* and steering closer to the bank to give the oncoming boat room to pass.

As the boat caught up with them, Alex and Alice could see five more people in the stern. Two, dressed in red-and-white striped tights, were juggling balls; two more, in clown costume, were blowing up red balloons to add to a cluster tied to the stern; and someone in a wizard's hat was steering the boat.

As he drew even with the *Ariadne*, Wonko stopped playing and called out, "Aleko and his fair Alice! Come, run away with the Gypsies! Join our circus! We're off to Banbury to the fair! Follow on, follow on, we're late!"

And before Alex could reply, Wonko resumed playing his fiddle, and the boat forged ahead up the canal.

"I have seen his troop in action," said Alex. "They are quite accomplished, actually, and very welcome at fairs because they do not charge for their services or even put out a hat for contributions like most buskers. They stroll about playing music, doing card tricks, juggling and mime - all for the fun of it. Would you like to go along with them to Banbury?"

"No," said Alice. "I've been to fairs and can always go to more, but I may not have a chance to be on the canal with you again. Let's stick to our plans. If you like, I will be a circus for you."

"What do you mean?" asked Alex.

"It's a very small circus, but I, like almost everyone, have a few tricks I can perform. Watch."

Alice wiggled both her ears, then one, then the other, and then both again. She arched one eyebrow and then the other, crossed her eyes, flared her nostrils, and stuck out her tongue, making a tube of it, and then touched her nose with the end of her tongue.

"Now, for a finale, all at once." She tried but couldn't do it, though the face she made in her effort made Alex laugh.

"There," said Alice. "It's the laugh that's the reward. There's more, but . . ."

"Keep going," Alex. "What else?"

"Well, I can dislocate my thumbs - see - and write with both hands in opposite directions. I can also stand on my hands and walk about twenty feet, do a back flip, balance a broom on my chin, juggle three oranges, do a puppet show with faces drawn on my fingers, and perform a few lame tricks with cards and coins. And I can tell a joke or two, recite limericks, sing Spanish lullabies, and read tarot cards."

"Here, on our small stage: The Amazing Alice," said Alex.

"No, not really. Most people learn to do things like that when they're young. Like unasked questions, it's just that these skills are not often volunteered or required. I was once stuck in an elevator for two hours with five other people, and while we were waiting to be rescued

I offered to do my circus act. And the other four people had tricks of their own.

"I remember one guy could burp the beginning of 'The Star Spangled Banner,' another could make the hair stand up on the back of his neck at will, and a lady could do birdcalls. We had a great time - laughed ourselves silly. The rescue people had to bang on the roof of the elevator to get our attention."

"You stir my memory, Alice. Will you take the wheel for a while? I will tell you my own circus story, but I cannot concentrate on steering at the same time."

Pleased to accept his confidence, Alice stood and took his place, while Alex sat beside her, closed his eyes and searched his mind for what he had not thought about in many years. Opening his eyes, he smiled, and began his story.

"I was in the circus once," said Alex. "As the assistant ringmaster of a flea circus. Most people think flea circuses do not really exist, but not so. Just last year I saw one in Montmartre in Paris and another one on the Rambla in Barcelona. I have even researched the history of flea circuses, and may start one of my own someday."

"Really? Tell me," said Alice.

"Well, then. When I was in the war in Spain we had long, boring weeks in the trenches, out of action far behind the lines. There was this Russian who was separated from his battalion. To pass away the time he collected fleas, which were easy to come by, and started a tiny circus. He had helped a cousin do it in Moscow.

"The scientific name of these fleas, by the way, is *Pulex irritans,* of the insect order Siphonaptera. These are not the same fleas found on dogs or the different species found on cats. Those fleas live *on* their hosts, whereas the human fleas live in dark, hidden places, and dine *out* - feeding off the nearest human. An altogether stronger, larger, more independent creature."

"You're not pulling my leg?" said Alice. "You really have been part of a flea circus?"

"Indeed. If we can find some fleas, we are in business," said Alex.

"Continue," said Alice.

"A *Pulex irritans* looks something like a tiny bee and is an eighth of an inch long, weighing about one fifth of a grain. Six extraordinary legs - like the legs of a crab - with which the flea can jump eight inches high and more than a foot in distance - one hundred times its body length. If you or I had such legs we could jump four hundred feet straight up, or broad jump seven hundred feet. Moreover, the human flea is strong - able to lift one hundred and fifty times its own weight."

Alex seemed to close his eyes again, but he was sneaking an anxious peek at Alice and the canal ahead. *She knows what she is doing*, he thought, and relaxed back into memory.

"Where was I? Oh, yes. Now, to train a flea you take advantage of these characteristics to make it react in ways that are natural to the flea but seem like human feats to us. The hardest part is getting a loop of very fine copper wire tied around a flea's neck. I will not go into the details, but it can be done - even though some fleas are, shall we say, 'eliminated' in the process. Each flea is taught only one trick. The Pavlovian strategies are employed: trial and error, reinforcement and reward."

"What are the tricks?" asked Alice.

"The simplest one is getting a tethered flea to catch a tiny cotton ball and throw it back. It looks like a game of catch, when in fact the flea is only getting rid of something it does not want stuck to its feet. After a few tosses, the trainer lets the flea have a little blood from his arm. The flea catches on quickly: catch, toss, catch, toss, eat."

"Forgive me for interrupting," said Alice. "There's a small motor boat coming around the bend ahead, and I'm slowing way down and giving him room to port. I just wanted you to know."

"Aye, you are the captain," said Alex.

As the small boat passed safely by and the *Ariadne* resumed speed, Alex reached out and touched Alice on her arm. "Well done, Captain - that is trickier than most people think. It is easy to put small boats awash."

She glanced at him and smiled.

"I *am* the captain. And you are the story-telling crew. Continue."

"Where was I? Tricks. Fleas can be trained to walk a tightrope, jump through a hoop; they can be attached to small costumes and made to dance. The 'dancing' is actually a lively reflex from having the metal plate they are standing on heated a bit beneath them with a cigarette lighter. The same method is used to have fleas race from one end of a bread pan to the other, pulling tiny chariots behind them."

"No!" exclaimed Alice.

"Yes, indeed. This was the primary use my Russian friend made of his fleas. Soldiers would wager on the fleas. It was my job to work the crowd in French, Spanish, Greek, and English - taking bets. Since the flea trainer knew just where and when to apply the heat, the race was fixed. We did quite well . . . until . . . a mortar shell landed on us one afternoon in the middle of a race."

Alice laughed.

"It was not funny. I had to give the money back.

"And my future in the circus business was over. My mentor and my trained fleas were . . . dead."

Alex closed his eyes.

He was in Spain now.

And Alice steered the *Ariadne* all the way to King's Sutton.

443

Pilgrimages and Fortunes

"Alex, we're coming up to King's Sutton. Help me through the turn-around. I haven't done it by myself before," said Alice.

"Right. You stay at the helm. I will be crew and stand by forward, with the barge pole."

"Even so, help me out if I need it. OK?"

But Alice negotiated the turn with skill - moving the *Ariadne* slowly forward and back and forward and back, in and out of the turning pool without touching either bank, and without a word from Alex.

As they floated in midcanal at dead-still, they exchanged admiring looks: Alex, pleased with her skill; Alice, pleased with his willingness to trust her.

Alex winked.

Alice winked back.

They were co-captains now.

As the *Ariadne* resumed cruising speed, Alex sat down by Alice and said, "When we find our moorage for tonight, we will still have time to go over to the village of Great Tew. It is called the 'place where time stands still' because the village has been restored to its condition at the beginning of the nineteenth century."

As time is standing still now, thought Alice.

"Vine-covered stone cottages, thatched roofs, and one of the finest old pubs in England, The Falkland Arms. It is said that Dr. Johnson himself frequented it, and you can still sit by the fire and have a tobacco-filled clay pipe brought to you for your pleasure, as was done in Johnson's day.

"They say the fire has been burning nonstop in the grate for more than a hundred years. I like the thought of a long-burning fire in a place where time stands still. It should be a place of pilgrimage."

How long will the fire burn between us? wondered Alice.

"Alex, will you take the helm for a while?" she asked.

"Gladly - you've done your share of the work."

Now it was Alice's turn to sit and close her eyes and think.

(Silence.)

She opened her eyes, but looked out over the passing fields, not at Alex. "I've been thinking of going on a pilgrimage," she mused. "I don't know why the idea appeals to me. In Japan I considered the temple route around the island of Shikoku established by Kobo Daishi.

"In Paris last Easter, I followed along for several blocks behind some pilgrims I saw on the Rue St. Jacques. They were walking from Paris to Santiago de Compostela in Spain. I felt a yearning to go with them."

(Silence.)

Alice stood by Alex, hand on his shoulder.

"A labyrinth is a pilgrimage on a smaller scale, isn't it, Alex?"

"Yes."

"And I suppose it's not how far you go or how long it takes, but what goes on inside you. The Japanese say it's not *finishing* a pilgrimage that's important, but *starting* it.

"And they say a pilgrimage starts in your mind - when you decide to begin. I think I have decided to begin, but I don't know when or where. It's like having a boarding pass for a flight to an unknown destination. I don't even know which plane is mine."

(Silence.)

"On the other hand, I don't really want to walk the path somebody else laid out. But I could establish a pilgrim route anywhere - one that would take as little as an hour to walk. Maybe that's what joggers do without consciously realizing it. The Buddhists say you don't have to go far away to find enlightenment - it may be found where you already are."

(Silence.)

"Or else maybe I just want to *yearn* for someplace - like Kyoto for example. Perhaps I would rather have the nostalgia of wanting to be there than to actually be there. I would yearn for it even if I were there. Basho, the Japanese poet, wrote a famous haiku expressing that."

(Silence.)

Alice sat down. Looked away. Looked back at Alex.

"Are you following this, Aleko, or am I just babbling on?"
"I am paying very close attention."
"Would it surprise you if I told you I went on a kind of pilgrimage last Easter – to Crete?"

"What?"
Alex almost steered the *Ariadne* into the bank of the canal.
"Surprised is not the word, Alice. I am . . . *astonished*. Tell me."

Alice stood again.
And once more put her hand on his shoulder.
She liked being in touch with him when she talked.
And she liked his willingness to let her talk, without interrupting her.
Among his many skills, Alex knew how to listen well.

"It's true. I flew to Heraklion from Paris, went out to see Knossos, walked around the outside without going in, and flew back the same night. You inspired the trip, you know. Max-Pol described your day with him at Knossos in his Chronicles. I knew you were both still in Crete, and I almost went looking for you. But, I didn't. Not the right time. But . . . maybe . . . sometime . . . you and Max-Pol . . . will take me."

"I am nonplussed," said Alex. "I started to say I can not believe you did that, but . . . I can believe it. Max-Pol would be . . ."

(Silence.)

Max-Pol, thought Alex. *Change the subject.*

"Did I tell you about the bunny in the Egyptian market in Istanbul?" asked Alex. "No, I am sure I did not. Well, then. This was years ago. You like Gypsies, and this is a Gypsy story."
Alice moved toward the bow and sat down on the deck, looking

back at Alex. She liked watching him when he told stories. His expressive face and gestures told as much as his words.

"Go on," she said.

"There was a Gypsy fortune-teller walking around with a tray hung from his neck by a strap. On the tray were five small boxes and one bigger box with a little door in it. While I do not believe in prophecy, I like those who are creative enough to make a living off the irrational needs of the public, especially when it is well and cleverly done.

"I watched while a woman gave the fortune-teller some coins. And suddenly, a little rabbit pops out of his box on the tray, looks at the lady, and hops over to one of the small boxes. The lady opens the box, takes out a slip of paper, and reads it with obvious pleasure. Good news. She gives the fortune-teller another coin and he gives her a piece of carrot for the bunny."

Alex paused to concentrate on a narrow stretch of the canal.

"Then what happened?"

"The bunny takes the carrot, bites the lady on the finger, and dodges back into his box. The lady shrieked, and berated the Gypsy and his biting bunny. She missed the point, I think. I doubt she understood it, but the lady had clearly been reminded that if one takes the sweet, one must also accept the bitter."

"Did you get a fortune?"

"Yes. I offer coins. The bunny picks the box. I open it for my fortune, which was written in Turkish. I show it to the Gypsy, who smiles and nods, indicating the fortune is good. I imagine all the fortunes were good, actually. Nobody wants bad luck. And the Gypsy had to stay in business.

"When he held out his hand for another coin to pay for the bunny's piece of carrot, I gave him the coin, took the carrot but did not offer it to the bunny. I did not wish to be bit. I ate the carrot myself, much to the surprise of the Gypsy, and the obvious disappointment of the bunny. I walked away. The Gypsy laughed."

"Do you know what the fortune was?"

"Yes. I kept it, and years later a Turkish friend translated it for me: 'Never trust the wisdom of a rabbit.' I still have the fortune."

(Silence.)

Alice walked back toward Alex. She climbed down to stand beside him again, hand on shoulder, while both looked up the canal ahead.

"Max-Pol sent me a Gypsy rug. A real one. Kostas gave it to him. Said he got it from a Gypsy who owed him a big favor. Woven of silk thread. Beautiful. Very old, I think. A Muslim prayer rug. Did he show it to you?"

(Silence.)

Max-Pol. Max-Pol. There is no escape, thought Alex, and said, "No, but let us take a short break. We will tie up under these trees ahead, and I will tell you more about Max-Pol."

205. Mill Lift Bridge
in Sunshine after a long night of rain

Lovely craggy oak tree

rounding corner to bridge 208
High Bush Bridge

-farm land with Tractor tracks-
New green wheat

449

Field of Goats
and one PONY

itch

nanny
trot

Free-RANGING
CHICKEN

Footpath

BLUE JOKE

When the *Ariadne* was loosely moored to two great willow trees, Alex fetched two bottles of India ale out of the galley. The two captains sat opposite each other in the stern, savoring the cold ale and the cool shade.

Alex broke the silence
"What would you like to know about Max-Pol?"

"Give me an example of Max-Pol's practical jokes," said Alice.

"Well, then. Here is one out of my undelivered funeral oration. As I told you, Max-Pol chauffeured Kostas and me around on what Max-Pol called the Isn't-Crete-Amazing Tours, which became tiresome I am sure, though he indulged us with a right good will.

"One day we were in the hills beyond Kolymbari when Kostas suddenly shouted for a halt. He pointed at three goats standing in front of a farmhouse. All three goats were blue. Not a shade of gray, but pale, sky blue. Of course we had to inquire. The farmer and his wife were not far away.

"The lady explained that her goats were a remnant of a very old, Egyptian breed of goats, and that they gave blue milk, from which she made blue cheese. And she went into her kitchen and brought back a glass of light blue milk and a small cheese of the same color.

"Needless to say, Kostas and I were both dumbfounded. We had never seen such things. The lady gave us quite a lecture about blue goats. I even took a few notes. And Kostas bought the blue cheese as a present for me.

"Max-Pol managed to say, Isn't Crete amazing? just once with a straight face, when laughter came from beyond a fence where the farmer had been watching. When Max-Pol and the lady began laughing, Kostas and I knew we had been set up, and we laughed as well.

"It seems that Max-Pol had become friends with the farmer, who turned out to be an English-speaking Dane married to a Greek wife. Since both were jolly types, Max-Pol talked them into spraying the goats with the blue hair dye favored by young travelers. He called the farmer and his wife before we left Hania. While we were en route, they staked the goats in the yard and dyed a glass of milk and the cheese with blue food coloring.

Alice drained the last of her bottle of ale, and raised her eyebrows in exaggerated imitation of Alex's style of expressing amazement.

"This is a side of Max-Pol I never imagined," she said.

Alex raised his eyebrows in reply.

"It is indeed his way. Unlike practical jokes that are cruel and destructive, Max-Pol's style is that of elaborate cleverness for the sake of an unforgettable moment of amusement. I am sure the story has circulated among the Cretan neighbors of the owners of the goats and their friends and relatives, because Kostas reports that people have passed by his store and *baaa*-ed at him, goat-style.

"There are more of these stories, but, as I say, that is the one I thought of for the funeral of Max-Pol. I hope I shall never have reason to tell it under such circumstances."

And with that somber turn of mood, Alex got up to release the mooring lines, while Alice took the wheel, throttled up the engine and resumed managing the onward course of the *Ariadne*.

THE FLOATING WORLD

That night after dinner, Alice offered to play her cello for Alex.

She sat in the stern cockpit and played in the dark stillness. When memories of the moonlit night on the hill above Giverny came to mind, her fingers began trembling and she stopped playing.

"Aleko?" she called, and felt his hand on the back of her neck.

(Silence.)

The light of the rising moon slowly lit the eastern sky.

"Would you like to hear a Japanese poem?" Alice asked. "It's from the world of ukiyo-e (the 'floating world') by a woman named Ikkyo Sojun. I memorized it when I was alone at a hot spring in the mountains above Kobe.

> *"Tsuki wa ie*
> *kokoro wa nushi to*
> *miru toki wa*
> *nao kari no yo no*
> *sumai naru keri."*

"Translate, please," asked Alex.

> "The moon is a house
> in which the mind is master.
> Look very closely:
> Only impermanence lasts.
> This floating world, too, will pass."

*

Late in the night, Alice was awakened by the moonlight shining through the porthole above her bed and falling almost palpably on her face. She sat up, put on her yukata, and went quietly out on deck. Slowly she turned around to take in the view of canal and field and

453

willows. Happiness and sadness washed over her at the same time, and she repeated to herself, *Only impermanence lasts. This floating world, too, will pass.*

As she moved around the deck, the words of an old piano bar tune came to her: "Grant me the right, to hold you ever so tight, and to feel in the night, the nearness of you . . ."

Wondering if Alex was also awake, she moved silently through the boat and into his cabin. She found him turned against the wall on the far side of his bed. She listened to his even breathing and decided he was asleep. The waves of happiness and sadness hit her again. She didn't want to leave, but she didn't want to wake him.

"Alice," he said softly. "Come."

Without a word, Alice dropped her yukata, and, in her nightgown, got into bed with Alex and once again curled up tight against him. When he felt tears run down his naked back, he wanted to roll over and take her in his arms.

But he did not.

Like a man on whose shoulder a rare bird has perched, he knew that any move he made, no matter how careful or benign, would be a wrong move.

He knew that her presence in his bed last night was for him - to meet his needs. Tonight, it was about her and her needs, which did not include Alex turning over and embracing her.

All that was needed was for him to be there and be still.

Alex did that.

When the moon was down, the two of them were still there, asleep.

In the morning Alice was gone when Alex awoke.

When he went to look for her, he found her in her bed, sleeping still, curled up, hugging her pillow, like a child.

Later, when she came out on deck, nothing was said about the night.

It was the morning of their last day together in their floating world.

Sunday, May 12

"Attention on deck. Now hear this!" announced Alex.

"We will not go far today by boat. We shall take our time, and mess about a bit in that beautiful stretch before Shipton Weir lock, where the Cherwell and the canal combine into one big slow-moving lagoon. The water lilies may be in bloom. It is a place Monet would like, I think."

The day was cloudless, calm, and unusually warm for May.

After Baker's lock, the *Ariadne* motored at slow speed into the loveliest part of the Oxford Canal system. The railroad and highways are out of sight and hearing, and the waterway is bound on either side by farms, fields, and woodlands. The suburban outskirts of Oxford are yet to be felt. A boat can be steered out of sight into quiet backwaters of the river where great willows line the banks.

Alex guided the *Ariadne* into a pool lined with thickets of reeds in which wild iris bloomed. Thoughts of the recent week in Giverny came flooding back to him. Cautiously, he nosed the boat into the soft mud of the bank just enough to make it temporarily fast.

"Let's go for a swim," said Alice.

"Not a good idea. Unfortunately, the canal is thoroughly polluted. If you fall in, you should hold your breath and not drink any of the water. As soon as you can you should get some antibiotics."

"But this is not the canal," said Alice. "This is the Cherwell - flowing river water. Just look at it. It's much cleaner and clearer than the canal."

"I still advise against it. Let us just sit here in the shade, have a gin and tonic, and enjoy the beauty of the place," replied Alex.

"I'd like to sit in the sun and tan up a little," said Alice.

She went below, changed into her swimsuit, and went out onto the bow. She quickly climbed up onto the roof of the boat, ran in Alex's direction, jumped off the roof, tucked her body into the cannonball position, and hit the water with such force that Alex was soaked.

"WHAT ARE YOU . . . ?"

Alex had not counted on her reckless courage and sense of mischief.

She swam around in the water, splashing Alex every time he poked his head over the rail to see where she was. Finally, she climbed up over the side. "I didn't swallow any," she said.

Alex went below to get dry towels. By the time he returned she had filled a bucket with water and climbed back on the roof above the door. When Alex came out on deck, she baptized him with the full bucket.

"I cannot retaliate now," he said, dripping wet and laughing, "but you have started something I will finish. Beware."

"I'm not afraid of you," said Alice. "Do your worst."

Nor am I afraid of you, thought Alex, and went below to change into dry clothes.

*

As he came back out of the cabin, Alex saw Alice's pale blue bathing suit hanging over the stern rail.

"I'm up here," she said, and he turned around to find her stretched out on a towel in the sun on the cabin roof.

Naked. Lying on her stomach, with her head toward him.

"Waiter, would it be too much to ask for a dry towel and to be served my gin and tonic up here?" she asked, lifting her head.

(Pause.)

Alex kept a grip on his composure. "Lime . . . or . . . lemon?"
"Lime, please."

Alex went below, mildly shaken. He was not prepared to see Alice naked. Pleased, yes, but not prepared. He cut his thumb while slicing the limes, and poured far too much gin in both their glasses.

Alice, he thought. *So much in character - this self-confident, careless, casual way of operating. No sense of danger or vulnerability, no matter what he said. Swim and strip off in the sun - why not?*

Taking a deep breath and determined to be nonchalant, he went back out on deck with her drink on a tray, one dishtowel over his arm, waiter-style; a paper napkin wrapped around his bleeding finger; and a dry bath towel over his shoulder.

"I hope Madame likes her gin and tonic on the strong side," he said, offering the towel and the tray. Alice sat up, wrapped the towel she had been lying on around her hips, and reached for the dry towel. Arranging it turban-style around her wet hair, she leaned back on her arms.

Alex stared at her bare chest. A crimson shape spread across the skin on the left side of her chest. *What had happened to her?*

She made no move to cover herself.

"I will answer the questions you have not asked. The condition you are looking at is called port-wine stain, a superficial malformation of the capillaries in the skin. People usually call it a birthmark if it's small and unobtrusive.

"I was born with it. Nothing can be done about it. My father always said I was lucky. Some people have things like this on their face. He told me to get used to it - and always keep my shirt on."

She sat up straight, held her arms out wide, and looked down at herself. "It's almost like a large hand across my left breast, which, as you can see, is smaller, wider, and flatter than the right one - as if the hand was pressing it down. Alice pointed to the other side of her chest. "The right breast is normal and not bad. If I had two of these, I would be a 'babe.' The first boy I slept with told me that.

"I would be lying if I didn't admit it took some getting used to - especially in adolescence. But I *am* used to it.

"It's the way I came into the world. It's not a wound or a disease, and it doesn't hurt. It's not a reflection of my personality or character. I feel about it the way you seem to feel about your leg: Love me, love my limp. Or, in my case, Love me, love my chest.

"This port-wine stain is part of the reason for my being interested in having a full-body tattoo, Japanese-style. I went to Morioka to see if he could do something old and beautiful incorporating this shape on my chest. He was intrigued, and promised to produce a design for me to consider the next time I am in Japan. The invisible tattoo I told you about was another matter altogether."

Alice stopped talking, picked up her gin and tonic, and looked at Alex with eyebrows raised.

(Silence.)

"You don't know what to say, do you, Aleko? I'm afraid I've become quite clinical and objective about it. But people who see it for the first time don't know what to say. Port-wine stains are not a chapter in the standard manual on topics for social conversation."

Alice looked down at her bare chest again.

"Alice, you underestimate me," said Alex, with conviction.

"I *do* know what to say, actually. Your bathing suit hides the stain. I would not have known. But you took it off because you wanted to show me something very private about yourself. Your clinical lecture masks the anguish you must have felt at times in your life.

"In every obvious way you are a lovely human being - especially striking with your fine features and white hair. You must know that. Yet, beneath your clothes you also know there is this red hand clutching your breast. It really is a kind of wound, and it must cause you psychological pain at times. You must have been teased about it when you were young."

Alice closed her eyes.

"And even now, it must be an uncomfortable part of buying clothes and underwear. Given the cultural standards of body perfection, it must always bother you a little that there are certain clothes you cannot wear without being self-conscious.

"I admire your courage in accepting what is you, and I am intrigued by your creative idea of incorporating the stain into a traditional form of Japanese art. When you do, I want to see it."

Alice opened her eyes, looking directly in his eyes.

"And even more - listen to me carefully, Alice - *even more*, I am moved by your deliberate exposure of what you feel is a significant flaw. Your candid explanation is useful, but what you have told me without words is a gift. I am not repulsed. You honor me, actually, with your secret."

She started to speak.

"Wait, let me finish. You have seen me naked, Alice. You have seen the stress marks of age, and the mangled condition of my leg. You know how I feel about it - how I try to rationalize and compensate - yet how it pains and vexes me. And now I have seen your nakedness . . . not by accident, but by design . . . and . . ."

"And?"

"That is that," said Alex. "One more thing not to fear between us."

Alice stood up, climbed down off the roof and onto the deck, and stood facing Alex, completely naked. She took his hand and placed it tenderly over the larger red hand on her chest. When she looked up at him, tears were streaming down her face. She turned away and went inside the cabin.

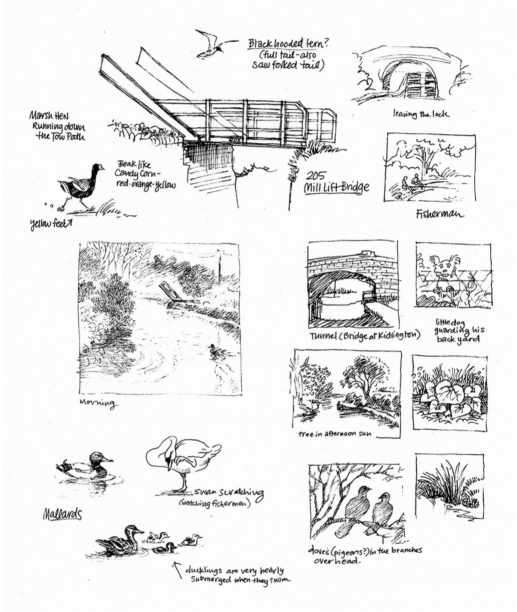

Black hooded tern?
(full tail - also
saw forked tail)

leaving the lock

Marsh Hen
Running down
the Tow Path

205 Mill Lift Bridge

Fisherman

Beak like
Candy Corn -
red-orange-yellow

yellow feet↗

Morning.

Tunnel (Bridge at Kidlington)

little dog
guarding his
back yard

tree in afternoon sun

Mallards

swan scratching
(watching fishermen)

↗ ducklings are very nearly
Submerged when they swim

doves (pigeons?) in the branches
over head.

460

Bridge 233

Duke's Lock

DONE

They moored once again at Thrupp, and went ashore to eat shepherd's pie in The Boat. Sunday night in the pub was peaceful. A few tourists, a few locals, but no weekend rowdies. And no Wonko.

Talked out, they went back to the *Ariadne* and retired for the night.

Alice lay awake in her bunk for hours.

Summoning the same courage it took to cannonball into the dangerous river water in the afternoon, she got up, went quietly into Alex's cabin, and stood still, not quite certain what to do next.

"Aleko?" she whispered, "are you awake?"

"Come," he said, and rolled over in his bed, leaving room for her.

Realizing she might never have a chance to be this close to him again, Alice took off her nightgown, lifted Alex's covers, and got into bed with him, skin to skin, spoon fashion.

Alice thought about the invisible tattoo she had sought in Japan.

Would this be the time she would like to have it? Would the intensity of passion come now that would make the tattoo visible?

No. This was something deeper, wiser, stronger. She only felt warm. And comfortable. And happy - like someone finally coming home to a longed-for reunion.

She put her arm over Alex's shoulder and held him close.

His hand reached for hers and held it tight.

She sang to herself, . . . *to hold you ever so tight, and to feel in the night, the nearness of you.*

Thus they fell asleep, as contented as ever in their lives.

When morning came, Alex awoke in bed, once again alone.

When Alice joined him in the galley to make breakfast, they talked about things to do with orange peel - dried, candied, dipped in chocolate - and marmalade. They talked about dish detergent and hand

462

lotion. They talked about Alex's 4711 soap. They talked about almost anything.

Except the unspeakable joy of the night before.

Each was content with the silence, the joy, and the resolution of the conundrum lying between them for the last two weeks.

Done.

MONDAY, MAY 13

By late afternoon the *Ariadne* was secured against the canal bank in Oxford where the trip had begun. When they had floated free of the last lock at Wolvercote, Alice sensed from the sound of the motor and the increase in speed that Alex was already in Oxford, working through a list of things to do when they arrived.

*

(Now, he has gone ashore to get mail and messages. He will look in on his bonsai and poppies on the way back. He is energized by having safely passed over dangerous reefs into calm waters. The Alice Question is settled. Now he knows what the nature of their relationship will be, and he is at peace with that. Is she? He will find out before the day is over.)

(Meanwhile, Alice was left alone to shower, change clothes, and shift her own thinking ashore, and onward. She will leave early Wednesday morning. She feels now as she had felt on the day at age eighteen when she successfully soloed in a small plane. She had proved she could fly - to go up and come down, safely. She knew even then that this was not the beginning of a career in aviation. Getting her pilot's license was not about flying. It was the satisfying conclusion of wanting to know something about herself:

Could she fly alone? Yes.
She never flew again as the pilot of her own plane.
But she would always know she could.)

*

Alice. Clean. Calm. Contented.

She sat in her favorite place at the stern of the *Ariadne*, a glass of Cretan wine in her hand. In years to come Alice will take out her memories of the past two weeks and live over each day as if feeling her way around an invisible komboloi. Two more nights - two more beads - and the keepsake will be finished. Max-Pol will be coming soon. Though she would like to see him again, she is not ready for the three of them to be together.

From beyond the greenhouse she could hear Alex coming, whistling his marching song.

"Alice, Alice, great news! Max-Pol will be here tomorrow," shouted Alex, as he came across the gangplank. "The three of us together, imagine!"

Alice reacted as if a large stone had been dropped in the tranquil pool of her thoughts. *Max-Pol . . . tomorrow . . . then I . . .*

"You are not pleased?"

"Does Max-Pol know I'm here?"

"How would he know? He only knew I had gone with you as far as Paris. I expected him around May 15. He is coming back early. Is this a problem?"

"Aleko . . . I think I should leave. It will be too awkward," said Alice.

"No. No. And again, *No.* I must be quite firm about this. There is one transcendent reason Max-Pol is coming early, and, for that same reason, you must stay, at least through tomorrow evening. You will miss a chance of a lifetime if you leave.

"Yesterday, as the gods of coincidence would have it, May 12, was the anniversary of the birthday of our own patron saint, Edward Lear. And I, the Lord High Panjandrum of the Spherical Learical League, have called a plenipotentiary meeting of the Jumwillies. We celebrate tomorrow. Those who miss the rites will be drummed out of the lodge - excommunicated - struck from the list. You *must* stay!"

"Yes, sir," said Alice, overwhelmed by Alex's emphatic enthusiasm.

Alex stood still, considering her, stroking the side of his face, as he often did when he was rummaging around in his mind, looking for just the right thing to say and do.

Finally, he sat down very close to Alice, picked up her bottle of wine, added some to Alice's glass, and filled a glass for himself. When he looked at Alice, he saw her eyes were closed.

She is afraid, he thought.

"I will be right back," he said, and disappeared into the boat's cabin.

When he returned, he sat down close by Alice, "Hold out your hand."

In his own hand he had a komboloi Alice had not seen before. He placed it in her open palm, folded her fingers over the beads, and wrapped his own large hands around hers.

"Well, then," he said, "You know that I have the disease of komboloi-mania. I collect them. I have many. But I have been attached to only three. Each one has a history. One of them I gave to Max-Pol, as you must know.

"It will tell you something about the depth of my feelings for Max-Pol when I admit that my mentor, Pendlebury, gave me that komboloi. I am sure Max-Pol has explained about Pendlebury to you, so I will not. Because I believe all lovely and important gifts should be passed on, I wanted Max-Pol to have it. In a way I think I am becoming to Max-Pol what Pendlebury was to me. I would have it so.

"Now, this komboloi I entrust to you. I have not had it long, though I had looked for one like it for many years. I will not pretend it was not expensive. For one thing, it is very old. It is quite valuable as the world counts value, because each amber bead has a fossilized insect inside.

"Millions of years ago, the insects got trapped in the sap of conifer-ous trees. The air and sun of that long ago summer were trapped with them. Through time and the pressure of glacial ice and debris, the am-ber formed. It was mined in the days of the Vikings, passed down the great rivers of Russia, across the Black Sea to Constantinople, cut and shaped into beads, which were strung together into a komboloi. I am sure it has been restrung many times, and prized by each of its owners. It is truly a rare komboloi. Beautiful. Powerful.

"I like it very much. I treasure it. And I will miss it.

"But, from now on, when I think of where it is and who has it, I will be profoundly satisfied, knowing that when you turn the beads with your fingers, you will think of me and these days we have spent together. Now it is yours."

"But also ours."

Alex turned his face away, tears filling his eyes. He cleared his throat, looked back to Alice, who had not moved. Her own tears ran down her cheeks and onto their clasped hands.

"Alice, we have not directly addressed one another with words about our feelings for one another. We have spoken more *by the ways we have been* together. But tonight I feel like telling you, before Max-Pol comes and before you leave, how it is with me. I will answer a question you have not asked.

"We have been dancing about, trying to settle affairs between us. It is complicated, because we are complicated people. First and foremost, it must be acknowledged that we are a man and a woman, and how that shall play out is always at the top of the list, whether we would admit it or not. Dr. Freud made the case for the truth of that.

"We settled that last night. And we have settled something else.

"I confessed to you that I was afraid. You did not ask what I was afraid of. And you did not console me falsely by telling me everything would be all right. All you said was, I know.

"Nothing anyone ever said to me gave me more comfort than those two simple words. I believe you *do* know. You *do* understand. As nobody else does. I cannot say how, yet I am certain of it. And I know you have been as afraid as I. I know too."

Alice started to speak, but Alex placed his finger over her lips.

"Just listen. All my life I have been perceived as large, strong, intelligent, confident, competent, full of health and energy, and above all self-sufficient. It has rarely occurred to anyone that I might need anything or anybody. I imagine the same can be said of you. Pendlebury saw through my disguise, I am sure, but he never said anything - he just helped me in ways I could not have helped myself.

"The truth is, I have run scared all my life. I began as an orphan with nothing. Yet, I have always been the one everybody else depended on. Always. This is my own doing. I could never admit I needed anything from anybody.

"Now, in these last years of my life, I feel more alone and more afraid than ever. My children have gone their own ways, never thinking I might need them. All my closest friends are far away, old and feeble, ill, or dead.

"And . . . I know my own physical health will fail all too soon.

"I am afraid of falling and breaking a hip, afraid of being bedridden, being senile, being out of control of my life, afraid of dying alone. It is not the dying. It is not the pain. It is not being afraid of being cared for at the end by strangers. None of that scares me.

"Here is the truth: I am afraid of falling into that final darkness all *alone*. And it is my *fear* that I am most afraid of. A fear that is a rabid dog barely chained in my basement.

"At the same time, I understand that this is the nature of our humanity - to ultimately go it all alone. But having another person recognize that existential reality, and out of their own fear and loneliness at least reach out and say, *I know*, means I am not alone, *alone*.

"Perhaps that is the essence of what Max-Pol means by being a Witness. You, Alice, are my Witness."

(Silence.)

"Witness. That is as good a word as any. I admit I have searched my brain for a label in English for what has come between us. What shall we call each other? Colleague, companion, co-conspirator, comrade, partisan, crony, collaborator, confidant, alter ego, ally, accomplice, soul mate, and on and on. None of those will do. Not even lover."

Alice had still not moved. Her tears continued to drip onto their hands.

"And you, Alice. You, who can be so forthright it scares me, have let silence speak for you. There is much I do not know in the way of facts. Moreover, you have not told me what you fear. You will if you wish, but it is not necessary from my point of view.

"What is unspoken may be understood even if not known in detail. There is a knowing that is beyond any words. I will be candid. You have found something in me you have needed and wanted but could neither name nor define."

Alice nodded her head. Yes.

"The first night you came to my bed, it was as a mother comforting a wounded child. No one has ever noticed the child in me that cries out to be held and comforted. Your intuition is finely honed, and you had the nerve to act on it.

"The second night, you came because you needed comfort yourself.

I felt it. There are few cracks in your defenses. But you are alone inside your castle, and even you get lonely. I know.

"And finally, last night you got into my bed naked against my nakedness, testing the heart of our alliance. Not for sex. But to allow us to be as close to one another as possible - not as lovers - as equals - as ultimate companions. And we walked across the coals without getting burned."

(Silence.)

"I am quite certain when I say we have not and will not ever have an experience exactly like this with anyone else. Nothing more need be said. Those nights happened. They will not happen again, but they were all we required."

Alex placed a finger under her chin and lifted Alice's face.

"Never forget this. I trust you, Alice, as I have trusted few. For the remaining years of my life, no matter where I am or you are, in times of being afraid I will think back to the nights you came into my bed, held me close, and we sailed away on the sea of sleep, the old owl and the young pussycat, by the light of the moon. That memory will always be a lifeboat for me in my sea of fear. As it will also be for you."

"I know," sobbed Alice, and leaned over into his arms, "I know."

He held her close - as tenderly as she had once held him - and rocked her gently back and forth. He looked at the pale beauty of the back of her neck. Once he had been tempted to kiss her there. He had not because he did not trust his intentions. He kissed her neck now, with certainty, as a seal on all he had just said to her. He laid his cheek on her neck and whispered:

> Surprising to find a Jumwillie here.
> Jumwillies come at the call of a tear.
> So Jumwillies must be nothing to fear.
> They belong to the lodge of our friend Mister Lear.
>
> Jumwillies, Jumwillies, all in a row.
> Jumwillies rain, Jumwillies snow.
> Jumwillies come and Jumwillies go.
> And nobody knows what the Jumwillies know.

"Nobody," whispered Alice, sitting up. "Nobody."

She leaned back away from their embrace, took his face in her hands, and kissed Alex tenderly on first one cheek and then the other, and then on his forehead.

She dried her eyes, picked up her glass of wine and handed Alex his glass. She held out her glass for him to drink, and Alex held his for her. Each drank from the other's glass. Then Alex crooked his arm, Cretan-style - Alice curled her arm through his, and they drank again.

(Silence.)

The one thing they did not say was the one thing they longed to say and hear, but which now seemed so ordinary in the face of their un-common bond. It was not enough. They did not say, I love you.

They thought it. They knew it. But they did not say it.

Alice put down her glass and picked up Alex's gift and considered it. She began humming her tune, marking time with the movement of the beads of Alex's komboloi as she moved them with her fingers. Click . . . click . . . click . . . click.

Alex chimed in with his marching song. The music fit together like spoons in a drawer. Like a man and a woman asleep in a bed - or an owl and a pussycat gone to sea.

That evening, Alex took Alice on a tour of the sights of old Oxford. Arm in arm they walked the cobbled lanes, peered in at the college quadrangles, and went as far as the Botanical Gardens by Magdalen Bridge.

The garden was closed, but the perfume of the flowering plants and trees came over the walls to meet and bless them. On the way back to the *Ariadne* they stopped to look in the windows of bookstores, but, like the events of the day itself, they were overwhelmed by the infinite possibilities inside, and passed on.

Weary, they walked back to the *Ariadne* talking about plans for tomorrow, when Max-Pol would come . . .

GOODNIGHT

Reluctant to go to bed, they sat side by side, in silence, in the dark, on the bench in the stern of the *Ariadne*.

"Aleko, what should I know about Max-Pol before tomorrow?"

Without thinking about it, Alex moved closer to Alice, took her hand in his, and began the comfortable conversation two people might have when they have successfully passed the same difficult examination.

"Alice, I am not avoiding your question when I say I will not tell you anything to prevent you from the pleasure of discovering Max-Pol for yourself. With all my heart, and out of my best judgment, I urge you to do just that. Whatever happens between you will be gain for both of you. I believe it. You have my blessing in this."

(Silence.)

"But, to be useful, I will say a few things. Max-Pol is on his way to living a much larger life than he ever imagined. I say that because he is a much larger person than he knows. He steadfastly rose up the escalator of academic, scientific, and cultural success. He became a doctor. For many that is enough. For Max-Pol it was not. At the top of that escalator is a small room where you will spend your days. The excitement is over.

"Max-Pol wants to live in a much larger world - and he has ventured out into it, willing to take substantial risks to determine what will engage him. Very smart people on a quest, and he is one, are exciting to be around. I have experienced this myself in the company of Max-Pol. I trust you will have the same experience. He is a catalyst for adventure. A match for you in this department, I might add.

"Lastly, Max-Pol is an honorable man. It is the highest compliment I can pay. He would not make it as a Cretan because he does not honor a certain kind of clever dishonesty as a virtue. He could not make a living as a horse trader. There is no duplicity about him - even in small things. Sometimes I think he is naïve, but then, I am older. And I am a Cretan man."

(Silence.)

"I will say no more."
Alice thanked him by squeezing his hand and laying her head on his shoulder. "Nor will I," she said.

*

They went to their cabins and to their beds alone.
"Goodnight, dear Alice," called Alex.
"Goodnight, dear Aleko."

As he closed his eyes, Alex thought, *Things are just as they should be.* And he went to sleep lying in the middle of his bed, knowing he would spend this night alone.

Sleep came to Alice almost immediately after she turned out her light.

Not the sleep of the emotionally exhausted, nor even the untroubled sleep of the contented. No. Sleep caught Alice up in its wings and took her soaring on the wind into imaginary landscapes.

Sweet dreams. She would not be back until morning.

TUESDAY, MAY 14

"Aleko, there's a very large rabbit in your poppy patch," called Alice, who was looking out the window while washing breakfast dishes in the galley sink.

"What?" Alex rushed on deck to see. Sure enough, the rabbit was there, and a very large rabbit it was. Actually, someone six feet tall dressed in a fluffy white bunny suit with great floppy ears and a round fluffy tail. Smoke seemed to be coming from its head. With its backside to the *Ariadne,* the bunny was inspecting the blue poppies and had just picked one.

"Hey!" shouted Alex.

"Hey, yourself!" shouted the bunny as it turned around. The man in the bunny suit was wearing a red rubber nose and smoking a large cigar.

"Max-Pol!"

"Aleko!"

CRASH!

In the galley, Alice had dropped a large bowl into a sink full of silverware and glasses. *My God, it's Max-Pol!* Drying her hands on a towel, she waved feebly at the bunny.

Here we go, she thought.

And then she remembered the fortune Alex had been given by the Gypsy in Istanbul: Never trust the wisdom of a rabbit. Laughing, she dashed out on deck to throw her arms around the big bunny as he crossed the gangplank.

*

To Max-Pol it seemed perfectly natural to find Alice with Alex aboard the *Ariadne.* Knowing Alex's affinity for surprises, here was one more. What did surprise him was the enthusiasm of Alice's welcome. He had not been hugged like that by a woman for too long.

When she released him, he stuck the blue poppy in Alice's white hair, put his red rubber nose on her nose, handed Alex a cigar, and began:

"From Seattle there came a big bunny."

"Whose nose was quite large, but not runny," added Alex.

"With ears large and floppy," said Max-Pol.

"He picked a blue poppy," said Alex.

"And turned an old maid into honey," said Alice, who was somewhat disconcerted at what popped out of her mouth. She blushed. And the invisible tattoo came to mind.

"Happy birthday, Edward Lear," said Alex.

And happy birthday, me, thought the bunny.

(Max-Pol had little use for what he called "the age days," and he managed to never mention his day of birth if he could avoid it. The attention that came with birthdays embarrassed him for some reason. Not since childhood had he or anyone else celebrated his birthday. He found if he kept his mouth shut about it, people did not ask, and he could avoid the matter. But, in fact, today, May 14, was his birthday. One to remember.

But he did not want this day to be about him. In time to come, he would look back on this May 14 and celebrate it as a special day for another reason - marking the beginning of having the answer to the question he had been asking himself for the last year, What am I going to do now?)

*

Max-Pol had brought special uniform shirts with him from Seattle.

Gaudy pink-and-orange satin bowling shirts, embroidered on the back in black, Victorian script: Spherical Learical League. He had intended sending one to Alice, but here she was. He had also brought matching baseball caps, with propellers on top that spun around with the breeze.

Alex put one arm around the bunny's shoulders and his other arm around Alice's waist, and, pulling the two close to him in the conspiratorial style of Wonko, he said, "Since I am the Undisputed Grand Pooh-Bah of this organization and we are in my territory, I hereby take command of the affairs of this day. In the spirit of British eccentricity, we shall wear our new uniform shirts and hats to amuse the natives. Put on your walking shoes and we are away!"

"Onward!" said Alex, Max-Pol, and Alice at the same time.

EDWARD LEAR AND ALEX EVANS

And so they set off in high good spirits - a three-person parade. Their wonky uniforms drew amused responses from other pedestrians, and friendly honks from passing cars and trucks.

Max-Pol dominated the conversation, chattering on about nothing in particular. He seemed both lighthearted and ill at ease.

What is going on with him? Alex wondered. *He is edgy. His good humor seems forced - as though he has something on his mind he does and does not wish to talk about. What happened in Seattle? Should I ask now or wait until Max-Pol and I are alone?*

Alex's mental committee replied as one voice: *Wait. Later.*

Let it be, then, thought Alex, because, most of all, he wanted to tell his two boon companions about Edward Lear as they strolled through the streets of Oxford, and then show them the art of Mr. Lear in the Ashmolean Museum.

*

(If asked what historical person he would like to be, Alex would have given the surprising answer, "Edward Lear - he is my alter ego."

Why does a man like Alex hold a man like Edward Lear in such esteem? If anything, at bottom, Alex is about sense. But Lear is known for his nonsense. Alex would have said, "Wrong. There is a great deal more to know about Mr. Lear." And, though he didn't say it, a great deal more to know about Alex Evans.)

*

Alex once wrote a short speech summarizing his thoughts about this man he so admired. He delivered his remarks over coffee, cognac, and cigars after an informal weekly luncheon with colleagues in a private room of The Old Bookbinders Ale House. His friends were not as familiar with Lear as Alex was, so when his turn came to hold forth, he was assigned the topic. The rule was: A brilliant five minutes.

"Well, then," said Alex as he began his speech. "Lear was a preposterous man who lived a preposterous life, leaving behind a preposterous legacy. He would have appreciated the summary use of a word that sums up all that is astonishing, illogical, eccentric, humorous, ridiculous, incredible, and, above all, nonsensical: Preposterous.

"His self-portraits are caricatures: a bald-headed, bearded, rotund figure, with a surprised expression on his bespectacled, owlish face.

"Well over a hundred years after his death at age seventy-six in 1888, his books of nonsense remain in print, and he remains the unchallenged laureate of nonsense. His poetry, alphabets, vocabularies, drawings, and his whimsical approach to geography, anthropology, and zoology still set the standard for the expressions of a playful mind.

"He is the godfather of the limerick, though he did not invent the form or even use the word. Perhaps it is more accurate to say he affirmed the state of mind out of which limericks spring: that pleasurable spirit of intellectual cleverness with words and ideas, which, in modern times, expresses itself as a succinct form of bawdy humor and social satire.

"Yet, for all the lightheartedness of his legacy, his was a sad and difficult life. Born the last of a family of twenty-one children, he was left to his own devices for education and income. He struggled with ill health - epilepsy, asthma, and chronic bronchitis - and insufficient income hampered him throughout his life. He did not have a home of his own until the last years of his life. He died unmarried and childless.

"Restlessly he wandered the world at a time when travel was hard: long journeys to Albania, Egypt, Italy, France, India, and the Mediterranean - notably Greece, and Crete.

"All the while, Edward Lear's sense of humor remained a refuge from the vicissitudes of his existence - an escape from his pains and sorrows and loneliness. It was as if there was an unrelenting gap between the life he lived and the life he wanted. He filled that space with amusements - directed as much at himself as at the world.

"Harvard University is the repository of an astonishing trove of material illustrating the complexities of his mind: volumes of journals and diaries, correspondence, sketches, songs, verse, and technically competent drawings of birds and animals.

"By profession he was an artist. A very talented artist. A painter of landscapes, an illustrator of his travels in many lands, and, for a time, the art instructor of Queen Victoria. He made his living from his serious art, not from his nonsense.

"His art work, especially his completed paintings, have long been scattered, but the great exhibition of his work at the Royal Academy in London in 1985 resulted in a renewed appreciation of the remarkable artistic talents of this man who had previously been remembered for apparent trivia.

"Above all, Lear was able to look at the world with open eyes and laugh at his preposterous place in it. He had the capacity to hold open house to all the characters on the stage of his inner life, and let them come and go at will.

"The breadth of his intellect, his sense of humor, and his unwavering nimbleness of mind endeared him to me.

"Nonsense fills the void between what you *want* to say and what you *can* say. Mr. Lear was the master of this fine art."

Alex had concluded his speech by quoting by heart several of Lear's limericks and the entire text of "The Owl and the Pussycat." His audience gave him a rousing ovation. "Bravo!"

*

And though Alex would not repeat his lecture for today's companions, he would throw in bits and pieces of information as the opportunity arose. He wanted Alice and Max-Pol to know without a doubt how much that rare Englishman, Edward Lear, was folded into the way in the world of an expatriate Cretan.

If only I could draw and paint, he thought, as they came to the steps of the Ashmolean Museum. If only . . .

THE MESSIAH

Often called Oxford's Attic, something of almost everything collectible has found its way to the Ashmolean since the museum's beginning early in the seventeenth century: archeological artifacts, manuscripts, portraits, coins, mummies, medals, religious objects, ethnic costumes, landscapes, sculpture, and odds and ends without category gathered by the most brilliant and eccentric of British characters on their forays into the ends of Empire.

Alex had spent many pleasurable hours in the great curiosity cabinet of the Ashmolean. As had Edward Lear.

However, bypassing all the collections on the ground and first floors, Alex led his companions directly to the Madan Gallery on the second floor. Here are works of Joseph Mallord William Turner. Lear had come to see these very same paintings and drawings when he visited Oxford in 1872.

Alex explained, "Lear admired these – Turner's watercolors of fish, a heron's head, and landscapes so purely composed of paint and light that when you look very closely, there is no 'thing' there – only what you were led to imagine. Lear also liked Turner's drawings of cows. I wanted to start this day by seeing the same Turners Lear saw."

Alice and Max-Pol were an attentive audience.

The museum guard in the Madan Gallery was also attentive – the Spherical Lyrical League shirts and propeller beanies were a suspicious sight. But the guard quickly realized that the League's leader knew his stuff, and followed Alex's commentary with interest.

"And now, over here, are three of Lear's own watercolors from his travels in Greece – one of a view from the mountains out over the plain of Marathon, and one of the Acropolis of Athens from the hill of Lycabettus. My favorite is this view of the Monastery of Arkhadi, the great symbol of Cretan independence. There is no nonsense in these representations. This is serious work.

"And finally, there is this great oil painting of Jerusalem.

"You would have enjoyed the company of Lear, Alice. He, like your mentor Monet, drew and painted out in the world, rain or shine. He, too, was *out there in it*."

"Yes . . . yes," said Alice, studying the painting. "You are right."

*

Alex had one more thing to show them - something Lear never saw.

"In a way it is the single most astonishing item in the museum," he said, "as unique in the world as Snowflake, the albino ape in the Barcelona Zoo. It is called *The Messiah*. Follow me."

He led them down one floor to the Hill Music Room. There, in the center of the room, suspended in a glass case, was an amber-colored violin in pristine condition. Its glow seemed to come from inside it.

They walked around the case slowly, awed into silence by the violin.

In a reverential voice, Alex said, "This was the creation of Antonio Stradivari in Cremona in 1716. Apparently prized by him, it was in his workshop studio when he died at age ninety-four, in 1737. Since that time, the violin has passed from collector to collector, but has never been played in public concert performance. Its name came from a comment that the violin's appearance in public, like the Messiah, has been promised but never fulfilled."

"That's hard to believe," said Max-Pol, shaking his head.

"It's true. The Hill family acquired the violin in 1890 and gave it 'to the nation' to be placed in the Ashmolean, never to be played, with the family retaining control over who even handles it. The family hoped that someday research capabilities would allow the construction and varnish to be analyzed, finally explaining the secret of its maker. That time has not yet come. And may never come.

"Now, it is the most famous and most valuable Strad of all. But nobody knows how it sounds when played. No great violinist has ever stroked a bow across its strings in public. It is mute."

As Alex unfolded the story of the violin, Alice and Max-Pol walked around the case, studying *The Messiah* from all sides. So close. So inaccessible. The essence of possibility unfulfilled.

"Many experts say an instrument's glory lies in both its maker and its players. The years of musical vibrations affect the wood, they say; the interchange with human hands and spirit affects the quality of the sound. Greatness in a violin depends on its use, they say.

"It is possible that this instrument may be *dead* because it has not been played. You may be looking at a profound tragedy: a corpse that will never sing. Like life, I think it cannot be saved for a better time - it should be played."

Alice and Max-Pol looked at one another while Alex spoke.
Something in each one of them was locked in its case.
Waiting to be played.

Alex, standing on the other side of the case, could see the two of them through the glass. He knew they were no longer listening to him. It was not easy being matchmaker to such intelligent people. The angle of approach had to be oblique, the suggestions subtle.
So far, so good, he thought.

At last, Alex led them down the stairs and out of the museum, avoiding the Arthur Evans Room, which contained many of the treasures Evans brought back from Knossos.

There were pots in there that Alex himself had found and re-assembled from shards long ago.

Part of the history of his own life was on display in that room.

He passed on by without comment.

This was not a day about Alex or Crete or even Lear, really. As far as Alex was concerned, this was a day about Alice and Max-Pol and possibilities.

Swinging his cane and pointing up the street like a drum major, Alex said, "Onward!" and began whistling his marching song.

THE PERCH

Hailing a taxi, Alex told the driver to take them to Binsey, a village on the Thames, northwest of Oxford town, on the far side of Port Meadow.

The Perch is there. A famous old pub with thatched roof, stone floors, and a garden leading down to the river. Alex had reserved a table outside on the terrace.

"Well, then. Lewis Carroll read portions of *Alice in Wonderland* to friends here in this garden," said Alex, when they were seated. "They say he read the story of the Mad Hatter's tea party. It is too bad that Carroll and Lear never met. Just imagine those two minds playing verbal badminton! With Lear's talent for music, they might have surpassed Gilbert and Sullivan."

The meal passed as the day had passed, with the fountain of Alex's knowledge splashing pleasantly on, spilling history and poetry and nonsense on Alice and Max-Pol, who were more than willing to be semi-silent partners in Alex's informal Lear festival.

He knew he was doing all the talking, and knew he was being affectionately indulged by his guests. He also knew it was time to leave them alone. At the meal's end, he excused himself.

"I must make some calls to arrange matters for this afternoon and evening," he said. "I will meet you at the edge of the great meadow in a few minutes." Alice went off to the restroom, and Max-Pol strolled through the gardens. He was sitting on a bench when Alice found him.

*

Alone. Together for the first time since Waterloo Station.

Alice sat down beside Max-Pol. She took a notebook and a fountain pen out of her purse. Opening the notebook to an empty page, she took the top off the fountain pen - a pen Max-Pol recognized.

She wrote: "Hello. It's me, Alice O'Really."

The same words she had written to him last summer, when he thought she was the mute blue nun.

All they knew about one another came to bear on this moment. Lightning did not strike them. But electricity was in the air.

With the same boldness with which she had approached him the first time, with the same audacity she had displayed walking across the labyrinth at Somerton, Alice laid the pen and notebook aside and moved over to sit close beside Max-Pol.

She took his hand in hers, interweaving her fingers with his, and leaned her head against his shoulder. She felt her skin flush.

(Pause.)

"Well, then," she said, imitating Alex, "shall we?"

This time Max-Pol was ready for her.

Leaning his head on hers, he replied, "Yes, anything's possible."

*

Well, well, well, thought Alex. *That did not take long.*

He had been watching from behind a hedge at the far end of the garden. He was content. His relationship with Alice was clear and lasting, as was his relationship with Max-Pol. Beyond doubt. Witnesses, all.

And as for what would come between Alice and Max-Pol? He knew he was the bridge between them. A bridge they could trust. What lay beyond the bridge was in their hands now - hands already entwined.

Alex walked down to the bench and sat beside Alice and Max-Pol, who did not move or change their positions. It was in this way that the possible shape of things to come was wordlessly acknowledged between the three of them. Alex shifted over to sit close by Alice. She took his hand in hers, and holding the hands of two men she cared for deeply, she said:

"Jumwillies, Jumwillies, all in a row.
Jumwillies rain. Jumwillies snow.
Jumwillies come and Jumwillies go.
And *nobody* knows what the Jumwillies know."

The three of them sat still, looking out at the clear, blue sky of summer, across the green emptiness toward the canal where the *Ariadne* was moored. They sat still, as in a theater, waiting for a long-anticipated play to begin.

Comedy? Or tragedy? Or Both?

THE WELL

Alex broke their reverie. "On! I want to show you a well."

He led them up the winding lane toward a church in a grove of trees, through a cemetery and around behind the church. There, down some mossy steps, is a well with a curious history.

Since the eighth century it has been claimed that the water of the well can heal afflictions, cure diseases, and enhance fertility. The water is also believed to be efficacious in affairs of the heart.

Legend says the patron saint of Oxford, the Princess Frideswide, prayed to St. Margaret of Antioch to provide a spring of water to heal King Algar's blindness. Oddly enough, the king had been struck blind as a result of an earlier prayer by the same princess, who had wished to prevent the king from abducting and marrying her. Lesson learned, the king regained his sight. The merciful princess remained a virgin. And the spring - now a well - became known for its miracles.

Henry VIII and his first wife, Catherine of Aragon, came to this same well at Binsey, where she was anointed with the holy water in hopes that it would aid her in providing a son for Henry. The water was not efficacious, and the rest of the familiar story quickly played itself out.

Not long after, the Roman Catholic Church and all its places of pilgrimage in England - holy wells included - were officially out of business.

A few visitors still come to the well at Binsey. Mostly tourists taking a look-around after a meal at The Perch. Perhaps secret believers also come, desperate for miracles.

And a few wandering agnostics attend - Jumwillies, for example - exposing themselves to whatever forces are at work under whatever name - be it coincidence or blind luck or fate. Multiple Working Hypotheses are the Way of the Jumwillies.

"It is not really a wishing well," explained Alex, as they stood by the holy site. "Still, I am sure people make wishes anyhow, just in case this well is the one with the power to make wishes come true. One would not want to miss out by being stubborn or narrow-minded about wish-granting."

Max-Pol thought about his own three wishes:
- to be free of his life with Laura,
- to leave medicine and go into voluntary exile,
- and to have a Witness for his ongoing life.

Though he did not take wishing seriously, nevertheless, all three wishes had come true. However, if he followed the rules of fairy tales, his wishes were used up.

Max-Pol considered Alice and Alex, as they peered into the well.
Perhaps they had wishes of their own.
Perhaps theirs would include him.

JUMWILLIES

From the well at Binsey, a taxi took them back into the heart of Oxford, to Blackwell Books, which has been serving the needs of Oxonians in its Broad Street shop since 1883. There is no finer English language bookstore in the world. Alex came to pick up gifts for Max-Pol and Alice: hardbound copies of Lear's book of nonsense and Peter Levi's biography of Lear.

"Since it is impossible," declared Alex, "to just pop in and out of Blackwell without browsing, I would like to direct the browsing, or else we will spend the rest of the day here. Come upstairs to look at the sections on ancient Greece and archeology – there are books on Crete – and Minoan art and history."

Two hours later they left, lugging six heavy bags of books. Alex could not help but notice that the volumes about Greece and Crete were chosen by Alice and Max-Pol together – obviously to be shared – since they had split the cost between them.

He took them next door to the White Horse pub, in business since 1591, to recuperate from shopping over pints of ale. Alex proposed a toast.

"Let us drink to the next meeting of the Jumwillies. In Crete in October."

"In October," said Max-Pol.

"October," said Alice.

"October, the first day, on the terrace of the Meltemi in Hania. I shall make the arrangements. Consider our table reserved."

That night they ate dinner aboard the *Ariadne*. Not wanting to spend the day cooking, Alex had ordered a Cretan meal brought down from Bunter's by his Greek friends: leg of lamb, pilaf, village salad, crusty bread, and yogurt with honey and walnuts for dessert. Alex's verbal fountain bubbled on during dinner, already laying out plans for Crete in October.

Alice and Max-Pol listened to Alex, but their eyes were on each other.

At bedtime, Alice insisted that Max-Pol move into the cabin she had been using, since it would be his for the coming week. Since she had to pack up anyway to leave early in the morning, she would sleep on the foldout bunk in the salon.

By unspoken agreement all three Jumwillies avoided any formal ending to the evening. They masked their farewell feelings with the busyness of getting three people settled in for the night in a small space.

Alex, exhausted from the emotional and physical expenditure of the day, was asleep moments after turning out his light.

*

Alice lay awake in the dark, wondering if Max-Pol noticed that she had not changed the sheets on her bed, and that she had lightly sprayed the pillow with the only perfume she ever used, a delicate scent of roses.

Once, when she was on a sailing trip in Tahiti, a French sailor had given her the perfume. She had considered falling in love with him, but did not. He was gallant. "Save it for a time when love does come to you," he had said.

Max-Pol pressed his face into her pillow and inhaled.

Roses, he thought, and was asleep.

Alice was still awake. She was thinking of two triplets in the collected sayings of Fabuliste Curnonsky:

> *In affairs of the heart, do not dismiss lightly these things:*
> *The delight of anticipation*
> *The pleasure of remembering*
> *The emptiness after fulfillment.*

> *Be forewarned. Do not forget:*
> *There are promises that cannot be kept*
> *There are questions that must not be asked*
> *There is truth that will not be told.*

As she drifted into sleep, Alice wondered, Would Jumwillies want to be able to count their chickens before they hatch? No. Jumwillies like being surprised.

WEDNESDAY, MAY 15

Daybreak.

Alice rose early. She dressed quickly and quietly. Barefooted, she carried her shoes and bags out the stern door of the *Ariadne* and across the gangplank to a bench on the bank of the canal, where she sat down.

Alex watched her through the porthole beside his bed.

Max-Pol was asleep in his bunk, encased in the concrete of jet lag.

There had been no goodbye the night before, and there would be none now. Even knowing it was likely that Alex was awake and watching, Alice did not look in his direction. She dusted off the bottoms of her feet, put on her red-leather sandals - one with buckles, one without - stood up, and walked away at a brisk pace.

She did not look back.

Later, when Alex put away her bedding he would find a small black folder on her pillow, tied with three long strands of her white hair. In the folder, two photographs - the irises of Alice's eyes.

Her way of looking back at him.

Tomorrow she will discover in her purse a small envelope containing pressed petals of blue Himalayan poppies. And in a small blue bag, one half of a pair of antique ebony dice.

His way of continuing to say, Hello.

At Walton Road, Alice saw a taxi coming in her direction.

Lucky me, she thought. Flagging it down, she got in and told the driver, "Railway station, please."

After two blocks, Alice recognized a familiar figure standing in the street, hailing her taxi. Wonko. "Stop," said Alice to the driver, as she rolled down the window. "Wonko. Are you weird or sane today?"

"Ah, Alice," he said. "Where are you going?"

"To the station," she replied.

"So am I, may I join you in your chariot?"

"Come on," said Alice, opening the door.

When Wonko sat down beside her, he seemed formal and distant. This was neither the loony clown nor the genial offstage actor. He looked at her solemnly, thoughtfully, and said, "I need to have a serious conversation with you, Alice, if you don't mind. It won't take long."

"Is it about Alex?" she asked.

"In a way."

"Go on."

"It's no accident that I'm here with you. At my request, Alex called to tell me you were on your way up from the canal. I've intercepted you because there's something you need to know before you leave Oxford."

Alice sat still and silent in her Mona Lisa pose.

"What I have to say may seem like something out of a novel or a movie, but I assure you it is part of this very real world. Beyond what you have seen of me in public and private, there is still another part of my life. I am a consultant for a private agency specializing in matters of economic security.

"You, yourself, have been working for fifteen years on security systems based on the iris of the eye, so you have some idea of what I'm talking about. Your world and mine have crossed. I would rather not tell you who I work for, but it is enough to say that they and I wish no harm to come to you, and that's why I want to talk to you."

Alice remained still and silent.

"Maybe it would be useful to verify that I know a lot about you.

"Here's a piece of paper for you to consider. On it you will find your passport number, social security number, bank account numbers, and a long string of other numbers - phones, fax, addresses and so on. Your blood type, bank balances as of yesterday in three accounts, and a few other items are there. You won't be surprised - you must know this information is not all that hard to obtain these days."

"Take a look," he said, offering the sheet of paper to Alice.

Alice read the numbers, nodded in recognition, but still said nothing.

"You either have one hell of a deep cover, along with truly eccentric habits, or else you are surprisingly naïve, despite your remarkable intelligence. You may be a liability to my client, or you may find yourself in some unexpected difficulty. Either way, I want you to see how your life looks through another lens. Let me tell you what I know, and explain how your life appears in the context of security concerns.

"You are one of the five or six people in the Western world who know just about everything important about security systems based on the iris of the eye. You've been involved from the very beginning - from elemental research to the development of high-resolution recognition devices.

"You know that these security systems are considered so foolproof that they have become a major tool in preventing espionage in the world of technology. Governments and their agencies increasingly rely on the same security systems. This explains why your own office building became a virtual prison.

"What you know is so sensitive and so important that not only would many companies and governments like to have access to it, they would also like to know how to circumvent it. I'm sure you have some sense of this, but I'm not sure you really comprehend the power of what you know, or how it is being used.

"It's no exaggeration to say you understand the combination to the lock on some of the most sensitive information in the world. Not only that, you know how the lock works - even how the lock is made."

He looked at Alice straight on, without turning away from her gaze.

"With that in mind, I come to your activities. This year you suddenly quit your job, cashed in your stock options, moved a lot of money into a French bank account, leased your apartment, and virtually disappeared.

"Your colleagues, friends, and even family were uncertain as to exactly why you left or where you were going. Europe, you told them, Back in a while. Very vague, but they all said, That's just Alice. Perhaps.

"You moved to Paris after going briefly to Japan, but you've also made many very short trips to places like Barcelona, Prague, Berlin, Vienna, and Crete - tourist destinations, but coincidentally places where it just so happens there are research laboratories working on security systems.

"You've traveled under a dozen false names, disguised yourself as a nun, a little old lady, a cellist, and a painter. You've sent mysterious packages to contacts in foreign countries. Finally, you often follow people around - but for no reason we have been able to ascertain.

"Now, most recently, you've made a sudden trip to London to meet an American man at Waterloo Station - your correspondent in Crete - who turned up in Oxford yesterday in a bunny suit.

"You've spent two weeks with Alex Evans, quickly becoming - how shall I put it delicately - his most intimate companion. And yesterday you were seen sitting between these two men, holding hands with both of them."

Alice relaxed, and smiled.
He doesn't know everything, she thought.

"We know Alex Evans has a wide range of friends in the Oxford/Cambridge academic community, including the scientific research institutes. And he just happens to have a social acquaintance with John Daugman, the Cambridge researcher who did most of the theoretical work on which iris identification is based. A man we actively protect, I might add.

"We know you have exceptional financial resources of your own. We know you are single and independent, with liberal political and social views, an extraordinary mind, and a creative imagination. We know you can fly a plane and skipper a boat. And . . . you are free to do as you choose. Your recent behavior is quite suspect - not normal behavior by any standard.

"Now, the question is, What are we to make of all this?"

Wonko may not have recognized Alice's Mona Lisa position, but he did notice her continuing smile.

"You may find it hard to believe that such close tabs have been kept on you. But trillions of dollars are at risk over the information you have. This is not a joking matter.

"If you don't understand this, it's time you gave it some serious thought. Given the stakes, it's a small cost to keep you and others like you under surveillance. I repeat for emphasis: This is not cold war spy stuff, not a novel, not a film. Protecting intellectual properties has become a matter of consequence."

Taking her continued silence for understanding, Wonko went on.

"So. There you have it," he said. I consider Alex Evans an astute judge of people. He's been helpful to me in the past, though he was probably not aware of it. I found it necessary to talk to him quite openly about you, respecting his condition that I let you know what I've just told you.

"He thinks you simply are not aware of your part in these matters. He's probably right. I want you to understand that I have no intention of either threatening you or frightening you, but I conclude that it's only fair to let you know you are of concern. The time might come when you may find that comforting, actually."

He paused. "You may need me."

Alice looked at Wonko shrewdly. Now she understood why he had turned up so often during the canal trip. He was shadowing her. And he may have even looked through the porthole when she was in bed with Alex. He certainly had drawn the obvious conclusions.

Yes, she thought again, *but he doesn't know everything.*

She laughed, and was still laughing when the taxi arrived at Oxford Station in a rain shower. Alice pulled a lightweight, black raincoat out of her shoulder bag and put it on. She took her time adjusting a black scarf over her hair and tying it under her chin.

Finally, she spoke. "How exciting all this is. You've given me much to think about, Wonko. I congratulate you on your own disguises, by the way. It's a memorable act: clown and musician, gentleman and under-cover agent.

"It's true you've told me things I didn't know. But I'm not as naïve and innocent as you may think. And I'm also not on the wrong side of things.

"I can't promise you I will be careful, because I'm often not. It's also true, as you observe, that 'normal' is not what I do. But I under-stand what you've said, and I accept the spirit in which you've said it. Thanks. I'll think about it. I suspect we'll meet again. I hope so. Here's my card.

"You obviously know how to get in touch with me, but you may not know how I think. There's a description of that drawn on the back of the card.

"And now, if I'm free to go, I must catch a train to London and then Paris. But I suppose you know that too. Would you like to come along?"

Swiftly opening the door without waiting for Wonko's reply, Alice picked up her bags, stepped out into the rain and walked away.

Wonko was both impressed and displeased. *One cool customer,* he thought. Had he learned anything? Hard to say.

He looked at the hieroglyphics on the back of the card.

What the hell? he said to himself.

He got out of the taxi, walked around the far end of the station and watched the platform until the last passengers boarded. He walked back to the taxi.

She was on it, he thought, because he had caught a glimpse of a woman in a black raincoat and black scarf, carrying a suitcase and a long black bag. *But then, how do I know she didn't see me, get on, wait for me to turn away, and then get off again? She's capable of that. I like her. I admire her, but I still don't trust her.*

The train rolled away down the tracks. Wonko went back to the station platform through the waiting room. No Alice.

In the women's restroom of Oxford station, Alice had opened a window just wide enough to give her a view of the parking lot. She saw Wonko get into the taxi and watched it move away toward town. She smiled.

Men, she thought. *How could he not check the ladies' loo?*

She combed her hair, refreshed her bright red lipstick, and considered herself in the restroom mirror.

So, John Daugman is still in Cambridge. The last time I saw him was at Toshiba in Japan. I should give him a call. It's been too long.

*

Outside, it was still raining. Alex was staring out one of *Ariadne's* starboard windows, watching the raindrops dappling the water of the canal.

He held Alice's iris photographs in one hand, and his ringing phone in the other.

"Hello?"

"Aleko? Wonko. Thanks. Everything went well, or at least I think it did. As you said, you can never be quite sure about her. That delights you, but troubles me. I explained my position but didn't ask any questions, and she had nothing to say by way of explanation.

"Puzzling. I thought she might be defensive – even outraged – about being somewhat exposed, but at times it almost seemed as if I was only giving her new ideas about what to do with what she knows. That really worries me."

"Perhaps she felt threatened," said Alex.

"Alice? No, not her. She wasn't intimidated, that's for sure. Anyhow, she got on the train for London and is headed back to Paris."

"Good." said Alex, "Thanks for keeping your promise."

"Aleko, a couple of things stick in my mind. She gave me her calling card. Just her name on one side, but on the back is a – I don't know what to call it – a design. She said it would tell me how she thinks. I don't get it. Have you seen it?"

"Yes, it is probably the same card she left for me on my desk, but I have not had time to figure it out either. I will let you know if I do."

"One other thing, Aleko. Do you know what she said after I laid out the whole picture for her?"

"No, I cannot imagine."

"She said, 'How exciting.' What do you suppose she meant by that?"

Alex laughed. And continued laughing.

Dear Alice, he thought.

"Wonko, she probably meant exactly what she said. She, unlike most people, often does. Just the thought of being *considered* capable of intrigue simply delighted her."

"Right," said Wonko. "They probably said that about Mata Hari."

"Now *that* is an exciting thought. Keep in touch, Wonko."

"And you do the same. I know your connections with her are personal, and I respect that, but you don't want anything bad to happen to her. Any help you can give . . . you never know . . ."

"That is certainly true," said Alex, laying the iris photographs alongside Alice's calling card. "You never know - but, somehow, I think Alice can take care of herself."

"You're probably right, Aleko."

"Goodbye, Wonko. My regards to your wife."

"I don't *have* a wife," said Wonko.

"I know," said Alex. "None of us are quite what we seem, are we?"

SNAPSHOTS

IN KYOTO, Morioka, the master of tattoo and calligraphy, visits his cousin, Iwai Hanshiro XI, the elegant young onnagata, backstage before the performance of *Kagotsurube,* in which he plays the female role of Yatsuhashi, a courtesan.

"Will Sanaa come back?" the actor asks, as he smooths white makeup on his face.

"Yes. She has written to say so."

"When?"

"Soon, I think."

"Will she get the invisible tattoo?"

"No, not this time."

"Someday?"

"Perhaps. It is not clear to me yet. We have not discussed the pain."

"Why, then, will she come back soon?"

"Because she likes who she is when she is in Japan. And she is interested in having a traditional Japanese tattoo to incorporate a birthmark she already has on her body. And also, I think, to have me paint another design on her flesh in ink the color of her skin. She liked that. I think she wants to see how it works with a man."

"Which man?"

Morioka smiled. "You, perhaps. I saw you together before she left."

The actor laughed.

"She only wanted to talk to me because she realized I must know much about women to play a woman for Kabuki. I suppose she thought I must be gay. Women feel safe with gay men, you know. Ha. I cleared that up. Now she knows. But lovers? Perhaps, but I think not."

*

IN ATHENS, Polydora Vlachou is showing a photograph to her companion, Maria. "This is the American doctor I was telling you about: Max-Pol Millay."

"I didn't know you cared for men."

"This one, he is not like the others. In some odd way he cares for me."

"Should I be jealous?"

"No, be excited. Maybe you will like him too. Keep an open mind."

"Ha."

"If the woman he told me about comes to Athens, I want to meet her."

"Now should I be jealous?"

"No. But I think any three of us could have a good time together."

"Three's a crowd."

Polydora giggled. "You can have a good time in a crowd, Maria."

*

AT TWENTY-NINE THOUSAND FEET over Greenland, Alice is looking down at the sea. She always likes this part of the flight to Seattle. In the far north, the sky is so clean - so clear - with sun so bright she must wear sunglasses to look out the window. The winter ice is melting on the sea, breaking up into complex patterns, moving with the wind-blown currents.

Like my life, she thinks. She leans back in her seat and kicks off her shoes: one white with black laces, one black with white laces.

In the far back of her mind, a small dark cloud of discontent is forming. She was surprised at the spontaneity of her response to Max-Pol.

Now, at a distance, she has doubts.

She feels as she did the day she met him at Waterloo and then encountered Alex. She had wept then. She did not weep now.

*

IN LONDON, Elliot Brownell, aka Wonko, is sitting in an oak-paneled office talking with a man in a rumpled black suit.

"So, we've misplaced her again? She didn't arrive at Paddington. And she didn't take the Chunnel train," said Rumpled Suit.

"Yes. Sorry."

Rumpled Suit tapped the fingers of his hands together.

"It's hard to accept that this is just one more example of her eccentric, spontaneous behavior. Where *is* she at this moment, do you suppose? Where is she *going*? And *why*?"

"I wish I knew," said Wonko. "She's easy to lose because she's unpredictable, but she's also easy to find because I think she's not really trying to evade us. She just doesn't operate out of a manual. Maybe we should accept that. Maybe we should try to recruit her."

"Now *there's* a brilliant thought. Recruit her. Maybe she would like working with us. At least we would know where she is. In the meantime, see if you can find her."

*

IN OXFORDSHIRE, aboard the *Ariadne,* Alex and Max-Pol are just approaching the lock at Duke's Cut.

"I want to push along and get as far as Somerton. There is a labyrinth there I want to show you," said Alex.

"I like mazes."

"It is not a *maze*, Max-Pol, it is a *labyrinth*. They are not the same. It is important to know the difference."

*

IN CRETE, it is the most beautiful time of the year. Clear, mild, sunny days - and the hills are carpeted with wild, red poppies. At the harbor in Hania, Kostas sits alone in the darkness of his shop, smoking a cigarette, and drinking tsikoudia. His eyes are red and puffy. He is dressed in black. The door is locked. The shop is closed. Kostas is in mourning. Yesterday, his mother died. He whispers to himself, "*Tora . . . eimai . . . orphanos* (Now I am an orphan)."

He begins singing softly to himself, *Vasilev ouranie . . .* - the prayer that begins both the liturgical service of the Greek Orthodox Church and the school day for all Greek children. Ancient Byzantine music. Solemn. Deep. It is an appeal to God: "King of Heaven, Comforter, Spirit of Truth."

Vasilev Ouranie

Va - si - lev ou ra - ni - e pa -
ra - kli - te to pnev - ma - tis
a - li - thi as

IN CRETE, very near the shuttered shop of Kostas, Ioannis, the owner of the Meltemi, is preparing the terrace tables for the tourists who, unlike the Greeks, come to eat at an early hour. As he sets out the knives and forks on the table nearest the harbor, he thinks of Alex. He wonders where he is. He admires and respects Alex, whose presence always adds a touch of class to the Meltemi.

When will Alex return? he wonders.

When Ioannis goes into the cafe to get glasses for water and wine, he pauses to read the poetry pinned to the wall beside the cash register. Alex gave it to him, saying it was the only poem he ever completed.

Ioannis reads the poem once again, reaching for its full meaning:

Οδηγίες Προς Οδοιπόρους

Θα σου δηλώσουν: Όλα τα ταξίδια έχουν γίνει.
Εσύ θα απαντήσεις: Εγώ δεν πήγα να δω ο ίδιος.

Θα επιμείνουν: Ο,τιδήποτε έπρεπε να πούμε, το είπαμε.
Εσύ θα απαντήσεις: Εγώ δεν μίλησα ακόμη.

Θα σου πουν: Ό,τι ήταν να γίνει, έγινε.
Εσύ θα απαντήσεις: Εγώ δεν τελείωσα ακόμη.

Σε προειδοποίησαν: Κάθε πορεία είναι μακριά,
κάθε πορεία είναι σκληρή.

Μη φοβηθείς. Εσύ είσαι η θύρα, εσύ κι ο θυρωρός.
Θα μπεις μέσα και θα προχωρήσεις. . . .

—*Αλέξανδρος Ευαγγέλου Ξενοπουλάκης*

"Ah, Aleko," Ioannis says aloud. "Come home. Come home soon."

LOUKA MAHDIS is the illustrator of the first volume of this book. Having read the manuscript, she was inspired to go to Crete to see its people and landscapes for herself. She began as a real person – a talented traveling artist with a sketchbook – and became a character in the novel. She has enriched the story with her sensitive eye; expressing with visual images what words cannot tell. Here is her self-portrait – combining the person she was and the character she is becoming:

SOTERIOS (SAM) TOURLAKIS composed and arranged the music for this book. He is a classically trained American musician. After reading the manuscript, traveling to Crete, and being immersed in Greek music, he, like his friend, Louka Mahdis, became a character in the novel. His music has been informed by his being tutored in the Byzantine liturgical tradition. In order to demonstrate the music in Kostas's mind, Sam had to cope with ancient and Modern Greek language, complex modes and notations, and then the intricate stages of translation into western forms of musical expression. His self-portrait is below – the Byzantine expression from which "Vasilev Ouranie . . ." was transcribed.

Δόξα καὶ Νῦν. Ἦχος λβ΄. Πα.

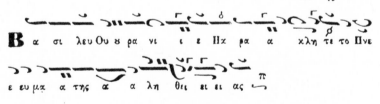